DEVILS IN THE MIRROR

DEVILS IN THE MIRROR

It is almost midnight on Halloween when firefighters find the body of Shayla Richards, a young black girl, high on Harden Moor, and photographs taken at the scene suggest a ritual sacrifice. As DI John Handford and DS Khalid Ali begin the murder enquiry they discover that Shayla had been at the centre of a previous police investigation with equally disturbing implications. The police find themselves caught between factions who insist the dead girl had been a compulsive liar, and Handford finds himself pursuing a man without a past. In fact there are those who wonder if he really exists...

DEVILS IN THE MIRROR

by

Lesley Horton

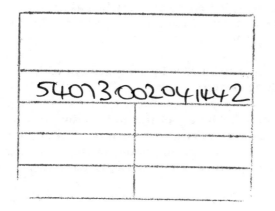

54073002041442

Magna Large Print Books
Long Preston, North Yorkshire,
BD23 4ND, England.

British Library Cataloguing in Publication Data.

Horton, Lesley
  Devils in the mirror.

    A catalogue record of this book is
    available from the British Library

    ISBN   0-7505-2555-X

First published in Great Britain 2005 by Orion,
an imprint of the Orion Publishing Group Ltd.

Published in Large Print 2006 by arrangement with
Orion Publishing Group

Magna Large Print is an imprint of Library Magna Books Ltd.

Printed and bound in Great Britain by
T.J. (International) Ltd., Cornwall, PL28 8RW

For Peggy Hewitt, my first creative writing teacher. From the beginning she believed in me and I thank her for her continued support and faith.

acknowledgements

Many thanks to all who supported and helped me throughout the writing of this novel. First to Detective Sergeant Colin Stansbie of the West Yorkshire Police, who has given of his time so generously to answer my many questions and to Simon Willis, former headteacher of Carlton Bolling College, Bradford, who explained the internal disciplinary procedures when a teacher is accused of abuse by a pupil. My thanks also go to Dr Gerald Partridge of the Holycroft surgery in Keighley, and to my daughter-in-law, Anne, for their expertise in all matters medical.

I would especially like to thank Joan Womersley and Marie Pattison who have read and discussed the manuscript with me and to members of the Airedale Writers' Circle who offer such support.

Extra special thanks to those professionals who have led me through the horrors of the unfounded allegations made against them. They wish to remain anonymous, but know who they are.

As always, I owe a debt of gratitude to my agent Teresa Chris who encouraged me through the problems of writing this book, to my incredibly patient editor, Kate Mills, and to Sophie Hutton-Squire, who corrected my mistakes and inconsistencies.

Finally, I thank my husband, Brian, without whose encouragement the daily task of writing would be so much harder.

Cliffe Top Comprehensive School,
Cliffe Top Lane,
BRADFORD
BD3 6TJ
Tel: 01274 635711

Headteacher: Mr B Atherton

16 October 2002

Mr Graham Collins
27 Silverhill Grove
BRADFORD
BD9 7NR

Dear Mr Collins

First let me congratulate you on behalf of the governors of Cliffe Top Comprehensive School on the satisfactory outcome of the hearing at the Crown Court. We are delighted you were exonerated from all charges. It is a sad fact of the times that teachers are vulnerable to allegations of abuse, particularly from young girls as unhappy as Shayla. Nevertheless, she finally showed considerable courage in admitting to the truth and thus brought the case against you to an end.

Now that the law has taken its course, it is

incumbent upon the governors of the school to conduct their own inquiry. We will obviously do this as expeditiously as possible, but in the meantime you will remain suspended on full pay. You are reminded that during the suspension you are not allowed to take on other paid employment or to work with children in any capacity.

Should you wish to discuss this letter, please do not hesitate to contact me.

Yours sincerely

Lawrence Welford

Lawrence Welford
Chair of Governors

chapter one

Eleven forty-five on the last day of October. Hallowe'en.

Children in robes and vampire masks demand a trick or a treat from long-suffering householders who, unwilling to risk the vagaries of the trick, opt for the treat. Tricks can be mean.

Shayla Richards had thought it was a trick – at least she had for a short while, until she realized it wasn't. And then it was too late. It had been played.

Firefighter Dave Crawshaw, too, had thought the 999 call was a trick. Three hoax shouts they'd had this month and now a fourth. Made by the same male caller, with the same deep voice, giving the same message: a fire up at Druid's Altar. The difference was, this time it was for real. Standing at the edge of the moor, he could make out a faint red glow above the slope and the breeze sifting through the trees brought with it the smell of burning wood. He stared into the darkness. A sense of unease came over him and he swallowed hard, tasting the mist that hung low over the ground.

'Anything?' The shout came from the direction of the fire engine, clear and loud. It made him jump.

A wall and a gate cut off the moor from the pathways. Unable to get any closer, the appliance

15

had stayed in the turning circle, its headlights penetrating the hazy darkness, throwing long shadows in front of him.

'Yes,' he shouted back. 'Hang on a minute; I'm going to have a look.' He picked his way over the damp grass and through the wintering bracken towards the giant outcrop of rocks that formed Druid's Altar. Stumbling and sliding over the large granite boulders embedded deep in the ground, he manoeuvred his way along the rough track. The glow from the fire remained steady, neither growing in intensity nor receding. It was eerie and for the first time in a long while his nerves began to take over. Perhaps the date and the place were firing his imagination? It was Hallowe'en and this was the site where in the past – and even now, if rumour was to be believed – gowned men performed their rituals. The wind whispered through the oak trees below in the valley and up the steep hillside. Dave shivered. He swung the beam of his torch over the moor as the altar came into view. It was always possible the hoaxer was still around. They usually wanted to watch, see a result, but up here there was nowhere for a person to conceal himself except in the rocks below, and Dave was damned if he was going to risk climbing down them at this time of night. Let the man have his fun.

He could see the fire now, a small one on the lesser of the two stones that made up Druid's Altar. He had no way of knowing when it had been set, but it was showing little sign of burning out. Probably built of peat and twigs. Whatever, it couldn't be left. He'd just get a bit closer to

16

check it, make sure it wouldn't spread – the last thing they needed was a peat-based moorland fire – then he'd call for one of the others to extinguish it.

He let the beam from his torch play on it for a moment, then swung it sideways. At first he thought the light had snared the fire raiser. Cheeky sod; he was there all the time, lying on the other stone, laughing at him. He took a step closer.

'Jesus Christ.'

A black girl was stretched out, her feet towards him. From his position he couldn't see her face, but her arms were crossed over her chest. He climbed on the rock. She was young, probably no more than fifteen or sixteen. Her hair, though black, was not Afro-Caribbean as the facial features suggested; it was too long and too straight. She was almost naked, wearing only a bra and a pair of skimpy pants. A lilac scarf was carefully tied round her neck, its corners splayed on her dark shoulders. He touched her arm. 'Come on, love, you'll catch your death here.'

No reply.

He'd almost expected her to jump up as a joke and frighten him, but she remained inert. He pushed at her, harder this time and her head lolled towards him, her eyes open and bulging and an expression of fear mingled with surprise on her face.

He fought to stifle the shock and the need to sit down. He had to attend to the girl, check she was actually dead – she might not be; she might need an ambulance. Touching as little as possible, he

17

leaned over her, pulled off his glove and felt for the carotid pulse. Nothing.

He could be wrong. Perhaps he was feeling in the wrong place, hadn't located it properly. He tried again, then slowly pulled his fingers away. He wasn't wrong; there was no pulse. He sat back on his haunches, suppressing the sadness that welled up in him. She was gone. There was no more he could do for her.

He stood up and scanned the neatly arranged body. Someone had taken time to do that, to display her as a sacrifice. A sacrifice to the gods? A pagan ritual in a place of pagan worship? It was spooky. Dave shivered and scrambled off the rock. He had to call it in.

It?

Her.

As his eyes followed the contour of her body, there was a flash of recognition. He knew her, or at least knew of her. She was the missing girl, the one in the red skirt and the grey puffa jacket, the one whose picture had been in the papers and on hoardings for weeks now, for so long you hardly noticed any more. But it was her, of that he was certain; it was the missing girl.

Shayla Richards.

Walter Heywood peered at the clock. Without his glasses the numbers blurred. It looked like eleven thirty, but it might not have been. It didn't matter. He didn't sleep well any more. Not since his wife died and not since he became old. It was when Edith died that he became old. Until then she'd kept him young. 'Eighty-four years young, that's what we are,' she'd say and laugh. And she was right because she had more energy than most. She shopped for the old folks, even though most were younger than she was. Each morning she'd trot out to the grocer or the post office to pick up their pensions and they'd tell her they didn't know what they'd do without her. Then in the afternoon the two of them would do the gardening, or go to the senior citizens club to play bingo or cards or to the tea dance at the church hall. In the evening after their meal they'd watch a bit of television. It was while they were watching television that she'd died, just slipped away soundlessly. Now without her next to him, he couldn't sleep.

A wind had sprung up since he went to bed and the curtain was billowing across the bedside table. He pulled himself from under the clothes, stiff from lying in one position too long, picked up his glasses and shuffled over to the window. The tall street lamps threw a hazy orange glow across the cul-de-sac and for a moment he stayed where he was, looking out onto the darkened road. The wheelie bins were out, he noticed. He'd forgotten his; he'd try and remember it tomorrow, not that there was much in it to be emptied. He stared at the houses across the street, semis with gardens back and front. The people who lived in them were good to him, kept an eye on him, checked he was up and about each day. But he knew they thought he was losing it, becoming confused, going senile even. Perhaps he was; but he wasn't confused about everything. He could remember the years he spent with Edith, all sixty-two of

19

them. He remembered courting her, asking her to marry him. He was twenty-one and she was twenty. He could remember as clear as day the tears she tried to hold back as he went off to war in 1940. He remembered their first house, their children, the smell of the washing each Monday and the baking each Thursday. What did it matter that he couldn't remember what he'd had for tea tonight? It wasn't important.

A movement from across the street broke his reverie. A cat, perhaps. He peered into the night. No, it wasn't a cat; someone was across at the Collinses' house. A man. It looked like a man. Mr Collins? He couldn't see properly. It was dark and whoever it was was partially obscured by the tree on his side of the road. Only the wheelie bin was in full view. He saw an arm stretch out and a hand lift the lid. Something was dropped inside; he didn't know what.

Then the person disappeared, probably down the path, but he couldn't be sure. Walter Heywood shrugged; it was none of his business what people did or when they did it. But perhaps he'd mention it to Mr or Mrs Collins tomorrow, just in case. If he remembered.

It was not so much the body of the dead girl lying on the huge block of millstone grit that disturbed Detective Inspector John Handford, but the silence of the crime scene officers. He was used to their chatter, their comments, their jokes even. That was their way of coping. You couldn't see what these people saw and not build some kind of defence mechanism against it. The worse the scene, the more inappropriate their remarks became – but not here. This was different and he wasn't sure why. Perhaps it was the place and the arrangement of the body in the sacrificial pose. Or perhaps they were cold and eager to get the job done. He pulled his coat round his large frame and ran his gloved hand through his greying hair. His craggy features crumpled into a frown.

He had been here since the early hours when the ebony blackness of the moor was streaked only by ribbons of light from the uniformed officers' torches and further away in the valley, patches of muted colour from the street lamps stained the darkness. Daylight had broken slowly and as the winter sun pierced the clouds, Druid's Altar was silhouetted against the Aire valley. Weathered with winter bracken and dotted with small trees, their skeletal branches straining against the wind, the moor stretched into the distance. Below them, blanketing the hillside, stood Altar Wood with its mass of oaks, some still in leaf in spite of the lateness of the year, and beyond that the valley, murky in the November gloom. Beneath the altar where the ground slipped down the hillside were large boulders long ago liberated then abandoned by melting glaciers, and round it embedded into the hardened earth the rocks had become a pathway for the legions of visitors. Those closest to the altars were inscribed, not with the usual girl-loves-boy messages, but with religious observations: 'Jesus loves you' and 'Christ is here' – not the kind of etching Handford was used to. Were they endorsing the site perhaps, ridding it of the age-old pagan rituals?

He wondered how many more such phrases would be needed to re-sanctify it after this.

As many ways on to the moor as possible had been closed off and officers posted to discourage press and onlookers. Lamps illuminated the immediate scene, the light harsh as it shone on the girl's body. The blue and white police tape separated the altar from the rest of the moor and outside its cordon Dr Jessop, the police surgeon, was in discussion with Detective Sergeant Ali. Handford watched them for a moment – the stocky doctor, slightly balding, and the tall, slim, much younger detective, his hair blowing across his face.

The two shook hands and Ali walked over to Handford. 'What's the matter with the SOCOs? I've never known them so quiet,' he said.

Handford ignored the comment. 'Any idea how she died?' He glanced over at the girl. There was nothing messy about her death, no obvious violence, no bone fragments, no blood, no gore. Quite the opposite. She lay on the altar, from this distance seemingly serene and peaceful, her arms crossed over her chest.

'Asphyxiated, but he won't say how. You know what Jessop's like: too cautious for an opinion. He says there are no obvious signs of a struggle – no defence wounds that he can see, no broken fingernails.'

That didn't mean she hadn't known what was happening, hadn't been afraid. Murder and violence were equal partners, however peaceful the victim appeared. In spite of the cold, the wind and the open air, it had a taste and a smell that lingered. Handford wanted to get on. Until the investigation began in earnest, when it became an academic exercise held together by rules and regulations, he was unable to detach himself from the person.

'Any sign of drugs, Khalid?'

'She doesn't appear to have been a user, although he won't rule it out. There are no obvious track marks. The post-mortem will tell us more.' Ali flicked onto the next page of his notebook. 'Rigor's well advanced so she's been dead at least ten to twelve hours. And she wasn't killed here – not on the altar at any rate. Lividity's wrong for the position she's in.'

'So she was brought up here dead?'

'Not necessarily. She could have been killed on the moor. She'd been lying on the bracken at some time. Dr Jessop found several small pieces caught in her brassiere straps, her pants and her hair as well as in her flesh. We'll have to wait to know whether she was dead or alive at the time. I've got a group of officers looking for the place where she may have been lying, but they're going to have to be quick before it rains.'

The forecast was for a wet and blustery start to the month, and the sky was heavy with cloud. It had also suggested mild temperatures, but it was cold up here and Handford pulled the collar of his coat more closely to him. He stamped his feet, releasing the rich aroma of the peat which lay close to the surface, and felt the rainwater seep round his Wellingtons. Even a thick pair of socks wasn't enough to prevent the cold perco- lating through to chill him.

Nor was there much to shield the girl. The edges of the lilac scarf stirred as a sudden gust cut across her. Handford turned to Ali. 'Why do you think she was left like this?' he said. 'It's almost as though she's been arranged in sacrifice.'

'I don't know. Whoever did it took their time; she's very neat.' Ali shivered and tied his scarf tighter round his neck. 'I just hope this isn't a pseudo-religious thing. That we've got a cult in the area that's suddenly decided to come out of its closet. One that offers human sacrifice.'

Handford studied his sergeant. As far as he knew there were no such extremists in the district, yet the serious expression that had covered Ali's gaunt features was now overtaken by another emotion – apprehension. Fear, even. The suggestion of a cult killing, although it had been his own, seemed to have unnerved him. Handford was surprised; he knew of some members of the Asian community who held the view that such groups were active, but he had never thought of Ali as being one of them. He had worked with him for a year now and respected him both as a man and a detective, the prejudices each had initially held against the other long forgotten. Yet Ali was a complex character and he couldn't help but wonder if this was another side to him, born out of his culture or his religion – another side Handford would find difficult to understand. His first reaction had been to scoff at the suggestion, but instead he made light of it. 'Don't jump to conclusions, Ali; there could be any number of reasons for this.'

'Like what?'

Handford frowned. 'A romp in the bracken with her boyfriend, a dare perhaps, on the scariest night of the year.' That was unlikely and he knew it. If it had been a joke or a dare, or even privacy for a bit of sex, then why arrange the body in this way? Why make it look like a sacrifice? Why not roll it down the embankment? It would have been months before it had been found – if at all. 'Come on, Ali. We have no reason to believe she was the victim of an unknown cult.'

'I suppose not,' Ali agreed. 'But look at her, John. Her death is clean, no sign of an attack and no obvious defence wounds. It's almost as though she didn't put up a struggle. And the arrangement of the body ... and the fire.' Ali shuddered. 'I tell you, this kind of thing scares me.'

Handford took a deep breath. The fire had been extinguished but the acrid scent of the ashes and burnt peat remained, teasing his nostrils. 'It's unusual, I'll give you that,' he said, 'but I'm not prepared to assume we've entered a world of weird factions or black magic. Let's try to keep it in proportion. Do you know anything about the Druids?'

Ali shook his head.

'Since we can't pretend they might not be part of this,' Handford continued, 'get someone onto checking them out. General stuff, what they believe, how they worship, if there are any modern-day groups in the area.' Suddenly he shivered himself, not sure if it was the cold or if the same someone who had walked over Ali's grave had walked over his. He said, 'Come on, there's not a lot more we can do here until forensics have

25

finished. We'll go and see the mother, tell her we've found her daughter.'

As they left he took one last look at the girl lying on the altar and shook his head. 'Who the hell would do something like this, Khalid? What kind of people has Shayla Richards been mixing with?'

If it was the silence that disturbed Handford up at the scene, it was the whimpering coming from the squat Afro-Caribbean woman rocking to and fro in the armchair opposite him that disturbed him now. When Evelyn Richards had opened the door and seen them, her face had suggested she expected good news – that they had found Shayla living rough somewhere. What they gave her was the worst possible news, followed by a little bit of hope when Handford asked if she was up to identifying the body.

'It might not be her? You think it might not be Shayla?' She was pleading rather than questioning. She didn't need an answer.

'Perhaps someone else could do it,' Ali said.

She looked up at him and suddenly anger flared. 'You think I don't want to see my own daughter now she's dead.'

Ali floundered. 'No, Mrs Richards ... that wasn't what I meant. I just thought...'

She glared at the sergeant, then turned to Handford. 'How did she die? Did someone kill her? Did she suffer?'

'We're not sure exactly how, but yes, someone killed her.' Handford replayed the image of the dead girl on the stone. 'And no, Mrs Richards, I

26

don't think she suffered. She looked very peaceful.' What was one small lie, if it eased her pain?

'When? When did she die?'

'Some time yesterday, we think. Perhaps during the evening.'

Grief etched into Mrs Richards' features. 'I was at bingo last night. It was a good night. I won sixty pound.' She pulled herself out of the chair and grabbed a Chinese vase from the mantelpiece. Taking off the lid, she snatched at the notes inside. 'This was for Christmas,' she screamed. 'This was for my Shayla's Christmas present.' Suddenly she threw the money at Handford. 'It's your fault,' she yelled. 'You didn't look for her when she was missing. I told you. I came to the station to tell you. If you'd looked for her...' Her voice descended to a whisper. 'Well, Inspector, she'll not trouble you no more now.'

What could he say? That they'd pulled out all the stops in their search for her? Shayla had been a girl who went missing periodically then turned up and mouthed off at the police that what she did and where she went was none of their business. They'd searched hard the first two times she'd disappeared, then after that they'd done the usual checks, and if she was gone for any length of time they had put up posters and asked uniform to keep an eye out for her. There was little point doing more; they knew she'd turn up – she always did – and anyway there were more urgent cases needing their attention.

Ali began to pick up the money and, all her energy spent, Evelyn Richards slumped back in the chair. Handford knelt next to her. They'd never found out why the girl had gone; it hadn't been up to them to determine why – they weren't social workers. Now it was pertinent to the inquiry. 'I know how distressing this is for you, Mrs Richards, but I need to ask you a few questions.'

'I don't want to answer no questions, not yet; I want to see my Shayla.' Her shoulders sagged so that her neck and chin seemed to disappear in her large bosoms. She attempted to stand up again. 'I'm going to get changed,' she said. 'I can't see Shayla looking like this.'

Handford placed a restraining hand on her. 'Mrs Richards, Shayla's still where we found her. When she's in the mortuary, we'll take you to see her. Please sit down. Would you like a cup of tea?' How crass, he thought.

She shook her head. 'I want to get changed; I've been at work.'

Handford pulled up a chair and sat opposite her. 'Where do you work, Mrs Richards?'

'Not full time. In the day I'm at the university; I study to be a counsellor. I want to help young kids.' Handford tried to hide his surprise, but she had noticed. 'I might be black, but I'm not stupid, you know.' She remained silent long enough for her comment to register, then she said, 'But I've got to get money, so in the morning and at night I clean some solicitors' offices in the city. Brown, Sutton and Miller right in the centre. And four times a week, when I'm not at the university, I clean people's houses.'

'Whose houses?'

She gave him a guarded look. 'Are you going to tell the tax people?'

He smiled at her. 'No, I'm not going to tell the tax people.'

'Some teachers at the university give me a job. Doctor Rowles – she works in Peace Studies, and Professor Adamson – he's in Pharmacy.'

Handford watched as Ali recorded their names. 'When Shayla went off before, did she tell you where she'd been?'

'She said she'd been staying with friends. But they're not real friends. They're bad company, make Shayla miss school, make her do bad things. You've got their names at your police station. The officers said they'd been to see them but she wasn't there. I don't think they had; I don't think they cared. What's one more black girl?'

'Did you contact them at all?'

'They said they'd seen her, been around with her during the day. One of them had let her stay at her house, let her sleep on the floor.'

'And this time?'

Mrs Richards stared beyond her interrogator. 'Not this time. She hadn't been with any of them. She'd not stayed the night at all. Right up to yesterday I was asking, but no one had seen her. I told the police, but they didn't care. They were bored with Shayla. "She'll turn up, Mrs Richards," they said. "She always does."'

This was not getting them very far and Handford changed the subject. 'Have you any idea why Shayla might go up to Harden Moor? Was it somewhere she liked to go, for a picnic perhaps or with a boyfriend?'

'What you suggesting? That my Shayla have sex with boys? No, never. She's a good Christian girl.'

29

A good Christian girl who was into petty crime, truanted from school and had taken to running away from home. Handford glanced around the room. Although the house was in one of the poorer parts of the city and appeared run down and dilapidated, inside it was neat and tidy. The three-piece suite was old-fashioned but not threadbare, the table and sideboard polished and the carpet cheap but clean. A television stood in one corner. Photographs of Shayla and her brothers covered one of the alcoves and on the mantelpiece was a picture of mother and daughter. They were smiling, seemingly happy in each other's company. What had gone wrong? Teenage years, or something more serious?

'I believe you're divorced, Mrs Richards. Can you tell me where Shayla's father is? We will need to talk to him.'

'He's gone. He's in Pakistan.'

For the first time since he had been rebuffed, Ali spoke. 'Pakistan? Why Pakistan?'

She glared at him again. 'Because that's where he comes from and if he's there he don't need to send me no money.'

'He's Pakistani? You married a Pakistani?'

Handford closed his eyes momentarily. Not again. The last case that had involved a mixed marriage had caused Ali all kinds of grief.

'Qumar thought he was the bees' knees, but he couldn't get custody of the kids. He wanted it – thought they'd be better off brought up in Pakistan. When the courts said no, he was on the next plane, didn't say goodbye, not even to Shayla, and she was his favourite. Then he wrote

30

and said he would get them one way or another. I wrote back and said I'd see him dead before he took one of my children away. Then I changed my name from Hussain back to Richards and I haven't heard from him since, and I don't want to, not never again.'

Handford stood up. 'A family liaison officer will be here soon. She'll stay with you, keep you up to date with what's happening. In the meantime, is there anyone you would like us to contact?'

'My brother, Calvin. You can tell him. He works at the hotel near the station. He's a chef. He'll be there now.'

Handford nodded. 'We'll make sure he knows.' As they reached the door, he turned and said, 'I'm sorry we had to bring you such bad news, Mrs Richards. I promise we'll do our best to find out who killed your daughter.' Her eyes filled with tears, but the tears didn't hide her distrust of them.

They were halfway to the car when the front door flew open. At first, light from the hallway filled the gap, then Mrs Richards' bulky frame. 'Hey, you,' she shouted. 'If you want to know who killed Shayla, ask that teacher, the one who groped her. You ask that Mr Collins.'

chapter two

Jane Collins held her breath as the blue line appeared in the window of the pregnancy testing kit. It didn't come as a surprise; she had suspected for a while. She must be all of four weeks because she knew when it had happened: October second, the day Shayla Richards was branded a liar and her husband found not guilty of indecent assault against her. They had held an impromptu party and afterwards had fallen into bed together, not even thinking about taking precautions. As far as they were concerned the nightmare was over, their lives could return to normal and nothing mattered.

But that was then; now it was different.

She looked again at the blue line and blinked away the tears. It couldn't have come at a worse time. As if it wasn't enough that the lying little bitch had ripped their lives apart with her allegations, the governors now wanted their pound of flesh. Two weeks of peace – that's all they had given Graham and her. Two weeks in which they held their meeting, composed their letter and posted it first class.

Dear Mr Collins, First let me congratulate you … it is incumbent upon the governors of the school to conduct their own inquiry… Yours sincerely, Lawrence Welford, Chair of Governors.

It swam in her memory – the off-white headed

notepaper, the black lettering of a laser printer and the neat signature of the chair of governors that brought with it memories of the harassment, the filth pushed through the letterbox, the graffiti sprayed on the car, and the names they were called as they walked along the road. She remembered word for word the headlines in the local papers when Graham appeared in the Magistrates' Court, followed by the Crown Court for the Plea and Direction hearing, then eventually the trial. Her husband was news. Salacious, lascivious news.

And now, again, they were living life on a knife edge, not knowing whether he would keep his job. The union rep told him not to worry, but it was all right for him; he had money coming in. If Graham were dismissed, branded unsuitable to work with children, what would he do? What would they do? They couldn't exist on her salary, certainly not with a baby. Midwives – even senior ones – didn't earn that much.

She put the testing stick back in its box and dropped them in the wastebasket. Her heart pounded in her chest and she took deep breaths to quell the panic that was rising in her. It wasn't just the loss of Graham's job and the money, although that was bad enough. It was Graham himself. The truth was she feared his reaction; he was on the edge. His moods had become wildly unpredictable, swinging from depression to explosive anger in a matter of minutes, sometimes over the most trivial things.

Fury rose in her. One girl had done this. One stupid, silly, lying slag of a girl. Damn Shayla

Richards, damn her and her lies. Damn her to hell.

Jane marched out of the bathroom, slamming the door behind her. In the bedroom she pulled on a pair of jeans and a sweatshirt and ran downstairs. The post lay by the front door. Not much – junk mail mostly. She gazed at it for a moment and as she bent down to pick it up she tried to ward off the familiar feeling of unease. She used to look forward to letters, but now she was nervous of them. Since the accusation had become common knowledge, they had brought either bad news or obscene messages. Did Shayla Richards have any idea what she was doing when she accused Graham, describing so graphically and so falsely how he fondled her breasts and genitals in the store adjoining his classroom?

Jane threw the letters on the kitchen table and opened the fridge. No milk; he must have forgotten to bring it in before he left for his run. She unlocked the front door and stepped outside. A steady drizzle was falling and the smell of autumn was in the air. As she picked up the bottles she saw Mr Heywood across the road pushing his wheelie bin to the edge of the footpath. She waved at him and he waved back. Poor man, he'd become so confused since his wife died. She'd been such a lovely lady who saw good in everyone and had never once doubted Graham. 'Such a gentle man,' she'd say, 'and a gentleman.' She'd even asked if it would help if she was a character witness, but had passed away before the case came to trial.

Jane returned to the kitchen, took the packet of

34

muesli from the cupboard and was about to pour some into a bowl when she heard the knock on the front door. Graham? No it couldn't be; he wasn't due back yet. Unless... Her heart missed a beat. He had gone out for his run early. She had begged him not to – it wasn't safe running in the dark she'd said – but he'd become angry and snapped that he wasn't stupid and knew how to take care of himself.

As she approached the door she could make out blurred shapes through the patterned glass and the familiar feeling of dread set in. Would she ever get over it? She turned the Yale and in front of her stood two men: one white, one Asian, both smartly dressed, their heavy winter coats buttoned against the weather.

'Yes?'

The older of the two spoke, his expression serious. 'Mrs Collins? Detective Inspector John Handford and Detective Sergeant Khalid Ali. Is your husband in?'

Ernest Heywood returned to the house. He was sure there was something he had to tell Mrs Collins. When she'd waved at him, some memory stirred at the back of his mind, but try as he might, he couldn't bring it forward. It was like there was a blank area in his brain, a black hole that events slipped through. Yet he was sure that whatever it was, was important. He shuffled his way back in to the kitchen. The house was cold and he pulled his cardigan around him. Edith would have told him to put the central heating on, and he would when they were further into winter. Technically, it was still autumn and for the moment his cardigan and the gas fire would do. It wasn't that he couldn't afford it, but there was no point wasting money when it wasn't necessary. He flicked the switch on the kettle and filled a pan with water. He always had a boiled egg for breakfast. His doctor told him it would be better if he cut down, prevent cholesterol clogging his arteries, but he'd ignored the advice. Did it matter at eighty-four? Did it matter now Edith was gone?

He watched the water begin to boil, the bubbles bursting and splashing onto the stainless steel of the hob. Carefully he lowered the egg into the pan and turned the timer to three minutes. As he took a slice of bread out of the packet, he wished he could remember what it was he wanted to tell Mrs Collins. Perhaps if he went into the front room and looked across at her house, he might remember.

The mist that had blanketed the road earlier was beginning to lift now, and the street lights were off. A car drove down the road and parked in the turning circle at the end of the cul-de-sac. The men, one white, one Asian, slammed the doors as they got out, then scrutinized the houses before walking towards the Collinses. Mr Heywood grimaced. Jehovah's Witnesses, Mormons, double-glazing salesmen; they had them all down here. He watched as they knocked on the door. He'd go across if it seemed they were harassing her. But he didn't need to because they weren't there more than a few minutes.

Funny, though. He could have sworn she

looked upset as she watched them drive away.

On his return from the abortive visit to see Graham Collins, Detective Sergeant Ali went straight to the incident room. Several officers assigned to the case from other subdivisions had already arrived and were standing in groups chatting. Others from Central joined them. He saw the copper-haired detective as he walked through the door and scrutinized the list, heaving an internal sigh of relief that Chris Warrender's name was not on it. To say he disliked the man was an understatement. The two of them shared an unpleasant history based on mutual dislike, Warrender's grounded in prejudice, his own in anger and frustration.

Ali walked over to him. 'What do you want, Warrender?' he asked, his voice hard.

The constable didn't seem to notice. 'I have a meeting with the DI,' he said.

'Why?'

Smaller and stockier than the sergeant, Warrender was dressed in a bottle-green crew-necked sweater and dark grey chinos. He sauntered towards Ali until he was close. 'I don't think that's any of your business, do you?'

Conscious of the sudden silence that had descended on the room, Ali stared at Warrender – a non-verbal reminder of their respective ranks, then moved to the table at the front of the room, picked up a clutch of files and said casually, 'Not if you're bringing him his sandwiches, but it is if you're joining the murder team. Are you, Constable?'

Warrender smirked. 'Joining the team? It would seem so, Sergeant.' He emphasized the final word.

Ali could feel hostility taking over and tried to keep his voice level. 'The DI asked for you?'

Warrender perched on the table. 'You wouldn't like that, would you, Ali? But don't worry, I requested a transfer; it came through the end of last week. Takes effect immediately.'

Ali frowned. Why wasn't the man's name on the list, and more importantly, why hadn't John mentioned it? He said, 'I'm surprised you wanted to come back here. I would have thought you were better suited to where you were – vice squad, wasn't it?' He knew he shouldn't let the man get to him, just assign him a desk and leave it at that.

Warrender slipped into the nearest chair and put his feet up on the table. 'That's right, but between you and me, Sergeant, I've had it up to here with prostitutes, pimps and kerb-crawlers. It's not all freebies when the toms are not too busy, you know. Then again you probably wouldn't. From what I've heard you lot take it when you want it, don't have to ask.'

Ali slammed down the files as his anger got the better of him. 'You lot?' he enquired, a steely edge to his voice.

Warrender smiled. 'Married men,' he said, his green eyes twinkling. 'Who did you think I meant?' The smile faded. 'The DI, is he in?'

Graham Collins leaned against the gravestone. The cemetery stood on the hillside and from it he could see the school: the buildings, the pupils, the staff. To look at the cars in the car park made

38

him feel better. He shouldn't be here. He'd been told to keep away, and at first he did. But eventually he decided the head and the governors might feel they had the right to take everything from him: his life, his job, his belief in himself. But they had no right to his freedom, particularly now that Shayla had admitted to lying and he had been found not guilty. He could go where he wanted.

The kids from the school used the cemetery as well. To them it was a place where they were unfettered by rules and regulations. It was where they came after they had registered in their classrooms. It was here that they bought and sold their drugs and sniffed their glue. There was no one here now, but he felt their presence, heard their voices – fuck this and fuck that – no reverence, no thought for the deceased's next of kin, just their own selfish pursuits. Scoring, shooting up. They had their own language, an ever-changing language, a language of those on the edge of self-destruction. He looked at his watch. Given another five minutes, they would begin walking out of school. Straight out of the front door, no attempt to hide and no one caring enough to stop them. Mostly the staff were glad to see the back of them.

But now it was peaceful and Graham leaned his head against the stone and felt its firmness. The iciness of the wet grass penetrated his jogging suit and he shivered. But he didn't move because both added to his discomfort proving that his physical senses had not yet been destroyed. Not so his emotions – they came and went. Sometimes there was nothing: no despair, no bewilderment, no anger; at other times all were strong, each vying for supremacy. Anger was the one he feared most, for when anger took over he knew that, given the right circumstances, the right time and the right place, he could not trust himself to walk away.

He closed his eyes tight to shut out the images: the girl in the shopping centre holding out her hand to him, then snatching it away, teasing him, laughing at him. Tears welled in his eyes. She shouldn't have done that; she shouldn't have humiliated him like that; it was no one's fault but her own.

As Warrender left him, John Handford picked up the phone, dialled Cliffe Top Comprehensive and asked to be put through to his wife. He had no idea how well Gill, as Head of English, had known Shayla Richards, but she might just be able to give him some initial information on her and on Graham Collins that he could take into the briefing with him. He drummed his fingers on the desk and as he waited he let his thoughts roam back to the interview he'd had with Warrender. There was no doubt the man would be a real asset to the team, but it was a pity he and Ali didn't get on. He was sure neither one of them would deliberately let their dislike of each other screw up the investigation. It would be up to Ali as the sergeant to make sure it didn't.

He heard the click of the receiver being picked up. 'Gill Handford.'

'Gill, it's me. I won't keep you long, but I need some information. What do you know about

40

Shayla Richards?'

'Shayla?' A heavy sigh blasted in Handford's ear. 'What's she done now?'

'She's dead, Gill. It was her body up at Druid's Altar.'

For a long moment there was silence. 'Are you sure?'

'Quite sure.'

'How did she die?'

'She was asphyxiated, but we don't know how until we have the results of the post-mortem.'

'John, that's awful.' She sounded distressed. 'How can I help? What do you want to know?'

'Something about the girl – anything. I need some background.'

'I don't have much; she's away from school more than she's here, particularly since she joined Kerry Johnson and her gang.'

Kerry Johnson. That name had cropped up on the list of friends he'd been given by the officer dealing with Shayla's disappearance. 'Did she have any other friends besides Kerry, do you know? Boyfriends perhaps?'

'She may have had. I can't say I ever saw her with anyone, but then, as I said, she was hardly ever around.' Gill hesitated. 'It was Graham Collins she had a crush on.'

'Yes, we know about him. She accused him of indecent assault, then retracted. What was the history between them?'

'No history. He complained once or twice she was stalking him and that he couldn't turn a corner without bumping into her. We told him to be careful and not to be alone with her, and her

41

head of year said he would have a word, but Graham made light of it, said she would get over it. To him it was one big joke.'

Not a joke then and certainly not a joke now.

'I know you shouldn't speak ill, John,' she went on, 'but she could be something of a bitch, our Shayla. I'm willing to bet her accusation was her form of revenge at being ignored, and to be honest, given everything that had gone before, I would have thought the officer who investigated would have had more sense than to take it all the way. At best it was her word against his.'

Suddenly Handford had the feeling he was on the wrong side of the fence. 'Am I to gather from that that the staff are closing ranks round Graham Collins?'

'All the more so since he hasn't been allowed back into school.' He could hear her anger growing. 'The governors and the education authority are holding their own internal inquiry first. They need to assure themselves that there is nothing else – you know, with other pupils.'

'Someone who may have been afraid to come forward before might do so now, you mean?' Handford paused for a moment. 'Could there be anyone?'

'John!'

Handford laughed. 'You're going to tell me he's a good man who couldn't kill if his own life depended on it. You're probably right, Gill. Even so, with the governors gunning for him, he can't be thinking too kindly of Shayla at the moment, can he?'

Her incredulity seeped through his earpiece.

'You mean he's under suspicion for her death?' Before he could tell her he had no suspects, merely people he had to talk to, she said, 'Don't be ridiculous, John. If he were going to do that he would have done it long ago. And like you say, he's far too gentle to raise a finger, let alone murder someone.'

Handford wished he could believe that. Gill was describing the man she knew before his world was turned upside down. Allegations and inquiries did things to you psychologically that changed you into a person you never thought you could become. He knew; he'd been through it a couple of years ago. There were times when he'd felt murderous, but he'd been fighting a community at his inquiry, not one person, and most of the time he'd felt impotent, powerless to sway the outcome. Collins on the other hand was fighting a young girl. In the right circumstances, he could be the dominant one. And if he wanted to pay her back, who knows what that would result in? Murder, perhaps?

This was too close to home and Handford moved onto ground that didn't awaken memories. 'Do you know anything else about Shayla, Gill – apart from the court case?'

'Not a lot. Her parents are divorced – a mixed marriage that didn't work out, I think. That's about it. I didn't come into contact with her that much. I'll have a word with her head of year if you like. Can I tell him why?'

'I don't see why not. It'll be all over the papers soon.'

'And so will your name as investigating officer.'

43

Her voice caught on the edge of her words and for a moment she hesitated, then she said, 'Can't you hand this over to someone else, John? Give it to Khalid. I'm bound to be given a hard time if you're involved.'

Handford was puzzled. 'Why? It's nothing to do with you.'

'Because I've been through it before.'

Been through it before? She'd never mentioned that or if she had he couldn't remember. 'When was this?'

'A year or two ago, when Graham was being questioned about the attack on Shayla. We could all see how badly it was affecting him, yet the officer didn't hold back. From what I can gather he gave him a really hard time before he charged him.'

'And the staff blamed you?' It appeared that even school staffrooms had their Warrenders.

'Some of them, yes.'

'That was a bit unfair.' He had been about to say childish.

'They were angry, John, and they needed to take it out on someone. I was the nearest thing to a police officer.'

Handford's voice softened. 'Why didn't you tell me, Gill?'

'I don't know.' She sighed as though she was trying to understand herself. 'I suppose partly because I feared you'd march in and make matters worse and partly because you were still getting over your own inquiry. But this time, John,' her voice became stronger, 'it's different. It's your case now and I can't argue that it's nothing to do with you. Everyone here has always been on Graham's side. There's even talk of industrial action if the governors go ahead with their inquiry and once you start to question him over Shayla's death they will be all the more determined. You and I will be under so much pressure – me from those here who will make it difficult for me if you treat Graham as a suspect, and you from your bosses and from Shayla's family and friends if you don't. Don't do this to us, John. Hand it over to Khalid, please.'

Handford's heart sank as he floundered in a mixture of exasperation and concern. Exasperation against a staff who seemed not to understand that a young girl had been murdered and her killer needed to be apprehended, and concern that because of him, his wife might become a whipping boy. He swallowed hard. For the first time ever his private life and his job were moving in opposite directions but in the same orbit. Sooner or later, inevitably, they would collide. He imagined Gill in her office, running her hand through her hair as she did when she was worried and he longed to go up there and put his arms round her and hold her close. But he couldn't; nor could he give her what she wanted.

'Khalid's a sergeant, and you don't give a murder case to a sergeant,' he said, the words sticking in his throat. 'You know how it works, Gill. It's my job. I promise I'll try to make it as easy on you as possible, but I can't hand it over just because you work with the man. The DCI wouldn't allow it. And what if Collins has an alibi? I'd look pretty silly demanding to be taken off the case if it's discovered he was at a church meeting at the relevant time.'

'I'm not sure he goes to church.' The ice-breaker. Gill was good at that.

He laughed. 'I'm sure it will be fine. We'll talk about it later. Perhaps we could have lunch. I'll come up to school.'

'No,' Gill said quickly – too quickly. 'No, I'll see you at Central.' A bell rang in the background. 'I've got to go,' she said.

Handford replaced the receiver. He had a bad feeling about this. Like it or not he would have to investigate Collins and already his own wife didn't want him around her at school. For her sake he would try to tread carefully but however careful he was, he was well aware that to her colleagues he would be the bad guy.

Kerry Johnson slouched across her desk, her head resting on her arm. The teacher kept looking at her, the one whose husband was a copper, but she didn't say anything. It was better like that, because it did 'er 'ead in when they were always on at her. The one who'd taken the register this morning hadn't been able to resist a dig. 'Kerry, it's nice of you to pop in. What made you join us today?'

'Because it's fucking raining outside. But that doesn't mean I'm stopping.' But she had stopped, although she might not have, had she known they were going to do Shakespeare. Romeo and Juliet. What wankers. The class was talking about arranged marriages because Juliet was being forced to marry some prince. No one would make

46

her marry someone she didn't want to, Kerry had said, and one of the Asian girls had insisted there was nothing wrong with arranged marriages. They worked.

'Only because the women daren't say anything if they don't.'

The teacher had stopped it there. She'd said they were getting away from the point. Yeah, and the rest.

They'd been given homework – an essay about how the nurse, the friar and the parents had been as much to blame for the final tragedy as the two lovers themselves had. She might do that one; it sounded just up her street. She could even make out a case that if they hadn't listened to any of them, they could have had it off in secret instead and not ended up dead.

Kerry thought little of marriage. She'd seen enough of it to last her a lifetime. Her mother and father had been married and never stopped rowing and fighting – real fighting with fists, until one Christmas Eve when Kerry was twelve. Her father had come home drunk and hit her mother, who'd fallen against the kitchen cabinet. She'd given her head a real crack and hadn't moved. He'd decided he'd killed her and ran off. He didn't stop to look. Kerry had rung for an ambulance straight away and when they came she could see the paramedics were trying their best, but it was too late; her mother died in hospital from a blood clot. Her father got life. She didn't miss him, but she missed her mother.

Social services took Kerry into care at first, but she didn't like it and went to live with Sean and

Glenys. The social worker said she seemed happy there and let her stay, then promptly forgot about her, which suited her fine – the more so when Glenys left. Even though he was her father's brother, she liked Sean, got on well with him. They had lots of laughs and he was not on her back all the time, insisting she went to school and the like. He gave her money when she needed it and taught her how to get it for herself when they were both really short. In return she gave him what he wanted when he couldn't find a woman. She didn't mind. It was only sex.

The class watched a video about Romeo and Juliet for the last half hour of the lesson. It had Leonardo di Caprio in it. Kerry liked Leonardo di Caprio, but thought Romeo was a wimp. The best bit was when Romeo and Juliet spent their first night together after they were married, and he woke up sprawled across the bed stark naked. Kerry wolf whistled. He had a lovely bum. The Asian girls looked away. For God's sake, it was only a bum.

This was ace, a lesson worth coming to again. There was more to Shakespeare than she imagined. She whistled again when Romeo pulled himself off the bed and walked over to the window. The Asian girls continued to sit with their heads bowed. They didn't know what they were missing. She waited with bated breath in the hope that he would turn round and give them a full frontal, but he didn't and when the classroom door opened and a teacher came in, stooped down and whispered in Mrs Handford's ear, the video was turned off. Kerry groaned. Trust a teacher to spoil the fun.

He stood in front of them. 'There's no easy way to tell you this,' he said. 'I'm sorry, but Shayla Richards was found dead this morning.'

The students turned to look at each other, Romeo and Juliet forgotten. A girl started to cry and someone put an arm round her.

'How sir? How did she die? Was it drugs?'

'I'm sorry, I don't know any more than that she has been found dead. Please can you pack up your things and return to your tutor room. There will be an assembly in half an hour.'

Kerry watched as the others filed out of the classroom. No one spoke to her; no one put an arm round her shoulder; no one cared about how she was feeling. Shayla had been her friend as well and no one gave a shit.

She turned in the opposite direction and walked out of school.

chapter three

Handford stared at the file in front of him, strain showing on his heavy features. He was attempting to go over his notes on policy decisions and strategies for the investigation, but could neither concentrate nor remember what he'd read. Gill's reaction worried him. They had been married almost twenty years, had two daughters of fifteen and thirteen and in all that time she had never once asked him to give up on a case. Surely by now she must know it was impossible. Even if he went along with what she wanted, he'd need a better reason than that his wife might be ostracised by her colleagues. The DCI would send him away with a carefully worded bollocking, and quite rightly.

He turned his attention to the list of actions. Towards the top was the intention to set a group of officers on interviewing all teachers at Cliffe Top Comprehensive who had a link with the dead girl. He knew that would make things worse, but it had to be done.

He shook his head; his brain was like mush. Early morning calls had never rested easily on him and he needed a dose of caffeine to revive him. He was just about to ring through to CID and ask someone to bring him a coffee when there was a knock at the door.

Before he had time to acknowledge it,

50

Detective Sergeant Ali appeared and strode towards the desk, a frown creasing his forehead. Handford groaned inwardly. That frown meant that he was not pleased about Warrender joining the team and had come to make his feelings known. He could do without this. Coffee was what he needed, not problems.

He thought of warding Ali off by asking him to bring him a mug, but seeing the expression on the sergeant's face, he decided against it. Instead he said, 'What's the matter?'

He saw the question dig into Ali's anger. 'Warrender,' he said.

'What about Warrender?'

'Is he on the team?'

Handford picked up his pen and clicked the top to retract the ballpoint. 'Yes, he is.'

'Permanently?'

The inspector kept his tone casual. 'As permanent as any of us ever are.'

At this Ali's fury spilled over and he leaned across the desk. 'Why?' he demanded.

Handford glared at him. There were times when dealing with Ali's paranoia was like pushing rocks up a hill. His words when he finally spoke were as cold as he could make them. 'I wasn't aware that staff decisions were any of your concern, Sergeant, but since you ask he's a very experienced detective. Both the DCI and I agreed he would be an asset to the team.'

Ali pushed himself away, turned and stood for a moment, his back to his boss. He was breathing deeply, trying, no doubt, to contain his anger. Handford waited.

Eventually, Ali turned round. 'He's a racist and a bigot, John,' he said quietly. 'And you know it. He doesn't belong on a case involving a black family.'

Handford sat back in his chair. 'Don't be ridiculous, Ali, we work in Bradford. If we took him off every case involving black or Asian families, he would sit twiddling his thumbs most of the time.'

'Then he shouldn't be a police officer.'

Perhaps not, but the beginning of a murder inquiry was not the time to debate staff appointments, however unpalatable. Everyone was aware of Warrender's racist and bigoted attitude, yet not only had there never been an official complaint against him from senior officers or the public, but also he was a good detective and popular in the station. If Ali tried to stir up trouble he would find himself in the same position with his colleagues as Gill feared she would be with hers.

He indicated the chair at the other side of the desk. At first Ali remained where he was. 'For goodness' sake, Khalid, sit down.'

Reluctantly, Ali did as he was told.

'I gather you two have had words,' Handford said. 'Has Warrender made comments to which you object? Because if he has, report him.'

'Warrender never comments, John, he intimates, and then suggests you have misunderstood. And don't ask if I did misunderstand. I know a racist remark that won't stand up to investigation when I hear one.' Handford saw him stiffen and his arrogance joined forces with his anger. 'I won't work with him. If he's on this case, then I'm not.

I'll go for a transfer.'

With an ultimatum like that there was no chance of a rational discussion, nor was Handford about to give him one. He didn't need to; Ali wasn't the token Asian in the station any more, needing to be pampered. There were two in CID, several in uniform and the new duty inspector was one Sayed Walid. If Warrender was a problem to Ali, then he would have to sort him out himself. Handford flicked shut the file in front of him, picked up his pen and pointed to the filing cabinet. 'Then you know where the transfer forms are. Take one and bring it back to me to sign.'

Ali's eyes widened in disbelief and when he spoke astonishment laced his words. 'You'd keep him and let me go?'

'If that's what you want.'

For a moment Ali seemed to struggle with his emotions. 'That's what they do in schools, isn't it?' he said bitterly. 'Get rid of the victim and let the bully stay. I'm the victim here.'

'Then deal with it, Ali. You're the sergeant; he's the constable. You outrank him.' Handford put his pen into his pocket and picked up the file. He fixed the sergeant with a hard stare. 'I understand you're looking to move up to inspector?'

'Yes.'

'Then learn to handle the Warrenders of this world, because until you do, I promise you, you'll not be given your two pips.' Handford pushed back his chair and stood up. 'You're a good detective, Khalid, one of the best, but you have a weakness, and Warrender is part of it. I'm giving you an opportunity to work on that weakness.

Take it, because I'm not going to do it for you.'

Ali remained silent as Handford walked towards the door.

'If you still want that transfer form, Sergeant, you know where it is. If not, let's stop wasting time and get on with the job we're being paid for.'

It was raining when Kerry Johnson walked out of the school's front door. She stopped for a moment to check no one was about to call her back, although she thought it unlikely the teachers would come after her, or even care that she'd gone. They'd never done before and this time they'd be too preoccupied with the news about Shayla to bother.

She pulled her collar round her ears, but it didn't prevent the wind biting into her nose and cheeks and she knew it wouldn't be long before they were red with cold. Tugging her anorak even tighter, she pushed her way through the group of journalists and photographers gathering at the front door. For a moment she wondered whether she should tell them that she'd been Shayla's friend, give them an interview, but then she thought of Sean and his hatred of the press and his anger if she got her name in the papers. So, as much as she would have liked people reading about her and her personal involvement with the murdered girl, she decided it was better to leave it to the teachers. Even though they knew the real Shayla, in a situation like this they'd have to make her look good. They would say she was a lovely girl who didn't deserve to die in this way and that everyone would miss her.

Yeah, right.

The fact was that the real Shayla would be missed by her family and by Kerry, but not by the kids in the English class who'd cried crocodile tears at the news or by the teachers who'd wiped their hands of her long ago.

The real Shayla was the one Kerry knew. The one who was a bitch with hardly any friends; the one who never stopped moaning about her life, boring everybody stupid; and the one who, when people stopped listening, downed a bottle of paracetamol and ended up having her stomach pumped, or accused teachers of groping her, as she had with Collins. How daft was that? And how daft was it that Kerry cared?

She set off down the hill, annoyed with her feelings and annoyed that there were tears running down her cheeks. She never cried – not even when her father killed her mother had she cried – and she shouldn't be crying now. She could pretend to the passengers who had got off the bus and were walking towards her that the tears were brought by the wind whipping in her face, but not to herself. Shayla was – had been – nothing but an attention-seeking cow, not worth anybody's time, and Kerry should have left well alone. But she hadn't. Instead she'd broken all her own rules and she didn't know why. And now Shayla was dead and she didn't deserve to be, and Kerry was crying. Angrily, she slapped away the tears and began to run – away from the school and the kids and from the teachers who didn't expect her to be upset and neither noticed nor cared that she was, and away from her memories of Shayla.

She'd been a gang member, useless at shoplifting, useless at mugging, but good at keeping
her mouth shut. Like a faithful dog, following and
doing whatever she was told. Desperately needing
to be someone's friend. As a gang member she
had a status she would have got nowhere else, a
status others wanted and had been refused. These
others, it suddenly occurred to Kerry, for no
other reason than they were jealous or malicious,
would take pleasure in telling the cops that she
and Shayla were friends and that Shayla had been
in Kerry's gang. Then they'd have the cops
buzzing round them like flies, involving her in the
police investigation, and because she was Sean's
niece, Sean as well.

He'd tried it on with Shayla once when she'd
first joined the gang and when Kerry wasn't
around, and the silly bitch had been so proud
that she mouthed off to everyone. Kerry had
given him and her what for afterwards, but if
anyone let it slip now the police would make two
and two add up to whatever they wanted them to
add up to, and she couldn't risk that. Without
Sean she'd be back in foster care. It wouldn't
matter that she'd been with him most of last
night and could give him an alibi; the cops would
hang on until they were a hundred and ten per
cent sure he wasn't implicated. It was inevitable
and it had happened before. Alibi or not, as far as
the police were concerned Sean would never
escape his past.

Kerry turned the corner, the wind buffeting her
as she struggled towards the bus shelter. Once
there, she sat down, pulled her mobile out of her

pocket and sent out four text messages: one to each of the gang and one to her uncle. When it came to murder, the living, she decided, were more important than the dead.

Khalid Ali leaned against the wall at the back of the incident room and watched Handford as he conducted the briefing. He struck an imposing figure as he stood at the front, tall and well built, cloned at a time when height and weight were all-important for a police officer. He was good at his job, too. He described Shayla Richards' murder and the state of the body without preamble or comment, then organized uniformed officers into groups, some to help with the fingertip search of the moor, keeping a special lookout for her clothes, others to make more detailed inquiries as to where she could have been while she was missing. He allocated teams to interview staff at the school and check on modern-day Druid groups, or any other so-called religious cult. 'I don't want us to make too much of this,' he said, 'and I certainly don't want it in the public domain, but we can't assume there isn't some pseudo-religious group practising human sacrifice in the district. I hope to God there isn't, but the location, the date, the arrangement of the body and the fire all suggest a religious ceremony of some kind. We can only rule it out when we find nothing to substantiate it.' He paused for a moment and stared hard at each one of them. 'This information is not to go out of this office. If I see a report of it in a newspaper or on a TV programme or hear it on the radio, I will find whoever has leaked it and pull

57

them apart .Understood?'

There were murmurs of 'Yes, guv.' Everyone in that room understood the importance of what he was saying. They respected John Handford. It was sad that his own respect for him had waned when he refused to back him over Warrender. Ali was speculating on his disappointment when he heard the silence and realized heads had turned to look at him.

'I know we were up early this morning, but try to keep up, Khalid,' Handford said.

'Sorry.'

Warrender tried to smother a laugh with a bout of coughing.

Handford fixed the constable with a hard look, then turned back to Ali. 'I was asking if there was any news about the postmortem.'

'Yes, sir. The body has been moved to the mortuary and the post-mortem is set for two o'clock this afternoon, but she hasn't been formally identified yet and the pathologist would prefer she was before he begins.'

'You'd better do that. In fact you and Warrender can go up to the house and meet up with the family liaison officer, who is...' He consulted his file. 'Connie Burns. You and she can take Mrs Richards to make the identification. In the meantime Warrender, check out the house, specifically Shayla's bedroom. It's probably a long shot, but see if you can find her clothes. When Sergeant Ali and PC Burns get back, I want the two of you to question Mrs Richards about her daughter as well as her own movements yesterday. Check she was studying at the university during the day and

58

cleaning there late afternoon, and that she really was at bingo last night. It should be easy enough if she won the money as she claimed. If Calvin is around, question him as well. If he isn't, find him and go through his movements from midday yesterday. He was at the hotel when we went to warn him of Shayla's death, but check with the head chef that he was there for the whole shift. And bring back his footwear for forensics. If he was up at Druid's Altar at all, there should be some sign of it on his shoes.'

While the constable murmured agreement, Ali made no reply. He couldn't believe Handford was expecting him to spend most of the day cooped up with Warrender and his prejudices. Was this his way of forcing the issue? Like the threat of him not getting promotion unless he learnt to work with the man? Deal with him, he'd said. Why should he? He wasn't the racist. The change in behaviour should come from the constable, not from him.

'Wouldn't it be better to bring Calvin in?' Warrender suggested. 'He's Afro-Caribbean and the fire report says that the caller's voice could have been West Indian. If we interview him on tape, his voice pattern can be examined against the 999 calls.'

'I hear what you're saying and I'm tempted,' Handford agreed. 'But I don't want to waste time and money if it isn't him. There doesn't seem much doubt that the same person made all four calls, yet if we're looking towards the uncle as a suspect, then two things worry me about them. Firstly, why three hoax calls before the genuine one? One, possibly two to test response times, but three smacks of someone out to make mischief for the fire service. Secondly, they were all made from the same box in Bingley. Calvin works and lives six miles away in Bradford. If he was working, even for some of the time, why go so far at that time of night to ring the fire brigade? Why not do it from the city?' Handford paused for a moment. When there were no suggestions forthcoming, he continued. 'Let's move on to Shayla, now. What would be Calvin's motive for killing his own niece?'

Ali pushed himself away from the wall and moved towards the front of the room. Against his better judgement he could feel the adrenaline surging. 'She accused a teacher of molesting her and then admitted she'd been lying. That must have caused the family some grief.'

'Enough to kill her?' Warrender said. 'Can't see it myself. They'd be more likely to knock her around or give her a good beating for lying. And from what the boss described, unless the PM comes up with something, there's no sign of that. Quite the opposite, in fact. Now if she'd been a Muslim, that would be different. She wouldn't be the first in this city to be strangled or suffocated for bringing shame on the family.'

Silence descended on the room.

Again the man seemed to be publicly damning his religion, not caring how offensive he was being. Angrily, he turned towards Warrender, but as he did so his anger drained away, for the constable was not smirking, but deadly serious and although he hated to admit it, right – it wouldn't be the first time such a death had occurred.

'She probably was Muslim,' Ali said. 'The husband would insist the children were brought up in his faith, and because of that, Shayla's original accusation and then her lies would bring shame on him. He might even feel the assault, if it happened, was her own fault, so even that would shame him. Warrender's right. If he has come back and murdered her, he would justify it as an honour killing.'

'Except,' Handford argued, 'Mrs Richards and the children have hardly heard from him since he took the first flight back to Pakistan after the hearing. Just that one letter–'

'In which,' Ali interrupted, 'he said he would get them one way or another. Perhaps he's come back intending to snatch them, except that he wouldn't want Shayla. She'd let him down, but worse still she'd let down Islam. He would see killing her as his only option.'

'So how do you account for the arrangement of the body and the 999 calls? What do they mean?'

Ali sighed. 'I don't,' he said, 'not yet.'

'A lot depends on the relationship between the husband and Calvin,' mused Warrender. 'They could both be involved.' He looked towards Handford. 'Do you want me to check them out, guv?'

'Yes. The former husband is Qumar Hussain. See if he is now, or has been back in the country recently. And if he is currently here, find him, although you'd better check all flights to Pakistan yesterday and today. If he was involved, then he's very likely fled already. Report back to Sergeant

61

Ali. If it turns out we're right and he has gone, you'll need to talk to the community relations officer.'

Ali nodded.

Handford walked over to the map of the district. 'The only feasible way to take a body up to Druid's Altar is by car and the shortest route is up Altar Lane, as ruinous as it is to your suspension. Otherwise it's a walk of about a mile and a half from the other direction, or a climb through the woods and up the hill. I wouldn't like to contemplate carrying a body either way at that time of night.'

'Unless she wasn't dead then. Perhaps she went of her own volition or was forced up there by the killer.'

'Perhaps. According to the police surgeon, Shayla may have been killed elsewhere, although he doesn't rule out that it could have happened somewhere on the moor. By the time he examined her, she'd been dead about ten to twelve hours. If she was with someone then we need to know who it was, whether he could have killed her and if he did why he waited until almost midnight to light the fire and contact the fire brigade. There's not much sense to any of this yet, but I must say what we've got at the moment smacks of it being a well-planned murder.' He turned to Ali. 'Anything to add, Sergeant?'

'Only that it's imperative we find out where Shayla has been since she disappeared. Uniform say there were no sightings of her at all, but given the girl's track record, I'm inclined to agree with the mother, that they expected her to turn up and didn't try very hard to find her. We have to know where she was. So we need to check out all her haunts and all the friends on the list, in particular Kerry Johnson.'

Warrender interrupted. 'Kerry Johnson; is that Sean Johnson's niece?'

'I don't know,' Ali said. 'Why?'

'Sean Johnson is a lifer on parole, has been for the past twelve years. He killed an eight-year-old kid when he was fifteen and did three years in a youth offenders' institution and five more in prison. Kerry went to live with him after her father killed her mother about three years ago.'

Ali was incredulous. 'Social services allowed her to live with a convicted murderer?'

Warrender shrugged. 'Apparently her social worker said she was happy there and they were around to keep an eye on her.'

'What about her father?'

'Got life.'

Handford asked, 'How did Johnson kill the eight-year-old?'

'She was asphyxiated – smothered, I think.' Handford and Ali exchanged glances and a buzz of conversation broke out round the room. 'He claimed it was an accident,' Warrender continued when there was silence. 'Said they were fooling about and it just happened.'

'A fifteen-year-old was fooling about with an eight-year-old?'

Warrender shrugged as though he didn't believe it either. 'That's what he claimed, guv.'

Handford turned to DC Clarke. 'Check it out. I want to know everything there is to know about

63

the Johnsons.'

'Guv.'

'Also, I want you and me to talk to Graham Collins. He wasn't in when Sergeant Ali and I called earlier. Let's see what he has to say for himself. The case file should give us some initial information.' He turned to Ali. 'Do you have it?'

'No, guv, we couldn't find it. It must have been misfiled. I've got a PC looking for it.'

Handford sighed. 'What about the officer dealing with the case? Perhaps I can talk to him – unless he's been misfiled too.'

Ali stiffened. 'I don't know who investigated, sir.' This was something he should have checked. He had intended to, but had become caught up with Warrender and it had gone clean out of his head. 'I'll get onto it, sir.' Even without the case file it was only a couple of years ago; someone must know.

'It was Detective Superintendent Slater, guv.' Heads turned towards Warrender. Ali groaned. He had to be the someone.

'Are you sure?' Handford was clearly astonished.

'Quite sure, guv.'

'But that's ridiculous,' Ali declared. 'Why should a superintendent investigate a case that any DC worth his salt could have done? Mr Slater would never involve himself in something so minor.'

It was Warrender's turn to glare. 'I'm only telling you what I know, Ali. If you choose not to believe it, that's up to you.'

'Stop that,' Handford snapped. 'How do you know, Warrender?'

'Because he asked me to check out Collins for him.'

'You?'

'Yes, guv.'

'And that's all you did: check out Collins?'

'His recent history; nothing further back. It didn't take long.'

Ali followed Handford into his office.

'Before we do anything, Ali, I have to know if you still want that transfer form. Because if you want to go, go now, not in the middle of the investigation.'

Ali didn't attempt to hide his annoyance. 'I don't know, sir, not yet.' He paused for a moment, then exhaled his frustration into the air. 'I don't want to go, John, and I certainly don't want to let you down, but you saw how he was with me – laughing at me, arguing with me.'

'You deserved to be laughed at,' Handford broke in. 'You should have had your mind on the briefing. And as for him arguing with you, all I saw was a man doing his job. He's a good detective with an analytical mind. Surely even you can see that.' Handford arched his eyebrows, demanding Ali's agreement.

'I do, but that doesn't mean I've got to like him or approve of him. But yes, I can't fault him as a detective.'

'Then that's all that matters.' Handford indicated he should sit down. 'You agree he has the local knowledge we don't have and that will be useful to us.'

Ali nodded.

Handford pushed further. 'Did you know about Sean Johnson?'

Ali shook his head.

'No, nor me. Warrender knows more about what goes on in this city than the rest of us put together, and whether you like him or not, we need him. Now let's get back to what's important.' Handford settled back in his chair. 'Can you think of any reason why Mr Slater investigated the assault on Shayla? It's like you said – any decent DC could have done it, yet he took it on. Why?'

'Short staffed?'

'I don't believe that. We're always short staffed but as far as I know he's never offered to help out before. No, there's something else. Shayla admitted to lying. If that was the case then an officer of Slater's experience ought to have been able to see through her, yet it went all the way.'

'It could be that the CPS were worried she was a black schoolgirl and if they didn't prosecute they would be accused of institutional racism. Their argument would be that it was in the public interest to bring it to court. Children's allegations against professionals who work with them have to be seen to go all the way. It might be nothing to do with Mr Slater.'

'No, but his decision to investigate instead of someone from CID had a lot to do with him.'

'So perhaps his reason had more to do with Collins than with Shayla Richards? You don't think they're related, do you? Or in the same lodge?'

'I don't know, but there's something. We need

66

that case file. We need to know why it went as far as the Crown Court.' Handford came to a decision. 'You check into Collins' background, Khalid – with a fine-tooth comb, please. I want everything you can dig up on him. And see how your PC is getting on finding the file; impress on him its importance. In the meantime, I'll have a word with Mr Slater.'

Ali stood up and put the chair against the wall.

Handford's telephone rang and he reached over to it, but didn't pick it up. 'You know, Khalid,' he said, 'we're only a few hours in and already I'm beginning to get a very nasty feeling about this case.'

chapter four

Warrender slid down in the passenger seat of the car and closed his eyes.

Ali glanced at him. 'Tired?' he asked.

The constable yawned. 'Overindulged last night, Sergeant. You know what it's like.' He opened one eye and squinted at Ali. 'But then, I don't suppose you do,' he said and settled down again.

They drove on in silence. It was easy for Ali to say he'd deal with Warrender, more difficult in practice. Regardless of Handford's opinion, the man was mocking him, putting two fingers up at his race and his authority, and he wasn't sure how to counter it effectively. Perhaps the best way for the moment was to ignore the comments and try to get to know him.

'You seem to know a lot about the area,' he said. 'Been in the district long?'

'I was born here, lived here most of my life; that's why I know a lot about it.'

'You're not married?' The question was clumsy and Ali knew it. Warrender sat up. 'You're asking a lot of questions, none of them any of your business.'

'Sorry, just interested.'

'In that case I'm not married. I'm not like you lot, have wives found for you. I prefer to find my own.'

Ali forced a smile. 'And so far you haven't?'

'No.'

The conversation was stilted and awkward and Warrender was keeping his answers to the bare minimum. Ali persevered. 'It's the job. So many broken dates and promises that it's difficult to commit.'

'If you like.'

Ali frowned. If you like? More a comment than an answer. 'What about family?'

Warrender sighed. 'My parents are dead and I have half a sister.'

Half a sister? He must have misheard, although he was sure he hadn't.

'Half a sister? What do you mean?'

Warrender turned to face him. Slowly and deliberately he answered the question. 'I mean I don't want to talk about it. I don't want to talk about me or my family, but particularly I don't want to talk about my sister, and especially not with you, Ali.'

'I'm sorry...' Ali's apology tailed off. 'I shouldn't have asked.'

His voice gravelly as though he had smoked too many cigarettes, Warrender said, 'No you shouldn't.'

They drove on in an awkward silence. War-render seemed angry, although at what Ali had no idea. Nor was he sure how or why he'd made a complete mess of his attempt at showing an interest in his colleague. His only consolation was that Handford couldn't say he hadn't tried.

The Richardses' house should have been no more than a ten-minute drive from Central, but traffic was heavy and it was slow going. As Ali paused at the lights, he wished he could say something to improve the atmosphere between them, but he was afraid any attempt at conversation might make things worse. He watched the Friday shoppers stream across the road intent on going about their own business. A few dashed across at the last minute, not caring that this was one of the most dangerous crossings in the city. Death and injury was something that happened to someone else, not to them. Had Shayla ever considered how her life would end? Doubtful; it was something old people thought about, not teenagers. As the lights changed to green, he pulled away and turned up the hill towards the Shipley–Airedale Road and from there on to Otley Road.

It was a dismal day. The sky was covered with a blanket of grey cloud and the rain, which had been heavy, now teased the air with the kind of light drizzle that wets, but does nothing to replenish half-full reservoirs. The wheels of the lorry in front of them threw sprays of grit onto the windscreen, distorting Ali's vision and he pressed the knob on the dashboard to clean it.

As they turned into Cliffe Top Lane on the approach to the house, Ali nodded towards the clutch of journalists outside the school. 'The papers will be full of this tonight. They'll have quotes from every schoolkid who comes out of that door.'

Warrender shrugged. 'Probably some at the Richardses' home as well. I just hope the FLO has kept the mother away from them.'

Relieved that they were at least being civil, Ali

said, 'Do you know Mrs Richards?'

'No, never had anything to do with her, although if she's like her daughter, I don't think she'll be much to write home about.'

'You've met Shayla, then?'

'I wouldn't say met exactly. Let's say our paths have crossed. I nicked her once when we suspected her of being involved in a mugging, but we couldn't make it stick. We thought she was part of Kerry Johnson's gang, but she didn't give anything away. Knew how to keep her mouth shut when it mattered, bloody lippy the rest of the time though.'

Ali remembered his own encounter with Mrs Richards. 'Her mother, too. She came at me like a charging animal this morning when I suggested she might prefer someone else to take on the task of identifying Shayla, then practically ignored me.'

'Of course she did, Ali, she's not going to be that fond of you, is she? You're a Pakistani. She's already divorced one; she's hardly likely to be thrilled to find another in her house.'

That was uncalled for. His anger against Warrender rising, Ali concentrated on manoeuvring into the spare parking place outside the Richardses' house. He brought the car to a stop and pulled at the brake harder than he intended.

Warrender looked down at Ali's hand, a smile curling along his lips. 'Careful, Sarge,' he said. 'There's a lot of hills between here and the mortuary; you'll need that brake cable.'

Ignoring the comment, Ali said, 'You researched Graham Collins for Mr Slater. What

71

exactly did you find?'

'Nothing much. Married three years to a mid-wife, no children. Not earning a fortune between them but comfortable enough to afford foreign holidays. Studied history at Warwick University, came out with a 2:1 degree and did his Post-graduate Certificate in Education at Leeds. Everyone I spoke to said he was a good student, but nothing special. I checked for a criminal record and for his suitability to work as a teacher. Nothing there, either.'

'You didn't trace further back than university?'

'No, Mr Slater didn't think it was necessary.'

'Or talk to any of the other pupils?'

'No, he told me not to.'

'Did you meet Collins?'

'There was no need.'

'You didn't go with Mr Slater then, when he questioned him?'

'No, all the super wanted was for me to do the legwork, find out a bit about him. He did every-thing else.'

'And you didn't think any of this was unusual?'

'Not for me to question why, Sarge.'

'No, but did you think it unusual?'

'Bloody unusual, but as you often remind me, I'm only the constable. I leave the decisions and the orders to those with stripes, pips and crowns.'

Ali smiled. 'Well, in that case, Warrender, the boss wants Collins researching more thoroughly. When we've finished with Mrs Richards and her brother and you've checked out their statements, I think you could make a start on it. Thoroughly, mind; go right back to his birth certificate.'

Warrender pulled himself straight. 'Christ, Ali, who do you think I am? Your white slave? That'll take for ever and I've got a date tonight.'

'Then cancel it. It won't do you any harm to have a celibate night in for once.'

Warrender unclipped his seatbelt. 'Screw you, Ali,' he muttered.

Ali was sure he was not meant to have heard, but he had and he wasn't about to let it go. 'I don't think so, Constable,' he grinned. 'I don't think so.'

Murder investigations, reflected Handford, fell into two categories: those solved in a few days and those that dragged on into weeks, months or even years, during which time they became cold cases. While not cold exactly it seemed to Handford that this case was already no more than luke-warm. There should have been some information on both Shayla Richards and Graham Collins from the indecent assault allegations but there was nothing. The case file had gone missing and so it appeared had the investigating officer. Detective Superintendent Slater had been sent to East Sussex to review a murder inquiry. This was not unusual; it often happened six weeks into an investigation, helped to bring new eyes to one that was floundering and give it a kick start. But since he'd gone four weeks in and, according to his secretary, at the request of the Chief Constable himself, Handford couldn't help feeling uneasy. Something was not right and his gut reaction was that it was to do with their case rather than that in East Sussex.

On the drive to the Collinses' house, Handford mulled over his concerns with Clarke. He and Andy had been friends since they joined the police service together as mature recruits, Handford having spent four torturous years teaching mathematics to teenage students who had little interest in anything, especially mathematics, and Clarke, five years his senior and a skilled engineer, choosing to avoid the inevitable as the industry began to slide inexorably into depression. Of the two, Handford had been the more ambitious and had risen through the ranks while Clarke had remained a constable. Nevertheless, there was no one on the squad whose judgement he trusted more than that of the man sitting next to him.

'There's something not right, Andy,' he said. 'It can't be a coincidence that on the very day Shayla is found dead both the case file on the original complaint and the investigating officer go missing.'

Clarke was phlegmatic. 'Yes it can, given that part of Mr Slater's job is reviewing other forces' ongoing cases.' He paused for a second. 'Although I can't speak for the file.'

Handford slowed the car to turn into the cul-de-sac. He drove along the road and parked at the edge of the Collinses' drive then turned off the engine and released his seatbelt. 'You think I'm making too much of this, don't you?'

Clarke smiled. 'I'm not into conspiracy theories, John, so yes I do, and if you think about it, you will as well. We had a complaint by a black girl against a white teacher at a time when racial

74

issues in this city were still raw. It doesn't matter whether the assault was racially motivated or not; it would have been too good an opportunity to miss to show that everyone got a fair deal when it came to the investigation of crime, so Detective Superintendent Slater was brought in. "You investigate this one, Slater. Let the black community see how seriously we're taking it."'

Handford had to agree, albeit reluctantly, that what Clarke was saying made sense. 'You think it was a PR exercise?'

'Yes, I do. The bosses were terrified of being seen to be racially prejudiced.'

Handford digested this for a moment. 'So what about the files?'

'Files go missing, John. It shouldn't happen, but it does. Talk to the CPS solicitor if you're still worried and if *their* files are missing then you know there is something fishy going on, otherwise forget it – it's not worth your time.' Suddenly he leaned forward and peered through the windscreen. 'Is that who I think it is?' he said.

Parked a hundred yards up the street was a red Fiesta and inside it a bespectacled man with wild bushy hair that never failed to remind Handford of an unkempt poodle once owned by an uncle of his. It had been called Fritz, he remembered.

Damn reporters. 'What's *he* doing here?' he groaned and pulled himself into the road.

As he approached the car, Peter Redmayne wound down the window. 'Hello, John. I thought if I waited long enough you'd pay Graham Collins a visit.'

Handford offered him a smile. Over time the

two had built up a grudging relationship occasionally bartering information. 'Hello, Peter. Not joining your colleagues outside the school or at Evelyn Richards' home?'

'No, I let the juniors do that. I go for the real story.'

'And you think the real story is here?'

'Don't you?'

Handford made no comment.

It was Redmayne's turn to smile. 'You can take that enigmatic look off your face, John; Collins is bound to be a suspect.'

'Routine inquiries, Peter, that's all. We're questioning all teachers who had a link with the dead girl.'

'Of course you are. You've no doubt got a team of PCs up at the school doing just that, whereas Collins warrants two plain clothes officers, one a Detective Inspector.' Redmayne returned the DI's gaze. 'Come on, John, I wasn't born yesterday. Shayla Richards accused the man of indecent assault and now she's dead.'

Handford prevaricated. 'That was some time ago and he was cleared.'

'Only by the courts. The governors are holding their own inquiry now; he could still lose his job.'

'Your point?'

'That girl had ruined his life once; perhaps he was afraid she'd do it again by changing her story. According to a neighbour she was a compulsive liar so it wouldn't have been beyond the bounds of possibility.'

You had to respect Redmayne. The news hadn't been passed on to the papers until Mrs Richards

76

had been informed of her daughter's death, yet he knew almost as much as Handford. He'd probably questioned more people than they had. The man ought to have been a detective instead of a journalist.

'At the moment we have no evidence to support any of that,' he replied stiffly.

Redmayne persisted. 'People who kill need only assumptions to support their paranoia, not evidence, and if you've spoken to Collins lately you'll know just how paranoid he is when it comes to Shayla Richards.'

'And you have?'

'Yes, I'm preparing one of those features on teachers who are wrongly accused of abuse by pupils and how it affects their lives. You know the kind of thing.'

Handford knew exactly what he meant – he had been through it when he had been falsely accused of racism a couple of years previously. It was something you never forgot, although no journalist had been interested enough to ask him how he had felt. He swallowed hard; paranoia was born of the bitterness at the unfairness of it all. Thank God the resentment he had felt had not developed into something worse.

'Without exception all have said the governors' inquiry is worse than the trial,' the journalist was saying. 'They fear the second time round the pupil might be believed – after all, it's drilled into professionals that we must believe children. They don't lie about something like this. Well, sadly, fourteen-year-olds do. At best they fantasize, at worst they lie, and Collins didn't trust Shayla not to change her story again. It wouldn't have affected the legal verdict, but it would certainly have put doubt in the governors' minds and they might just have given her the benefit of it. People have killed for less, John; you should know that. And for what it's worth Graham Collins is frightened and angry. His wife is afraid he'll harm himself, but I've been with him a lot over the last week and I wouldn't like to take bets on whether it's himself he's likely to harm, his wife or Shayla Richards.'

Handford frowned. Redmayne's logic was persuasive and he was inclined to believe him. The man was a good investigative journalist and his arguments were based on sound research and always well reasoned.

'How did you find out about the inquiry, Peter? Was it Collins?' As far as he knew the governors' inquiry was not in the public domain – according to Gill, they preferred to keep it in-house.

'No, it wasn't. When I asked him about it he refused flatly to comment and given the chair of governors is Lawrence Welford, I wouldn't put it past him to have threatened Collins with instant dismissal if he mentioned it. It makes you wonder doesn't it, whose interest Welford has at heart – his, the school's or the pupils'? Certainly not Collins. So, no names, but it *was* a member of staff who rang me. He said the public ought to know how they felt about what they consider the unjust treatment being meted out to a colleague, and...' Redmayne paused, seeming to grapple with how he should continue. At first Handford thought he had changed his mind and was going to leave it at that, but then, suddenly, he reached over and opened the passenger door. 'Get in, John.'

Handford did as requested and when he was settled he said, 'What?'

'That's not the only thing they're angry about.'

Handford felt his stomach lurch. 'Go on,' he said.

'They're angry that the husband of one of their own is investigating the case. My understanding is that Gill asked you to hand it over to someone else, and you refused. The feeling among the staff is that it's an underhand method by CID generally and you in particular, to gain inside information. To put not too fine a point on it, Gill is your snout. I gather you've already asked her for the low down on Shayla Richards and Graham Collins?'

Handford listened, aghast. How dare they? How dare they discuss Gill and him at all, but particularly with a reporter? Handford's anger got the better of him and he snatched at the door handle. 'What is it you want, Redmayne – a quote? Well you're not getting one, not from me.' He pushed open the door and wrenched himself out of the car.

As he strode away, the journalist called after him, 'I'll take that as a no comment then, shall I?'

Handford turned and walked back to the car, his grey eyes blazing. 'Take it as whatever you like, Redmayne, but I warn you, leave Gill out of this.'

Graham Collins was taking a phone call in another room when his wife showed the two detectives into the lounge. As they waited for him, Handford wondered if he was in conversation with Peter Redmayne and cursed his earlier anger. By letting his temper get the better of him, he'd given the journalist what he wanted. He doubted he had enough to make a story out of it yet, but he was pretty sure it wouldn't take him long to do so. For Gill's sake, Handford would have to set about limiting the damage as soon as he could.

He glanced at Clarke, who grimaced as he took in their surroundings. Handford knew instinctively what the constable was thinking. They'd both been in homes before that seemed to be doomed and brought only bad luck to the occupants and this was one of them. It was a troubled house; he'd felt it as soon as he entered, for there was a bleakness about it that was almost palpable. Other than that, it was the kind of dwelling in which you would expect to find a professional married couple.

Handford had been surprised at its size. From the outside the garden and frontage was that of a typical semi, but inside it was bigger than he expected. The room they were in was open plan, comprising large lounge and an equally large dining area, both generous enough to be divided off from each other and still have two good-sized rooms. French windows opened onto the back garden, which stretched from the patio on to two terraced lawns. Hard work to maintain, Handford thought, but they were in pristine condition so someone had done a good job.

The interior was immaculate, the decor tasteful, the lounge and dining room suites of good quality, and while they were not top of the range, the widescreen television, the video and DVD player were definitely twenty-first century technology. A computer, printer and scanner nestled on a desk in one corner of the dining room, presumably where Collins had prepared his work for school. Handford wondered when they had last been used for anything other than games and the Internet.

There was no doubt the couple had a comfortable lifestyle here, but it would take two salaries to sustain it and given what had happened it was not surprising Collins had become a frightened and angry man. He and his wife had a lot to lose. At the moment he was still on full pay but if the inquiry decision were to go against him, he would be sacked. Whichever way you looked at it, Shayla's death was timely. She was out of the way and the governors' premise that if there were other victims an inquiry would flush them out was now no more than a vain hope. Vulnerable kids would be more likely to link the allegation with the killing and keep quiet, and why not? As Redmayne had intimated, it was one of the first things the police had to rule out.

'My wife said you wanted to see me.'

Graham Collins' entrance startled them. Neither had heard him come in, so either the carpet had snuffed out his footsteps or the man was naturally stealthy.

Handford's eyes met his. That Graham Collins was handsome wasn't in doubt. It was no wonder pupils had crushes on him, stalked him even. Going on six foot, with dark hair, classical features and deep-set eyes, he was the trim but muscular kind of man seen on some TV adverts. There ought to be a law against teachers looking like that, Handford thought and wondered fleetingly if Gill fancied him. He couldn't blame her if she did, although if she saw him now, she'd more likely feel sorry for him.

Here was a man going under. He looked exhausted: his features were strained and his eyes, surrounded by dark purplish circles, seemed to have sunk deep into his skull. He had lost weight too, for his clothes didn't quite fit. There was only so much anyone could take and Collins had taken it; everything – his expression, his physique and his body language – suggested he was at the end of his tether. If Shayla Richards had been lying, she had a lot to answer for.

As Handford introduced himself and Clarke, he attempted to lessen the burden, if only for a brief moment. 'Just routine inquiries, Mr Collins,' he said.

The man had obviously prepared himself for the visit; his voice, though quiet, was surprisingly firm. 'I don't believe in routine inquiries, Inspector, certainly not when an officer of your rank is making them.' It could almost have been Redmayne talking and Handford wondered if he had warned Collins about Shayla's death.

'I've been here before,' Collins went on, 'as I'm certain you know and although I was assured then that the inquiries were only routine, I can promise you they were very far from that. So before I answer your routine inquiries, I want to know what has happened and why you have come to me.'

Handford, however, was not to be rushed; he needed a few answers to a few questions first. 'Perhaps we could sit down.'

Collins indicated the chairs. When they were settled, Handford said, 'Can you describe your movements between midday and midnight yesterday?'

Collins leaned back in his chair, his expression one of concentrated reflection. 'The same as yesterday and the day before and the day before that,' he said finally. 'Why?'

Clearly he was not going to be cooperative and why should he? He had had one bad experience at the hands of the police. And if he knew about Shayla's death, perhaps from colleagues or even from Redmayne, he would want to distance himself from it. 'Could you be more specific, sir?' Handford asked.

'No, Inspector, not until you tell me what is going on.'

What was left of Handford's patience from his altercation with Redmayne was melting fast. 'In your own words, Mr Collins, you've been here before, so you know the score. I ask the questions, you answer them and when I'm ready, and only then, I tell you why I've been asking them. So what were your movements between midday and midnight yesterday?'

For a moment Collins seemed to reach down into himself as he struggled with his emotions. Handford felt sorry for him, but he was having to do enough fighting for information as it was. He waited, then Collins said, 'My wife's car was in the garage for a service and she wanted to do the supermarket run in her lunch hour, so I picked her up at the hospital about one o'clock. We went to the supermarket and afterwards I dropped her back at work just before two and drove home. I put the shopping away, had a bite to eat and watched a bit of television.' His eyes met Handford's. 'Have you any idea how dire afternoon television is, Inspector?'

Handford had, but this was not about him.

'Then about half four I went out for a run.'

'Where?'

'Calverley Woods.'

'That's quite a distance from here.' And about as far away from Harden Moor and Druid's Altar as you could get.

Collins shrugged. 'I'm training.'

'Training?'

'I take part in fell races. My aim is to win the big one at Burnsall and the best place to train apart from the fells is through woods and over the moors.'

Handford nodded as though he understood, then said, 'Even when darkness is falling?'

'Better still – your feet have to learn to understand the ground.' The man had an answer for everything.

'It must be hard work.'

'That's why I do it. Fell racing is hard, the terrain can be difficult and the woods and the moors are one way of getting used to it.'

Handford paused, considered, then asked, 'Do

you ever go up to Harden Moor to train?'

'Sometimes.' Collins compressed his lips. His expression suggested he was aware the interrogation was becoming more specific, leading somewhere. The question was did he know where?

'But not last night?'

'No.'

'Did you see anyone while you were out?'

The air between them began to thicken. 'No, Inspector,' he said scornfully, 'you're not likely to meet anyone in the woods when it's getting dark. I prefer to be where there are no people. People recognize me. Some of them still think I'm a pervert – and when I'm among them, I can't tell the difference. I don't know who does and who doesn't, so I try to keep away from them all, particularly when I'm alone.'

Handford stifled a sigh. He appreciated Collins was antagonistic towards the police and that he may be unaware of the reason for today's questions, but he was not stupid and must realize his answers could rule him out of whatever it was they were investigating. Or perhaps he was shrewder than Handford was giving him credit for and appreciated that vague answers containing some truth were difficult to either confirm or contest. According to him most of the time between noon and midnight yesterday, no one had seen him and he had seen no one. No wonder he preferred it that way. What was certain was that Collins had not been at church as Handford had joked to Gill and that meant he could not be ruled out. He shuddered to think what that could mean for his wife.

Clarke took over. 'What did you do after your run?'

Collins turned his head towards the new interrogator. 'I came home, had a shower, prepared our meal, then picked my wife up from the hospital.'

'Which would be what time?'

'When she'd finished her shift. Just after eight o'clock.'

'And then?'

'We ate our meal. We had just finished when the hospital rang and Jane was asked to go back into work. Apparently they were particularly busy and someone had called in sick. I was furious and we had a bit of an argument. She hasn't been looking well lately, and I told her she shouldn't go, but she said she couldn't let them down and she could catch up on her sleep today – it's her day off,' he added.

Handford said, 'You drove her to the hospital?'

Collins looked back at the inspector. 'No,' he said, 'her car was back from the garage and she drove herself. I was still angry with her and thought if she could go out, so could I. Petty, I know, but there you are; that's what you become when you've gone through what I've gone through. Anyway, I rang a friend and we met in the pub. We had a couple of drinks, talked, played a few games of pool, then he said he had to get back and left. I stayed for a while, then came home.' A sardonic smile ran along his lips. 'And before you ask, Inspector, because I know you will, the pub was The Four Feathers and the friend Peter Redmayne.'

Handford could feel his anger against the journalist rising again. Redmayne had been with Graham Collins the previous night and hadn't thought to mention it when they were speaking. No, he was more interested in making something of Gill's current relationship with her husband. He swallowed hard as he attempted to remain inscrutable. 'Peter Redmayne, the reporter?'

'Yes. He's doing a feature on me and he said any time I was feeling low or wanted to talk I should ring him. I'd had a row with Jane and I wanted some company. I'm not supposed to contact teaching colleagues and they've been warned against contacting me, so hc was the best available.'

'What time did you leave The Four Feathers?'

'Eleven.'

'Did you come straight home?'

'No, I stopped for a while, had a walk round the park.'

Did the man have a death wish? He seemed to be doing nothing to help himself. 'Why?'

'I didn't want to be in the house on my own.'

'You should be careful, Mr Collins. Wandering the park at that time of night could suggest you were up to no good,' Clarke broke in. Handford smiled to himself. Andy sounded like some of the old coppers who took it as part of their job to offer advice to the foolhardy.

Collins shrugged. 'Most people think that anyway.'

'So what time did you arrive home?' Handford asked.

'Quarter past midnight or thereabouts, just

after Jane. Ask her.'

Handford let his eyes rest on Collins' face. Even though he understood where he was coming from and sympathized with his situation, he was beginning to dislike the man. 'When we arrived this morning, you were on the phone. Were you talking to Peter Redmayne?'

'No.'

'Who were you speaking to?'

'Jane's mother rang me. Her washing machine is on the blink and she asked me to pop round. Suspension means I'm always available, you see,' he added bitterly.

Handford smiled briefly at the addendum then nodded to Clarke who got up and left the room. Collins' eyes followed him until he disappeared, then he said, 'I've answered all your questions, Inspector. Are you going to tell me now what all this is about?'

The time was just about right and Handford leaned forward in his chair. 'Shayla Richards was murdered yesterday some time between noon and eleven p.m., Mr Collins. Her body was found on Harden Moor late last night.' He watched as the teacher's expression changed from one of mild curiosity to abject horror, for whatever Collins had expected it wasn't this. For the first time since the detectives' arrival, his composure slipped. 'My God, first I'm charged with indecently assaulting her and now you think I killed her.'

When Handford didn't reply, Collins jumped up and took a step towards the inspector. He bent over him, his knuckles turning white as his hands gripped the arms of the chair, his face so close that Handford could see the beads of sweat forming on his forehead. 'Do you?' Collins hissed, the words catching on his breath. 'Do you think I killed her?'

Handford searched the man's eyes. 'I don't know, sir,' he answered quietly. 'Did you?'

On his way to the kitchen, Clarke picked up the telephone from the table and made a 1471 call. He copied the recited number into his notebook.

Mrs Collins was squatting on the floor next to an open cupboard, from which she was pulling dishes and stacking them next to her. On the table were bin liners bulging with rubbish. She looked round as he tapped on the door.

'You look busy,' he said as he entered.

'I've got to do something,' she said. He couldn't be sure whether she was angry as she spoke or just plain frightened. Either way, the antagonism was obvious in her voice and her body language.

'The cupboards need cleaning and it's better than doing nothing.' She grabbed hold of the edge of the kitchen unit and pulled herself upright, then stepped round the crockery to get to the sink, where she picked up the wet cleaning cloth. Suddenly her anger got the better of her and she threw the cloth hard into the water, which fountained over her and the work surface and ran down the cupboard door to the floor. She stood immobile for a moment, her head lowered, breathing heavily. When she was more in control, she spun round and glared at Clarke. 'What's going on?' she demanded. 'Why can't I be with my husband? Why are you questioning him? Don't you think we've gone through enough?'

Clarke watched the damp patches from the soapy water darken on her sweatshirt. 'Just routine enquiries, Mrs Collins. Nothing to be worried about.' He hoped he didn't sound patronizing; she'd been through it too many times to be sweet-talked. 'The inspector's nearly finished.' He pulled a chair out from the table and sat opposite her. 'I think both he and your husband could do with a cup of tea if you don't mind making one.'

Jane Collins smiled suddenly. 'I expect you want one too.'

Clarke's eyes twinkled. 'I wouldn't say no,' he said.

She flicked on the kettle, then busied herself taking mugs and sugar from one of the cupboards and milk from the fridge. When she finished she sat down. 'Please tell me what this is all about.'

Clarke let his gaze wander over her. In spite of her earlier resentment, she was different from her husband. Her expression was softer, less bitter – but the same fear was deep in her eyes and he was sure only the truth, whatever it was, would do.

'Shayla Richards was found murdered up on Harden Moor late last night,' he said. 'We're questioning anyone who knew her, including the staff at the school.'

For a moment she sat quite still. Her face had paled even more if that were possible, and she put her head in her hands. She remained like that for some moments, but when she looked up again her eyes burned with anger. 'And my husband wins the jackpot, I suppose,' she said bitterly. 'An inspector comes to question him?'

Clarke understood how she felt, but it didn't make any difference. 'I'm afraid so,' he said.

'Then whatever you think, you're wrong,' she blurted out. 'He hated what Shayla had done to him, to us, and I can't say that either of us will be sorry she's gone, but he wouldn't have killed her.' Her eyes met his. 'I don't suppose that's enough for you though, is it?'

He shook his head.

The kettle clicked off and she pushed back her chair. As she poured the water into the teapot, she asked, 'You need me to corroborate what he's told you?'

'Some of it, yes.'

As he put the questions to her, she verified her husband's account as far as she could. Her car had been in the garage for a service and he had picked her up from work at one o'clock so that they could go to the supermarket; afterwards he had dropped her back at the hospital. He met her again about eight o'clock after her shift finished and drove her home.

'How did he seem to you?'

'He was wet and he was cold, but otherwise he was fine, no different from usual, whatever that means.'

Clarke frowned. 'What does it mean?'

'That since Shayla Richards made her allegation he has not been the man I married. He has withdrawn into himself, doesn't seem to have much purpose in life.' She paused for a moment. 'And he's angry, so angry.'

'With whom?'

'With everyone. With his headmaster, with the governors, with the police, the courts, the newspapers, the people out there who believed he could do something like that.'

'With Shayla?' Clarke asked quietly.

'Of course with Shayla; she started the whole rotten mess,' she said with candour. 'But not enough to kill her, Mr Clarke; he wouldn't do that.'

Clarke allowed the silence to digest what had been said. Whatever the outside world might think, Jane Collins believed implicitly in her husband – he hadn't assaulted Shayla Richards nor had he killed her – but then Shipman's wife had the same unshakeable belief in her husband.

'After you got home, what happened then?'

'We ate and then I was called back into work for a couple of hours. Graham was furious and we had an almighty row, but what else could I do? We're very short-staffed. When I got back around midnight he wasn't at home, although it wasn't long before he came in.'

'Did he say where he'd been?'

'No, and I didn't ask. I could tell from his manner that he was still angry with me and frankly I didn't care because I was exhausted. I went straight to bed. He'd already gone out on his run when I woke this morning so I didn't see him until after nine. Mr Handford and the other detective had been by that time and rather than wait they said they'd come back later, so I never got the chance to ask him and anyway we were more concerned about what the police wanted than where he was last night. Nothing else seemed important – nothing, even...' She stopped.

'Go on,' Clarke urged.

'No,' she said, 'it's nothing.'

Whatever it was, he could tell by her face that it was important, but at the moment she wasn't prepared to go any further. Perhaps later. Clarke opened his pocket book and read out the telephone number he had picked up from the 1471 call. 'Do you recognize this number?'

'It's my mother's. Her washing machine has broken down and she thinks it will help Graham if he has something to do. I sometimes think she breaks things on purpose just to keep him busy,' she said.

'My mother-in-law's the same,' Clarke commented with a smile.

Jane Collins stood up. 'I've got to get rid of this rubbish,' she said, picking up a couple of the bulging liners. 'The dustbin wagon is due any time.'

'Here, let me help you; we've just about finished anyway.' He followed her out of the front door to the wheelie bin.

It was cold and Clarke shivered as the November air penetrated his jacket. Mrs Collins didn't seem to notice. She walked up the drive to the pavement, opened the bin and started to push down the rubbish to make room for the new bags. Suddenly, as though it was burning her fingers, she let the lid drop and her hand flew to her mouth. 'Oh God,' she exclaimed. She took a step backwards, then crumpled into herself and leaned against the garden fence, moaning, 'No, no, no.'

Clarke dropped the waste sacks he was holding and ran to the bin. Lying scrunched up on top of the debris were a red skirt and white blouse. They were all too familiar. He turned to Jane Collins. As she looked up at him, he saw the fear in her eyes.

'They're Shayla's,' she cried hysterically, tears coursing down her cheeks. 'She was wearing them on the posters. They are, aren't they?'

'I think so, yes.' Gently, Clarke manoeuvred her through the gate. 'Go back in the house, Mrs Collins,' he said. As she hesitated he repeated more harshly, 'Please, go back inside.'

She pulled away from him and as she ran he could hear her shoes slapping the concrete of the drive. Once she was out of sight, Clarke pulled his mobile from his pocket and pressed a number with his thumb. 'Get out here, John,' he said urgently when the call was answered. 'I think we might have found Shayla Richards' clothes.'

chapter five

A visit to the mortuary to identify the body of a child had to be every mother's nightmare, yet Ali never failed to admire the dignity and composure they held until they saw the child lying on the trolley. Evelyn Richards was no exception, for she had taken time to prepare her outward appearance as if she were attending a wedding. The smart dark purple suit and a grey blouse hugged her large figure and her make-up, though discreet, had been carefully applied. The delicate perfume that seemed to surround her clung to the car's upholstery long after the visit had ended.

During the journey she maintained a composed silence: no words, no weeping. It wasn't until she saw her daughter through the viewing-room window that she uttered any sound, then she gave out a series of moans that transmuted into a crescendo of screams as she flung herself at the glass. She beat her fists against the barrier keeping her from her daughter and demanded to go to her and to take her home. She was finally led away sobbing by the family liaison officer, Connie Burns.

For Ali the death warning and the identification were the worst part of any murder inquiry. Once it was over he would forget she was the mother of the victim and treat her as any other witness, accomplice in the murder, or even the perpetrator. Grief-stricken mother she might be, but statistically Shayla was more likely to have been killed by a family member than by a stranger, and until it was proved otherwise even Mrs Richards had to be considered a possible suspect.

By the time they arrived back at the house, however, anger had set in and the Evelyn Richards Ali had encountered earlier in the day surfaced.

'Why has he been in Shayla's room, going through her things?' she demanded as she saw Warrender coming down the stairs with evidence bags in his hand. 'You've no right.' She lurched at him. 'Give me them back. Give me back my Shayla's property.'

So upset was she there was little point Ali reminding her that he had told her before they left for the mortuary that DC Warrender would check Shayla's room while they were gone and that Calvin would be with him the whole time. He could understand where she was coming from, for when he had said it, her daughter's death had not been real to her. Now it was. All privacy melted away in a murder investigation and, as unsympathetic as it might seem to onlookers, the sooner Mrs Richards accepted that, the easier her ordeal would be. 'We need to know as much about Shayla as we can,' he reiterated as they moved into the sitting room and sat down – Mrs Richards in one of the armchairs, Ali opposite her and Warrender and Calvin at the table.

'You don't need to take her things away,' she insisted. 'I can tell you about Shayla. She was a good girl; she tell me everything.'

'I'm sure she did, Mrs Richards, but sometimes there are things teenagers like to keep even from their mothers, personal things which are private to them. That's why DC Warrender has been looking in her room, to see if we can find anything like that. I assure you it may help us to find who killed her.'

'You know who killed her,' she growled. 'It was that Graham Collins.'

'We don't know that, Mrs Richards,' Ali said patiently.

She pushed herself out of the chair and as she moved towards him he stood up. 'You know nothing,' she spat at him. 'Nothing. But I tell you; he took her purity, then made her lie to the court and now he's killed her. I tell everyone.'

'You really mustn't do that, Mrs Richards,' he said, a warning note in his voice. 'I know you're upset, but you can't go round accusing people. You'll get into a lot of trouble.'

Evelyn Richards leaned forward and thrust her finger into his chest. 'Don't tell me what to do. No Pakistani tells me what to do no more, not after *him*.' She spat out the last word.

Ali took a step backwards and spread his hands in resignation. 'Perhaps you'd rather talk to DC Warrender,' he said.

She turned to look at the constable. 'You kept Shayla's room tidy?' she asked.

The dispute between him and Ali seemingly forgotten, Warrender smiled at her and his voice was gentle as he consoled her. 'It's just as she left it, Mrs Richards.'

She seemed at a loss and Calvin put his arm round her and led her back to her chair. 'Come on, Evie,' he said. 'Answer the detectives' questions.' Then he nodded to Ali, who regained his seat.

Her responses were short and to the point and the information she gave regarding her movements on the day of Shayla's death was no different from that she had given Handford. They would check of course, but Ali was sure it would be corroborated.

Warrender turned to Calvin Richards. 'What about you? Where were you between midday and midnight?'

'I worked a split shift yesterday: breakfast then dinner in the evening. I was in the hotel kitchen by six in the morning, off at eleven then back on at three. We finished round about half eleven. I went straight home to bed because I was on breakfasts again today and I needed my sleep.'

'What did you do between eleven and three?'

'I went out looking for our Shayla. I do – did – it every day. Every spare minute.'

Warrender's voice softened. 'Where did you go?'

'Manningham.' A district on the edge of Bradford, Manningham had once been the haunt of prostitutes and pimps and then in July 2001, the seat of the riots. Since then money had been pumped into the area to improve it and the lot of those who lived there and things had settled down. Inevitably, there remained pockets that were a haven for drug dealers and addicts, so it was no real surprise that Shayla might have been there. 'Someone said they'd seen her in a cafe, and I went to look.'

'Alone?'

A fleeting expression of concern crossed Calvin's face and he hesitated before he answered. 'Yes.'

Warrender frowned, but let the hesitation pass. 'What was the name of the cafe?' he asked.

Calvin relaxed. 'Stella's.'

'But you didn't find her?'

'No. If she'd been there, I'd have brought her home and you wouldn't be here.'

Ali turned to Mrs Richards, who suddenly stood up and stretched over to the alcove to pluck a photograph of Shayla as a child and thrust it in front of the sergeant. He took it from her. She must have been only nine at the time, ten at the most, and was wearing a red swimming costume and clutching a large trophy in her hands. She was smiling widely. 'Tell me about the photograph,' he said.

'It was taken when she won the inter-schools' swimming competition,' her mother replied. 'She was the best swimmer; she got the most points of everyone. She was a good girl then.'

'Then?'

'Before...'

'Before what, Mrs Richards?'

'Before she grew up,' Evelyn Richards' tone was wistful, as though everything would have been all right had her daughter stayed a little girl. 'Before she became a woman, before that teacher took advantage of her.' She looked up at Ali. 'I tell you, he's the one who's taken her away from me.'

There was no point arguing. Nothing Ali could say would change Mrs Richards' mind. She was filtering out the negatives, and the fact that

99

Shayla had admitted to lying made no difference. Instead he said, 'Tell me something about Shayla's friends. Who did she go out with?'

Mrs Richards' eyes lit up for a moment. 'She's popular, my Shayla; she has lots of friends. They go round in a group together, but her best friend is Kerry Johnson. They're always together.'

This was getting them nowhere. She was seeing her daughter as she would have liked her to be, not as she was. As much as he would have preferred not to be, he had to be tougher. 'This morning,' Ali reminded her, 'you said her friends were not real friends, that they were bad company, that they persuaded her to truant and got her into trouble.'

Mrs Richards glared at him. 'It was not bad trouble. If Shayla thought it was bad, she wouldn't do what they wanted.'

Warrender followed Ali's lead and leaned over the table so that he was closer to her. 'I arrested her once in connection with a mugging,' he said. 'That's bad trouble, Mrs Richards.'

She glared at him. 'Why you do that?' she shouted. 'Why you make my Shayla look bad? Is it because she's black?'

Warrender sighed. 'No, Mrs Richards, it's because she was mugging an old man and trying to steal his money.'

A heavy silence spread between them and it was a moment before anyone spoke.

Suddenly Calvin's deep voice echoed across the room. 'Tell them, Evelyn. Tell them what she was like. They'll find out sooner or later. It's better coming from us.'

100

But disloyalty wasn't part of Mrs Richards' make-up and she wasn't about to allow anything detrimental to be said about her daughter. She snatched the photograph back and turned it towards them. 'Look at her,' she entreated, pointing to Shayla's image. 'This is a good girl.'

Calvin stood up and walked over to his sister. 'I loved Shayla as though she was my own,' he said quietly. 'But she was sick and you know she was.' He looked up at the detectives. 'Things haven't been good for some time. She ran away, never let us know where she'd been and she didn't seem to care she was hurting us. We tried, but nothing we did was ever enough.' He turned back to his sister. 'We've got to tell them the truth.'

Ali and Warrender watched as the tears began to run down Evelyn Richards' cheeks and when Calvin faced the two detectives again, his eyes, too, were wet.

'Shayla became difficult after Qumar left. She loved him and couldn't understand why he had gone, leaving her behind. We tried to explain that he couldn't take her with him to Pakistan, but she was no fool; she'd seen what was happening, had been in the court when he was refused custody. As far as she was concerned he hadn't fought hard enough for her. From then on, she wouldn't do anything we asked of her, refused to eat the food Evie cooked and fought against going to the Christian church. She became a problem at school and got in with the wrong crowd. The teachers were always ringing up and complaining about her, so she stopped going altogether until a welfare officer came round to see us – then she went sometimes. She was as bad at home; she screamed and shouted at Evie, called her terrible names.' Up to this point his voice had remained quiet, but suddenly it changed as he began to intone as if he were preaching hellfire and damnation. 'This girl,' and he picked up another, more recent photograph. 'This girl had devils inside her. We are good Christians and we tried to rid her of them. But they were eating her up from the inside.' His voice became louder. 'She turned from our God and her punishment was to die with her face still turned from Him. She died with her devils, in a place of devils. I tell you, Sergeant, it was the right place for her to die.'

Walter Heywood watched the activity at the Collinses' house through his lounge window. First, two men arrived and went inside. A while later four or five more people drove up in a van with POLICE in large blue letters across the side and the bonnet, clambered out, pulled on white coveralls and disappeared down the path into the house. One remained outside. He, or she – Walter wasn't sure which – was more interested in the wheelie bin and it was as the lid was opened that the old man remembered what it was he'd wanted to tell the Collinses.

Handford left Clarke with the scene of crime team at the house and returned to Central to write up his policy notes before meeting Gill for lunch. He had debated whether or not to bring Graham Collins back with him, but in the end had chosen not to. There were sound professional reasons for not doing so. The skirt and blouse could have been bought anywhere by anyone, and until there was scientific evidence they belonged to the dead girl he couldn't assume they were hers. As for the neighbour, Walter Heywood, he had been very vague about what he had seen and since both Collins and his wife had denied all knowledge of the clothes, Handford couldn't prove anything different. As Collins had said, 'If I had killed Shayla, would I have been so stupid as to put her clothes with my own rubbish?' It was a good point, to which Handford hadn't replied. Instead he had asked him once more for his movements the previous evening. His answer had remained the same: he'd arrived home just after midnight, gone to bed and not roused until about half past seven, when he'd set out for his run. His wife had corroborated his story. Until more evidence surfaced, Handford wasn't prepared to start the clock ticking by arresting him. Indeed it would have been premature, not to say foolish to do so. Instead, he left Collins with Clarke to watch the SOCO team systematically search his house and his belongings. If Shayla *had* been there, they'd find the evidence and then he'd bring him in.

So why couldn't he rid himself of the feeling that Gill's fears had impinged on his final decision? Was he afraid that if he arrested Collins, Gill's colleagues would close ranks against her and she would blame him? Although he was aware that in an investigation the job came first, family second, he was having difficulty coming to terms with it. He'd expected Ali to deal with it a few months ago when family loyalty had been at odds with that of the police service. 'If you can't hack it, Ali, get out, because otherwise you're a liability,' he'd said – words which were coming back to haunt him. Perhaps he ought to tell that to himself with the same firmness, and if he couldn't hack it he should be honest enough to do what Gill had wanted him to do in the first place and talk to DCI Russell about relieving him of the case.

As she turned her key in the lock, Kerry Johnson sensed the familiar feeling that enveloped her each time she entered the house. Even in strong sun the hallway was dark, and apprehension pawed at her from every corner. She flicked on the light in the hope that it would melt away in the semi-brightness of the sixty-watt bulb, but it didn't and it wouldn't because it was part of her.

It had happened almost four years ago and in a different house, but still Kerry couldn't rid herself of the violence of the argument and the ear-splitting pitch of the scream. She felt her father push past her and saw her mother stretched out on the floor between the kitchen cabinets, blood seeping into the curls of her hair. It was almost as though she was watching a play from somewhere high in the theatre, with herself as the main player. The man who had answered her 999 call said it was good that her mother was bleeding; it showed she was alive. So she had sat next to her and held her hand until the ambulance arrived, assuring her that everything would be all right, and praying at the same time that the blood

would not stop. Prayers hadn't helped though –
her mother had still died and she'd had to live
with the pictures etched into her brain. They'd
sent her for bereavement counselling. The lady
assured her that the images would dim in time,
but she was wrong, for they hadn't; they were
always there, garish and vivid. She doubted the
vision of her mother with the hideous gash
furrowed deep in her head would ever fade.

The house was silent and there was no sign of
Sean; he was probably sleeping it off. He had
drunk himself into a state of near paralysis the
night before, first at the King's Arms and then
when they threw him out of there, at home. In
the early hours of the morning, when she finally
managed to persuade him to bed, he had made it
up the stairs by crawling on all fours. He was a
big man, built like a prop forward, and she'd had
to help him on his way by pushing him from
behind, swearing at him as they went. Once at
the top he'd curled into a ball and it had taken all
her strength to drag him the last few feet across
the landing, into his room and on to his bed. Had
it not been so sad, it would have been funny, but
Kerry wasn't one to laugh at drunken antics;
she'd seen too much of them in her father before
he'd killed her mother. So, having hauled Sean
into bed, she'd walked away, closed her bedroom
door and slept with a pillow over her ears.

Standing on the bottom step, she called his
name and listened, hoping he hadn't gone out,
for she would rather he learned about Shayla
from her than from a newspaper hoarding. He
would take it badly; he always did when it was a

kid, because he knew what that meant, and this time it would be worse for him because he'd known her. They weren't going to be able to keep that from the cops for long; they'd be round here to question him quicker than it took them to switch on their little blue lights. It was better she told him now and took the brunt of his frustration and fear, than he found out from the television and hit out at some poor sod in the pub. It was as much for her as for him, though, because she couldn't take the risk of him breaking his licence conditions, going back inside and social services putting her with some do-gooders of foster parents again.

She mounted the stairs and as she neared the top, she heard the toilet flush and the bathroom door open. Sean staggered out. The big man she knew as her uncle, who had cared for her all these years, was a wreck. He stood swaying by the bathroom door, appearing to consider the possibility of movement, then decided against it and slid down the door jamb to slump in a heap on the floor. Unkempt and looking like death, he was dressed in the clothes he had slept in. His dark hair, which was usually slicked back, stood in dishevelled clumps and he needed a shave.

She called up to him. 'Did you get my text?'

He grunted and she wasn't sure whether it meant yes or no. Looking at the state of him, she suspected the latter.

'They've found Shayla Richards' body, Sean, up on Harden Moor. They say she's been murdered.'

Sadness crawled over her young, delicate

features as she watched his body quiver when the words penetrated. He lifted his head and his glazed eyes tried to focus on her. But the effort was too much and with a moan he pulled himself up and disappeared into the bathroom again.

Kerry grimaced. Why had he chosen last night to go on a bender? If she was to get anything useful through to him, she'd need to sober him up. She turned into the kitchen where she filled the kettle and put it on the gas. Then she pulled a black bin liner out of a drawer and wandered into the sitting room. It was much as it had been left last night – empty cans squashed and strewn on the settee and the chairs, the stench of beer mingling with the permanent staleness of the room. A quarter-full bottle of whisky lay on the floor. She picked it up. She hadn't realized he'd drunk so much of it, but then last night had been a binge night. Things had got on top of him and he hadn't able to control himself. He drank less when she was with him, so she'd stayed and listened to his alcoholic ramblings. He talked about the little girl he'd killed, as he always did when he went on a bender. It was because of her he got drunk, more often than not on the three anniversaries: of her death, of his conviction and worst of all on her birthday.

'Catherine, that's what she was called. Have I ever told you she was called Catherine? She was pretty. It would have been her birthday today; she'd have been twenty.' And so it went on for most of the night, first him claiming he hadn't meant to kill her, and then moaning that the cops had no right to fit him up every time there was a kid involved. By one o'clock, she decided she could stand no more and forced him up to bed.

For a moment she sat on the edge of the settee immersed in her thoughts, then twisted round to gaze out of the window onto the road. The grubby net curtains and the dirt on the glass added to the gloom that hung over the street and for a moment it seemed to Kerry that even the weather was mourning them all – her, Sean and Shayla.

A car's horn blared suddenly and a voice yelled obscenities at the driver. Kerry stood up and pulled the curtain to one side. An old man was shaking his stick at the disappearing vehicle. The lady from next door was running towards him. She put her arms round him and manoeuvred him towards the pavement, taking them out of Kerry's sight.

That's what she had to do for Sean: manoeuvre him out of sight. She couldn't prevent the police knocking on their door, but she could pour enough coffee down him to make sure he was sober. Even with her as his alibi, he'd need all his wits about him when the cops came to question him.

Warrender and Ali updated Handford on their interviews with Evelyn and Calvin Richards.

'I tell you, boss, it was weird,' Warrender said. 'Calvin stood in front of us like some kind of evangelical preacher and announced that Shayla was inhabited by devils. You wanted to laugh, but he was so serious you couldn't.'

'How did Mrs Richards react?'

'She cried – loudly – but she didn't contradict him. She wasn't prepared to admit to Shayla's state of mind, though. All she wanted to do was preserve her image of her daughter.'

Handford glanced at Ali, who nodded in agreement. 'There's no doubt Shayla was a very disturbed girl or that Calvin believed in what he was saying.'

'Too right,' Warrender said. He leaned forward to emphasize his point. 'And if it's true, I don't think it's a coincidence she was found on Druid's Altar set out like a sacrifice.'

'You mean there's a link between where she was found and the devils Calvin claims lived inside her?' Handford asked. He tried to keep the amusement out of his voice, imagining what he would write in his policy book if it were true.

If Warrender noticed, he showed no sign of it. 'Yes I do, boss; there's got to be a link somewhere,' he said seriously. 'According to Calvin they did everything they could, conventional and unconventional, to rid her of these devils.'

'Such as?'

'They sent her to a psychiatrist for a while, but she didn't seem to be getting any better, so they asked the vicar of their church to exorcise them from her.'

'And did he?'

'He certainly carried out an exorcism.'

'Which obviously didn't work?'

'According to Calvin the devils had such a tight hold that Shayla wasn't receptive enough. He tried to persuade the vicar to have another go, but he wasn't keen and she kicked up a big fuss, said it was rubbish and she wasn't going to go along with it. It was then she ran away – at least that's what Calvin says.'

'Could Richards have found her and killed her?'

Ali answered. 'He says not; but yes, I'd say it was possible.'

'Could he have been the hoax caller?'

'He could have been,' Ali said, 'but it's difficult to say without a voice-pattern analysis.'

'Okay, we'll have him in, talk to him on tape. We need to check out his alibi first, though. Have you done it yet?'

Ali smiled. 'That's Warrender's job.' He turned to Warrender, a gleam in his eye. 'And given the circumstances, sooner rather than later.'

Warrender glared at him. 'Just going, Sergeant.'

As he pushed back his chair, Handford said, 'Before you go, Warrender, you said the vicar was asked to perform another exorcism and that was when Shayla ran away.'

Warrender nodded.

'You sounded sceptical, as though you didn't believe Calvin. Why?'

'I'm not sure, boss. I didn't know Shayla that well, only came across her once and I know she ran away from home from time to time, but...' he hesitated, 'I just felt that this was not a situation in which she would have done that. She'd have told Calvin and the vicar where to go, mouthed off at them, but not run away. I think there was another reason why she fled and Calvin's not telling us.'

chapter six

Handford had intended that he and Gill should eat in the canteen, but by the time she arrived he'd decided he wasn't in the mood to be surrounded by a herd of police officers. What he wanted was a drink and enough privacy to explain to his wife why he intended to stay on the case. He would tell her he was sorry, but he couldn't be dictated to or even blackmailed by the teachers at the school, and there was no doubt in his mind that by using her that's what they were doing.

The city-centre pub was filling up with lunchtime drinkers and diners, but they managed to grab a table tucked away in the no-smoking zone, where they could talk without interruption. As Handford ordered sandwiches at the bar and waited for their drinks, he wondered if the staff at the school had already begun to give Gill grief. He glanced over to her and as she pulled off her hat, unwound her scarf from round her neck and finally shrugged off her coat, he thought she looked pale, but that could have been the lighting.

He paid the barman and pushed his way back through the crowd, holding the drinks up high. When he reached the table, he lowered them down carefully, then slid Gill's towards her.

She took a sip of the white wine and said, 'You're not going to, are you?'

The meaning was clear and in spite of himself

he smiled. He'd never been able to get anything past her. He sat down. 'No,' he said.

'Have you spoken to Mr Russell?'

He studied his beer, wishing he could give her the answer she wanted. 'No,' he said. 'I can't. I'm sorry.'

'Why, John? Shayla was found on Harden Moor: that's the Bingley area and Bingley isn't on your patch. There's no reason at all why you should be investigating officer.'

'And ordinarily I wouldn't be, but she lived round here, her family lives here and she's on our books as a Misper.' Misper was CID-speak for a missing person and it made sense that if she came from their area and was missing from their area and they had been keeping an eye out for her for the past few weeks, they should stick with her now she was dead – it was the least they could do. 'She was our case before this.'

A woman in a striped pinafore appeared with their sandwiches and they lapsed into silence as she placed them in front of them.

The occupant of the adjacent table pulled a folded newspaper out of his pocket and opened it up. MURDERED. The headline screamed out at Handford. Underneath in smaller print, but equally as bold, it read, 'Body of missing girl found at local beauty spot'. There was the picture of Shayla that had been used in the missing posters, probably the only one the local paper had been able to get hold of at such short notice. He couldn't read the rest, didn't know whether he wanted to, but about halfway down the second column was an insert in bold lower case letters:

'The police didn't do enough to find my Shayla.'

Typical. Before her body had even been examined, they'd got to her mother, who, in her grief, had given them a quote damning the police. Within a couple of days the media would want to know why they were no nearer making an arrest and the more scurrilous amongst them would suggest that it might have something to do with institutional racism within the police ranks. After all, Shayla *was* black. They might even go so far as to bring up the internal inquiry into Handford's alleged racism in his handling of the investigation into the murder of Jamilla Aziz two years ago, although they'd conveniently forget that he was exonerated. Not-guilty verdicts make poor copy.

Gill smiled as she thanked the waitress, but when the woman had gone her smile faded. She leaned over the table towards him. 'But that doesn't mean *you* have to be the senior officer, does it?'

'It's been assigned to me, Gill. I don't have a sound enough reason to do anything about it. Come on, you know how the police service works.'

She sat back. 'I most certainly do,' she said bitterly, pushing a recalcitrant brown curl behind her ear.

'I'm sorry, Gill,' he said. He stretched over and covered her free hand in his. He gave it a squeeze. 'Come on, we've got through worse than this.'

She made no reply, but neither did she pull her hand away.

He said, 'Are there any signs of animosity against you at school?'

She sighed. 'Not as such, not yet. Everyone is still in shock. But there are rumblings. Shayla's head of year wasn't happy about giving me information to pass on to you.' She bent down, took an A4 envelope out of her bag and handed it to her husband. 'He did in the end but, well, he wasn't keen. He mumbled something about confidentiality and the Data Protection Act and me doing your dirty work, but in the end he told me what he knew. If you want official documents though, you'll have to go through the Head.'

Handford opened the envelope and pulled out several sheets of paper. 'I'll go through these in detail later, but for the moment tell me what you know.'

'You've probably got most of it by now,' she said. 'Her mother is Afro-Caribbean, her father Pakistani. They divorced shortly before Shayla's thirteenth birthday. By all accounts she was very close to her father and was devastated when he went back to Pakistan.'

'And that was when she began to rebel?'

'No, we saw signs of it when she transferred from primary school. Her form tutor said it began after her parents separated. From what I gathered from Philip Sutton, her head of year, her problem was more complicated than a parental break-up, although that was at the core. The children – there are two boys as well – were brought up as Muslims–'

'That's what Khalid said would have happened.'

'Yes, but as soon as the father left, Mrs Richards insisted they all reverted to Christianity. It didn't seem to worry the boys; they were younger, more adaptable. But not Shayla. At a time when most teenagers are coming to terms with who they are, trying to find themselves, her life fell apart. She didn't know who she was any more; she wasn't even sure of her nationality, her religion, even what food she could eat. She seems to have been pushed into a completely new world and then to make matters worse the father she adored went back to Pakistan, leaving her behind.'

As Gill was talking, Handford flicked through the notes she had made. 'It says here that she attempted suicide a couple of times. Were they serious attempts or just cries for help?'

'Who knows? She took paracetamol. You only need a few to kill, although I don't know whether she was aware of that. As far as she was concerned her life was impossible. She was forced into a situation she didn't want by a mother who showed a lot of bitterness towards Shayla's father and was determined to rid the whole family of him. It must have been like being deposited in a foreign country with no means of support. Somehow she needed to find someone who could nudge her into a world she could understand. It's not surprising she cried out for help.'

'Did she get any?'

'After the second suicide attempt I think she saw a psychiatrist. I've no idea how that went, because shortly afterwards she accused Graham Collins of indecent assault and we saw very little of her.' Gill glanced at her watch. 'Look, I must go.'

As Handford was helping her on with her coat,

115

he said, 'You liked Shayla, didn't you?'

She thought for a moment. 'Yes,' she said. 'Yes, I did. Before all this she was a bright girl who could have done well and she was fun to have in the classroom. What she did was wrong, but she had her reasons, screwed up though they were.'

They moved out of the pub. It was raining more heavily now and Handford wondered if the forensic team had finished up at Druid's Altar. Unlikely; it was an open scene with a lot of area to cover. They could be there two or three days. Rather them than me, he thought as he pulled his coat collar round his ears. Together, arm in arm, they manoeuvred the various crossings to where Gill had parked her car.

When she stretched up and gave him a kiss on the cheek, he resisted the urge to take her in his arms and hold her tight. Instead he opened the car door for her. She climbed in, lowered the window and looked up at him. 'I may have liked Shayla,' she said, 'but she had a vivid imagination, she made up stories, fantasized, told lies, call it what you will, and she was very good at it. She fooled the officer who investigated her allegation. I didn't believe for a minute that Graham Collins had assaulted her. I didn't think it should have got as far as the magistrates' court, let alone the Crown Court; none of us did. And now he has an internal inquiry to look forward to.' She turned on the engine. 'I tell you this, John: it you make him into a suspect, the staff will close ranks round him and treat me like a pariah. If you've got to be the investigating officer, promise me you'll be discreet when you question him. Don't bring him

116

into the station.'

Handford crouched down. 'I can't promise that, Gill,' he said quietly. 'We found Shayla's clothes amongst the rubbish in his wheelie bin.'

Warrender smelt the rich aroma of fried food as soon as he opened the door. Stella's cafe was a typical greasy spoon: a menu of all-day breakfasts and chips. Warrender loved greasy spoons. Chips with everything was his normal diet, except on a Friday when he went out with the lads for a curry and much as it hurt him to say so, he had to admit the Asians could make a good curry.

Warrender had timed his visit to Stella's to coincide with the dinners. Ali wouldn't like it, but who cared? He had to eat and since it was dinnertime, Stella would be too busy to answer his questions immediately. So he might just as well keep out the cold while he had a good meal, then talk to her. The cafe was basic but clean. The eight tables were covered in yellow plastic tablecloths, which were wiped down as the customers left. In the centre of each stood blue salt and pepper pots, a vinegar bottle, sugar basin, a small vase of dusty plastic flowers and a foil ashtray. Stella's clientele tended to be the kind who smoked and ate – sometimes at the same time. Warrender grimaced. He had many vices, but smoking was not amongst them.

He ordered at the counter and when Stella brought his meal to him, he let her see his warrant card and asked if he could have a quick word when she was less busy. He assured her it was nothing to worry about, only a few questions, but she didn't seem concerned anyway. She'd lived and worked in the district for too long to worry about the police. She ran an honest business – too busy and too tired most days, she said, to have to be worried about being collared by the law. And anyway, her nephew was a policeman in the Met; she wouldn't want to bring disgrace on him, would she?

It was half an hour later when she brought two cups of tea and sat down at his table. She pushed one towards Warrender. 'On me,' she said.

She looked tired, ready to sit down. Warrender didn't doubt she worked hard, was on her feet most of the day. Her wiry frame suggested that she burned off more calories than she ever put on. They didn't stand a chance of staying with her long enough to make her acquaintance. She pulled out a cigarette. 'You don't mind if I have a fag, do you?'

He did, but shook his head.

'A three-a-day girl, me,' she said as she lit it. 'One first thing when I get up, one after I've finished the dinners and one when I get home and put me feet up. Did you enjoy the meal?'

'Just how I like it.'

She drew on her cigarette. 'Now, what was it you wanted?'

Warrender added two spoons of sugar to his tea and stirred. 'Do you know a man called Calvin Richards?' he asked.

'West Indian, big fella. Comes in looking for his sister's girl. She's forever missing. Gives them loads of grief.'

Obviously she hadn't heard. 'Not any more she

118

doesn't, my love,' he said. 'She's dead. We found her body up on Harden Moor last night.'

'No! Poor sod. He'll be shattered. Murdered, was she?'

'Yes, she was. The thing is, Stella ... did you see Mr Richards yesterday?'

She pulled on her cigarette again. 'Yeah. Yeah, I think I did. He came in because someone said they'd seen her in here.'

'What time?'

'Not sure; about half past two. I'd finished with dinners, I know that.'

'And had they? Seen her in here?'

'Don't know, love, they might have done. I'm too busy to notice most of the time. People don't register with me when I'm run off my feet. Orders do. I can tell you which table ordered what, but not who. I'm never wrong,' she said proudly, 'unless they change tables.'

Warrender indicated to the poster on the wall. 'You have her picture up over there. Surely if she was here, that would have rung a bell with you.'

'That's what the other fellow said, except not so polite, miserable git. I told him, "If you speak to me like that again, mate, you're out of here."'

'The other fellow?'

'Yes, he came in with Richards. He's always with him. A Pakistani. Tall, thin, well-dressed, about thirty. Very concerned about the girl, he was. More than Richards himself, I'd say.'

It was well past lunchtime when Sergeant Ali walked into CID and poured himself a coffee. He glanced round; it was empty except for Clarke. It

119

appeared the team had taken Handford's words to heart and were out interviewing.

'Busy?'

'Just got back from the Collins house. Thought I'd catch up on paperwork,' Clarke said without looking up.

Paperwork was the bane of a policeman's life. There was too much of it, and it took good detectives like Clarke away from what they did best. Ali watched him for a moment. He'd been in the job a long time, had worked at Central for some of it and in the city for all of it. He would probably know something about Warrender, something that would help Ali understand the man. Half a sister – he was sure he hadn't misheard. He pulled up a chair next to Clarke's desk and sat down. 'You know Warrender?'

'Mmm.' Clarke didn't look up.

'Well?'

Clarke stopped typing into the word processor. 'Why?'

Ali shrugged. 'If I'm to work with him I want to get to know him better. I tried this morning but he wasn't having any.'

Clarke took a deep breath, blew it out and then sat back, his hands clasped on his head. 'What can I tell you? He's been in the job for about ten years, never been promoted, although he passed his sergeant's exams first time.'

'So why isn't he a sergeant?'

'He should be, but you've seen him: he's a good detective, but he fools around a lot. He's got views that would – shall we say – be considered un-politically correct in a sergeant. Basically, he's his own worst enemy.'

'So why is he still in the job?'

'You'd have to ask the bosses that, but as far as I know there's never been a complaint made against him. They can't sack him on what they think they know. They need evidence.'

'What about his family?'

'He's not married; his parents are dead.'

'Brothers and sisters?'

Clarke sat up straight and for the first time looked uncomfortable. 'No brothers, one sister – twin, I think.'

'Half a sister, he told me,' Ali said, scrutinizing Clarke's face. It showed no surprise.

'You asked him about her?'

'Just the questions I'm asking you. I was trying to be friendly.'

Clarke frowned. 'Look, Khalid, I think you should ask Warrender to explain, not me.'

'I've tried.'

'Then forget it. It's not your business.'

'That's what he said, but I think it is. He treats me like dirt, is prejudiced against me and I'm told to deal with him. How can I do that if I don't know why he's like this? If it's just my race he doesn't like, then fine, I know where I stand and I'll go ahead with my request for a transfer.'

Clarke looked surprised. 'You asked for a transfer?'

'This morning.'

'What did the boss say?'

Ali studied his fingers. 'He told me where the form was and said to bring it back for him to sign, then said if I wanted my promotion I had to

121

learn to deal with the Warrenders of this world.'

Clarke stifled a smile. 'Yes, I imagine he did.'

'You think he's right?'

'It doesn't matter what I think.' Clarke steepled his fingers and considered. After a moment, he spoke. 'I shouldn't do this, but if I tell you about Warrender so that you'll understand, I want you to promise you never heard it from me.'

Ali nodded.

'Say it. Because if they ever find out, Warrender'll have my balls and the boss will chew up what's left of me and spit me out. And I wouldn't want that.'

'I promise.' Ali placed his mug of coffee on the edge of the desk and sat forward.

'Warrender's parents are dead; that much you know. What you don't know is that they were killed in a car crash and his sister was badly injured. Warrender was driving–'

'And he blames himself?'

'Probably, but it's not as simple as that. It was his parents' twenty-fifth wedding anniversary and they'd all been away for the weekend. They were on their way home, it was late, not much traffic but the vehicle that hit them on the corner was travelling too fast on the wrong side of the road. It was a horrific accident but it wasn't Warrender's fault; he couldn't have avoided it. His parents died at the scene and Katie was taken to hospital. He walked away with whiplash and a few cuts and bruises. Katie sustained massive injuries and for quite a long time it was thought she wouldn't recover. When she did, she was unable to walk; the crush injuries had been severe and her spinal cord had been severed. She's paraplegic, as well as having other problems. A nurse cares for her during the day and Warrender the rest of the time.'

'Which is why he called her half a sister?'

'She was a brilliant tennis player, had a real future ahead of her. The driver of the other car ended that and Warrender is not very forgiving.'

'I can understand that, but I can't see the connection between the accident and his feeling towards me, unless...'

'Unless... Yes, the other driver was a young Pakistani lad. No licence, no insurance, no MOT and he ran away. When he was picked up he denied having been in the area, but there was considerable forensic evidence to put him in the car and at the scene and Warrender was able to describe him. Even then the lad's friends tried to frighten Warrender into retracting his statement by intimidating Katie while she was ill. It only happened the once – after that the nurses were told not to let anyone of Asian origin in to see her – but once was enough. The driver got six months. When the verdict was announced his friends and family in the public area cheered. That's what Warrender can't forgive: six months for his parents' lives and his sister's half-life and their elation that it was so lenient. As he was taken downstairs, the driver gave Warrender the thumbs up and grinned at him. Then to add insult to injury as Warrender left court there was a delegation of youths outside to meet him. They grunted and yelled "pig", then cheered. There was no sign of remorse, just jubilation that it had happened to a policeman. It was

123

a long time ago and people have grown up, race relations have come a long way, but it's still raw to Warrender because he goes home to it every night. That's why he has no time for you, Ali, because he has no time for anyone of your race. It's nothing personal, but it's not going to go away.'

Ali sat for a long time digesting what Clarke had told him. Eventually he said, 'Why has no one ever mentioned this to me?'

'No one knows. You know what Warrender's like. A girl on every street, his little black book in which he registers their score. He wants to be one of the lads, not the butt of their sympathy. He got the insurance, enough to let him buy a bungalow that he customized to Katie's needs, and hire a nurse so he could carry on working, but you've seen how tired he is sometimes. The nurse works during the day and he cares for her at night, except on a Friday when he goes out for a curry. That's the measure of his social life, Ali – a curry on a Friday night.'

'If no one knows, how come you do?'

'I was the officer who dealt with it. I've known all along.'

'And who else is party to the information?'

'The DI and the DCI.'

Ali felt tension closing on the back of his neck. He didn't know whether to be relieved or angry. He settled on the latter; it was easier. 'Shouldn't I have been told, given I'm the one in the firing line?'

'No. We promised Warrender. I've broken my promise, because I know you: you wouldn't have let it go and the deeper you dug, the more trouble you would have caused, and it's not going to make any difference to what he feels about your fellow men. And remember this, whatever he's putting you through, it's nothing to what he's been through and is still going through.' Clarke returned to the computer keyboard. 'It's his call, Ali, not yours. He has a right to his privacy.'

Handford rarely attended a full post-mortem. He would show his face, watch until the external examination of the body was over, then disappear, leaving his junior officer to pick up any immediate information. He hated everything about them: the coldness of the room, the line of white porcelain sinks and the stainless steel table where the body lay. Worse still was the sound of the drill boring into the skull. The first time he'd heard it as a young DC he'd passed out and had vowed when he came round that he'd avoid all post-mortems if he possibly could. For Shayla Richards it was not possible. He had to be there. It was stupid, melodramatic even, but he felt he owed it to her. Yet if he was going to get through the next hour or so, he would have to put his feelings aside, be dispassionate and divorce the lifeless body from the girl Gill had described – bright, lively, but at the same time unhappy and confused. As he'd walked back to Central after lunch, he'd tried to imagine Shayla's feelings as she accused Graham Collins of assault and her shame when she admitted in court to lying. Now he couldn't do that because all there was in front of him was an inert, unseeing, unfeeling carcass.

Yet he should try, for only by understanding her would he find her killer.

As the pathologist worked on the body, Handford found himself concentrating on a spot of blood on one of the wheels of the trolley on which she was laying and wondering who it had belonged to. It seemed to go on for ever: cutting, drilling, weighing and slicing the organs until she was a dissected, empty shell. Finally the pathologist stood back. Probably in his late fifties, early sixties, he must have performed thousands of post-mortems. Now it was all in a day's work.

'Well,' he said. 'As you would expect for someone of her age, she was an extremely healthy young girl, didn't smoke or, as far as I can tell until we have the test results, take drugs. Sexually active though, sadly not unusual for a teenager in these days. There are signs, however, that she was roughly treated in that area.'

'What signs?'

'Bruising. Some of it fairly recent.'

Handford frowned. 'Some of it?'

'Mmm. There's recent bruising and not so recent bruising. My guess is that she has either been abused systematically or she was into frequent, boisterous sex.'

'Can you say which?'

The pathologist studied Handford intently with a mixture of resignation and pleading. 'You know I can't tell you that, dear fellow,' he said. 'My work ends with the what; yours is the who, the why and the when.'

It had been worth a try. 'Any DNA?'

'On her underclothes probably, and there were

126

a couple of pubic hairs that didn't belong. But you'll have to wait for forensics.'

As always. 'So, cause of death?'

'Respiratory failure, but not strangled. There are no signs of bruising round her neck or on the floor of her mouth, the epiglottis or the lining of the larynx, there is no damage to the thyroid cartilage and the X-ray shows the hyoid bone is intact.' He moved over to the viewer and switched on the light. Handford followed him. 'Look, no break at all,' he said, pointing to the negative. 'And there was no water in her lungs, so she wasn't drowned. No, this young lady was suffocated, probably with a pillow or a cushion or some such object. I've taken fibres from her nasal passages and her mouth; she would draw them in as she was fighting for breath. The scientists should be able to give you some idea of their origin.'

'You don't think she was killed on the moor, then?'

'Most probably in a house – on a carpeted floor or a settee. There are suggestions of the skin on her back having come into contact with a rough surface like carpet pile or upholstery. It's not easy to see unless you're looking, but I can fairly well guarantee the imprint was there prior to the bracken piercing her skin. And that happened post-mortem. No blood,' he added by way of explanation.

The mortuary assistant began to cover the body, but the pathologist stopped him. 'Just a moment,' he said, then turned to Handford. 'Come over here, Inspector.' When he was close enough to see, the pathologist lifted the girl's arm from under the sheet. 'There are no defence wounds as such, but there are abrasions on both arms, here between the wrist and the elbow. Can you see?'

Handford nodded. 'What does that mean?' he asked.

'Smothering tends to be associated with the very young or the elderly. It's difficult to achieve when the victim can fight back. And that's what's happened here – she's tried to fight back. The bruising is a result of being held tightly to stop her struggling.' He placed her arm back under the sheet and nodded to the attendant, who wheeled her away.

'So what are you saying?'

'I'm saying that it took one person to hold her down while another held the cushion over her face until she stopped breathing. I'm saying, Inspector, you're looking for two perpetrators, not one.'

'I didn't kill Shayla Richards. I swear I didn't,' whispered Graham Collins. He had barely moved from the lounge chair since the scene-of-crime team had gone. He looked up at his wife, his eyes pleading. 'I promise you I didn't.'

Jane crouched in front of him and took his hands in hers. 'You don't need to promise me anything. I know you didn't. You're not a murderer, any more than you were a sex attacker. We'll get through this, Graham, just like we got through the court case. You and me, together.'

'She admitted to lying at the court case, Jane, but now she can't say anything. She's of no use to me at all. And how did her clothes come to be amongst our rubbish? As far as the police are concerned it was me who put them there. Even Mr Heywood couldn't be sure it wasn't.' A wave of tiredness engulfed him. 'I thought it was all over, Jane. It was, almost.' Anger began to build in him and he banged his fist on the arm of the chair.

Jane startled, stood up and took a step backwards.

'How could the stupid girl get herself killed?' he yelled. 'Didn't she know what it would do to me?' He was being irrational and he knew it. It wasn't Jane's fault; it wasn't even Shayla's fault; but he had to blame someone. He leaned back and covered his face with his hands. It was a nightmare, a never-ending nightmare.

Eventually he pulled his hands away and looked up at Jane. Her face was creased with anxiety. He knew he wasn't the only one carrying the burden, but he couldn't help her. He didn't have the strength.

'What about the governors' inquiry?' he said. 'This is going to give them all the ammunition they need – a teacher who is accused of sexual assault and then of murder. They're not going to keep me on after this, whether I'm innocent or not. The doubt will always be there. Parents are not going to want their children taught by me. For God's sake, Jane, there are still some who believe I got away with it the first time, that I forced Shayla into the confession.'

Jane tried again to reassure him. 'We'll deal with it, Graham, just like we did before.'

But he wasn't listening. 'And I suppose we'll

129

deal with me out of a job, never being able to get another one, because no employer will ever be sure of me.'

'We'll fight for compensation. They can't sack you because of something you haven't done.'

'Can't they? I wouldn't be the first. And even if they don't sack me they can keep me on suspension. You read the governors' letter. While on suspension I can't take on any other paid employment. I could be in that situation for years.' He took in the look of disbelief that covered her face. 'You don't believe me?' He jumped up from the chair and searched through the pile of newspapers in the rack. Pulling one out he snatched at the pages. 'Look,' he said as he found what he wanted and read out the headline. 'Scandal of the doctors suspended for years.' He threw the paper at her. 'Read it,' he ordered. But before she could he grabbed it from her. 'This man has been on suspension for ten years following a complaint from a patient. It says that even though he has been exonerated he has not been allowed back to work.'

'But that's doctors.'

He heard the break in her voice, but by now his anger had taken over. 'You think it can't happen to teachers?' She backed away as he closed in. 'Of course it can.' As he watched her everything became clear to him. It was as though a taut elastic band had snapped in his brain. For a moment it stung in his mind, but as the pain died so did the mist that had been clogging it for all those months and out from behind the mist flooded the anger at those who were trying to destroy him – the governors, the police, those who still didn't believe him, and most of all, Shayla Richards. He observed them as they slid one by one into the person standing in front of him. He was afraid of what he was going to do to her but knew he couldn't stop himself even when he saw the fear in her eyes as she pleaded with him.

'Graham, don't; you're frightening me. Please don't.'

He advanced towards her, forcing her backwards until she was pressed hard against the door, then when she could go no further, he grabbed hold of her chin between his thumb and first two fingers and squeezed, digging his nails deep into her flesh. 'It's your fault. Don't deny it. You spend your days up at that hospital bringing the little bastards into the world, the kids who grow up to tease and then lie just to destroy me.'

He banged her head against the door, then swung her round and threw her towards the chair. She slipped and fell over its arm and as she tried to pull herself up he towered over her. He could smell her fear.

'Don't Graham,' she screamed. 'Please don't hurt me. I'm pregnant.'

For a split second he stopped, then he lifted his arm and hit her hard across the face. 'You stupid bloody bitch,' he yelled at her. 'You stupid bloody bitch.'

chapter seven

It was all very well Clarke telling Ali it was Warrender's call and he had a right to his privacy. *He*
had a right to be treated with respect, whatever the
circumstances. In truth, Ali could understand why
Warrender felt as he did, and although he thought
he was wrong, he couldn't say he blamed him.
What he found difficult to comprehend was why,
knowing the situation, John Handford hadn't
warned him. Surely he was owed that much.

Handford had been hard on him that morning,
told him to deal with Warrender. And he had
tried; God knows he had tried, but dealing with
Warrender was like dealing with a boomerang.
Each time he thought he had Warrender's regard
– at least as his senior officer – the man's aversion
towards him came whizzing back.

He had, he decided, a choice. He could carry on
as he was – him scoring points some of the time,
Warrender the rest of the time – or he could do
something that would make a difference. What, he
wasn't sure. He didn't relish the idea of facing up
to him, partly because that could produce more
problems than it solved, and partly because he
didn't want to break Clarke's confidence. Nor did
he want to go back to Handford. Since he'd threatened to transfer, the rift that had been there when
he and Handford had first met had resurfaced.

He began collating the morning's statements,

most of them from the school. That the staff were backing Collins to the hilt was plain. Detectives had returned complaining that getting information from some of the teachers had been like pulling teeth. It appeared they were angry that the husband of one of their own was in charge of the investigation. For some reason they seemed to see it as a breach of her loyalty. A teaching assistant, Jaswant Siddique, had been especially vocal and had refused to answer any questions at all until Handford was taken off the case. Apparently, he saw Gill as her husband's informant. It was ridiculous. The DI was nothing if not sure of his duty; he would never allow himself or his team to let his family affect his job. Ali knew that, to his cost. He could still feel his embarrassment at his boss's words when he had committed that particular sin. 'If you can't hack it, Ali, get out, because otherwise you're a liability.'

Ali was deep into the paperwork when Warrender sauntered into the incident room and without a word, sat down at his desk.

'Where've you been?' Ali tried to make the question sound innocent.

'Doing what you told me to do: checking out the Richardses' movements.'

'And?'

Warrender rested back in his chair and stretched his legs out in front of him. 'Evelyn Richards checks out to the letter. When she wasn't at the university she was going or coming from her cleaning jobs. I doubt she would have had time to kill her daughter and anyway I don't think for a minute she'd harm Shayla, whatever she'd done. In fact, I admire the woman. She's a hard-working single mother trying to better herself for her kids' sake. She's lived in fear of Hussain coming back and taking the children away so that she'll never see them again. Her view is that if she can get some decent qualifications, she can move away and start again without that worry hanging over her. By all accounts she had a bloody awful marriage. He treated her like a skivvy most of the time and when he wasn't doing that, he was bullying her into converting to Islam. But she's a strong woman, certainly stronger than he expected and she refused to be browbeaten by him, continued to attend her own church in spite of him. Even threatened she'd go to the Race Relations Board if he tried to stop her worshipping in her own way. She couldn't prevent him from brainwashing the kids, though.'

Ali ignored Warrender's choice of words and said, 'I'm amazed you think so highly of her, Warrender; when I met her she seemed more like a hellcat than a woman.'

'She's grieving for her daughter, Ali. She's doing it in her own way, that's all. Deep down she blames herself for Shayla's death, but it's easier on her if she can throw that blame onto us in whatever form is available at the time. You were a Pakistani and you were there. It became your fault, but it wasn't personal.'

'It felt personal,' Ali said, remembering how she flared at him.

'So what did you do – back off?'

Warrender could have been talking about the two of them, rather than him and Mrs Richards.

Backing off was exactly what he did with the constable and what he'd done with Mrs Richards. He made no comment, knowing that his silence confirmed it.

'Then you shouldn't have; you should have taken time to listen to her instead, then you'd have realized. The trouble with you, Ali, is that you're all career policeman. You weren't interested in her, just what she was doing the day Shayla was killed. Someone like her needs careful handling. You ask Connie Burns.'

Listening to Warrender, Ali felt like a naughty schoolboy who had to be told some home truths. He'd shown his authority by demanding to know where the man had been, and now – again – he was losing the battle.

He tried not to sound hostile. 'You don't think much of me, do you, Warrender?' He wasn't sure what he had meant to gain from the question, but the man's silence was all the answer he needed and since there was nothing more he could say, he asked, 'What about Calvin?'

'I checked his movements at the hotel and his shifts were as he said. The head chef was called into a meeting so he can't be sure exactly what time Calvin left. The kitchen was clean and ready for the lunchtime staff, so whatever time he'd gone, he'd finished his work. There's a conference at the hotel and they were quite busy. The head chef thinks Calvin can't be far out in his estimate of when he left.'

'He doesn't have to clock on or off?'

'No, he's second chef and as such is considered management, so we can't be absolutely sure.'

'Second chef – what does that mean?'

'Assistant head chef if you like; takes over from him when he's away, on a day off or at a meeting.' Warrender grinned. 'A bit like you when the DI's not here, except he probably has more responsibility.'

Ali wondered why he was even trying. He shot Warrender a look, which he hoped would penetrate the constable's thick skin. 'Anything else?'

'Well, he didn't tell us the whole truth. He visited Stella's for the reason he gave, but he wasn't alone; there was someone else with him. An Asian, Stella said, tall, thin, well-dressed, about thirty. According to her, he seemed more upset about Shayla's disappearance than Calvin.'

Ali was interested. 'Qumar?'

'That's what I thought, so I showed her the photograph I got from Shayla's room. She didn't think so, but...'

Ali smiled. 'I know,' he said. 'All Asians look alike to her.'

Warrender sighed as though he was dealing with a recalcitrant teenager. 'What I *was* going to say, Sergeant, was that when I spoke to Calvin, he denied absolutely being with another man, said there were some Asians in the cafe but none of them were with him. He said Stella was busy at the time and could easily have been mistaken.'

Warrender had wrong-footed him again and Ali tried to hide his discomfort. 'Could she?'

'Unlikely. An Asian in a greasy spoon? I can't see it, can you?'

Ali shook his head. Perhaps the younger ones, but not someone well dressed and in his thirties.

136

A member of the community with that kind of description would have been obvious. No, she couldn't have been mistaken.

'Anyway, the man spoke to her, said that given she had a poster of Shayla in her cafe, she must have noticed her if she came in. Stella said she hadn't and it became quite heated by all accounts. But even when I put this to him, Calvin wouldn't give in, still insisted he was alone, so I've brought him in.'

Ali's eyes widened. Handford had said to wait before bringing him in. 'You've brought him in? Don't you think you ought to have cleared that with me first?'

'I didn't need to; I rang the DI and cleared it with him.'

'You rang the DI?'

Warrender smiled. 'You're beginning to sound like a parrot, Ali. Yes, I rang the DI.'

'I'm your sergeant, Warrender. You should have contacted me first.'

'Yeah. And you'd have told me to wait while you spoke to the DI to ask him what to do, and then you'd have had to get back to me. What were Richards and I going to do in the meantime – play cards? No, I talk to the organ grinder, Ali–'

'As opposed to...?' Ali broke in.

'His assistant.' Warrender grinned, pulled his legs towards him and stood up. 'Now are we going to question Richards or are we going to stay here arguing?' He inclined his head towards Ali. 'Or do you want to clear it with the DI first?'

Peter Redmayne hunched forward over his

137

computer screen and screwed up his eyes. He knew better than to sit this way, but he was neither typing nor reading what was written there. He pushed his large spectacles up his nose and sucked at a pencil. The reporters' room was a beehive of activity, but he caught none of it, too concerned was he with the fact that he was becoming more involved with Graham Collins than he would have wished. He was breaking the journalists' law – get close to the story, never to the person. It was a good law when it worked. Today it hadn't.

He had spent the past hour with Graham Collins and was deliberating what he should do with the information gleaned: write it up, parcel it away for future use, or pass it on? His mind was a whirl of questions to which he had no answers and of information that was rapidly transforming itself into concern at what the man might do. By the time he had left for home, Collins had appeared calm, but what if he wasn't? What if the calmness was a mask to hide the hatred and the fear still bubbling away inside? What if his wife *was* at risk?

The woman in reception had described Collins' manner as frenzied when he had rushed into the newspaper's offices, pushed his way to the front of the long queue of waiting people and demanded to see Redmayne. She had rung up to the reporters' room. 'I think you'd better see him, Peter; he's in a terrible state.'

He surveyed Collins through the pane of glass in the door leading to the foyer for a few minutes, watching as he paced backwards and forwards,

138

obviously agitated, then forcing a smile he stepped into reception. 'Graham, what can I do for you?'

The greeting had scarcely been uttered when Collins threw himself at him, almost bowling him over. 'I hit her,' he blubbered, hysteria mounting in his voice.

At first Redmayne wasn't sure what he meant. Whom had he hit? Shayla Richards? Was he confessing to murdering her? Collins had been dragged into the abyss over the past months; it wasn't beyond the bounds of possibility that he had cracked completely. Redmayne had intimated as much this morning when he had met John Handford. *I wouldn't like to take bets on whether it's himself he's likely to harm, his wife or Shayla Richards.*

But this wasn't the place; people were looking. Gently he manoeuvred Collins into an interview room and onto one of the chairs. 'I'll get you a glass of water,' he said.

When he returned a few minutes later, Collins was standing at the window, his back to the door. Breathing deeply, his head was bowed and his arms spread wide as he clung on to the sill. Redmayne walked over to him and touched him cautiously on the shoulder. 'Come on, Graham. Drink this.'

Collins turned, more composed, and took the glass from him.

'You said you hit her. Who are you talking about?'

Collins took a drink and scrutinized the glass. 'Jane,' he whispered.

It was almost a relief. 'Jane? Is she all right?'

Collins slumped into the chair. 'I don't know,' he said, his voice barely audible.

Redmayne ought to have asked someone to check on her, make sure she was not too badly hurt, but Collins was talking so he kept his fingers crossed and listened. Bit by bit he described what had happened. There was no excuse, Collins said, he'd lost it; it was like a fireball had burst in his head. He made his hands into fists and banged them against each other. 'She said she was pregnant. How could she become pregnant? How could she do that to me?'

At first Redmayne thought that perhaps Collins was not the father, that Jane had been having an affair and that was why he was so angry. But, as with everything about the man at the moment, it was not so simple.

'How could she bring more Shayla Richardses into the world, more kids to taunt and accuse.' He was a man obsessed. Shayla Richards filled his whole world. There was no room for anyone else; he saw her everywhere – even in a cluster of cells.

Redmayne was concerned. Collins had had two years of hell, followed by a couple of weeks of euphoria after he had been exonerated, then the blow of another inquiry to face and now Shayla's murder had taken more than its toll. Not even the news of a child of his own made a difference – indeed it had only served to push him over the edge.

Redmayne tried to reassure him. 'Graham, you're being irrational. You've devoted your working life to teaching and you want to return to it, so you must know that not all children are like Shayla Richards. And as far as your own are concerned, they'll never be in the situation she was in; they'll not live a life in which they'll have to fantasize to gain attention. You and Jane will make sure of that.'

For a short moment that seemed to soothe him and he opened his fists and let his hands drop onto his lap. 'Perhaps,' he said. Silence drifted between them until Collins lifted his head. 'Do you think I should tell the police what I've done?'

'No,' Redmayne said swiftly. A confession of that nature would not augur well if Collins was near the top of the police list of suspects. 'No, if Jane hasn't called them, you say nothing. It's zero tolerance towards domestic violence in this neck of the woods and you'll be in court as fast as they can get you there. Leave it. Go back to Jane; make sure she's all right and try to show her how sorry you are.' He pushed on his glasses. 'I assume you are sorry?'

Collins nodded. 'Yes.'

Redmayne wasn't sure if he was entirely convinced. Collins had been fighting his monsters for so long that he was in danger of becoming a monster himself. He said, 'If she wants to press charges, there's not a lot you can do, but if she doesn't, then thank your lucky stars.' He let his eyes meet Collins squarely. 'But I tell you this, Graham: as much as I understand what you've been through, you touch that wife of yours once more and *I'll* make a complaint to the police.'

141

Grief shrinks people. Big man though he was, Calvin Richards seemed to have shrunk to manageable proportions while he had been waiting in the interview room. He sat, his shoulders hunched, a nearly-empty Styrofoam beaker in his hand, and stared at the chairs opposite. When Ali and Warrender entered the room, he made to stand up and as he did so the sleeve of his coat caught the beaker, which fell on to its side to roll backwards and forwards on the table until it came to a stop. Calvin grabbed it and, looking away from the detectives, he brushed at the errant drops of liquid with his fingers, then wiped them against his trousers.

Ali was sympathetic. 'Don't worry about it, Mr Richards,' he said in a tone that suggested he understood Calvin was nervous. People often were when asked to come into a police station to answer questions. 'Would you like another coffee?'

Calvin shook his head.

'I am sorry to have kept you waiting, but we have a problem with what you told us this morning and we need to clear it up,' Ali explained, as the two detectives settled themselves in the chairs opposite him. 'It's nothing to worry about.'

Calvin watched as Warrender began to tear off the transparent film on the tapes in his hand. 'You going to record what I say?' he asked, his eyes widening.

Ali smiled at him. 'It will make it easier for all of us if we do. Then there can be no mistake about what you have said. You keep one of the tapes; we keep the other.' He pointed out to Calvin that he was not under arrest and that he was free to go at any time, which seemed to calm him a little, then continued with the formal caution. When that was over, he leaned forward as though taking the man into his confidence. 'You went to Stella's cafe between shifts because you had been told that Shayla had been seen there?'

'Yes.'

'And you say you went alone?'

'Yes.'

'Our problem, Calvin, is that the owner of the cafe is adamant another gentleman accompanied you – a Pakistani, tall, thin, well-dressed, about thirty. Do you know anyone of that description?'

Calvin shook his head.

'Can you answer for the tape, please?'

'No.'

'DC Warrender met the owner and he thinks she is telling the truth. In fact she has no reason to lie and he has no reason to disbelieve her.' He gave Calvin time to digest his words, then he said quietly, 'Who was this man?'

His only reply was to moisten his lips with his tongue.

Ali tried again. 'I understand you're upset and a little nervous, but I've got to warn you we're not going to let this go. We'll find out sooner or later who he is, and given we're hunting your niece's killer, don't you think it would be better if it were sooner?'

Still he maintained his silence.

Ali glanced at Warrender, and lobbed the questioning to him.

'If it was your ex-brother-in-law,' said Warrender, 'I can understand why you might want to keep quiet, given your sister's hostility towards him, but we need to know. Was it Qumar?' His voice had an edge to it.

Calvin picked up the beaker and began breaking off the edges around the lip. Eventually, he shifted his gaze to the recorder. 'You turn that off?' he asked.

Ali shook his head. 'No, sorry.'

Defeated, he drooped. 'His name is Shahid Mustafa. He was helping Shayla when she was filled with the devils.'

'Is he the psychiatrist who counselled Shayla after her suicide attempt?' Ali asked.

Calvin shook his head and said, 'No, she was no good. She didn't help Shayla at all. Mr Mustafa is a man with real powers to help people.'

Ali was cynical. 'What do you mean, powers?'

'Powers given him by Allah.' Calvin reached into his jacket pocket and pulled out his wallet from which he took a black-edged card. He handed it to Ali, who read it and passed it over to Warrender. As the constable scrutinized it, his eyes widened. 'You don't believe this rubbish, do you?'

Calvin bristled, his face tightening as he shielded his beliefs against the implied criticism. 'He's helped many people,' he said defensively.

Warrender read from the card. 'Become healthy from sickness of all kinds?' He threw it on the table. 'I wish,' he said derisively.

Ali frowned. He picked up the card, glanced at it and then said, 'He claims he can cast out evil spirits. Is that how he was treating Shayla?'

'They were hurting her. She needed to be rid of them.'

'How did he do it?'

'I don't know; I was never in the room. But it *was* beginning to work. Shayla screamed and screamed while he was casting them out. He told me not to worry about the noise. It can be painful for the victims as the devils leave the body. Some patients remain quite still, others shake and those like Shayla who are gripped so tightly by them scream and shout.'

Ali frowned. 'That must have been very distressing for you, Calvin. I'm surprised you didn't ask to go into the room with her.'

'He wouldn't let me. He insisted that if it was to work they had to be alone. They needed to concentrate, he said, and you can't do that if there are people watching.'

Warrender snorted impatiently. 'I bet you can't,' he murmured.

Calvin glared at him then, in a sudden show of exasperation, he lifted his arms and banged his large fists down onto the table. Ali grabbed at the recorder to prevent it bouncing to the ground, and Calvin half-stood to lean over to Warrender. 'Don't mock me, man,' he threatened, his eyes narrowing. 'When you know what it was like, you can comment, but until you do, keep your mouth shut.' He remained in that position for a few moments, then sat down and wiped his hands over his face. Eventually, he looked towards Ali. 'We were at our wits' end with her. We didn't know what to do. Anything was better than what was happening, and I tell you, whatever *he* thinks...' He shot a look of disdain at Warrender. 'Shayla *was* beginning to get better.'

But Warrender was not impressed. 'How do you know she was?' he asked.

'Mr Mustafa said.'

The constable lifted his eyes to the ceiling, maintaining his show of disbelief. 'Mr Mustafa seems to say an awful lot. I think it's about time we had him in and he said it to us.'

At this Calvin's nerves took over. 'No,' he pleaded. 'No, you can't.'

'We can.'

'No, he doesn't want to be involved. That's why I didn't tell you about him.'

Warrender bent forward. 'I don't care what he wants; he *is* involved. He has been doing God knows what to your niece and for all we know you might have been too. We've only your word for it that you were the other side of that door.'

Calvin snapped. 'I wasn't there. She was alone with him and he was helping her.' He stared at Warrender, daring contradiction.

The constable sat back. 'I hope you're right,' he said quietly. 'But we shan't know unless we talk to him, so what's his address?'

Calvin smiled smugly. 'I don't know. He always came to us. If you want him you'll have to find him.'

Warrender picked up the card. 'Oh, we will,' he promised. 'We'll keep this card for the moment and check his address through his mobile phone provider.'

Gill Handford poured herself a large glass of red wine as she waited for the local news to begin. It had been an awful day, the worst ever. The children had been upset and there was little the staff could do to comfort them. She had wanted to hug tight some of the girls who were particularly distressed, but that was against Union advice. Never touch a pupil, no matter how much you feel it would help. It could be construed in the wrong way – and even though Graham Collins had been cleared, there were some parents who preferred to believe other teachers would take physical contact too far if they got the chance. So the children had had to cry alone and gain comfort from each other.

As the news began, she turned up the sound. Shayla's murder was top story. The presenter gave out as much information as he had which was no more than that her body had been found just before midnight at Druid's Altar. 'She was formally identified by her mother, Mrs Evelyn Richards, this morning,' he said. He went on to explain to viewers that Shayla had been missing for some time. 'At a press conference held earlier, Detective Inspector John Handford, who is leading the investigation, had this to say.'

The screen filled with a view of the press office at Central. John sat with DCI Russell at the table, behind them a blue screen in the centre of which was the West Yorkshire Police badge. The camera zoomed towards him. Gill knew how much he hated being the centre of attention at these con-ferences and saw the signs of discomfort – sitting on his chair as though he were chained to it and from time to time playing with his earlobe. Once he began to speak, however, his nervousness receded and he became the calm professional.

'What we need to know,' he said, 'is where Shayla was during the weeks she was missing. Extensive inquiries failed to find her, but someone must know, either because they were shielding her or perhaps hiding her. If anyone saw her, however fleetingly – even if you're not absolutely sure it was her, please come forward and tell us. You may hold the clue we need which will identify her killer.'

The cameras remained on her husband as the journalists threw questions at him. 'What was the cause of death?' 'Is there likely to be an arrest soon?' He answered them as succinctly as he could, telling them no more than he wanted them to know, until Peter Redmayne said, 'Shayla Richards was a pupil at Cliffe Top Comprehensive?'

Gill caught her breath.

'Yes.'

'Is it true that your wife is a teacher there, Inspector?'

'Yes, it is.' John's eyes were wary.

'Couldn't it be said that since I assume all members of staff at the school will be under suspicion, at least for the moment, you have a conflict of interest here? Should you be leading this investigation?'

John stirred in his chair. 'I can promise you there is no conflict of interest,' he declared, probably more tersely than he intended.

Redmayne pushed further. 'My understanding, Inspector, is that the teachers at the school think there is.'

Gill kept her eyes on her husband's face. She recognized the cold stare, the frigid smile and the icy tone. He was not going to let the reporter get away with it, for she knew that he was trying to protect her as well as himself.

'Then as always, Mr Redmayne, you know more than me.'

There was a ripple of laughter, but the journalist was not to be embarrassed or silenced. 'Could you confirm then that the dead girl is the girl who brought the allegation of sexual assault against Graham Collins, a teacher at the school?'

Handford was now visibly angry. 'No, I cannot, Mr Redmayne. The identity of the complainant cannot be divulged for legal reasons as well you know, and if you insist on forcing the issue you will almost certainly be held in contempt of court.'

Gill could take no more as fury wrenched at the knots in her stomach. She couldn't blame John; he had done well within the parameters allowed to the police these days, but the ideas had been planted and the public would believe the journalist. By next week she would be the enemy in school, Graham Collins would be the number one suspect and Shayla would not be allowed to rest in peace.

Angrily Handford pushed back his chair. He was furious with Redmayne. The DCI had congratulated him on keeping his cool and deflecting the journalist's questions, but he didn't feel it was deserved. Without giving Redmayne a single straight answer he'd handed him the information he wanted on a plate, and the rest of them the story by default. They couldn't print it of course, neither the fact that the staff at the school wanted Handford off the case, nor that Shayla had been the girl who had made the allegations against Collins. But good journalists had ways of hinting, and that would be sufficient.

He'd had enough of today, he decided. He wanted to go home to Gill and the girls, try to have a family evening. Unfortunately, he couldn't, not yet; he would have to wait in case anyone rang in. If they were going to get anything of any use it would be now, straight after the broadcast. He was about to leave the room to return to his office when Redmayne caught up with him.

'We need to talk, John,' he said. 'The Globe at seven?' And without waiting for a reply he walked out of the building in the direction of the newspaper offices.

chapter eight

Sean Johnson's hands trembled as he lit his cigarette. He pulled at it, allowing the hot smoke to curl round his mouth and sting the back of his throat. The news on the television was full of Shayla Richards and watching the press conference had made him nervous. He wished he'd never met the girl, that Kerry had never brought her home when she'd first joined the gang, that he'd never tried it on with her. Someone would be bound to remember, then they'd talk to the cops, who would make up a story to fit the facts. They'd say he'd had another go, that she'd wanted none of it, he'd got mad with her and killed her. It had happened before, hadn't it, with the eight-year-old? But that was different; she'd threatened to tell her parents. He'd only wanted to frighten her to stop her from talking. It was her own fault that frighten had had to turn to quieten. He was fifteen and hadn't known what to do when she'd started screaming, so he'd put his hand over her mouth and held it there until she stopped, but his hand had been too big and had covered her nose as well. At first she'd struggled, then she'd gone limp and it had taken him a little while to realize she was dead. When he had, he'd panicked and pushed her body into the canal. It had been three days before they'd found her.

He felt sick at the memory and mashed out the

cigarette in the ashtray he'd pinched from the pub.

With Shayla it had been different. She wasn't a little girl; she'd been up for it, would have gone all the way if his probation officer hadn't come calling. Just passing, she'd said, then eyed him up and down and told Shayla she ought to be at school. Shayla had mouthed off at her, but had left anyway. When Kerry had come home, she'd given him a tongue-lashing and said she would make sure he wouldn't have the opportunity again.

He opened his tobacco tin and pulled out another roll-up. He'd said nothing to anyone at the time but Shayla had been so proud that someone had made a pass at her, she had crowed about it. He'd been the laughing stock of the pub after that – 'Can't get it on with a real woman,' they'd mocked. 'Still after little girls?' It would be too much to hope with the girl dead that they wouldn't want to tell their story. The cops would be all over him like a rash and they'd reflect on their ages – her a minor at fifteen and him thirty-five. That would clinch it; Sean Johnson had killed again. After all, it was only a matter of time.

Kerry came out of the kitchen with two mugs of coffee. She handed one to Sean. 'Drink that,' she said. 'I'll go to the chippy later.'

His hand trembled as he took it and he had to use both to steady the mug while he took a sip. The coffee was hot and its bitterness masked that of the cigarette. 'Why is our life always so fucking awful, Kerry?'

She looked at him, sadness clouding her eyes.

'It's not,' she said gently. 'We're doing all right, you and me.'

But Sean was not to be appeased. 'All right? I kill a kid, your dad kills your mum, the police are never off our doorstep and now Shayla Richards.'

Kerry placed her mug on the floor and leaned towards him. 'Now you listen to me, Sean Johnson,' she said firmly. 'You need to forget that kid; it happened years ago. My mum's dead and I can't bring her back, and as far as I'm concerned I haven't got a dad. As for Shayla Richards, we knew her; so what? So did lots of other people, including every teacher in the fucking school.'

His voice cracked. 'They didn't try it on with her though, did they? I did and that'll be enough for the cops.'

'What you did six months ago hasn't anything to do with what happened to her yesterday. You didn't kill 'er, so there's nothing to worry about.'

He pulled on his cigarette, 'But even so...'

'There *are* no buts, Sean. I was with you last night except when you were at the pub, and lots of people will vouch that you were there. Even the cops can't make something out of nothing. And anyway, you weren't the only one to try it on with her. Collins did.'

He frowned. His head still ached from last night's binge and he was having difficulty thinking clearly. 'But he was found not guilty. Shayla said she'd lied.'

'No,' Kerry broke in. 'Shayla came up trumps. She knew which side her bread was buttered.'

Sean panicked. 'She can't this time though, can she? She's dead.'

153

'Then we'll have to do it for her.' Kerry's voice was ominously quiet. 'I'm not risking Collins going down for life.' She stood up and pointed to his mug. 'Finished?'

Sean nodded. 'I'm scared, Kerry. I'm scared if they let Collins off, they'll fit me up and send me down.' He flicked at his lighter and relit his cigarette. 'I can't go back inside. You know what they do to child-killers.' He dragged on the roll-up as though it was his last. Roll-ups were his legacy from prison; he couldn't smoke normal cigs any more – they made him feel sick. That's what prison did to you: stop you being normal. Smells, noise and constant fear. No one, inmates or screws, cared that he'd only been a kid himself when he killed her, or that he hadn't meant for her to die. They had their own rules and their own form of justice in there.

Unable to sit still any longer, he pulled himself out of the chair and walked to the window. It was dark, but he could feel the energy of the street. The lamps threw smudges of light onto the ground and parked cars lined the pavement. There were more than usual; probably there was something on at the school. Unless the police were still there, searching, examining, questioning, getting closer to learning about his dodgy relationship with Shayla. He shivered and turned back to Kerry, whose gaze was concentrated floorwards. 'I can't go back inside,' he pleaded. 'It's got to be Collins.'

She lifted her head and he saw the flicker of alarm in her eyes. 'Sean, Collins can't go down. If he does we lose...' Determination took over as she stood up and approached him. 'We will only

154

lose what we've got if your bottle goes.' Now her eyes had hardened. 'And that's not going to happen, is it Sean?'

Defeated, he shook his head and gave a last drag on his roll-up.

With her gaze still firmly on her uncle, Kerry picked up the mugs and handed them to him. 'Wash those up,' she ordered. 'It'll give you something to do. Then for God's sake, have a bath 'cos I'm not staying in with you if you're going to stink the house out.' She unhooked her coat from the back of the chair. 'I'm going to the chippy and I'll get a video while I'm out, one that'll cheer you up. Then, after that,' she grinned, 'if you play your cards right, you can sleep in my room tonight.'

Khalid Ali caught up with Warrender in the car park. 'Sorry if I've spoilt your date,' he said. He hoped he sounded genuine.

Warrender turned to face him. 'You haven't, at least not all of it. I'll miss the beers, but I'll catch up with the lads later at the curry house.'

Ali remembered his remark about the constable having a celibate night in for once. 'Sorry, I thought…'

Warrender grinned at the sergeant's obvious discomfort. 'I know what you thought,' he said, then stabbed a finger towards him. 'You really should be more careful, Ali.' His voice hardened. 'Since you know nothing about me, you should learn not to jump to conclusions; you might get it seriously wrong one day,' and with a curt nod he walked on.

And you, thought Ali as he followed him, should

stop fantasizing about your lifestyle and tell the truth about your sister if you don't want people to jump to conclusions. But to say it would alert Warrender to what he knew and he didn't need the argument. Better a smug detective constable. Instead, he quickened his step to catch up with Warrender and when he was alongside, said, 'We'll put our energies into finding Shahid Mustafa tomorrow, although I can't say I'm looking forward to meeting him.'

'Why?' Warrender exclaimed, his tone incredulous. 'Because according to him, he,' he recited the words on the card, 'can help sustain and enliven love, get rid of bad luck, cast out evil spirits and has black magic capabilities? You don't believe that rubbish, do you, Sarge?'

'No Warrender, I don't,' Ali replied firmly, his patience beginning to wear thin. 'But Calvin does, Mustafa does and whoever killed Shayla probably does, given the sacrificial arrangement of her body, and personally, I have difficulty coming to terms with talk of devils, evil spirits and black magic; it's way outside my understanding.'

'It's way outside all our understanding, but then most of what we come across in this line of work is. Just keep it simple, Ali. There *were* no devils or evil spirits in Shayla Richards, except of her own making, or that of her family. It's not rocket science if you bother to consider what she'd been through. She was a disturbed girl.' He tapped his head. 'It was all in her mind. If they'd left her with the psychiatrist, perhaps she'd have been able to do something for her; instead of which they put her through an exorcism, threatened her with another and then when that didn't work they brought in Mustafa and God only knows what he was doing to her. It's not surprising she went potty.'

Of course it wasn't. Put like that it made perfect sense. Except ... except since the start of the case nothing had been straightforward. The location, the arrangement of the body, Collins, even Gill Handford was being dragged into it. Ali had watched the press conference broadcast and he felt for her. If Redmayne and the media had their way, she could be in for a rough time. Perhaps he'd ask his wife to give her a ring. They'd become good friends after an evening spent at the Alis' during his first case at Central, and he was sure Amina would be happy to support her.

As they approached Warrender's car, Ali said, 'Have you come up with anything on Graham Collins yet?'

'Not yet, but I'll work on it tonight. A drink at The Four Feathers, I thought.'

'The Four Feathers?'

'Collins' local. A bit of watching, listening and talking where he drinks and you can learn a lot. Although I suppose you can't, can you? Being a Muslim.' He grinned again and pressed the electronic key fob. The orange sidelights of the car flashed in reply.

'I can always have an orange juice.'

Warrender guffawed. 'Not with me you don't, Ali. If you go into any pub with me, it's as my sergeant, not as a drinking partner. I want to get information from the people there, not frighten them off. See you and they'd run a mile. No, you go home to your obedient little wife and leave this to the big boys.' He opened the car door and slipped into the driver's seat. 'I'll bring you back a packet of crisps,' he promised as he clipped his seat belt into position, then he put the car into gear and with a wave drove off.

As John Handford struggled against the wind buffeting the car park of The Globe public house, he asked himself for the dozenth time why he had come at all. He didn't usually accept ultimatums from journalists, particularly after the kind of aggravation he'd had to endure at the press conference. But he was curious. Redmayne had been so determined they meet he hadn't given him the opportunity to refuse, and although Handford doubted the reporter would break his silence on the identity of the informant at the school, he hoped he would have something useful for him. He was also keen to know why Redmayne hadn't disclosed his date with Collins the night before.

The Globe was Redmayne's local and it was here that he and Handford always met. As a free house, it offered a variety of beers, including real ale, a passable restaurant and bar menu and a congenial atmosphere. Even on a filthy night like tonight it was impossible not to be cheered by the deep red carpets, the dark oak furniture and the real log fire. As Handford walked through the door, he felt its welcoming warmth immediately. The ends of his fingers began to tingle as the blood returned and he rubbed his hands together to quicken the process. He scanned the room and saw Redmayne wave to him from a corner booth, indicating at the same time that he had already got John's drink in for him. He pulled off his coat, shook it and made his way to where the man was sitting.

The reporter half stood as he greeted the policeman. 'Glad you came,' he said. 'I wasn't sure whether you would.'

'I wasn't sure either, but you didn't give me much of an opportunity to refuse.'

'No, sorry about that. It was deliberate though; I have something to put to you and I needed to see you alone.'

Handford sat down. 'If it's about my being relieved of the investigation or you acting as mediator for members of staff who don't want Collins questioned, then forget it, I'll have this half and go.' He picked up the glass and as if to prove his point, took a long drink.

Redmayne grinned and pushed his spectacles back up to the bridge of his nose. 'It's an interesting thought,' he said. 'But no, that's not it.' The smile faded. 'But it *is* to do with Collins, and if I tell you, I want you to promise you'll not act on it.'

Handford could feel his hackles rising. The arrogance of the man. Just how important did he think he was? 'For goodness' sake, Peter, you can't ask me that. If it's relevant to the inquiry, I have to. We've a dead fifteen-year-old – or have you forgotten?'

Redmayne remained silent for a moment. 'No,' he said, then, 'I'm sorry, John, but like you and

159

your policeman's hat, I can't take mine off completely either. I've got nothing I can print yet, but if anything comes of it, I want you to promise me first refusal.'

The pub's atmosphere was beginning to work its magic on Handford and he relaxed and smiled at the reporter's request. 'As always, Peter,' he said as he picked up his beer again. 'However, before you tell me, I'd like to know why, when I met you this morning, you didn't mention that you'd spent last evening with Collins.'

'You didn't ask.'

Anger sparked in Handford's face; that was the kind of reply he expected from a seventeen-year-old delinquent. Holding himself in check, he replaced his glass carefully on the table. 'It wasn't up to me to ask about something I had no knowledge of,' he said quietly. 'It was up to you to tell me. Knowing you had been with him would have helped – not just me, but Collins as well.' He glared at Redmayne, who shifted his eyes onto his own beer. 'This isn't a game, Peter, and you'd know that if you'd been up on Harden Moor this morning with a dead girl. Instead of trying to dredge up a story on my relationship with my wife, you ought to be doing what you do best, reporting crime. For Christ's sake, man, you know as well as I do how the most insignificant piece of information can turn out to be vital. It can count someone out of or into an investigation and stop us wasting our time. You had something relevant on a man you obviously believed would be a suspect or you wouldn't have been sitting outside his house waiting for us to appear when all your colleagues were at the school. In future, Peter, when you have information you pass it on. You don't wait for me to ask you.' He could have said more, but his outrage against the man was subsiding. 'You come into the station tomorrow and make a full – and I mean a full – statement.'

For a few moments Redmayne offered no comment, exhaled heavily as though to rid himself of the onslaught, then said, 'My God, John. I bet your detectives are terrified of you when you're in this mood. I haven't been told off like that since I was a junior reporter.' He pulled himself out of the booth. 'I need another drink. You?'

Handford shook his head; it didn't seem fair to expect the man to buy him one after the dressing-down he'd given him, even if Redmayne *had* deserved it. He leaned against the hard wooden settle. It had been a tough day, he was tired and for a moment he closed his eyes. His mind whirled with pictures of Shayla's body on the altar, of Collins and Redmayne and of Gill – particularly Gill. Through no fault of her own, she was being dragged into a side of the case that shouldn't even be there, and in spite of his rebuke, he couldn't be sure Redmayne wouldn't still make a story of it. He'd heard nothing from his wife since lunchtime and although he would soon be home, he suddenly felt the need to satisfy himself that she was coping. He reached into his pocket for his mobile, but as he looked up he saw Redmayne weaving his way between the tables, sipping his drink as he walked, and with a sigh he replaced the phone.

Redmayne slid into the booth and for a few

moments the atmosphere between them was strained, neither of them knowing quite what to say. Eventually Handford asked, 'What was it you wanted to put to me?'

For the first time since he had known him, Redmayne wasn't sure of his ground. 'Can I ask a couple of questions first?'

It was the least Handford could agree to, although whether he could answer them was a different matter. 'Go on,' he said.

'I gather you've searched Collins' house?'

'Yes.'

'Because you found some of Shayla's clothes among his rubbish?'

'On top, rather than among. Whoever left them had made no attempt to hide them.'

'So they could have been put there to frame him?'

'It's always a possibility, although to be honest I can't think of anyone who would want to, can you?'

Redmayne shook his head. 'The only people who might would be those who believe he got away with assaulting Shayla, but to frame him they would have to have been involved in her death somehow and that doesn't make sense. Unless...'

Handford was one step in front of him. 'Yes, unless it's family, and we're working on that, although currently there's nothing concrete to prove they were implicated. The fact is, Peter, we're sure Shayla wasn't killed on Harden Moor, so it had to have happened elsewhere and at the moment we have no idea where.' He drained his

162

glass. 'What we believe to be some of her clothes were found in Collins' wheelie bin, so we searched his house knowing that if Shayla had been there, we would uncover the evidence.'

'And have you?'

'If we had I wouldn't tell you, but the truth is I don't know yet. We're looking for minute traces – fibres, hairs, that kind of thing – and it'll take some time for the scientists to sift through what, if anything,' he emphasized the words, 'was found.' He paused, regarded his empty beer glass and wished he'd let Redmayne get him another. 'I've answered as many of your questions as I'm prepared to for the moment. It's your turn to give me something.'

In spite of the awful weather, the pub was beginning to fill up. Regulars stopped to have a few words with Redmayne and a group of young men sat in the booth in front of them. Handford wondered if they would have more privacy in his car, but was reluctant to brave the wind and the rain just yet. Redmayne leaned forward as if to keep the conversation confidential. 'It's Collins. Something happened today that has got me worried. I know I should have told you about our meeting yesterday evening, and it wasn't that I didn't want to, it was just that I needed to learn more about the murder first.'

Handford cocked an eyebrow and Redmayne spread his hands in defeat. 'All right, John, I admit it. *Mea culpa.* I'll tell you what I know and you can make of it what you will. Collins rang last night and asked me to meet him at The Four Feathers. His wife was at work; he was depressed and needed company. Nothing new there. We had a few drinks and played a game or two of pool and we talked, mostly about Shayla. There was nothing unusual in that either, it was par for the course, but last night he seemed especially angry with her, took it out on the pool balls, slapping them all over the table. I thought at one time the landlord was going to stop us playing.'

'Did he explain why he felt as he did?'

'No, and I put it down to a bad day. He has a lot of them. But now ... well, I'm not so sure any more. I told you this morning he was living on a knife-edge and if he were tipped over, I wouldn't like to take bets on whether it would be himself he would harm, his wife or Shayla Richards. Last night, when Jane had to work, he was teetering, but he rang me and I was there for him. At the moment I'm interested in him, I listen to him and that's what he wants – someone to listen. It doesn't even matter to him that I'll probably use what he says in a feature. Today your visit and the search of his house tipped him over and there was no one around to help. The result was that after your officers left, it wasn't pool balls he took his anger out on; it was his wife.'

Handford closed his eyes momentarily. He knew that not bringing Collins in when they found the clothes would backfire on him. His reasons were sound, but they were pitted by his concern about possible repercussions on Gill. The result: he'd tried to avoid hurting his own wife, to have Jane Collins harmed instead. Ali would have a field day if he knew. Redmayne, too. 'Is she all right?' he asked.

'I went to check on her before the press conference. She's shaken and not a little confused, but otherwise she's fine and refuses to make a complaint. Collins is full of remorse of course, although he blames Shayla, the school, the governors, the police, anyone and everyone, for his behaviour.' Redmayne ran his hands through his mop of hair, making it more unruly than ever. 'Bad as it is, it's not that that worries me, it's his reason for the attack. After your lot had left, she tried to reassure him that she knew he hadn't killed anyone, that they would get through and he would soon be back teaching. The kind of reassurance you expect a loving wife to give – and make no mistake. Jane Collins loves her husband very much. But Collins is unpredictable and talk of the job sparked his anger. Apparently, he'd read a newspaper article a few days earlier about a doctor who had been kept under suspension by an NHS Trust even after he'd been exonerated ten years ago; since then he's been drawing full pay and not allowed to work anywhere else. Presumably Collins saw his life stretching out in front of him in the same way. His anger flared, he lost control, grabbed hold of her and forced her back against the door. She begged him to stop, said he was frightening her, but either he didn't hear her or he was too far gone, so she screamed at him that she was pregnant and pleaded with him not to hurt her. That should have brought him to his senses, and for a split second, he said, it did, until for some reason which he couldn't or wouldn't explain, he completely lost it, accused her of being a stupid bitch and then hit her –

hard, by the looks of it. She has quite a bruise on her cheek.'

For a while Handford made no comment. Sometimes he wished life had a rewind function. He had sensed when they were questioning him that Collins was being ultra calm, holding himself in check, and he ought to have guessed that eventually the man would blow, that the stress he was under could turn to sudden, violent anger. He'd seen it happen before and he'd seen the human tragedy it left in its wake. But the notion that the pregnancy was its detonator was deplorable. Jane Collins ought to have her husband charged with ABH. Unless there was something else, something they didn't know about? Reading between the lines, Redmayne seemed to think there was.

'I assume she *is* pregnant? It wasn't just a ploy to get him off her?' Handford asked.

'Oh yes, very early stages, but she is pregnant.'

'And the child is his?'

'I wondered that at first, but yes, it is.'

Having disposed of the obvious, Handford said, 'It sounds to me that Jane having a baby was the last straw for him. Why do you think that was? I would have thought it was the first good thing that had happened to them in a long time.'

'He saw the pregnancy as her attempt to bring more kids like Shayla Richards into the world. It was almost as though she'd done it to spite him. He said there would be even more kids to taunt him and lie about him. The man's in turmoil. He's all over the place and as guilty as hell at what he's done. Jane insists he's never hit her before, but

166

he's so obsessed with Shayla and what she's put him through that I wouldn't trust him not to do it again. It's almost as though Shayla Richards is with him all the time, that she's haunting him – his own personal devil if you like, which I suppose in a way she is. How do you rid yourself of someone or something like that?' There was a roar of laughter from the boys in the next booth and Redmayne's voice faded to a whisper. 'I'm no psychiatrist,' he said. 'But given Collins' state of mind, it seems to me he has two choices: either he kills himself or he kills her. I hope I'm wrong, John, but I have to ask myself – if he could attack his wife so violently, what more could he have done to Shayla Richards?'

Evelyn Richards sat on her daughter's bed and rocked backwards and forwards. She cuddled the photograph of the nine-year-old Shayla clutching her swimming cup. The frame was cold, as cold as Shayla had probably been, except they wouldn't let her touch her. It was all she had left of her little girl and this was how she wanted to remember her – excited, happy, alive. Although try as she might, the only image Evelyn carried was of her lying on a trolley covered by a white sheet. The policeman had been right; she did look peaceful – more peaceful than Evelyn had seen her for a long time.

Was all this her fault? Shayla had taken the break-up of the marriage harder than the boys had. She blamed her mother, but it was Qumar who had disturbed her peace, not leaving them alone, demanding residency, then going back to

Pakistan without a word when it was refused. It was during that time the devils had taken over Shayla's life. They were insidious, creeping into her dreams when she was asleep and into her mirror when she awoke.

Evelyn pressed the photograph hard into her breasts until they hurt. She began to sob, but not so loudly that the policewoman would hear and come in.

Calvin had said they ought to let Qumar know. It was his right, he argued. But she'd said no, not yet. Later, when they'd buried her according to the Christian faith, in consecrated ground with a cross on her headstone, where Evelyn could go and visit her and talk to her. They would tell him after she was buried. If they contacted him now, he would want her interred according to his faith and he didn't have the right. He'd lost any rights over her when he'd gone and hadn't sent money to help care for her. If he'd done that it wouldn't have been so difficult to manage because money would have been one less thing to have to worry about. Evelyn could have given her daughter what she wanted. If she'd done that, perhaps Shayla wouldn't have turned to Collins. You should be able to trust teachers, and Shayla thought she could. Instead he'd taken advantage of her youth and her innocence and deflowered her, taken away what peace was left to her. Now, finally, he'd killed her and taken away her mother's peace as well.

She'd told the detectives, but they'd refused to listen. The Pakistani sergeant had insisted they didn't know who had killed her, but Evelyn

168

Richards did and she was going to make sure everyone knew so that they could help her gain retribution. She had lots of friends – at the church, at the university, here in the street where she lived. They would follow her to Collins' house, congregate round it, force him out, force him to confess. In her mind she imagined the crowd surrounding his house, waving pictures of her daughter in her swimming costume, clutching her cup. She heard the crash of the glass as they hurled stones at his windows, and their chants of 'Murderer, murderer.' As she rocked her baby, safe in the wooden frame, the roar of their abuse intensified in her head along with her own sobs. She would avenge Shayla's death, even if the police wouldn't.

It was the only thing she could do for her daughter now.

chapter nine

To Warrender The Four Feathers was pretty much like most pubs, worse than some he had had to visit as a police officer, better than others. It stood on its own land facing the main road, a tarmacadam car park to the side. Outside the door garish boards advertised Sizzling Steaks for £5.99, Happy Hour every Thursday six to seven and Quiz Nite each Monday.

Warrender wasn't sure what, if anything, he'd get from being there, but everyone would have opinions and once they were stored in his brain, he could set about extracting the fact from the fiction. It would take time, but it was the kind of police work he enjoyed. Also, he was determined to show Ali what being a good detective was all about. The man thought he was God's gift and he needed to learn that he wasn't. But then in Warrender's experience they all did, thought they were above the law. Could say or do anything they wanted and get away with it. The wisecrack about having a celibate night in for once still rankled. If only Ali knew. Warrender had been angrier than he was prepared to admit and had related the comment to his sister, together with a few expletives. 'Tell him, Chris, not me,' she had said wearily. She had heard it all before and it didn't solve anything. 'At least then he'll have half a chance of understanding.' But Warrender didn't want the sergeant's understanding – it would stick in his throat.

The pub was dark. Dark wallpaper, dark furnishings, subdued lighting. It was also almost empty. At one end of the room a couple were deep in conversation, seemingly oblivious of their surroundings, and at the corner table a man was equally engrossed in the book he was reading. He carried the look of someone who lived a harassed existence, probably needed to get away from the kids with their loud music and their quarrelling, make his own space, read in peace. As Warrender watched him, the man's fingers groped for the pint glass on the table in front of him, his eyes never straying from the page. To the side of the curved bar, a couple of middle-aged men peered into the gloom as they played a game of darts. The pool table at the far end of the pub stood empty.

The landlord was leaning on the bar reading the local paper and barely moved as Warrender ordered a pint. He was a young man with a shock of black hair and bushy eyebrows and, although it was November, he was wearing a short-sleeved black shirt, thus exposing the intricately designed tattoos along his arms. On each knuckle of his left hand was a single letter, which when put together spelled out the name JUNE. Probably his girl-friend, or even a former girlfriend. That was the problem with tattoos: they stayed with you. One reason why Warrender had never succumbed.

'On your own?' the detective asked as he placed the money on the bar.

'No, June's upstairs putting the little 'un to bed and Brenda will be in later.'

Warrender looked around. 'You're not very busy – weather, I suppose.'

'Aye, it can keep some away.' The landlord passed Warrender his drink, slid the coins into his hand and rang them into the till. 'Most of the regulars don't come in until half eight, nine o'clock. It'll get busier.'

Warrender glanced at the paper. Shayla Richards was front-page news. 'Bad business, that,' he said, nodding at it.

'It is that.' The landlord stepped sideways to the optics and released a single shot of brandy. 'She were a little tart, though. I've chased her out of here more than once. Flaunting herself around she was, pretending she were eighteen. She must 'ave thought I were born yesterday.' He drained his glass as though he wouldn't get another opportunity – or perhaps he didn't want June to see him drinking the profits – then drew another, a double this time. 'No one's surprised she came to a sticky end, at least not round 'ere they're not. Though in all conscience, she didn't deserve this.'

Warrender hitched himself onto the high stool and leaned across the bar. 'I'd heard a whisper that she's the girl who accused the teacher of a sexual assault.'

'You heard right, mate. It's not supposed to be common knowledge, but everyone round here knows. Graham Collins – that's the teacher – he's one of our regulars. Which was another reason I wouldn't have her in here, coming in winding him up so that he couldn't even have a quiet drink. A lovely chap, he is; wouldn't hurt a fly. But I tell you, she's near on destroyed him. He

172

was a real jovial type before it happened. Now he hardly has a civil word for anyone, but we're all on his side.'

'You think she was lying about the assault then?'

'Yeah, course she was. Well, she said she was, didn't she? Not that we believed it right from the beginning. And I'll tell you something else for nothing.' The man was getting into his stride, just as Warrender wanted. 'He didn't murder her, neither. Apart from anything else, she were killed last night and he was in 'ere,' he finished triumphantly.

Warrender grunted as though in agreement. 'You know him well?'

'Only as a regular since he came to live round here.'

'So he's not local, then?'

The landlord gave Warrender a suspicious look. 'You're asking a lot of questions; you're not a reporter, are you? 'Cos he's had his fill of them.'

Warrender smiled. 'No, nothing like that.' He leaned even closer. 'To tell you the truth,' he lied, 'I'm a mature student up at the university and I'm working on a dissertation on the psychological effects of false accusations, particularly on professionals.' He wasn't sure if the landlord had understood a word he'd uttered, but it didn't matter because he seemed impressed, so Warrender went on. 'I was hoping to talk to Mr Collins himself, but if he's a suspect in that girl's murder, I doubt the police will let me. It would be good, though, if you could tell me something about him. I promise you it'll go no further than me and the university.'

The landlord took Warrender's glass. 'Another?' he asked. 'On the house.'

'That's very civil of you. Just a half.'

For the next quarter of an hour the landlord sipped at his brandy and Warrender asked questions.

'You said he hasn't been here very long. Where was he before, do you know?'

'He's been here four years, give or take. I think he'd been in other schools somewhere else, because he wasn't new to teaching. He's married as well, a lovely girl; she's a midwife, works up at the hospital, delivered our little 'un. But I don't know nothing about her.'

'Do you know where Mr Collins comes from originally? Not round here?'

'No, he's too posh for that. Mind you, with his background, it's not surprising he's posh. Not that he talks much about it. Doesn't seem to want anyone to know, and that's what we like about him: he doesn't flaunt his upbringing. From what I can gather he moved around a lot. I think his father was in the army or something. He talks a lot about Germany and how he was sent to boarding school so as not to disrupt his education; that's probably where he got his posh speech from,' he added knowledgeably. 'Desmond over there might know a bit more.' The man with the book. 'I'll see if I can get him to have a word.'

Just then the pub door opened to let in a flurry of cold air and three youths sauntered through, approached the bar and ordered three pints and a whisky chaser each. Warrender doubted any one of them was eighteen and had he not been a mature student at the university he would have sent them packing. He watched as they carried their drinks over to the pool table.

'Keep your glasses off the table, lads,' the landlord shouted over to them and one of them raised a hand in acknowledgement. 'You can't take your eyes off them; got to watch them all the time,' he said, then went to the other end of the bar and shouted for Desmond. The man looked up from his book, placed a marker in it and laid it on the table with his half-finished drink. 'You spent a lot of time with Graham,' the landlord said, when he joined them at the bar. 'Do you know anything about him before he came here? This fellow was asking.'

Desmond, who was less garrulous and more suspicious than the landlord, stared at Warrender. 'So who are you?'

Warrender hoped against hope that Desmond did not work up at the university and begin to ask difficult questions, like who his professor was. With his fingers metaphorically crossed, he explained again. Desmond seemed satisfied and Warrender swallowed his relief.

'I wouldn't normally talk to strangers about him, but the murder is a step too far. We need to support him and Taffy is right, I probably know him better than most.' Taffy? The landlord was no more Welsh than Ali was. 'His father was in the army – a major, I think. Graham was sent off to boarding school somewhere in the Cotswolds, he said, but I can't remember the name. Anyway, after Saddam invaded Kuwait, his father was sent to the Gulf. Graham was expecting to go to university but postponed it after his father was killed. Shortly afterwards his mother was diagnosed with breast cancer. Apparently she'd known about the lump all the time her husband was away and after his death she was in too much of a state to do anything about it. When finally she saw a doctor, it was too late. Graham was quite cut up about it, said it was his fault he hadn't noticed something earlier. He'd thought the rapid loss of weight was because of his father. He looked after her until she died, then went to Warwick to study history. Poor man, he's had a rough time one way or another.'

The pub was beginning to fill up and June had come down into the bar, the little 'un no doubt asleep now.

Warrender's stomach was beginning to crave the curry his friends would be devouring. He doubted there was much more to learn here, and he'd given enough of his free time to Ali. Tomorrow there would be a lot of digging to do back at the station. He hoped there weren't too many private schools in the Cotswolds. He would have to look back into army records too and wondered who was going to give permission for that. Not the superintendent; he wasn't there, and anyway he'd been adamant last time that Warrender was to go no further back in his research of Collins than his years at university. He had thought it odd at the time, but decided it wasn't for him to question a senior officer's decision. That said, had he not been so busy with another case, he would probably have ignored the order and delved deeper. He'd never tell Ali this, but he was quite grateful to the sergeant for giving him the opportunity to do it now. As Ali came back into his mind, he remembered something. 'Give me a packet of crisps,' he said to the landlord as he put on his coat. 'Salt and vinegar should do it.'

Graham Collins walked back into the lounge, looking gaunt. Whoever the phone call had been from, it was not good news. Jane regarded him with a depth of compassion she had never felt before. He couldn't take much more. She fingered her bruised cheek – a symbol of the physical and emotional hurt she was feeling.

'That was Lawrence Welford, chair of governors,' he said. 'They've postponed the internal inquiry. The police won't let them hold it while the investigation into Shayla Richards' death is ongoing. It could be months, Jane. What if they never find out who killed her? What happens to me then? I'll never get my job back.' He leaned against the wall. 'It's like living in a nightmare.'

What could she say that hadn't been said a hundred times over? He was right. Often she'd gone to bed at night, hoping that when she awoke in the morning everything would be back to normal. Instead it got worse. She'd heard it said that everyone goes through bad patches in their lives, but 'bad' was no description of what was happening to them – it didn't even come close. Graham shouldn't still be living with this; Shayla had lied, and he had been found not guilty. The judge had said that he could leave the court without a stain on his character. Except for the stains formed by other people's judgements – stains that discoloured both their lives, for although she'd never mentioned it to Graham, she'd been on the wrong side of people's assumptions and preconceptions, too. A woman in the final stages of labour had refused to let her deliver the baby. She wasn't going to have the wife of a pervert near her, she'd said. What kind of a woman stays with someone like that, she'd asked between the screams and shouts. When Jane had attempted to defend herself and Graham, the woman had cursed and snarled that there was 'no smoke without fire'. The nursing manager had tried to laugh it off and put it down to the pain talking, but she'd moved Jane to another patient nevertheless.

Graham slumped into the chair opposite his wife. 'He didn't say so in so many words, but Welford thinks I killed her,' he said. 'In fact he probably hopes I did, then I wouldn't be a problem any more.' He leaned forward to take her hands but as he touched her, she flinched and he pulled back. 'Even you're not sure, are you?' he said bitterly.

'Yes I am,' she said and as if to show she meant it, she bent towards him and clasped his hands in hers. 'I *am* sure; I know you didn't assault her and I know you didn't kill her, but you hit me, and at the moment I'm finding that hard to forgive. It's only because you've been through so much that I'm not leaving you.' Her voice hardened. 'But if it happens again, Graham, I will. I'm not prepared to be a battered wife, whatever the reason.' She pulled away from him again and for a few moments they sat in silence while both tussled with the significance of her words.

Graham sat as if fixed like stone. 'I'm so sorry, Jane.' He was almost inaudible. 'What I did was unforgivable. No reason I can give excuses it. But somehow, I promise you, I will make it up to you.'

For a moment she needed to put some distance between them. She stood up and walked to the window, opening the curtains. It was dark, the only light coming from the few street lamps and the houses opposite. Not for the first time, she envied their occupants their neat, oblivious lives. She and Graham didn't belong in the same world any more.

Suddenly, she asked, 'Do you want this baby?'

He jumped up and hurried towards her, grasping her by the shoulders as he turned her to look at him. 'Of course I do, Jane. If you don't believe anything else, you must believe that. We've always wanted a baby together. It's the only good thing to come out of this mess.' He took a deep breath, then let it out slowly. 'It was just ... that ... I don't know ... that Shayla Richards has spoiled everything for us and I wanted to get back at her. I've tried to keep it together for so long but this afternoon I couldn't hold on any longer. All I could see was me out of a job, you working to keep us, and a baby I couldn't provide for. All these images were beating at my brain; I could see them and feel them. Then suddenly there she was, taunting me and laughing at me because she'd won, and I hit out. I hit at Shayla, Jane, not you.'

When she made no reply, he said, 'Please don't

179

leave me. I'll do anything you want: see a doctor, a counsellor, a psychiatrist if you want, but please, Jane, don't go.'

As much as she didn't want to give in to him, to make it plain that she wouldn't stay with a husband who hit her, she couldn't stop herself. She put her arms round his neck and said, 'You've got to accept that we're living this together, Graham, and it's hard for me too. If you act as if you're the only person involved and that everyone else is your enemy, it will break us up. Don't let it do that, particularly now.' When he made no comment, she pulled away. 'I've had enough,' she said. 'I'm tired; it's been a long day and just for once I want to do what normal people do, relax, watch television, listen to music, anything but talk about Shayla Richards.'

Collins closed the curtains. 'Then that's what we'll do,' he said. When she was settled, he kneeled in front of her and placed his hand on her stomach. 'This baby is going to make our lives better and nothing Shayla Richards or the governors or the police can do is ever going to change that. Tonight, I promise, I'll look after you and for once we'll be Mr and Mrs Boring spending our evening quietly at home.'

He was about to kiss her when the brick crashed through the window, followed by a blast of cold air as the curtains billowed against its force. Glass showered onto the sill and for a split second they froze. Simultaneously, they jumped up. The curtains were blowing in the wind and as Collins caught them and pulled them open, he made out the figures silhouetted in the light of the street lamps and heard the rising chant of 'Murderer! Murderer!'

Handford hadn't known quite what to expect when he arrived home. Given the time – well past eight o'clock – there could be no doubt in Gill's mind that he was still on the investigation and not much doubt in his that he was letting his wife down the first and, as far as he could remember, the only occasion she had ever asked something of him in relation to his job. In the event there had been no time for recriminations or apologies since as soon as he was in the door his phone had rung. The duty inspector thought he ought to know about the vigilantes outside Collins' house and the brick through his window. The group, small, female and vocal was led by one Evelyn Richards, and had still been there when the police arrived. Unfortunately, the inspector said, they'd had to arrest Mrs Richards, who had sat down in the road and refused to move unless they took Graham Collins into police custody for murdering her daughter. If she had been reasonable they would have sent her home, but the silly woman had kicked the constable assigned to remove her, so they'd been obliged to arrest her for assault.

Handford had no choice but to return to the station, where the constable in question said he was not interested in bringing charges against Evelyn Richards and she was released with a stern warning not to take the law into her own hands and a promise from Calvin, who had arrived a few minutes earlier, to keep an eye on her. Handford also suggested that the duty inspector have a word with the FLO, reminding her to do the same.

From Central he had driven to the Collins house. Before he knocked on the door, he examined the gaping hole surrounded by spider-web fractures in the centre pane of the front window. Someone had attempted to shield it with plastic sheeting, although how secure it would be in the wind which was beginning to blow more fiercely now, Handford couldn't be sure. It was better than nothing, however, until a glazier could come the next day to replace it.

As he entered the house the same aura of hopelessness he had encountered when he had visited during the morning washed over him, but this time something more stalked the room: fear. It was as tangible as the furnishings it clung to. Little attempt had been made to clear the glass, and slivers still lay on the sill and the carpet. Graham Collins had let him in to the lounge, where Jane sat on the settee. She was chalk white as she sat hugging herself, her arms caging the shock and the tears, her gaze fixed on something beyond him. Both were badly shaken by the turn of events; whatever they had expected to happen, it hadn't been this. Perhaps Handford ought to have warned them of Mrs Richards' state of mind, although he couldn't believe that Collins had been so naive not to think she would consider him a suspect.

'I'm not a suspect, Inspector,' he had said quietly. 'To her I'm a murderer. How do I fight that?'

Handford had murmured something about him

not having to – the police would make sure she didn't bother him again. He hoped he sounded reassuring, but he doubted it. Collins had been there too often over the past couple of years to be comforted. So Handford left them, knowing there was little more he could do; he hadn't come to question the man, merely to make sure that he and his wife were unhurt and to suggest that they should stay somewhere else overnight – at Jane's mother's perhaps. They refused, partly because they felt the house was more vulnerable without them and partly because Graham Collins was insistent that no one was going to turn them out of their own home. Handford gave them his card and told them that if there were any more problems they should contact him. He hadn't commented on the bruise on Jane Collins' face – that would keep until later.

When he arrived back home Gill was in bed and when he left for work early Saturday morning, she was still asleep. He ought to have waited, gone in later, but it was the beginning of a murder inquiry and there was a lot to do. If he let too much time slip away, the chances of catching the perpetrator would recede. At least it was the weekend and by Monday when Gill was back at school, things might be very different. He met up with Ali in the car park.

'Mrs Richards has set up a group of friends as vigilantes,' he told him. 'Made quite a mess of Collins' front window.'

Ali groaned. 'I told her yesterday not to take the law into her own hands.'

'Obviously not strongly enough.'

'Obviously. Warrender thinks I can have no influence over Mrs Richards – wrong race, apparently. And also I'm not interested in her as a person, just as a witness. He thinks she needs careful handling, that she's grieving for her daughter and that I ought to spend more time listening to her and less time being a career policeman.'

Handford smiled. 'That's what he called you?' Like the constable, he wasn't keen on coppers on accelerated promotion. Too busy fast-tracking and building up brownie points to gather real experience. Warrender was right; you often learned more by listening than by questioning. He was afraid he and the DC were a dying breed in the new police service.

As they were climbing the steps up to CID, Ali said, 'Warrender said he was going to Graham Collins' local – you know, to mingle, see what he could pick up.'

'Good idea. If there is anything, he'll have found it, although I wouldn't look too closely into his methods, if I were you. And it would be sensible not to send him back there as a police officer, at least not for the moment.'

Ali held the door open for Handford. 'You approve of the way he works?'

Handford could feel a sigh building. He walked into his office and put his briefcase on his desk. 'Not always,' he said, taking his coat off, 'but sometimes a little bit of subterfuge works wonders. It's a quick way of getting information and even you must admit there's precious little of it around about Collins.'

Ali's expression suggested he wasn't convinced.

'Oh, come on, Khalid. Would you feel the same if it was Clarke or me doing it? I doubt it. We all break the rules at times, even you; it's the only way to get the job done. And a white lie about why he's in a pub is hardly a hanging offence.' Handford chuckled. 'I wonder what he told them.'

'I said I was a mature student researching the psychological effects of false accusations on professionals, guv. I tell you, they were very impressed.'

The laughter that followed Warrender's comment went some way to dispelling the team's frustration at having to work through the weekend. There were advantages, the big one being that they would earn overtime, but there were disadvantages too: weekend working, dates broken, rows and arguments. Handford needed to get them out doing something, to make sure their interrupted lives yielded something positive. He allowed the amusement and the various comments to subside before asking Warrender to tell them what he had found out.

'According to the regulars, his father was a Major Collins – I don't have a Christian name – who died in the Iraq war in 1991 and the mother followed him some months later from cancer. There was no mention of brothers or sisters. I've already been in touch with the military police and they're looking into Major Collins for me. I'll check on the various birth, marriage and death certificates on Monday as well as tracking down the school Collins attended in the Cotswolds.

185

But I'm going to need something to flash in front of headteachers who might be afraid they're breaking the Data Protection Act by passing on information.'

Handford made a note. 'I'll have a word with DCI Russell,' he promised. 'Anything else, Warrender?'

'Not really, except that Collins is well-liked at the pub. No one would hear a word against him, which is more than can be said for Shayla. They had no time for her at all. According to the landlord she was often in the bar flaunting herself, pretending she was eighteen; he said he'd had to throw her out several times, although I guess that was more out of loyalty to Collins than her age because in other circumstances I doubt it would have stopped him from serving her. To my knowledge he supplied three underage lads with a pint and a whisky chaser each while I was there, and probably more after I'd gone. Which reminds me...' He opened his drawer and pulled out a small packet, which he threw at Ali. 'The crisps I promised you, Sarge. I hope you like salt and vinegar.'

Ali caught them and although he laughed with the rest of the team the sentiment didn't quite make it to his eyes.

Handford watched his sergeant and wondered what was going on in his head. Did he consider Warrender's action a slight against him and his race, or an attempt to undermine him? Probably both, but if he commented, he would be the loser, considered someone unable to take a joke. To his relief, Ali said nothing and he waited for

186

everyone to settle down again. 'Anything on the Druids?' he asked.

A detective at the back of the room held up his hand. 'We do have a small group in the district, sir, but they have alibis for Thursday. Their leader, Paul Ritchie, was horrified a body had been found up at the altar. I didn't tell him anything, Boss, just talked generally about the cult to see if there was something that would tie them in with the murder, but there was nothing. It even appears there's a big question mark over Druid's Altar itself. According to a local historian I spoke to, apart from the discovery of a few flints and axe heads, there's no real archaeological evidence that anything Celtic or occult ever happened there. Not that any of this stops the modern day Druids from believing in the site. There are ten of them in the group. Normally they would have celebrated Hallowe'en up at Druid's Altar, but this year they didn't. All except one of their number joined another group on Ilkley Moor, where there's a Druidical dial circle called the Twelve Apostle Circle. It's a bit like Stonehenge apparently. I talked to the absentee as well...' He flicked over the pages of his notebook. 'Jacob Priestley – but he has a solid alibi. He was rushed into hospital on Thursday morning with appendicitis, so he was either in the operating theatre at the relevant time or recovering. To be honest, sir, I think we can rule the Druids out of this.'

As stupid as it made him feel, Handford was relieved, yet the image of Shayla spread out on the stone still made the hairs on the back of his neck stand up. He tried to ignore it. 'Yes, I agree,'

187

he said, 'although it begs the question as to who would know they would not be up there and that it would be a safe place for them to leave the body as well as have the time to arrange it as they did.'

'Unless it never occurred to them in the first place that there might be Druids there. Perhaps they considered it as no more than a local beauty spot.'

'I'd go along with that had it not been for the way the body was left. Someone knew the purpose of that stone. Even so, there's got to be a rational explanation and we need to find it. In the meantime we stop concerning ourselves with weird factions and black magic and investigate this as a straightforward murder–'

'Except for Shahid Mustafa, guv,' Warrender broke in.

'Except for Shahid Mustafa,' Handford repeated with a sigh and looked towards Ali. 'What do we know about him, Khalid?'

'Not a lot, except that he's a self-styled counsellor cum psychic cum solver of any problem you can name. He also purports to have black magic capabilities. He was brought in by Shayla's uncle to cast out the evil spirits in her. Calvin claims it was beginning to work when Shayla disappeared. As yet, we only have a mobile number for him and that seems to be permanently turned off. Since Calvin insists he has no idea where Mustafa lives, we haven't been able to make contact. I suspect Calvin warned him of our interest and he's lying low. Anyway, we've got the phone company onto it and I should hear something soon. Interestingly, I can't find him on the electoral roll, so I imagine Shahid Mustafa is his professional name.'

'Then find him, whoever he is. Anything from the school, Ken?'

The DS in charge of the relevant team looked up. 'We've interviewed all teachers who came into contact with her,' he said. 'But she truanted so much, particularly after the allegation, that most of them hardly knew her. It wasn't easy up there. I can't say they were actually obstructive because they answered our questions, but they were furious that Collins was being targeted again. Apparently they were about to take on the governors to stop them holding an internal inquiry and were prepared to strike if he wasn't reinstated. They may still, even though the inquiry has had to be put on the back burner for the moment. What I can't get my head round though, guv, is that the man organizing the protest isn't a teacher, but a teaching assistant – Jaswant Siddique. Perhaps he has more time than the teachers or perhaps he feels more strongly. Either way, he has the ability to persuade. He's part time, so we weren't able to speak to him. He'll be in on Monday, so we'll pop in then and if necessary we'll check him out.'

Handford closed his notebook. 'Do that, Ken,' he said hoping fervently that it wouldn't backfire on Gill. He really did need to talk to her. 'The rest of us can concentrate on the victim and her friends, the family and their friends and Graham Collins. We also need to make it a priority to find out where Shayla was when she disappeared. She must have been somewhere, with someone, and so far we have absolutely no idea. Clarke put out a request for media help on this. Visit everyone she knew; put a bit of pressure on. Also keep an eye on Mr and Mrs Collins – we can't be sure there won't be more repercussions. Warrender, I gather from Sergeant Ali that you have built up something of a rapport with Mrs Richards. Visit her and make it clear that if there is a repetition of last night's events we will arrest her. She is to leave the Collinses alone.'

Graham Collins waited until his wife had left for work before reading the text message: *meet u monday 8 same place don't b l8.*

There was no signature, but he didn't need one. He knew exactly who it was from. She wouldn't leave him alone, particularly now; she'd be worrying herself sick wondering if he'd killed Shayla. Perhaps just for once he wouldn't go, wouldn't dance to her tune. Let her worry. It would do her good to sweat.

He sat down at the kitchen table and put his face in his hands. If only he had had the courage to go along with what he was thinking. But it wouldn't be a good idea; he'd have to meet her – there was no saying what she'd do if he didn't. She held all the cards, cards that could destroy him more surely than any police investigation. *They* needed proof; she, on the other hand, had all the proof necessary.

chapter ten

Kerry Johnson picked at the burger in the Styrofoam carton in front of her. The others ate theirs as though there was no tomorrow. She felt sorry for them. As she watched them scoffing the quarterpounders and chips she wondered if they'd eaten at all today or just been given some money and pushed out of the door. She'd seen it happen to Kylie and she wouldn't be surprised if it didn't happen to Gemma and Lindsay, too. Sean might not know a lot about parenting, but at least he fed her.

She hadn't wanted to come into town today – it didn't seem right now Shayla was dead – but it would have looked odd if she hadn't turned up and also she needed to get away from Sean's whingeing. She liked him; it might even be true to say she loved him, but sometimes she questioned who was doing the looking after: him or her. She had hoped last night's sex would have calmed him down a bit, but by this morning he was still whining that it was only a matter of time before the police came to question him, so eventually she'd decided she couldn't stand any more, had told him to go to the pub to watch the match and she'd come into town.

The four of them always met up in the shopping centre, but the place was crawling with coppers showing photographs of Shayla and

191

asking if anyone had seen her over the past few weeks and if so where. Some people must have thought they had, because the police looked interested and jotted comments on the forms on their clipboards. When Gemma had said she was going to talk to them, tell them that she had known Shayla, Kerry grabbed hold of her, ordered her to forget it and pulled her towards the entrance. The other two followed. It didn't do to argue with Kerry.

It was almost dinnertime when they reached McDonald's and the place was filling up, but they managed to find a free table where they could sit together and decide how they were going to spend the afternoon. Shoplifting and pinching bags were out – it would have been asking for trouble with so many police around, and anyway Kerry wasn't in the mood. Lindsay wanted to go to the pictures, but Kylie said bowling was more fun. Gemma was still moaning about not being able to talk to the police because she'd had her eye on the particularly good-looking one. She'd happily have spent time with him, she said, giving him anything he wanted, and she shivered in anticipation of what might have been. All except Kerry laughed; she didn't feel like laughing.

'Why are you being like this?' she said. 'Don't you care what's happened to Shayla?' When no one answered her she said, 'She's not just disappeared this time, you know; she's dead.' Her tone matched the hostility flashing in her eyes.

Unconcerned, Gemma picked up a chip, dipped it in the tomato ketchup and sucked at it slowly. 'I'm not going to pretend that I'm going to miss her or that I liked her,' she said eventually. 'None of us did. She was only with us because you felt sorry for her. She never did get the hang of shoplifting and she was no good at pinching bags; we'll be better off without her.' And as if to demonstrate her indifference she indicated Kerry's food and said, 'Do you want that burger?'

Kerry pushed it towards her. 'Am I the only one who cares about Shayla?'

The others didn't reply, but it was obvious they agreed with Gemma. Eventually Lindsay said, 'We care that she's dead, but we won't miss her from the gang. Gemma's right – none of us liked her; she was only let in because of you. If you'd asked us we'd have said no. You're too soft, that's your trouble,' and she smiled at Kerry. She was probably right. Kerry had looked after them ever since they got together, and she'd felt the need to look after Shayla; sometimes she thought she was more like their mother than their friend.

They ate in silence for a few minutes, until Lindsay said, 'I wonder who killed her.'

Kylie sniggered. 'Probably someone she'd been having it off with, or turned down. You know what she was like: get them worked up and then walk away.' Her gaze flickered towards Kerry. 'Or perhaps it was Sean. He tried it on with her once and didn't get anywhere. Try it again did he and she didn't want him, so he killed her? It wouldn't be the first time.' She took a bite of her burger. 'I bet the police think that; he could be down at the nick when you get home.'

Kerry's eyes narrowed down into slits. 'You keep your mouth shut, Kylie Moore,' she warned. 'Or I'll shove that burger right down your fucking throat. Sean was with me on Thursday night – all night,' she added, daring them to argue.

Kylie flinched. 'All right, no need to go ballistic,' she said. 'It was only a joke. Can't you take a joke?'

Kerry regarded Kylie with distaste. If anyone else had made comments like that, she'd have had her out of the gang as soon as look at her, but Kylie was the best shoplifter of the four of them and the best at snatching bags and disappearing before the victim had time to realize what was happening, although to look at her you would never have thought she'd have either the skill or the speed. Anyone less like a Kylie she couldn't begin to imagine. Her mother was fourteen when she was born – a time when Kylie Minogue was a big star in *Neighbours* – and as the nurse handed over her eight-pound dark-haired daughter wrapped in a towel, she thought that the name really suited her. If it had then, it didn't now, for she had grown into a large pasty-faced girl who drank too much, smoked too much and wore too much make-up. Her brassy blonde hair high-lighted the dark brown roots and she plucked her eyebrows into pencil-thin archways because she thought they looked sexy. Kerry had always thought a Yorkshire pudding would be sexier than Kylie, but she'd never said anything.

Lindsay, on the other hand, would have made a brilliant Kylie. She was petite with fine features and skirts so short that they showed more of her backside than was decent, even in Kerry's eyes – although secretly she wished she had a bum she could show off like that. But when, as much out of jealousy as anything else, she had made disapproving noises, Lindsay had said that she might run the gang, but she didn't own her and what she wore was her own business, and anyway short skirts were easier to run in when they needed to get away from the security guards and coppers. Kerry couldn't and didn't quarrel with that. Of all of them, Lindsay was the one she liked best. She wasn't the brightest, but she was the one she was most able to confide in, knowing that anything she said wouldn't go any further. Not that she'd tell her everything. There were some things you kept to yourself.

Kylie pulled out a packet of cigarettes. 'Anyway,' she said as she lit up, 'it was probably Collins that killed her. After what he did to her, I wouldn't put it past him.'

Gemma frowned. 'She said he didn't.'

'Yeah, that's what she said, but I don't believe her. Why would she wait so long before changing her mind if he didn't do it? I bet he frightened her into it. And I bet she said she was going to tell everyone what he'd done and he killed her to stop her.'

Lindsay sucked at her Coca Cola, dragging the last drop up through the straw. 'I like him,' she said when she had finished. 'He's really fit and that smile... Someone with that smile couldn't do anything like that.'

'How would you know?' Gemma sneered. 'He's a man, isn't he? And anyway, you're never at school. How many times have you seen him?'

'Once or twice. I quite liked history.'

'Yeah, and the rest,' Gemma scoffed.

Kerry had to stop this. It didn't matter whether Collins had killed Shayla or not; she needed him kept out of prison and to do that she had to get them all on his side. It didn't matter that they didn't know why – the reason was nothing to do with them. 'He didn't assault her. She told me he didn't,' she said finally, and when Kylie opened her mouth to protest, she added, 'and I don't believe he killed her either, so we're not going to say he did.' She glared at Gemma. 'You'll keep that mouth of yours shut if you know what's good for you. You don't talk to the cops unless they come to you and even then you tell them nothing about Shayla and him. And that goes for the rest of you.' For the moment that would be enough, but they had to remain focused. 'I tell you what,' she said. 'It was on the telly that the teachers think that that English teacher's husband shouldn't be on the case and one of the cleaners was in the chippy last night and she said they were going to march to stop him hassling Collins and to force the governors to let him back into school. Why don't we join them, set up our own demonstration?'

'Why should we?'

'It'll be something to do.'

'You want us to be on the side of the teachers? We 'ate 'em. And it'll not stop the police; they'll still have to find out who killed her.'

'But they won't be using a copper whose wife works in the school. There's no saying what he'll make her tell him about us and Shayla – and I don't want the hassle.'

Kylie looked puzzled. 'Why? You've never been bothered about the cops hassling you before. And why should Handford tell him anything about us, anyway?'

Kerry sighed. Sometimes Kylie was even thicker than Lindsay. 'For fuck's sake use your brain, will you? This is a murder, not a bit of shoplifting. This'll be a different kind of hassle and we don't want it. You especially; they'll only have to put you in one of them rooms and you'll tell them anything they want to know and more besides, just to make you look good. And Handford'll let on about us because she's married to him and because Shayla was in our gang.'

Kylie tried to get back some credibility. 'Other people know; they can tell as well.'

Gemma raised her eyes to the heavens. 'Yes, but only if they're asked. She'll tell him because she's married to him.'

'From what the cleaner was saying,' Kerry added, 'the teachers aren't being cooperative with the cops, but she will be. She'll be his snout.'

She watched their faces. Gemma was with her and whichever way Gemma jumped, Lindsay would follow. Kylie still seemed hesitant; she needed something more. 'We've got to give shoplifting and pinching bags a miss anyway while the fuzz are crawling about everywhere and this'll give us something to do.'

Kylie succumbed. 'I will if we can carry placards and things.'

Stupid tart. 'So you're all in?'

197

They nodded.

'The only thing is,' Kerry said cautiously, 'it'll mean being in school.'

'You're joking!'

'We've got to be; we don't have to bother with lessons, but we can't get others on our side if we're not there.'

Kylie pouted. 'I'm not wearing uniform.'

Kerry glared at her. 'Whatever,' she said. 'Are we on then?'

Lindsay said, 'I am. My mother's had a letter saying they're taking her to court if she doesn't make me go to school. She might go to prison. So, I'm on.'

Kerry looked at Kylie. 'Go on then,' she said reluctantly, 'but someone'll have to bang on the door otherwise I'll never get up in time.'

'How is she?' Warrender asked FLO Connie Burns as she opened the door to him.

'Coping. She has the boys; she needs to stay strong for them.'

'Where are they?'

She closed the door. 'With Calvin; he's taken them ice-skating. Dion has gone quite happily – it's an adventure for him – but Aaron took some persuading; he wanted to stay with his mother. He's taken Shayla's death very hard.'

'Have you managed to get anything from her?'

'Nothing of any use. She insists she has no idea where Shayla was over the past few weeks; although, to be honest she's so grief stricken, and so sure Graham Collins killed her, that she probably thinks he was holding Shayla.'

'Then put her right. We don't want a repeat of last night.'

'I don't think you need to worry on that score – not for a while at any rate.'

Warrender studied the policewoman, tried to tune in to what she was thinking. 'I hope you're joking,' he said.

'I hope so too,' she answered with the same seriousness.

He changed the subject. 'What about Calvin? Would he know where Shayla was?'

'Difficult to say. Sometimes I think he ... I don't know ... I think he might have a suspicion.'

'Has he said something?'

'No, it's more what he hasn't said, or rather what he's stopped himself from saying. It's just an instinct. I've nothing concrete, but I'll keep working on it.'

'You know the pathologist said it would have taken two people to suffocate Shayla. Could the two have been Calvin and her mother?'

'I'd be surprised, but I can't rule it out. They believed in the devils inside her, and they were frantic to rid her of them. Perhaps in the end they thought peace would only come with her death and that killing her was the way to free her. I tell you this though, Chris: if they did it's tearing them apart.'

'Yes, I imagine it is. Look, I need to have a word with Mrs Richards. The boss wants to make sure she understands there is to be no repeat of what happened last night.'

'She's in the sitting room, but go easy on her.'

'Don't worry, I'm not going to read the riot act.

199

I'll have a chat, see what I can find out, and slip it in so she'll hardly notice.'

Evelyn Richards was sitting in a chair clutching the photograph of her dead daughter, her eyes fixed on a point somewhere across the room. Warrender doubted she was actually seeing anything, except perhaps for a hazy image of Shayla transmitted from her mind like a film from a projector.

'Hello, Mrs Richards,' he said softly.

She looked up at him, her face streaked with tears. 'You come to tell me off,' she said. 'Like that inspector last night.'

He took the chair opposite her. 'No,' he said. 'Nothing like that. Although it would be better if you left Mr Collins to us.'

For a second her eyes brightened and she sat forward. 'You believe me; you think he killed my Shayla?'

'I don't know, Mrs Richards, but if he did we'll get him. For now though, promise me, no more demonstrations.' When she didn't answer, he arched his eyebrows in warning.

'If I do promise,' she said, 'you'd better arrest him quick.' Then she collapsed back into the chair, the effort of speech seeming to have sapped her energy. The photograph slid from her grasp and Warrender bent to pick it up.

'She was a very pretty girl,' he said as he looked at it.

'She was a good girl too, not like what people have said about her. She slipped, that's all. We all slip sometimes, don't we? She got in with bad company. They turned her from me, but I always loved her, always took her back.'

'That's what mothers do, Mrs Richards.' He handed her the photograph.

'You've got children?' she asked.

'No.'

'Married?'

'No.'

'A girlfriend?'

'Too busy.' Warrender didn't want to talk about himself, didn't want to tell her that he couldn't – wouldn't – commit to a relationship any more, that he was strictly a one-night-stand man, so instead he said, 'What kind of things did Shayla like doing?'

'Sports. She was good at games, especially swimming. You seen her photograph?'

He nodded.

'She liked reading too; she was always down at the library and sometimes she would go and help out at the shelter. That was good. "We'll look after her," they used to say to me. "Don't you worry about her, Mrs Richards, she's safe with us."'

'Which shelter?'

'At the church. They open up in the daytime and feed those less fortunate. Sometimes they let them sleep there if the weather's bad. Shayla used to like to help.'

'She would stay over, sleep there?'

'Sometimes.' Her eyes flashed in anger. 'Why not? She was doing good work, helping those less fortunate.'

This was a new side to Shayla. 'I'm sure she was. You must have been very proud of her.'

She picked up the photograph again and smiled sadly. 'I was always proud of her. Always. You ask the minister what Shayla did for people. He will tell you. She wasn't bad, she was good; she slipped, that's all, she slipped.' Her eyes filled with tears. 'What am I going to do without her, Mr Warrender?' she asked him. It was a question he couldn't answer. It would have seemed trite to suggest that only time would help, because time didn't always heal, so he shook his head.

'She changed so much,' she said, the words catching in her throat. 'What happened to her?'

He would like to have told the truth, that she lost her father at a difficult time in her life and then her mother forced her to lose her identity. Instead he said, 'She grew up, Mrs Richards – I expect that's what happened to her.'

He wasn't sure how she would take what he was going to ask next and hoped he wouldn't alienate her. 'Did she lie about Mr Collins assaulting her, like she said?'

Evelyn Richards evaded the question, instead saying, 'She had a schoolgirl crush on him, I knew that. She cried a lot after it happened. She said she loved him, but that he shouldn't have done what he did.'

'What do you think she meant?'

'She was in the shower when I got home. She was crying and screaming. She said she was dirty, that Graham – she called him Graham – had made her dirty, and that she had to wash herself, clean herself. What else could she have meant? He deflowered my little girl; he made her unclean.'

'Was the allegation her idea or yours?'

'He had to be punished. I couldn't let her go through life thinking that what he had done was right.'

'So it was yours?'

Again she didn't answer him directly. 'Calvin went mad. He wanted to kill him. He should have done. It should have been that teacher who died, not Shayla.' She rocked in the chair. She was in pain, he knew, but none of this was going to go away. He watched as she moaned and listened as her memories became scrambled as they tumbled from her. 'The policewoman who came said she shouldn't have washed, but she had to. She had to become clean. But it was no good, it was too late. The devils were in her; he had put the devils there with his dirty ways.'

'So, why did she change her mind at the trial?'

Mrs Richards stared at him as if she had forgotten his existence.

'It was that Kerry Johnson – she made her change her mind. She forced her to say she'd lied. It's Kerry's fault she's dead. He killed my Shayla because Kerry told her to change her mind.'

'Why should Kerry Johnson force Shayla to change her mind about the allegation?'

'I don't know, boss.'

It was gone six and the rest of the team had finished for the day. Handford would have liked to go home too, but this needed discussion; it might even mean someone visiting Kerry this evening.

Ali handed each of them a mug of coffee then

perched on the edge of the table. 'You're sure this wasn't the ramblings of a grief-stricken woman? I mean she's been throwing accusations in all directions since it happened,' he said.

'No, I don't think it was,' Warrender argued. 'Evelyn Richards might be upset, and she might be wrong, but she's not stupid. She believes firmly that Graham Collins did assault Shayla and is adamant he killed her, probably because she was about to change her mind again. It wouldn't have made any difference to the court's verdict but it might have affected the governors' decision. Mrs Richards' rationale is that if Kerry Johnson hadn't persuaded her to change her mind about the allegation in the first place, Collins would have been in prison and Shayla would be alive today.'

'Do you think Kerry was instrumental in Shayla changing her mind?' Ali asked.

'I don't know, Sarge, but I think she could have been. What I don't understand is why.'

Handford said, 'What more do we know about Kerry, Khalid?'

He stretched over to pick up his notebook and flicked over the pages. 'Not a lot. She's fifteen and an only child. Her father killed her mother when she was twelve. It was an accident by all accounts and would have been a manslaughter charge had he called an ambulance instead of running away from the scene, leaving her to die. Afterwards Kerry was placed in care and was with a series of foster parents before she went to live with Sean. She refuses to have anything to do with her father, has never visited him in prison.

She's a chronic truant and into shoplifting and street robbery, but doesn't have a record because she's hardly ever been caught, and on the few occasions she has been picked up, we've never been able to make it stick.'

Warrender said, 'She's a cunning little piece and intelligent with it. Not a good combination. I suspect she's the boss in the Johnson household and she certainly keeps her gang on a tight rein; they do exactly as she tells them. I tell you, Guv, she's tough and if she doesn't want to, she'll not admit that she persuaded Shayla to change her mind about the allegation. We'll need to go in with a lot more than Mrs Richards' intuition.'

'So, where do we go from here?'

'We talk to Kerry anyway,' Warrender said. 'And we talk to Collins again.'

'What about Mr Mustafa?' Ali broke in. 'I've received his mobile account address from the phone company and they said they'll have a printout of his calls with us after the weekend.'

Handford made notes in his file. 'You see him tomorrow, Khalid, with Warrender...' He glanced over at the sergeant, whose face remained expressionless. Perhaps he and Warrender were beginning to come to some kind of understanding at last. After the weekend he'd have another word, check out Ali's reaction. 'Clarke and I will visit Kerry and Collins. And it might be a good idea for you to talk to the minister at the shelter where Shayla helped out. So far everything we've heard about her is negative. It'll be good to see her from another perspective.'

Warrender grinned. 'Can't do that tomorrow,

boss – it's his busy day.'

Handford stood up from his chair and handed his mug to the constable. 'You're absolutely right, Warrender,' he said. 'We'll leave it until Monday. Now go home the both of you and do whatever you usually do on a Saturday night.'

Warrender's grin became wider. 'I don't know about you, Sarge,' he said looking straight at Ali, 'but I doubt I'll be having a curry tonight. I told you that's Fridays, didn't I? Saturdays it's the dessert.'

Ali arrived home in a temper. He'd tried to put Warrender's comment about Saturday evening being the dessert out of his mind, but he couldn't because he knew the man had made it purely to offend him. And he had succeeded; he had found it offensive. It wasn't his fault Warrender's sister had been killed by a man who happened to be an Asian. He was as appalled as anyone by that kind of crime and with the leniency of the sentences handed down.

Ali's foot skidded on a pair of small wellingtons which had been abandoned on the front doorstep.

'For goodness' sake, Amina,' he grumbled as he walked in the door. 'Can't you make the children tidy their things away before I come home?'

Amina, who was at the cooker, turned. 'Sorry,' she said. 'Bushra and Hasan were playing in the puddles and Bushra fell in. She needed drying down, and I completely forgot about the wellingtons.'

'They shouldn't have been playing in puddles;

206

they should be doing something more worth-while.'

'It's the weekend, Khalid. They were outside enjoying themselves. What's so wrong with that? They're upstairs playing at the moment, but if you think they ought to be doing something more worthwhile perhaps you can read them their story while I finish preparing our meal.'

'You mean they're not in bed yet?'

Amina stopped what she was doing and faced him. 'No, they're not in bed yet; they were waiting for you. Bedtime is the only time they see you. Don't deprive them of it, Khalid, just because you're in a bad mood. *I* appreciate you're at the beginning of a murder investigation, but they don't. Go upstairs, read them their story and let them work their magic on you. By the time you've done that and had a shower, the meal will be ready.'

Magic was exactly the right word, for as soon as he walked into the children's room he felt better. They were delighted to see him, their faces lit up and they jumped up from playing with their toys to grab him.

'Come and see what I've built,' Bushra cried.

'She's only built a house, but mine is a castle,' Hasan said.

He bent down to inspect their creations. 'They're both wonderful,' he said. 'Your house is like that in the story I read to you last night, Bushra, and Hasan, your castle is quite magnificent.'

'Are you going to read us our story tonight?'

'I've come home specially to do that. Come on

207

both of you, into Bushra's bed where we can all cuddle up together.'

They scuttled into the bed and Ali sat next to them. He was only halfway through the story when their rhythmic breathing told him they were asleep. Carefully he lifted Hasan into his own bed, kissed them both softly on the forehead and tiptoed out of the room.

Amina was right; it wasn't fair of him to take his temper out on the children. His bad mood was not their fault. In fact it was probably no one's fault but his own. He shouldn't let Warrender get under his skin, but he didn't seem able to prevent it. It ought to be easier now that he knew why Warrender acted as he did. Perhaps it would be. Perhaps he *would* be able to take his remarks less personally. Except that they felt personal. He could shake off insults from suspects and prisoners without difficulty, but not those from a colleague – and particularly not from Warrender. From the first time they'd met there'd been bad feeling between them and he'd assumed the constable's dislike of him was a case of jealousy combined with blatant racism. Now he knew differently, but it didn't make it any easier to take.

By the time Ali had showered and dressed he was no further on in solving the problem, but he did feel better and he went downstairs ready to eat humble pie.

Amina was sitting at the table. He put his arms round her shoulders. 'Sorry,' he said.

She placed her hand on his and said, 'Is this murder getting to you? There's been a lot about it in the evening paper.'

He pulled away from her and sat down on the dining chair. 'Not really; no more than any other murder. No, it's Warrender.'

Amina served out the curry. 'Oh, Khalid, not again. What is it this time?'

Ali took his plate and placed it on the table. 'It's not what you think. Well, in some ways it is, but it's more complicated now.'

'For goodness' sake, Khalid, you're talking in riddles. Just tell me.'

As he talked, her face saddened and from time to time she interjected with, 'Poor man.' Finally she said, 'To lose your family like that, and then to find that their lives were not worth more than a six-month sentence. How does he cope?'

'He copes by taking it out on the rest of the Asian community. Why can't he let it go, move on and accept that we're not all the same?'

Amina poured him some water. 'Probably because he goes home to it every night.'

'That's what Clarke said.'

'Then believe it. Imagine what it would be like for you if every night you had to come home to me in a wheelchair, and worse, to know that you were probably the only one who cared. Certainly the man who ran them down didn't, or his family, or his friends. Warrender's mistake is to keep it all to himself. Are you sure no one else knows?'

'Just John and the DCI. I think that's what hurts. They knew and didn't think to tell me, even though I'm the butt of his comments. Even when...' He put down his fork and stared at his plate. 'I didn't tell you yesterday, but when I knew Warrender was to work with me, I asked John for a transfer.'

'Oh, Khalid! Why?'

'I thought if I threatened to go, John would refuse to accept it and transfer Warrender instead.' He looked up at her. 'I know, I know, it was childish and stupid and a little bit arrogant and I deserved John's reaction.' He smiled at her. 'He told me where the transfer forms were and then said if I wanted my promotion I had to learn to deal with people like Warrender. And at the moment he's forcing the issue by sending me out with him.'

'Good for him. You know, when it comes to understanding you, John is a very wise man. He knows exactly how to deal with you.'

She was right, of course; she usually was. John Handford wasn't the only wise one in his life. Amina stood up and began to clear away the plates. 'Go into the lounge and I'll bring the coffee,' she said.

Ali wandered through the glass doors that separated it from the dining area. The room had a cosy, lived-in feel to it. It never worried him that there were signs of children everywhere, because even though he jealously guarded the time he spent alone with his wife, the boxes of toys against the walls and the beginners-music on the piano meant they were building a family, and that was important to him. He warmed himself in front of the coal fire that glowed in the hearth and wondered what Warrender was doing at this moment. The same as Amina, probably, except while his wife was caring for children of six and eight, he was tending to and supporting a grown woman.

It was raining heavily as Handford pulled on the handbrake at the bottom of his drive. The security light swathed the area in brilliance and as he got out of the car, Brighouse, one of their two cats, scuttled from the bushes and demanded loudly to be let in.

'What are you doing out in this weather?' he asked him. 'You're wet through.' He slipped his key into the lock and pushed open the door. The cat ran into the lounge and by the time Handford had taken off his coat and hung it up, Brighouse had installed himself on the hearth and was licking his wet fur.

The room was warm in the glow of the fire and the shelter of the heavy velour curtains that shut out the blustery introduction to winter. Gill was comfortable on the settee, her knees pulled towards her, a clutch of A4 handwritten sheets resting against her thighs. She looked up from her marking and her brown eyes clouded over, the smile and the whisky with which she normally greeted him, absent. 'Have you eaten?' she asked briefly.

'No,' he said and when she didn't move he added, 'I'll get something out of the freezer.'

'No need. If you can wait until I've finished these A-level essays, I'll cook us something or we can send out for a pizza if you like. The girls have had theirs and are watching television in Nicola's room,' she added.

He scrutinized her as she concentrated on her work, occasionally pushing a stray wisp of hair behind her ear. Her features were as strained as her voice and he knew she felt let down by him. He wished it could be different, and he supposed it could if he gave up the investigation.

'Any good?' he said and nodded towards the papers.

'Not bad.'

'Let's have a pizza tonight. I'll order it then pop up and say hello to the girls, leave you in peace.'

His daughters, Nicola and Clare, were fifteen and thirteen respectively and growing up quickly. Nicola was the image of her mother, striking with her brown curly hair and large brown eyes. Though younger, Clare was taller than her sister and had his grey eyes. Her hair, which had been blonde as a baby, had darkened over time and was without any trace of a curl. She had grown it long and had developed the same habit as Gill of periodically tucking it behind her ears, almost without realizing it. They were involved in the television programme and except for a swift 'Hello, Dad,' their attention remained firmly fixed on the screen. He watched it with them for a while until he felt his eyes closing and his body relaxing into sleep, when he dragged himself from the chair and went back downstairs. The delivery boy was at the door and Gill was packing the completed scripts into her bag. 'I'll get some plates,' she said.

Handford paid for the pizza and garlic bread and took them into the lounge. They always ate pizza in there. It was pleasant, homely and relaxed. He placed the boxes on the coffee table. The aroma of the pepperoni and cheese made his mouth water and he realized how hungry he was.

As was always the way at the beginning of a serious investigation, there had been no time to sit and eat a decent meal and as usual he had staunched the hunger pangs with coffee and the odd biscuit.

'Do you want wine?' Gill shouted from the kitchen, 'or would you prefer a beer?'

'I'll have a beer.'

She came back carrying plates, an unopened bottle of red wine, a can of beer and two glasses. 'Fingers or knives and forks?'

He smiled at her. 'Fingers I think, don't you?'

She smiled back at him and the tension was broken. For most of the meal they made small talk, mainly about the girls, until he asked, 'Do you know Jaswant Siddique?' It was a question he shouldn't have posed and he regretted it the moment it was uttered.

At first she took it on face value and answered him. 'He's a part-time teaching assistant at school. Why?' Then, realizing its implication, she said, 'You're asking me as a policeman, aren't you? It's part of the case.' She shook her head. 'Don't do that to me, John. He's a colleague; don't ask me to discuss a colleague with you.'

'I'm sorry,' he said. 'I shouldn't have done.'

She was visibly angry and his apology was not enough to appease her. 'No, you shouldn't. If you're determined to carry on as investigating officer, I can't stop you, but don't use me as your informant.'

His snout, Redmayne had called her, and the words swirled in his head. Handford pushed his plate away and picked up his glass. The beer was

213

cold, but far from pleasing him it added to the chilled atmosphere that had surfaced again between them.

Gill stood to collect up the plates. 'You surely don't think he had anything to do with Shayla's death? You can't.'

He tried to recover some credibility. 'I don't think anything at the moment, Gill, it's just that he's the man organizing the protest at the school and when he was questioned, while he was not obstructive exactly, he was certainly unco-operative. I have to ask myself why.'

Her eyes blazed into his. 'Then ask yourself, John, but don't ask me.'

He could have been questioning a reluctant witness or a recalcitrant villain, but he wasn't, he was talking to Gill and what was happening was something he had always feared: the job causing a rift between him and her. It happened so often to police officers, but he had been lucky. Although she hated the way his work elbowed its way into their lives without so much as a please or a thank you, she understood how much he loved it and she lived with it. Now it was affecting her more directly and in spite of all the support she had given him over time, he couldn't return the favour. The image of Shayla Richards stretched out on the altar, her arms crossed on her chest, was still so clear in his mind, and he knew he had to be the one to find her killer. When it was over, he would ask for some leave, take Gill away and try to explain why he had felt as he did and why for the first time ever she was coming second in his life. He hoped she would understand and forgive him.

'I will have to speak to Siddique,' he said as he avoided her gaze, 'see him for myself. If I can't get him at home, it might mean coming into school. I'll try to avoid that but I'd rather not bring him in to the station, even if he agreed to come of his own volition; as things are, it would be too heavy-handed.' He stood, took the plates from her and replaced them on the table, then he clasped her hands in his and eased her back onto the settee. She made no attempt to pull away. 'I'm not a predator, Gill, stalking and tearing apart anyone I think might be involved,' he told her earnestly. 'But I *am* a detective and I *am* investigating the murder of a fifteen-year-old who was a pupil at Cliffe Top Comprehensive and I can't help feeling that the link in all this is the school. I don't know what that link is yet, but I do believe Graham Collins and you are the excuse, not the reason for an uncooperative staff and a part-time teaching assistant who has the ability to persuade sixty or more teachers to his point of view and who is, for his own reasons, determined to organize a protest against the governors, the police in general and me in particular. I owe it to you and Shayla to carry on. I'll shelter you as much as I can and I promise you I won't use you as my informant again, but I'm not stepping down.'

chapter eleven

It was a few minutes past ten on Sunday morning when John Handford knocked at Sean Johnson's door. The house seemed quiet, the curtains drawn across the window. He took a step backwards and craned his neck to check for movement. Nothing. He knocked again, louder. A light came on but the curtains remained drawn. Eventually Sean Johnson's bleary-eyed features appeared and he flung open the window and looked down.

'What do you want?'

Handford held up his warrant card. 'Detective Inspector Handford,' he said. 'This is Detective Constable Clarke. We'd like a word, if you don't mind.'

'I do mind,' Sean snarled. 'It's the middle of the bloody night.'

'For you maybe, Mr Johnson, but for the rest of us, it's ten o'clock in the morning, so are you going to open the door? We can shout at each other if you'd prefer, but I'm not going until I've spoken to you. Come on, Sean, you don't want me to drag you down the station, do you? The parole board wouldn't be too pleased.'

'Keep your fucking voice down, can't you?' He banged the window shut.

It took a few minutes before the door was opened by a man still groggy from sleep. He was attempting to tie the belt of a grimy green towelling dressing gown around him, but it kept slipping from his grasp. Giving up the challenge, he let the two ends drop and the gown hang loosely, revealing a pair of boxer shorts and vest of indeterminate colour, and opened the door wider to allow the two detectives inside. Kerry Johnson came into view at the top of the stairs.

Clarke looked towards her. 'Get him a coffee, love,' he said. 'I think he could do with one.'

She didn't reply, but sauntered down the steps and into the sitting room where she bent over to switch on the gas fire. Her short nightgown rode up her backside to show a pair of skimpy knickers. For a moment she warmed herself in the flames, then moved towards the door.

'You want a coffee, Sean?' she asked.

He grunted an answer which she obviously took to be in the affirmative because she walked from the sitting room into the kitchen, her eyes showing contempt as she passed the detectives.

Sean slumped into the chair and felt along the arm for his packet of cigarette papers and tobacco tin. He pulled out a paper, smoothed it, lined it with tobacco and skilfully rolled an emaciated cigarette, which he lit and drew on. The ends of the paper sparked into the air and fell still glowing onto the pile of the towelling robe where they were extinguished.

The shabby sitting room, furnished with a red two-seater settee, two mismatched armchairs, a rectangular coffee table and a television and video player, was cleaner than it deserved to be, a state no doubt due entirely to Kerry. Two of the five centre lightbulbs were dead, and the room was murky. Clarke drew back the curtains.

Sean blinked. 'Do you 'ave to?' he said. 'I'm still 'alf asleep.'

'Then we need to wake you up.' Clarke leaned against the wall and opened his notebook.

Sean took another drag on his cigarette and contemplated his knees. 'You've come about that girl,' he said. 'The dead one. Well, I didn't kill 'er.'

'No one said you did, but we've got to ask,' Clarke said phlegmatically.

'You always bloody do. Any kid and it's like she's linked to me with a piece of string. Well, not this time. I didn't kill her.'

'But you knew her?'

'So? I know a lot of people. Kerry lives with me; she's got friends and they come here sometimes, but it doesn't mean I kill 'em.'

'So where were you on Thursday, between midday and midnight?'

'Here – some of the time, anyway.' He sighed as if he was tired of having to explain himself. 'I went to see my probation officer about two o'clock. You can check that. Then I played a bit of snooker and came back for me tea. You can check that, too.'

'We will, Mr Johnson.'

Kerry came into the room carrying two coffee cups. She hadn't made any for the detectives. 'After that he was with me until he went to the pub,' she said as she handed one to Sean. 'He called in at the offy for some cans on his way back and we were here together for the rest of the night. Look,' she added, 'he couldn't have killed anyone on Thursday; he was on a bender, blocking out an anniversary. There are three of those in his life: the day he killed that kid, the day he was sent down and the day that would have been her birthday. Thursday was her birthday and he got drunk. He was out of it. You ask anyone who saw him.'

'It's good that he cares,' Clarke commented.

'Well, he does.'

Handford watched her as she spoke. She was approximately Nicola's age, but she had a toughness that his daughter neither possessed nor needed. Nicola had had her ups and downs, but she lived a comparatively normal life with two parents. With Kerry's mother dead, her father in prison and an uncle on life parole, he doubted she knew what a normal family was. Whether she cared or not was a different matter.

'So what were you doing when Sean was seeing his probation officer and playing snooker?' he asked, his voice as gentle as he could make it. 'At school?'

'School? Don't be stupid. I don't go to school unless they come looking for me and then only for a day.' She didn't mention Friday.

'So where were you?'

'Out and about.'

'Where?'

'Here, in town. A bit of both.'

'With anyone? Members of your gang?'

'No.'

Handford smiled at her. 'Not much of an alibi, is it?'

She grinned. 'Didn't know I'd need one,' she said. 'Do you want a coffee?'

219

'Yes, why not?'

'You'd better sit down then. Won't be long.'

Handford moved newspapers and magazines off the settee and made himself comfortable in the corner. Clarke pushed himself away from the wall and sat next to him.

While they had been talking to his niece, Sean had remained hunched in the chair, looking at no one, his roll-up held between the tips of the first two fingers and thumb of his tight hand. From time to time he had pulled on it; once it had gone out and he had had to relight it. His coffee remained untouched. Now he was on his own with the police he shrank further back in his seat and threw furtive glances at the two detectives. Eventually he said, 'I knew you'd come.'

'I expect you did,' Clarke answered.

'You always do.'

'So you said earlier. We visit everyone known to us who has had some involvement with crimes against children. It's procedure. But you've got an alibi, Mr Johnson, so you've nothing to fear.'

'That won't stop you thinking it's me.'

Handford had had enough. He could understand his paranoia, but it was tiresome. 'Actually it wasn't you we came to see. It was Kerry,' he said.

For the first time Sean made eye contact. 'Kerry? Why Kerry?'

'She was a friend of Shayla's – you said so yourself. She might be able to tell us something about her that only a friend would know.'

Sean returned to his cigarette. 'You won't want me, then?'

'She's only fifteen so I'd rather you stayed, but it's not essential.'

Kerry pushed open the door with her bottom, carrying two mugs. She handed one to Handford, the other to Clarke, then sat down.

'Tell me something about Shayla,' Handford asked without preamble.

'There's nowt to tell.'

'There must be something.' He smiled at her. 'I've heard that you don't take just anyone into your gang, so there must be something about her that made her one of you.'

Kerry shrugged. 'I felt sorry for her.'

'Why?'

'I dunno. She'd had a hard time. Her dad had left her.'

'And that was the reason?'

Kerry shrugged again as though she didn't care, yet Handford was convinced she did. Tears faltered on her lower eyelids, but didn't spill over and he didn't want to make this any harder for her than it obviously was.

'Did she have any other friends?'

'Not that I know of. People got tired of her whining all the time.'

'About what?'

'Her dad, her mum, everything.'

'Did she have any boyfriends?'

'She'd go with any boy who'd have her, but there was no one special.'

Handford appeared to take Kerry into his confidence. 'She'd had sex with someone before she was killed. Do you know who that could have been?'

She picked up her coffee mug and stared at it. 'Could have been anybody; she wasn't that fussy.'

'Why do you think she accused Mr Collins of assaulting her?'

'Probably because she wanted 'im to. She was always saying he was fit and she wouldn't mind a go with him.'

'Do you believe he did?'

'He might 'ave. He's a man isn't he? He wouldn't be one to waste an opportunity.'

Poor kid, so cynical at fifteen. Handford didn't know why it affected him because he'd seen it all before. 'But he's a teacher.'

'What's that got to do with anything?'

'Did you like him?'

'Hardly knew him. I don't do school. I told you that.'

As Handford watched her he remembered why he'd left teaching. Kids who made his life hell because they didn't care. How did Gill put up with it? Kerry was exactly the kind of pupil who had driven him to distraction, yet his wife seemed to thrive on the challenge. If he dared to bring up the subject at the moment, he wondered what she would think about someone like Kerry. Hard on the outside, soft at the core?

Kerry stared at him, her expression mocking. 'You're that copper whose wife teaches at the school – teaches English.'

'That's right.'

'Your snout, is she? Tells you all about us?'

'No, Kerry, she doesn't.' He felt his anger rising. It was bad enough journalists and the staff at Cliffe Top Comprehensive thinking they could be judge and jury on his relationship with his wife, but he wasn't about to take it from a pupil. 'Why did you tell Shayla to change her mind about the allegation she made concerning Mr Collins?' His voice was curt.

'I didn't.' Her gaze hardly faltered.

'Mrs Richards thinks you did.'

'She would, the stupid old cow.'

'*I* think you did.' He knew he shouldn't provoke a minor like that and he could feel Clarke's eyes boring into him.

Kerry was less concerned. 'Then you prove it, copper, if you can,' she scoffed. 'But since the only person besides me who would know is dead, I think you're on to a loser, don't you?'

At the same time as Handford and Clarke were knocking on Sean Johnson's front door, Khalid Ali and Chris Warrender were on the fringes of the city, pondering Shahid Mustafa's residence, an expensive dwelling hidden from the main road by a deep border of tall trees.

Warrender leaned his arms on the roof of the car. 'We're in the wrong job,' he said as he looked towards the large detached house. 'Casting out evil spirits and performing black magic must be profitable. I wonder how much he charges the poor sods who come to him.'

Ali made no reply; he couldn't be sure what, if anything Warrender was intimating by his observation. Last night, Amina had said he was being paranoid about the constable. She was right. He had to admit that Warrender had been doing no more than reflecting his own thoughts.

Embarrassed, he slid back in the car. 'Open the gate, will you?' he said.

Warrender pressed the intercom at the entrance and when the disembodied voice answered, he introduced himself. The lock on the gates clicked and he pushed them inwards. 'Let's hope he hasn't a couple of Rottweilers waiting for us,' he said as he climbed back into the passenger seat.

Mr Mustafa was standing at the door as they drew up. 'I've been expecting you,' he said, his English impeccable. 'Calvin informed me you had taken my card, and I don't suppose it took you long to find my address from the mobile number. You know I never did believe that one's house was one's castle.'

He was a tall, thin man dressed in a dark-grey suit and crisp white, collarless shirt. His black shoulder-length hair was expertly cut and his fingers were long and thin with finely manicured nails, as expressive in their movement as the deep brown eyes which penetrated those of the detectives. He led them into a large, brightly lit lounge, which it seemed to Ali had come straight from the pages of a glossy magazine. The generous four-piece suite was silver-grey and the carpet deep terracotta, as were the curtains. A fire burned in the white marble Louis XVI fireplace, either side of which bronze statuettes of elegant ballerinas stood on plinths in deep alcoves. On the mantelpiece were several photographs of young boys. At one end of the room was a state-of-the-art music centre and at the other a grand piano, which the musician in Ali itched to play. His was second hand and although it served its purpose while the children were learning, his dream was to own a baby grand. There was no television, at least not one Ali could see. Porcelain vases and figurines were safely stored in the glass-fronted alcoves either side of the bay window, and the walls were studded with original water-colours, oils and acrylics, adding a fusion of colour and warmth to the room. Not a family room certainly, much more that of an English gentleman. Perhaps that was what Shahid Mustafa was trying to become.

He indicated that the detectives should sit down. 'Would you like coffee?' he asked.

Ali was about to decline when Warrender said, 'Yes please, I would.'

Mustafa excused himself. 'I'll pop and ask Mrs Harris to bring us some,' he said and left the room.

'Didn't take him long to suggest we were in the wrong – abusing his human rights by checking his address through his phone account,' Warrender grumbled.

Ali ignored the remark and stood up. He wandered around, taking in the artwork. 'Looks like he's a collector,' he said. 'These are originals.'

'Know anything about paintings, Sarge?' Warrender asked.

'Not a lot. My wife dabbles a bit, both landscapes and portraits, but she'd love this.' He pointed to the tall rectangular picture in varying shades of blue, deep at the base climbing to fronds of a lighter colour, representing what? He wasn't certain – the force of the wind blowing long hair or tall grasses yielding against its strength. He supposed it could be whatever the onlooker wanted it to be.

Mr Mustafa came into the room. 'It is beautiful, isn't it?' he said 'So calming, yet such movement.'

Ali resumed his seat. 'You know something about modern art, Mr Mustafa? These are all originals.'

'I am a collector, Sergeant. I have a few prints, but I much prefer originals and I think I have an eye for what is good and what is second rate. Many of these artists were unknown when I bought their pictures; now they are not and their work has risen in value. Not that I would sell. Beauty is meant to be seen and savoured, not haggled over.' He settled himself in the armchair opposite Ali then, with a sweep of his hand, pulled down the cuffs of his shirt to show the gold links beneath his jacket.

'I hope you have good security, Mr Mustafa,' Warrender remarked, looking around. 'This room is a thief's paradise.'

'Of course, Constable, and considerable insurance too.'

'Do you live here alone, sir?' Ali asked.

'Yes, I do.'

'You're not married, then?'

'Yes, I am, but my wife does not like England and so spends much of the year while the boys are at boarding school with her family in Pakistan.'

Ali frowned. 'And you are happy with that?'

'Our marriage was arranged. I did not dispute my parents' choice, nor did Nadirah. She is from a good background, has given me the children I

226

wished for and is here when the boys are at home. I am happy with the arrangement, as is she. What more could I want?'

'So who looks after the house?'

'I have a live-in housekeeper, Mrs Harris. She was my daily for five or six years, but when her husband died it seemed sensible that she should sell her own home and take the flat that was built onto this house by the previous owners. She is quite self-contained, but here when I need her.' He smiled as the door opened and a woman in her late fifties or early sixties, dressed in a winter coat and hat, appeared with a tray of coffee. 'She is what the English would call a treasure, I think.'

Mrs Harris blushed. 'Don't take any notice of him,' she said. 'He's always saying that. If anyone is a treasure it's Mr Mustafa. Now, have you got everything? Because I want to get to church.'

'That's fine, Mrs Harris. I'll see you later.' He handed out the coffee. 'Help yourselves to cream and sugar.' He regained his chair. 'I assume you didn't come to talk about me, rather about Shayla?'

Ali spooned sugar into his cup. 'When was the last time you saw her?'

'The eighth of October.'

Warrender and Ali exchanged glances. 'You seem very sure, Mr Mustafa.'

'I'm sure because it was the day of our last session and the day before she disappeared. That's something you don't forget; after all she was a patient of mine. Calvin rang me on the ninth to say that her bed had not been slept in and they were worried about her. She had been very depressed when I saw her; she thought she was never going to be free of the devils eating away at her. There was little I could do to reassure her, so when I learned she had not been home I was naturally worried.'

'What did you do?'

'What I could. I helped in the search for her, went with Calvin to see her friends, visited the shelter, kept an eye out for her.'

'Why should you do that? You were her counsellor; I wouldn't have thought you would become so involved.'

'I'm involved with all my patients, Sergeant. It's my job to heal them and although I thought she was improving, it was obvious that I was in fact failing Shayla. The least I could do was to find her and continue to help her. Also I was a friend of her father. Before he returned to Pakistan he asked me to keep her safe.'

'Did her mother know this?'

'No. Nor did Calvin, and I would rather they didn't. Mrs Richards in particular hated Qumar. Had she had the slightest inkling that I was watching over her daughter for her husband she would not have let me help her when she became so ill.' He replaced his cup on the tray. 'When Qumar left, he wrote to his wife to warn her that he would get back his children one way or another. It was no more than a threat in the heat of the moment, but had Mrs Richards known of our friendship she would have assumed I was in a plot to kidnap Shayla and the boys and she would never have let me near her daughter.'

'And you're not. In a plot, I mean.'

He began to play with his fingertips. 'No, Sergeant, I am not.'

'Have you been in touch with her father since Shayla disappeared?'

'No. I tried, but he was working away from home, somewhere in the north of the country I think, and I wasn't able to get a contact number for him. I told his firm what had happened and they said they would pass on the information. I've heard nothing from him since. According to Calvin, Mrs Richards refuses to tell Qumar about Shayla's death in case he demands a burial in the Muslim tradition, but as her father, it's his right to know.'

He stood up and walked over to the fireplace, where he rearranged the photographs. Ali watched him. He was debonair, suave in movement, mellow in voice tone. His language was polished, he knew when to smile, when to frown, and his timing in answering questions would be the envy of any performer. Ali was in no doubt Mustafa was giving a performance, probably the same one he used on his clients. Yet there were signs of anxiety that he couldn't control: a slight but obvious tremor in his hands, tiny facial movements, the tension in his shoulders and an occasional reluctance to make eye contact, particularly when Qumar Hussain was mentioned. He was concerned, but about what Ali had no idea. The counselling sessions, perhaps, or, in spite of the denial, had he been helping Qumar regain his children? It was more than possible that a man like Mustafa would have the contacts for such an operation. Here was a man who needed investigating and once back at the station, Ali intended to put someone on to researching his background, his associates, his work as a counsellor and any peripheral activities he might be into. But that was for later. For now Ali looked towards him, smiled and said, 'Don't worry, sir, we're in touch with the police in Pakistan. They will inform Shayla's father. But if he does contact you, perhaps you can give me a ring.'

Mustafa relaxed and sat down. 'Of course,' he said.

Ali replaced his cup on the tray. 'Can you tell me why you didn't get in touch with us when the news of Shayla's death broke? You're obviously an intelligent man and you must have realized that the more we knew about Shayla, the more chance we would have of apprehending her killer.'

'There's nothing sinister about my reasons, Sergeant. Confidentiality is important in my work and a lot of what she told me about her life and her family was confidential. Until I had permission from her parents to reveal it, my hands were tied. I have done that, and they have given me their permission, but unfortunately,' he smiled, 'you found me before I could come to you.' He glanced at his watch. 'Now, gentlemen, if there's nothing else, I do have to be somewhere.'

Warrender, who had been quietly taking notes while Ali asked the questions, sat forward in his chair. 'If I may, sir,' he said. He looked at Mustafa for a long moment, then said, 'How much do you charge for your sessions?'

A chill enveloped the room like a cloud, and

anger flooded the face of their host. His eyes were cold and threatening and his voice when he spoke was steely. 'I do not think that is any of your business, Constable, do you?'

Warrender agreed. 'Probably not,' he said, 'at least not for the moment. Perhaps you can tell me instead, then, whether your patients come here to be counselled.'

Mustafa gained control before answering and when he did, the smooth quality of his voice had been re-established. 'No. I go to them. It's better for them to be in familiar surroundings; they are usually more comfortable that way. If that's not possible, I have rooms in the city and I meet them there.'

'And they are where?'

Mustafa pulled out a card and pen from the inside pocket of his jacket. 'I'll write the address on the back.' He handed it to Warrender, who said, 'Where did you counsel Shayla?'

'The first sessions were held at her home, but it soon became obvious I couldn't work there, so we moved into my rooms.'

'Why couldn't you work there?'

'Because her mother wouldn't leave us alone. Both I and my patients need privacy and she wouldn't give us that.'

'Shayla came to the rooms on her own?'

Mustafa's cheeks tinged with anger again. 'Of course not. What do you think I am? She was a minor. Calvin brought her and stayed in the waiting room.'

'Do you have a receptionist to make appointments?'

231

'No, I always organize them myself. I find it better that way.' When Warrender looked puzzled, Mustafa sighed and said, 'The fewer people involved, the less intimidated the patients feel.'

Warrender sat back more comfortably in his chair. 'I'm interested, Mr Mustafa. How did you conduct the sessions with Shayla? What did you do exactly?' His tone had become confidential.

'We talked about her and her life, what were her fears, her aspirations, and eventually when she began to trust me, what it was that had allowed the devils to take hold.'

'Did she tell you?'

'Not really, although there was no doubt her unhappiness stemmed from the break-up of her parents' marriage and the fact that she wanted to remain a Muslim. She didn't want to be a Christian. She didn't believe in the religion and she concluded that the devils had come because she was forced by her mother into the church and she was, therefore, by definition, bad.'

'So she rebelled? Attempted suicide? Made false accusations against one of her teachers?'

'I'm not sure they were false, Constable. She insisted to me that he had assaulted her and it was her friend who had persuaded her to change her story.'

'Why should the friend do that, do you think, and why should Shayla agree? After all, at best it made her into a liar, and at worst she could have been charged with wasting police time and that of the courts.'

'I don't know and I don't think she knew.' Mustafa became impatient. 'We hadn't got that far.'

'Just for the record, Mr Mustafa,' Warrender said. 'Can you describe your movements on Thursday?'

'I was working – all day.' Mustafa's tone became heated. 'And no, I will not tell you who my clients were. If you want that information, you'll have to get a warrant.' He stood up. 'Now, if that's all, officers...'

As they moved towards the door, Warrender stopped. 'Just one more thing, sir. Your card says you have black magic capabilities and Calvin told us that Shayla screamed and shouted during some of her sessions. Were you using black magic then, sir? Were you frightening the poor kid to death? Was that why she ran away, do you think? To get away from you and your approach to counselling?'

'Don't you think you were being a bit aggressive with Mustafa?' Ali said as he slammed the car door and turned to Warrender. 'Asking about his financial affairs, then suggesting Shayla had run away from him because he was using black magic on her. We came here to find out more about the victim, not to treat him as a suspect.'

'Oh, come on Ali, you know as well as I do we treat everyone as a suspect at this stage of an investigation.'

Ali turned the key in the ignition and put the car into gear. 'We keep an open mind, Warrender, until we have some evidence to lead us to suppose someone might be involved. Then, and only then, do we treat them as a possible suspect.'

'That came straight out of a textbook, did it?'

The gates at the end of the drive were open and they drove out into the road. Ali could feel his anger flaring; he didn't have to take that. He was tired of the comments and the insinuations.

'No, it didn't come straight out of a textbook, and just remember who you're talking to,' he snapped. He slowed and indicated he was pulling into the side of the road. When he had stopped, he unclipped his seatbelt and shifted round to face Warrender. 'I don't care what you do when you're on your own – it's your throat you're cutting – but when you're with me, we go by the book.'

'None of us go by the book all the time, not even you, Ali. We all know that.'

Yes, he'd cut his own path more than once and been reprimanded for it, but this was not about him. One way or another, Warrender had to show him – or at least his rank – some respect. 'I mean it, Warrender. By the book. I hope I'm making myself clear.'

Warrender grinned. 'As crystal, Sergeant.'

Ali started up the car. He wasn't sure he'd won the argument, but felt better at having made his point. For a while they continued in silence. Eventually, Warrender said, 'Mustafa is guilty of something, Sarge, I'm sure of it.'

'But not necessarily of murder.'

Warrender gave in. 'All right, not necessarily of murder, but I tell you, he's not what he seems, and if you think he is you're not looking at him as a detective. Surely instinct counts for something. You saw him, his house, his pictures, the figurines. He's loaded. Counselling must be a bloody good business.' He paused, waiting for a reaction. When none came, he said, 'Look at the way he works. He uses only a mobile number as a contact; he doesn't have a receptionist in his office in the city. What kind of a professional is that?'

For a while Ali pondered Warrender's words, then said, 'Actually, I agree with you. Mustafa does need some research.'

Warrender became thoughtful. 'I wonder how much he does charge for his services.'

'However much it is, Calvin seemed to think he was worth it.'

'Calvin was so worried about Shayla he would have paid any amount to anyone, providing they were showing some progress. That was one of the reasons why the Richardses took her away from the psychiatrist – because she wasn't working a miracle. The vicar obviously couldn't, so in comes Shahid Mustafa, who, unknown to them, is a friend of Evelyn's former husband. They take him on, and after a few sessions he persuades them he is making progress; the devils are tumbling out of her with screams and shouts. Suspicious or what?'

Ali smiled. 'All right, Warrender. Put like that it does seem suspicious.'

With the air of a victor, Warrender settled back in his seat. 'I wonder how Calvin heard about Mustafa in the first place?'

'From one of the Asian papers, perhaps. There are lots of adverts from people who claim they can solve these kinds of problems.'

'No, that's too hit and miss. Shayla was

235

precious to them and he would want to know who he was getting. I think this was something Mustafa planned. It's too much of a coincidence that he is friendly with Qumar. I think he contacted them with some kind of story, saying he had heard of their problem with Shayla and schemed his way into the family. He would meet them face to face, give them the same perform-ance he gave us, and they'd be hooked. When in fact, what he was actually doing was what he said Mrs Richards could have feared – hatching a plot to kidnap Shayla and the boys. In fact I would go so far as to suggest he's a high-class bounty hunter. It would certainly account for his wealth.'

Ali shook his head. 'I understand what you're saying and I might even agree with you. I just don't think you've got the evidence to sub-stantiate it.'

Warrender yawned as though he was becoming bored with the conversation. 'Then get it, Ali. Your community has a nice wide circle. Ask around until someone comes up with something. I go to the pub to get my information; you must have somewhere you can go to do the same thing.' As Ali opened his mouth to argue, Warrender said, 'We've got to start somewhere.' He slid down in his seat and closed his eyes. 'And while you're about it, keep this question in mind. Mustafa lives alone in that big house with an elderly house-keeper. He sees his wife only during the school holidays. What does he do for sport?'

'Sport?'

'Sex, man. You can't tell me he's celibate for four-fifths of the year, because I don't believe it;

he didn't look as though he was chewing his fingernails. So either he's gay and wanders one of the parks for young lads, or he has some woman on the side, or he uses prostitutes, *or* he uses the girls he counsels.'

Ali stared at the detective, who opened one eye. 'That's typical of you – you've a one-track mind. You think everyone is like you. Where is your evidence for any of that, for God's sake?'

Warrender pulled himself upright, a smile playing on his lips. 'I haven't any, Sergeant; that's for you to find.'

Ali turned the car into the parking area in front of the police station and as he slid to a stop, Warrender said, 'Calvin told us that Shayla shouted and screamed when she was alone with Mustafa. Why do you think she was doing that? I'm damned sure it wasn't the devils fighting their way out of her soul. More likely she was fighting someone off.' When Ali made no response, Warrender went on, 'She'd had sex before she died. Perhaps it was with him. Perhaps he killed her when she wouldn't play along.'

Ali shook his head. 'Not on his own. The pathologist said it took two people to smother her. Who was the other one?'

'I don't know. Calvin, perhaps. He was loath to tell us about Mustafa.'

'You said a while ago that Shayla was precious to them. Now you're saying that Calvin went along with Mustafa having sex with her. Do you really believe that?'

Warrender sighed. 'No, not really. Not unless Mustafa persuaded him that that was the only way to rid her of the devils.' He glanced at Ali and grinned. 'I know, it's far fetched, but everything about this case has been far fetched, from the devils inhabiting Shayla to the arrangement of the body. And before you ask, yes, I can see Mustafa arranging the body like that. He's arrogant enough. It would be his way of mocking the religion Shayla had been forced into. Putting two fingers up at her mother and showing his support for her father.'

chapter twelve

The cemetery was a stupid place to meet. Kerry thought so every time she sat there waiting for him, but it was close to home and school and Graham Collins didn't seem to mind. He'd been here for some time; Kerry had been sitting on one of the benches watching him. He was in his running gear, probably the only way he could get out of the house without arousing suspicion – saying he was going for a run.

He seemed nervous, couldn't settle: he wandered backwards and forwards across the path, sat down on one of the gravestones, then stood up and paced again. She hoped he wasn't psyching himself up to say 'no more, not another penny'. She didn't need that, partly because in another eighteen months she would have the money she wanted to get out of here, and partly because if he did she would have to carry out her threat and she didn't want to do that either; it might backfire on her and land her back in care.

Sometimes she wished she'd never got involved, but at the time it seemed too good an opportunity to miss. When she'd first collared him and told him what she knew, he'd denied it. Then she'd explained how she knew and he'd gone white and hadn't denied it any more. Instead he'd scoffed and told her she'd never be able to prove a thing and the papers wouldn't be able to print it anyway. She'd said it didn't matter; rumour would be enough. Already there were people who thought him a pervert and it wouldn't take more than a whisper to cause trouble for him. It didn't matter what the courts said – it was what the people around here would say if they knew, what his wife would say if *she* knew. His marriage would be over, and he would be finished in teaching. They'd never have him back once it got out. They wouldn't be able to risk it.

When she'd thought about it later, she realized she'd been either brave or stupid, because given his track record he could have done anything to her. She could have been dead now like Shayla. But he hadn't. Instead, he'd crumpled and pleaded with her not to tell anyone, said he'd give her anything she wanted if only she'd keep it to herself. So off the top of her head, she'd said she wanted a hundred quid a month. It wasn't a lot for a teacher; he could pay that with his eyes shut – and anyway his wife was working, so he'd got her wage as well. Call it justice, she'd said. She was doing no more than exacting justice.

Kerry strained to see what he was doing now. For a while he remained still, and then pushed himself away from the gravestone and looked at his watch. How long would he wait? It would be interesting to find out, but not a good idea. Better not give him any more time to brood. His back was towards her. She sneaked up behind him and tapped him on the shoulder.

'You got it?' she said.

He spun round. 'Don't do that,' he spat. 'Don't

creep up on me.'

She wagged a finger at him. 'That's the problem with people who have something to hide; they're always nervous.'

'I'm not nervous. I just don't like people creeping up on me.'

She took a step back. 'You look knackered,' she said, not without some sympathy. 'Let's sit down.'

'Someone will see us.'

'So what; they'll see us, walk past and forget us. If you stand there and pass out, they'll come up to us, ask what's wrong and never forget us.' She set off towards the bench she'd left. He followed her. 'And anyway,' she said as she sat down, 'who in their right mind comes into a graveyard at eight in the morning in November?'

He didn't answer but perched a couple of seat lengths away from her.

'Have you got it?' she repeated.

He nodded but made no attempt to move.

'Come on, then. I haven't got all day.'

Momentarily, he remained where he was, then stood up, unzipped the pocket of his jogging suit trousers and pulled out a brown envelope. For a split second he hesitated and his tongue flicked over his lips. She'd been right. He was going to tell her this was the last payment. She'd left him too long, given him time to psych himself up.

No way.

'The police think you assaulted Shayla,' she said abruptly, her eyes never leaving the envelope in his hand. 'Probably that you killed her as well. Did you?'

He glared at her. 'No, I didn't,' he said, his voice surprisingly quiet. Then, 'How do you know that's what the police think?'

'They came to see me yesterday wanting to know about Shayla. Thought me being a *friend...*' She emphasized the word to make sure he understood the implication. 'I'd be able to tell them about her. They asked me if I thought you'd poked her, and whether I'd told her to change her mind about what she'd said about you.'

He began fiddling with the envelope. 'What did you tell them?'

She grinned. 'Don't worry. I stood up for you. Can't have you losing your job, can we?' She allowed her smile to fade as she stood up and stepped out onto the path. She turned towards him, stretched out her arm and palm upwards, jiggled her fingers. 'Come on, hand it over. I've got to get to school.'

For a moment he hesitated, then, making sure there was no one to see, he handed it to her. Stimulated by his unease, she made only a cursory attempt to keep it out of sight. Leaning against the side of the gravestone, she opened it, flipped through the contents, closed the flap and thrust it into her bag. 'I'll trust you it's all there, because if it isn't...' She leaned over him, her face so close she could smell his breath. 'It will be easy to tell them what I know.' And before he could comment, she pushed herself upwards and said, 'You haven't asked why I'm going to school.'

Weariness edged back into his voice. 'Presumably to make some poor teacher's life a misery or to see who you can fleece next.'

She grinned. 'You *would* think that, wouldn't you? Well, you're wrong – at least about the last bit. I don't think there could be anyone else as easy as you to fleece, and you know me. I'm not one for hard work. But you're right about us making a teacher's life a misery.' She nodded towards the school. 'They're doing it for you, you know.'

He frowned. 'What do you mean, doing it for me? Who's doing what for me?'

Obviously no one had thought to tell him. 'The teachers don't like the way you're being hassled, so they're going to have a protest to get rid of the copper and force the governors to let you back into school. We – me and the gang – thought we'd lend a hand, set up our own demonstration, show how much we miss you. It'll mean giving that English teacher a hard time because she's married to the copper, but so what? She's a teacher, isn't she? Hard times go with the job. No point wasting any sympathy on her.' And with that she turned and walked to the gate, stretching her arm upwards to wave at him.

For a long time after Kerry Johnson had gone, Graham Collins remained on the bench in the cemetery. His brain was reeling. He didn't know whether to feel excited that his colleagues were supporting him, or concerned about what they would do to Gill Handford. He didn't want anyone to go through the kind of trauma he had endured, least of all her. Without reaching any conclusion, he shifted his position to the gravestone from which he could watch the kids and the teachers walk into school. Monday morning. At the best of times no one liked Monday morning – back to work after the weekend – and for Cliffe Top Comprehensive, this particular Monday morning would be anything but the best of times. They would be struggling to get back to normal. Love Shayla Richards or hate her, she was one of their own who had been murdered and that would take some coming to terms with.

As he watched, Kerry Johnson met up with her gang and walked through the front doors. They were not supposed to use that entrance; it was for visitors, senior pupils and staff. Not that rules had ever bothered either Kerry or the other three who always followed her lead.

Earlier, he had been made to wait for her. Eight o'clock, she'd said. It was at least quarter past before she showed. Not that time mattered any more. He hadn't been ruled by it for a long while now. Keeping him waiting had been a pathetic show of her power, and by remaining until she came he had acknowledged it. It was difficult to know how much she knew about what was happening. Did she know, for instance, about Shayla's clothes in his wheelie bin? Had the police mentioned that? Surely not. The truth was, it didn't matter what she knew and what she didn't know. She'd rendered him so uncertain, she could do or say whatever she wanted and he accepted it in case it was the truth. He could never take the risk with her. He had been going to tell her to stuff her blackmail, but when it came to it he had drawn back. One comment from her was all it took for him to lose his nerve: *the police think you*

244

assaulted Shayla, probably that you killed her as well.

He pulled his knees up to his chest and shivered. He wasn't cold, for although it was the first week in November the air was warm. Jane was on the late shift this morning and he'd left her grumbling that it was so mild she didn't know what to wear. He'd tried to persuade her not to go in, but she'd insisted she felt fine. For the sake of the baby she needed to rest, he'd said, but that wasn't what he'd meant. The bruise on her cheek was still all too obvious and whatever excuse she gave for its existence, her colleagues were experienced enough to know the difference between a husband's fist and a doorjamb. He doubted any one of them would understand or care what had happened to him in that split second when he had lost it or that he was so ashamed of himself that all he wanted to do was crawl away and hide.

The ground was damp and he was beginning to feel its chill seep through the seat of his jogging suit. He stood up and leaned against the headstone. As he stamped his feet, the moisture in the grass bubbled around his running shoes. He needed to get home, have a shower, change – shake off Kerry Johnson.

The staff car park was filling up. He watched as Gill Handford climbed out of her Golf. A few steps from the car she turned to press the electronic key and stood for a moment as the lights flashed. Then she left the parking area to walk to the front entrance. Before she could go in her way was barred by Jaswant Siddique. For a while, they held what seemed to be an animated conversation, then plainly annoyed, Gill propelled him aside, wrenched at the door and pushed her way through, letting it go with such force that it swung back in his face and he had to thrust out his hands in defence.

Collins frowned. He'd always thought Siddique prone to getting above himself, acting as though he was a teacher rather than a teaching assistant. But Gill's response surprised him. It wasn't like her to show aggression – she was assertive, not aggressive. Whatever he said, it must have angered her very much to provoke such a strong reaction. Could it be that he was giving the English teacher a hard time because she was married to the investigating detective, as Kerry Johnson had said? Was Jaswant Siddique involving himself in that?

As Gill disappeared, the door opened again and Kerry Johnson came out. She walked up to Jaswant Siddique and stood talking with him for a few minutes. They looked towards the cemetery. The chill around Collins' feet seeped upwards and he felt his body quiver. Surely she wasn't dropping him in it. Both of them waved up at him and the teaching assistant ran across the road. He stood at the edge of the pavement and looked up. Collins wasn't sure whether Siddique could see him, but he shouted nevertheless. 'Don't worry, Graham, we'll sort it. We'll have you back in school in no time.'

Following the Monday morning briefing, John Handford returned to his office to try to make sense of what they had gleaned so far. Amidst an assortment of gut instincts, hunches and question marks only four concrete facts emerged. First, Shayla had been suffocated, probably – definitely according to the pathologist – by more than one person; secondly, she was not a virgin and had had sex, forced or otherwise, on the day of her death; thirdly, there were no reported sightings of her during the three weeks she was missing; and lastly, her clothes had been found in Graham Collins' wheelie bin. Who had put them there was an issue he hadn't yet taken up with Collins in any great depth. Today he would have to, if only to assuage Ali's suspicion that he was dragging his feet to protect Gill. The sergeant was wrong; he was, as he had said, waiting on the report from forensics before he questioned the man, but that was in now and the results were inconclusive. He couldn't deny he was concerned about his wife, though. He hated that the inquiry was coming between them. Last night it had hung there, unspoken and unresolved, but tangible.

Handford stood up, stretched, and walked over to the window. Resting on the cusp of winter, the weather outside was as dreary as his thoughts. A blanket of grey hung low over the buildings and misty rain teased the air. A few people were killing time outside the theatre opposite and others trudged up the hill towards the college and the university. Students, probably. They chatted to each other as they climbed, and he wondered if they were talking about the cleaner whose daughter had been murdered. He doubted it but found it satisfying that even now, after all his years as a detective he could still think like that; that he was not, as Warrender had described

247

Ali, a policeman more concerned with people as witnesses than as human beings. He smiled to himself as he remembered the sergeant's expression of disbelief as he recalled the comment.

It was a more relaxed Handford who returned to his desk, picked up the phone and asked the officer who answered to bring him in a coffee. He turned his attention to the notes he had made at the briefing. Most of the trace, investigate and eliminate actions (or TIE in police jargon) had been completed. It hadn't been difficult to trace those who had known Shayla – teachers, friends, neighbours – and they had interviewed and eliminated the majority from any involvement in her death. No one knew where she had been during the weeks she was missing and the majority didn't care. What was obvious was that generally, and certainly since her father's departure for Pakistan, there had been little in the way of sympathy for or friendship towards the dead girl. Few had liked her, some had tolerated her, most had ignored her. Except for Kerry Johnson.

He settled back in his chair and clasped his hands behind his head. Kerry Johnson. Now there was a girl who warranted a question mark or two. She was very intelligent. Streetwise, self-centred and self-seeking, she seemed cautious on the one hand, loyal and compassionate on the other. Why else would she support her uncle and stick by Shayla, take her into the gang? Unless she had another agenda? Perhaps that was it. Perhaps she had persuaded Shayla – forced her, even – to admit to lying about the allegation of sexual assault for her own reasons, reasons that had nothing to do with the dead girl.

A knock on the door broke into his thoughts and Clarke came in carrying a mug of coffee. Handford pointed to an empty space on the desktop. 'Thanks,' he said, then as the detective was about to leave he asked, 'You busy, Andy?'

'Not especially so, boss. I'm helping Warrender check Graham Collins' background.'

'Getting anywhere?'

'No, not yet. So far we haven't found him in any of the current boarding schools in the Cotswolds. I was just about to try those that have folded for one reason or another. It's not going to be easy, though.'

'In that case take a rest from it and help me out here. Do you want to get yourself a coffee?'

'No thanks, I'm drowning in the stuff.' Andy Clarke pulled up a chair and sat down. 'What was it you wanted my expert opinion on?'

'Who killed Shayla Richards?'

Clarke smiled. 'Nothing much, then?'

Handford laughed. 'Toss ideas about with me.'

'Okay. You think it goes back to the assault, don't you?'

'Don't you?'

'I think it might do, yes, and I think he might have done it.'

'So if he did, why did Shayla change her mind? Did Kerry Johnson frighten her into it? And if so, why?'

'I don't know, but I think we ought to bring Collins in. It seems to me he's very close to the edge; a bit of hard questioning might just do the trick. Do it by the book, insist on a solicitor, but go in hard. You could try his wife as well, but not here. She's been very loyal to him up to now, but her husband's fist in her face might just have dented that and in softer surroundings she might well open up.'

Andy was right, of course. He thought logically, didn't let his emotions confuse the issue and Handford was grateful for that. He glanced at his watch. Time was passing, both in hours and in days, and it wouldn't be long before his bosses would want to know how he was progressing – did he have any idea who had killed the girl? He let his eyes wander over the confusion of information that littered his desk.

'Even if he did assault her,' he said, looking up at Clarke, 'we can't assume he killed her, nor can we discount Calvin Richards, Shahid Mustafa or even the hoax caller if it comes to that. The voice analyst tells me she needs more time to be sure, but the way it's progressing she thinks it unlikely that he and Calvin are one and the same. Having said that, neither his nor Collins' or Mustafa's alibis are sound. There are windows in which any one of them could have killed her and taken her up to Druid's Altar. Although why they left her as they did...?' Handford shook his head.

'Do you think Warrender might be right and that Mustafa was helping Qumar get his children back – the two boys in particular? The chances are he wouldn't have wanted Shayla, tainted as she was – she was hardly marriageable – but the boys, he'd want them; and once they were in Pakistan, Mrs Richards would have the devil's own job to get them back, even with a residency

250

order from the court. Perhaps Shayla found out what was happening, that she wasn't included, so she threatened to tell her mother. Perhaps Mustafa had to kill her to keep her quiet. I can see him arranging her body on the altar, if only as a sick form of revenge on Evelyn Richards.'

Handford swallowed the rest of his now cold coffee. The picture he was getting was neither black nor white, but rather like an old photograph – a delicate shade of sepia. Nothing standing out clearly. Few facts, but several suspects with motive and opportunity. Means was more of a problem because if the pathologist was right, two people had come together to kill her. Two with reasons enough to want her dead. Who were they, these two? Calvin Richards and Shahid Mustafa; Calvin and Evelyn Richards; Graham and Jane Collins; or was it persons unknown? Someone she had slept with or rejected – the hoax caller, perhaps? Whose idea was it to leave her on the stone up at Druid's Altar? And why?

He paused to consider what he should do next – talk to Jane Collins, then, as Clarke suggested, bring Graham Collins back to the station and record the interview? His stomach curled. It would cause trouble. Collins' followers – colleagues – would show their displeasure and Jaswant Siddique would lead them, probably with some display of togetherness or even industrial action and Gill would have to ride the storm. Perhaps he ought to go up to the school first, warn Siddique that he had no intention of giving up the investigation and if he continued to be uncooperative and intimidating, he would charge

251

him with obstructing the police in the execution of their duties as well as with harassment. He doubted the CPS would go with it, but it sounded good and might just be enough to quieten him.

The telephone interrupted his thoughts, startling him. Clarke responded with a grin and a mimed statement that he was going to get on.

Handford indicated his thanks and as the door closed, he picked up the receiver and said, 'Handford.'

The voice at the other end was unexpected. 'This is Brian Atherton, headteacher at Cliffe Top Comprehensive.'

The bitterness of the coffee bubbled in Handford's stomach. Was this to do with Gill?

'I wonder,' Atherton continued, concern twitching at his vocal cords, 'could you come up to the school? I have something here which I think maybe you ought to see.'

chapter thirteen

Brian Atherton, a small, balding man, bustled towards Handford to greet him with outstretched hand. In spite of his attempt at politeness, he looked and sounded worried and as he neared the detective, his eyes scanned the foyer as if to check no one was around to recognize his visitor.

'Please, come to my office,' he said, his voice breathless, ushering him into a room sparsely furnished with a desk, an education-issue grey filing cabinet and several school chairs which stood against the wall to be drawn up closer whenever necessary. The cream walls were bare except for a large colour-coded timetable and a monochrome aerial photograph of the school and surrounding district. On the desk a combined television and video machine was positioned to face the head's high-backed black leather chair on one side and the smaller visitor's chair uphol-stered in bright orange moquette on the other; this he offered to Handford.

'It's good of you to come at such short notice,' he said. 'I wasn't sure what to do, but given the circumstances I thought I ought to let you see it.' Then as an afterthought, he added, 'Oh, I'm sorry, would you like a coffee?'

Handford shook his head. 'Not for me, thank you,' and before the headmaster could ramble on further, he asked, 'Perhaps you could explain what it is you want me to see, Mr Atherton?'

The headteacher picked up a videotape from his desk. 'This,' he said, 'It's from the cemetery.'

Handford's patience was wearing thin. 'The cemetery?'

Set on the hillside overlooking the school, the city's Victorian cemetery was of considerable historical value, housing the remains of rich and famous inhabitants from as far back as the nineteenth century. Still in use, it was now massively overcrowded but the proximity of the graves and the larger headstones afforded those intent on sexual encounters or drug dealing the privacy to carry on unnoticed and unhindered.

Brian Atherton leaned forward and spoke in a tone that suggested what he was about to say was confidential and should therefore remain a secret between them. 'For some time now, Inspector, we've been having problems with pupils going into the cemetery before, during and after school hours. More often than not they sit and talk and smoke, but occasionally they take drugs and from time to time dealers meet up with them. Sadly, there have also been incidences of vandalism to some of the headstones. Recently it was decided by the cemetery's owners to install CCTV cameras, and, in the hope of curtailing this behaviour, either I or one of my deputies agreed to take a look at the tapes each morning, to ascertain which of our students, if any, are showing anti-social tendencies. Sometimes we get something, more often than not we don't – at least not now people have realized they can be caught on film. Anyway, today we came across this.' He pushed the cassette into the video player and pressed the play button.

The film was surprisingly clear and Handford watched as a man in a jogging suit paced backwards and forwards along the pathway, occasionally disappearing from sight behind one or other of the ornate Victorian monuments to reappear again a few moments later. At one point he turned towards the gate, giving the camera a good shot of his face.

'That's Graham Collins,' Handford said. 'What's he doing in the cemetery?'

Brian Atherton paused the recorder for a moment. 'It's not unusual for him to be there first thing in the morning. Generally he's by himself and seems to be doing nothing more than watching staff and students arrive at school.' He shook his head sadly. 'I suppose it's his way of still feeling part of us.'

'And it doesn't disturb you he's doing this?'

'Of course it does; he shouldn't be there. He's been told to keep away until Shayla's allegation has been resolved–'

'Surely it has been now,' Handford interrupted. 'The case collapsed when she admitted to lying. The judge directed the jury to give a not guilty verdict. In law, he's an innocent man.'

Atherton's voice, which up to now had been smooth, became more defensive. 'In law he might be, Inspector, but the governors have to assure themselves there is no likelihood of similar allegations from girls who were too afraid to come forward initially.'

'Is that likely?'

255

'No, but we can't take the risk. Can you imagine the uproar from the press and the public, not to mention the parents, if we do nothing and someone did do so? Like it or not, we have to cover ourselves. But as you so rightly said, in law Graham is an innocent man and while we can prevent him from coming into the building, we can hardly stop him frequenting a public place, even if it is a cemetery, and even if it does overlook us. If I did so the reaction from the staff would be terrible. They're restless as it is. They feel Graham has been badly treated. If I report him, they are likely to take the industrial action they have been threatening and I can't risk that. Had he made any attempt to approach the students, I would have asked for him to be moved on, but he leaves once our day begins and as far as we know he has never met up with any of the pupils. Until this morning.'

He released the pause button and the image was set in motion again. A figure emerged from the right. Handford leaned forward to get a better view. He was looking at what was possibly a teenager dressed in dark trousers and an anorak. He or she tapped Collins on the shoulder and he spun round, whether in surprise or anger Handford couldn't tell. They spoke for a few moments and then moved towards the bench. When they sat down, Kerry Johnson's features became more discernible.

'It's what you'll see on the next frames that made me call you,' Brian Atherton said. 'Watch them.'

The two players sat either end of the bench and

256

from their body language it became apparent that this was no friendly meeting. Eventually Collins stood up, unzipped the pocket of his jogging trousers and took out an envelope. They spoke for a moment before Kerry stood up and held out her hand. Collins handed her the envelope and she flipped through the contents, put it in her bag, and then leaning very close, appeared to whisper to him. There was no indication as to what she said, but she gave him little chance to reply before she stood up and stepped back. They talked for a few more minutes until she turned and walked down the path to the gate, waving at him as she went.

Atherton pressed the stop button and leaned over to take out the tape, which he slipped into its box. As he switched off the television, he said, 'That didn't seem to me to be a very friendly meeting.'

'No,' Handford said pensively. 'It didn't.'

'What do you think Graham gave her?'

Handford remained thoughtful. 'I don't know. Could have been anything, although by the way she checked the contents I would say it was probably money. I would like to take this tape back with me if you don't mind. I'll have it enhanced; it might give us more when it's clearer.'

'Why should he give her money?'

'A good question, Mr Atherton. Why should he give her money? Tell me, what do you know about Mr Collins?'

Atherton pondered for a moment. 'Not much, actually. Married, no children. His parents are dead, I think. He's a very private person, doesn't talk about his background, but as far as I under-stand it, he is the product of an army family who moved around the world quite a lot so he was educated at a boarding school – Beech Tree Grove – in Stow on the Wold in the Cotswolds. I remember that particularly because it's unusual to employ teachers in this school who have been educated privately. If they come into teaching at all, they prefer to remain in the private sector. I felt we were lucky to get him. He has an excellent degree and came to us highly recommended from his first school. He's been on the staff for about four years. He's a good teacher, you know; got an excellent OFSTED report and was very popular with the students.'

Handford rubbed at his temple with his fingers. 'Do you think he assaulted Shayla, Mr Ather-ton?'

The headteacher was firm. 'No, I don't. I always believed Shayla was lying. Why she should have done so I don't know; it would need a psychiatrist to work that out. And before you ask, Inspector, nor do I think he killed her. Why should he? He was close to being cleared by the governors.'

'Even if he was, his reputation had been tarnished and may never be restored.' Handford had gone through an inquiry of his own for alleged racism some years previously when he had arrested a young Asian boy for the murder of his sister and the community had rioted – a riot for which he was blamed. The inquiry had exonerated him but in spite of that, promotion had passed him by and it was only comparatively recently that his bosses had begun to show trust in him again.

'What will be his chances of promotion now, Mr Atherton? The teacher who was accused of an assault against a pupil and got away with it. There are people in this city who not only think he did but also that he killed Shayla. He had a brick through his window at the weekend, you know.'

For a few moments neither man spoke. It was obvious all this was new to Brian Atherton and he was struggling to come to terms with it. 'I didn't know,' he murmured. 'Poor man.'

Poor man he might be, but he was a poor man who needed investigating. Until a suspect was cleared, sympathy could not be allowed to intrude, and whether Cliffe Top Comprehensive liked it or not, Collins was nowhere near that stage. Gill hadn't wanted him to come into the school, but he was here now and it was time to make his intentions clear and show the staff that he would not go away. He pulled out his metaphorical knife and scratched the surface, trying not to draw blood.

'I don't know whether Mr Collins killed Shayla or not, Mr Atherton, or indeed whether he assaulted her or not, and I'm never going to find out if your teachers insist on blackmailing me, through my wife, into withdrawing from the case. Gill has no means of influencing the choice of investigating officer or of persuading me or my bosses to hand it over to another detective. I *will* continue to work on this case whether the staff like it or not and I *will* do it in my way. I don't tell them how to do their job, so please make sure they don't interfere with mine, because I promise you if they do I will come down heavily on them.

Perhaps you can make that clear.'

The headteacher stiffened. 'I will certainly pass on your concerns, Inspector, but a school isn't the police force; I can't give orders like that. Mr Siddique in particular feels very strongly about you harassing Graham Collins, who is a personal friend. It will be difficult to stop him.'

'Then *I* will tell him, Mr Atherton. I will warn him that he is the one harassing and that harassment is a criminal offence and I'll do it now, because if he's in school, I can't see much point in my coming back, can you? My sergeant tells me Mr Siddique has been less than cooperative but the questions still need to be answered. Perhaps you could have him brought here now.'

At first Handford thought the headmaster was about to refuse, but after a short pause he picked up the phone. 'Ask Mr Siddique to pop along to my office would you?'

Ask Mr Siddique? How about tell Mr Siddique? Who's the head here?

While they waited, Handford said, 'What is Mr Collins' relationship with Kerry Johnson?'

Atherton frowned. 'I didn't know until this morning that he had one. Like Shayla, she's hardly ever in school. I'm not even sure he taught her. I can find out if you like, go through past timetables, but it will take time.'

Handford relaxed a little. The tautness had gone from Atherton's voice. 'I would be grateful,' he said and smiled. It was time to plaster over the knife wound. 'Can you think of any reason why he should be giving Kerry money, if that was what he was doing?'

'I can't; I wish I could. Kerry's in school today if you want a word with her as well. I'd have to stay, of course.'

There was no point filling in the abrasions completely. 'No, I don't think so, not yet. I'll see her at home once I know more.' There came a knock at the door. 'That will be Mr Siddique. Do you have a room I could use?'

Atherton sighed. 'Use mine, Inspector. I'll need to go to the deputy's office to check the timetables for you.' He made for the door. 'Try not to antagonize him, will you? I shouldn't condemn my staff, but Mr Siddique can be,' he paused as he searched for the right word, 'opinionated, shall we say. He could cause a lot of trouble in school.'

As Brian Atherton opened the door to Jaswant Siddique, Handford smiled and held up the CCTV tape. 'Thank you for your cooperation, sir, and for this,' he said. 'I don't know what any of it means yet, and it may not be of any relevance, but you were right to call me in.'

Tall and dressed in a black T-shirt and jeans, Jaswant Siddique appeared gaunt as he stood in the doorway, silhouetted by the bright lights from the foyer. His hair, which was pulled back in a ponytail, was receding at the temples, accentuating the length of his face, and his deep brown eyes held an aura of threat. As Brian Atherton introduced the teaching assistant he scowled and Handford was unsure whether his anger was directed at him as the investigating officer, or at

261

the headmaster for cooperating with the enemy.

'Please come in and sit down, Mr Siddique,' Handford said as he pulled up one of the school chairs. 'I won't keep you long.'

Siddique remained standing. 'You have no right to pull me out of the classroom and I certainly don't have to answer any of your questions.' His voice, though smooth, had a steely edge to it.

'I am investigating a murder, Mr Siddique,' Handford said, his tone just as dangerous. 'I have every right to bring you from your classroom to interview you, although as you said, you don't have to answer my questions if you prefer not to. However, if you refuse, I have to ask myself why you are doing so and what you have to hide.'

Anger blazed more brightly in the teaching assistant's eyes. 'The last time you interrogated us you put Graham Collins in court on a trumped-up charge. We're not going to let that happen again.'

'I had nothing to do with the first inquiry, Mr Siddique – they were not my questions and it was the CPS who decided on the charge, not the police. This is different.'

'Yes, this time they've given us the husband of one of our teachers. God only knows what they'll be expecting you to drag from her.'

Handford's eyes narrowed. 'I strongly suggest you leave my wife out of this. What and who I investigate has nothing to do with her.'

Siddique stared at him with a touch of insolence. 'Shayla Richards was a liar and none of you could see that.'

'She's not a liar now, sir, she's dead. She can't

tell us anything.'

Seconds passed and Siddique shifted uncomfortably. Eventually he said, 'You can ask your questions but I can't promise to answer. I'm not saying anything that will incriminate either me or Graham.'

Handford raised his eyebrows. 'Are you aware of anything which is likely to incriminate you both, Mr Siddique?' His tone was dangerous.

'No, of course not.'

Handford stored the comments away to be used at some other time, because for a man with the kind of arrogance Jaswant Siddique was exhibiting there was always another time. He said, 'Then you have nothing to fear. Now, please sit down; it will be more comfortable for you and I won't have to strain my neck looking up at you.'

The man perched on the edge of the chair.

'You're a teaching assistant here, I understand?'

'Yes.'

'Part time?'

'I work Monday and Tuesday all day and Wednesday morning.'

'What do you do Thursday and Friday? Do you have a job in another school, or any other work?'

'I study.'

'Where?'

'At the college.' He stood up. 'Look, is all this relevant?'

'Please sit down.'

Siddique took a step towards the door. 'No, I won't sit down. Isn't it enough that you're harassing Graham, without starting on the rest of us? None of this is relevant.'

Handford looked up at him. 'Then let me ask you something that is relevant. Where were you last Thursday?'

The man's eyes mocked. 'So, now you think I killed her? Typical.'

'I don't know who killed her yet, Mr Siddique. But if you insist on being uncooperative and I can't eliminate you, then I have to think you might be involved; it's in your own interests to answer my questions. Here would be better, but I can take you to the station if you prefer.'

'No, I do not prefer and if you want me at the station you'll have to arrest me and you have no grounds for that.'

Handford leaned back in his chair. 'Obstructing the police, harassment. Take your pick.'

The teaching assistant remained silent. Handford had given him something against which he couldn't argue. Now was the time to be the nice guy. 'Look, Mr Siddique, a fifteen-year-old girl has been murdered. She was a pupil at this school. Surely you want her killer caught?'

Siddique clicked his tongue derisively. 'I don't give a shit about Shayla Richards; her father had brought her up as a Muslim and she renounced Islam in the worst possible way. She uncovered herself, she slept around, she defiled her body and her soul.'

'Then you know more about her than the rest of the staff. My understanding so far is that she was hardly ever in school. No one here knows her well enough to be able to give us anything concrete about her lifestyle – except, it appears, you. You must be well acquainted with her to do that.

You worked with her?'

'I support students with special educational needs. She wasn't considered to come into that category, so no, I didn't work with her. But you don't have to know someone to know *of* them, particularly in a school, and particularly with a slut like Shayla Richards. Her lifestyle was common knowledge,' Siddique scoffed. 'Just because none of us mentioned it to you, doesn't mean it didn't happen. She was a tart and a liar; she ruined Graham Collins' career. No male teacher was safe with her around. She deserved everything that was coming to her.'

'Those are very strong feelings, Mr Siddique.'

Jaswant Siddique stood up. 'Of course they're strong feelings, and they're the feelings of all the right-thinking teachers and the pupils in this school – except of course, those who consort with the police.' He walked to the door and pulled it open. 'I warn you, Handford, before I've finished I'll have both you and your wife out of Cliffe Top Comprehensive, and I won't do it quietly.' As if to prove his point he slammed the door behind him. His anger seemed to remain, reverberating round the small office for several minutes after his departure.

Handford walked away from the school, his mobile to his ear.

'Ali, bring Collins in,' he snapped.

'You want Collins in for questioning?'

'Yes, with his solicitor.'

'Under arrest, or just in?'

'Just in, not under arrest.'

265

There was a pause at the other end of the phone until Ali said, 'Are you all right, John? Has something happened?'

Still angry, Handford didn't want to discuss it. 'I've spent the last quarter of an hour trying to interview a particularly objectionable man and got nowhere. I'll tell you about it later,' he said. 'In the meantime, just do as I ask, will you?' He hadn't meant to be so terse.

Ali seemed to ignore it. 'Are you coming in, sir?'

Handford took a deep breath in an attempt to dissipate his anger. 'No, I'm going to talk to Jane Collins up at the hospital. Let me know when Collins and his solicitor are on their way. And Khalid...'

'Yes sir?'

'Put someone on to finding out about Jaswant Siddique.'

He could hear Ali chuckle. 'Am I to take it he's the particularly objectionable man?'

'You are. He's a part-time teaching assistant at the school. I want to know all about him. Everything. He should have been at the college on Thursday. I want to know if he was there, when he arrived, when he left and anything else they can tell me.'

'Do you have an address for him?'

'No. Atherton wasn't prepared to hand out staff addresses, quoted the Data Protection Act at me. We'll have to get a warrant for those. See to that as well, will you?'

'Yes, sir.'

'Oh and tell Clarke that Collins was at a board-

266

ing school near Stow on the Wold,' he glanced at his notebook, 'Beech Tree Grove School.'

'Sir.'

Handford ended the call and made for his car. As he passed by the staff parking area, he caught a glimpse of Gill's Golf. The lights were on in his wife's classroom, which faced the main road, and he wondered if she had seen him as he walked into the school. If she hadn't then he was pretty sure it wouldn't be long before she knew of his visit. Jaswant Siddique would see to that.

Bloody man. Just who did he think he was? A jumped-up teaching assistant who thought he was running the school. Did he really believe he could stop the police investigating a murder? Even if by some miracle he managed to get Handford off the case, there'd be someone else. But that someone else wouldn't have a wife who worked in the school. That was obviously his objection, although why he didn't know. Handford thought back to what Gill had told him about the investigation into the allegation. Understandably the staff had closed ranks round Graham Collins then and he didn't blame them for doing so now, but Siddique's reaction was excessive. He wasn't just organizing a protest against the governors, the police in general and him in particular, he wanted Gill out as well. Why? Did he think she knew something detrimental to him? Had something happened which he thought she knew about, perhaps from the original inquiry? Oh God, if he went down that road, it would mean asking Gill and she'd already made it clear she wasn't prepared to discuss a colleague with him.

It was a pity Siddique wasn't as loyal to her as she was to him.

Then there was his reaction towards Shayla to consider. Certainly he held nothing but contempt for the girl and her conduct. There was no doubt her lifestyle left much to be desired – even Kerry Johnson had suggested as much – but generally the teachers who had had contact with her had seen her as a vulnerable and unhappy girl, so why not Jaswant Siddique? He worked with special needs children; he of all people ought to have had some compassion for her. Yet he had used words like slut and tart. She was only fifteen and fifteen-year-olds rebel. How had he described it? *'She deserved everything that was coming to her.'* Why? What had she done that had driven out his compassion? Had he been one of the men who were not safe with her, perhaps? Was he someone who needed to cover his own back, even two years after the complaint against Graham Collins? There by the grace of God...? Was the man's anger ruled by fear for himself, rather than resentment for a friend?

Handford smiled to himself. No evidence, just another hunch, but worth pursuing.

He unlocked his car, threw the CCTV tape on the passenger seat and climbed in. He glanced at the white box. Now *that* held evidence, although of what he wasn't quite sure yet. Was Kerry Johnson blackmailing Collins? What did she know about him that he would want keeping secret? Perhaps they would throw more light on that at the station when they questioned him.

The midday traffic was heavy and the journey to

the hospital slow. The greyness that had blanketed the sky early that morning was rapidly being overtaken by the deep blue-black of storm clouds, and the former mildness in temperature was giving way to a stifling humidity as flashes of lightning preceded rolls of thunder in the north-west. Handford counted the seconds between the two. One second, one mile, that's what his mother had always said. Eight, nine miles away from the city. A storm at Druid's Altar, perhaps, washing away whatever was left of any evidence. It didn't matter because the scenes of crime officers had finished, but the cordon had been left and the public were still refused access. Normally he couldn't see why anyone should want to be up there at this time of year, but a body had been discovered and there were always the ghouls who wanted to see for themselves, or the friends who came to pay their respects by placing flowers where she had been found.

As he manoeuvred the car round the back streets, Handford turned up the volume of the cassette player so that the golden tones of the Brighouse and Rastrick brass band filled the car. Before he had joined CID and the job had taken over, he had been a member of a local band; sadly, now all he had time to do was to buy CDs for the home and tapes for the car and enjoy the music. If nothing else it soothed away his anger at Jaswant Siddique and his concern over Gill and focused his mind instead on Jane Collins. He hoped that through her he might be able to understand her husband. He would try not to upset her, but he couldn't guarantee it, for the fact was Graham Collins was becoming less and less clear to him. Initially he had been a man mauled by a young girl and the system, then he had become a suspect in her murder. Her clothes were found in his wheelie bin and he didn't seem to want to help himself with a decent alibi. He followed that by violently attacking his pregnant wife, whom he referred to as a bitch, and now, this morning, it seemed he was being black-mailed by a young girl for a reason Handford couldn't begin to explain.

As he parked the car in the hospital grounds and climbed out, the black clouds released their load and large raindrops bounced around him. He scrunched up his eyes and looked skywards. Like his meeting with Jane Collins, the change in the weather would either clear the air or muddy the ground beneath his feet even more.

chapter fourteen

The hospital canteen wasn't the best place to meet. A quieter side room would have been better, but Jane Collins worked in the labour suite and since they were busy, there were none available and anyway, if Handford were honest, the cries emanating from behind the closed doors disturbed him more than the background babble of conversation, canned music and clatter of crockery in the canteen. Give him the shouts and abuse from the cells any time; he pushed those into the background, hardly heard them.

Handford looked across at the woman sitting opposite. 'Just a chat,' he'd said, but he knew and she knew it would be more than that. Detectives didn't have chats. They asked questions, gnawed away at your private life and discovered things you didn't want anyone to discover.

A deep frown furrowed her forehead and her fingers alternated between playing with her wedding ring and feathering her cheek.

'It's a nasty bruise,' he said.

Jane Collins nodded.

'I won't insult you by asking how you got it. I do know.'

'Peter Redmayne?'

He made no reply, but he knew that as far as she was concerned he didn't need to.

'Even if he is your husband, you don't have to

put up with his violence,' he said. 'Report it and we can charge him with assault – actual bodily harm, even.'

'No, I can't do that; not now. I've warned him if he does it again I'll leave him, but that's as far as I'll go. He's on the edge, Inspector. I'm not sure what he'll do next, and to be honest if it comes to killing himself or hitting me then I'd rather it was the latter.'

'You think he is likely to kill himself?'

'Don't you? You've seen him. He can't take much more.' She took a sip of her coffee. 'He goes running.'

'I know.'

'It's his salvation. It helps diffuse his anger and his hurt, because he's been dreadfully hurt by the school, the governors and the people out there who still think he assaulted and now murdered a pupil. He's desperately worried he'll never get his job back. He loves teaching, although God knows why.'

Handford grinned. 'I often think the same of my wife.'

'She works at Cliffe Top doesn't she? Graham mentioned her once or twice. He liked her.'

'Did he ever mention a Jaswant Siddique?'

Jane Collins thought for a moment. 'No, I can't say it's a name I know. Is he a teacher at the school?'

'A teaching assistant. You're sure Graham never mentioned him?'

'I'm sure. Why?'

'Because according to the headteacher he's a personal friend of your husband, and he's

272

certainly pulling out all the stops to support him and get him back into school.'

'That's kind of him.'

Handford wasn't sure 'kind' was the word he would have used. 'What about Kerry Johnson – do you know her?'

There was no flicker of recognition at the name, no sudden upsurge in her level of anxiety. 'Is she a teacher?'

Unless she was a very good actress, Kerry Johnson was a name of which she was not aware. 'No, she's a pupil. She was a friend of Shayla Richards.'

'I'm sorry. I've never heard Graham speak of her.'

Two people with some kind of a relationship with Graham Collins, and his wife had no knowledge of them. Handford doubted Siddique cared a jot about Collins; the man was snide and sneaky and more than likely using the situation for his own ends, whatever they were. But Kerry Johnson was different and if she was blackmailing Graham Collins and his wife had no idea, there was something in his life she knew nothing about either. There were times when Handford hated this job. If Graham Collins supported his theory then her world was about to come crashing down again. It was always the innocent who suffered and it seemed to him he was always the one to bring that suffering into the open. Much as he disliked the idea, it was his job to do exactly that.

'Tell me about Graham. How long have you been married?'

'Three years. I met him at a hospital dance while I was training as a midwife at Leeds General. He was studying for his PGCE and was invited along with other students from the university. It was his smile I fell for first.' She surveyed her cup, as though embarrassed at what she had just said. 'He has the most engaging, appealing smile. Everyone says so; at least they did until someone suggested it was that that lured Shayla into his stockroom.' Her voice broke and the words bubbled in her throat. 'Now he hardly ever smiles.' She stopped for a moment to compose herself. 'Anyway, we started dating and got engaged after he qualified and began teaching in Huddersfield. A couple of years later, I was offered a senior midwife's job in Bradford, and a month after that the history post came up at Cliffe Top Comprehensive. Graham applied and got it. We'd been in Bradford a year when we married and moved into our house. Until Shayla Richards we had a good life.'

'What about his family? Does he have any brothers and sisters?'

'No, he's an only child. His parents are dead. His father was killed in 1991, in the Gulf war and his mother died of breast cancer. If it hadn't been for friends from school there'd have been no one on his side of the church at the wedding. It's sad really.' She patted her stomach. 'This little one will have no paternal grandparents or aunts and uncles; it'll have to make do with mine. Did you know I was pregnant?'

Handford nodded.

'Peter Redmayne again?'

He smiled his agreement. 'He mentioned it when he told me about the bruising. I'm sorry, that's what we detectives do: get information out of people.'

'It doesn't matter. If it hadn't been Peter, someone else would no doubt have told you. At least he's on our side.'

Handford didn't want to talk about Peter Redmayne and sides and he brought the conversation back to her husband. 'Tell me more about Graham, about his childhood, for instance.'

'I don't know much. Apart from the fact that he went to boarding school near Stow on the Wold and from there to Warwick University, then Leeds for his teaching qualification. He doesn't talk much about his past.'

'Doesn't that worry you? That there might be something he doesn't want you to know?'

'We all come into a relationship with baggage, Inspector. I'm willing to bet there are things about you before you met your wife that you wouldn't want her to know. It doesn't matter what happened before we met. We love each other and in spite of everything he's a good and decent man. He's not a sexual predator and he's not a killer. I'd know if he was.' She pushed back her chair. 'We'll get through this. Battered and bruised,' she let her fingers whisper along her cheek, 'but we'll get through it.'

Handford stood up. It was only fair to tell her that the battering and the bruising was about to begin. 'I'm having your husband brought into the station for questioning.'

Her eyes widened in horror and she slumped back onto the chair. 'Why?'

He regained his seat. 'The clothes in the wheelie bin, for one. I need an explanation for those. And, I'm sorry, but his alibi is weak. I need to go through it with him in detail.' He refrained from telling her about the meeting with Kerry Johnson. She'd enough to cope with.

'You'll arrest him?'

'No, he'll not be under arrest, just helping—'

'Helping the police with their inquiries,' she broke in. 'A euphemism for we suspect you, but we can't prove it yet. No one, except perhaps his colleagues, will believe now that he hasn't killed her.'

He made no reply. She was right. Suspicion stuck to a person who had been 'helping the police with their inquiries', more so if that person had already been charged with a criminal offence – even if he *was* found not guilty.

'You do realize this may tip him completely,' she said bitterly. 'He needs someone to believe him.'

'I'm sorry, but I must record the interview. I can only do that at the station.'

'And if his alibi remains weak and he cannot account for Shayla Richards' clothes in our wheelie bin, you'll arrest him?'

'I don't know, Mrs Collins. If he gives me no more than I've already got, then no, I won't have the evidence, but I have to warn you that I'll continue to look for it and if it's there I'll find it.' He wanted to say that if he was innocent he'd have nothing to fear, but given the past two years it would have been crass, not to mention cruel. Instead he said, 'As much as you hate Shayla, and I know you must, she *is* dead and someone killed her. If she were your daughter, you'd want her killer found, wouldn't you?' He leaned over and touched her arm. 'There's no point telling you not to worry because you will. I would in your shoes. All I can say is that I hope for your sake it turns out as you want it to, but I can't promise anything.'

It was lunchtime when seven members of staff, all known militants – troublemakers, some would call them – came together to insist on the reinstatement of Graham Collins, make plans for a vote of no confidence in Brian Atherton and ask that either Gill Handford's husband be taken off the case or her taken out of school until Shayla Richards' killer was apprehended.

Jaswant Siddique chaired the meeting. He was sure they'd be with him; he'd picked them carefully.

As expected, they were all in agreement that the continued harassment of Graham Collins by the governors and the police should be rejected and that he should be given all the support at their command, including, if necessary, strike action, although they hoped it wouldn't come to that. None were in any doubt that this would be accepted by the staff and according to Siddique the pupils were prepared to help too; they were just as angry, he said. Even Kerry Johnson and her gang had come into school to be part of it.

'My God, they must think it's important if they're blessing us with their presence,' chortled the P.E. teacher.

The bearded science teacher wasn't too sure. 'I'm not sure we need the likes of them becoming involved.'

'Once it's sorted, they'll be back truanting again,' Siddique cajoled. 'For the moment they'll have their uses, whip up support among the rest of the kids. They'll do a good job, and it'll look better if they do it themselves than if we get involved; it will be seen as an unprompted decision on their part.'

'Even so, it would be better if it was someone else rather than Kerry Johnson.'

The second item on the agenda, a vote of no confidence in Brian Atherton, was not an issue either. They had always considered him a weak headteacher. Of all people, he should have backed Graham Collins, no matter what. He was as much aware as anyone else that Shayla Richards had been a liar and a troublemaker. To believe her instead of him and then cooperate with the police was, in their opinion, a sign of disloyalty. Now, according to Jaswant Siddique, he was doing the same again. It was one thing the police coming into the school after her murder to make rudimentary inquiries of those who had known her, quite another for the head to invite them in to hand out information. Handford, he said, had almost crowed in front of him as he waved the videotape and thanked Atherton for his cooperation. Siddique could only guess at what it contained, but given that Graham Collins had been in the cemetery earlier, it didn't take a rocket scientist to work out that it might have had something to do with him.

The second resolution was passed without argument.

The third was not so easy. Militant as they were,

the other six were not convinced it was necessary to ask for Gill Handford to be removed.

'I doubt the staff will go for it,' argued the NUT union rep. 'She's popular and very few are going to condemn her for being married to a detective. You'll have to have a better reason than that.'

Jaswant Siddique was not to be mollified. 'He'll use her as his informant. God knows what tales she'll be telling.'

'What can she tell? There is nothing to tell, unless you know something we don't.'

Siddique backtracked. 'That's not the point. It's the principle. One of our pupils has been murdered; one of our teachers is in the frame; and the head of English is married to the investigating officer. He shouldn't be on it. It's a conflict of interest.'

'Only if she's a suspect,' the union representative insisted. 'And I can't quite see calm, gentle, middle class Gill Handford killing someone, can you? No, Jaswant, you're on a hiding to nothing with this one. All four unions have agreed that you call a full meeting tomorrow regarding Graham and Atherton if that's what you want, but I tell you they won't go for a witch hunt, nor will the majority of the staff. If you want Gill Handford out, you're going to have to think of something else.'

When Handford stepped into interview room two followed by Sergeant Ali, Graham Collins' solicitor was pacing the floor. He was plainly angry. 'I hope you have a good reason for bringing us both down here, Inspector,' he said. 'I'm a busy man and don't take kindly to being ordered to the station at a moment's notice.'

Handford glared at him. Obviously he'd decided attack was the best form of defence. 'I haven't ordered you anywhere, Mr...?' He raised his eyes interrogatively.

'Bayliss, Leo Bayliss.' He made no attempt to shake hands. 'National Union of Teachers' solicitor.'

'I need to question Mr Collins in relation to the death of Shayla Richards,' Handford said coldly, 'and I suggested he bring his solicitor with him. It's in his own interest to do so. Had you been too busy, Mr Bayliss, we could have postponed until you had more time to devote to your client. But since you're here, perhaps we could get on.' He gave the solicitor a curt nod, which the man returned with a look that challenged Handford to cross him again if he dare.

Graham Collins, still in the jogging suit of this morning, sat at the table, staring at the coffee stains and the graffiti, unmoved by the duel of words. Bayliss took a pace towards Handford and said, 'I'm not sure my client is well enough to be questioned. Look at him.'

Handford was inclined to agree. 'I can have him medically examined if you wish, but it will mean waiting for the doctor and I don't know how long that will take.'

At this, Collins jumped into life as though someone had plugged him in to the electricity supply and he ran twitching fingers through his thick, dark hair. 'For God's sake,' he shouted. 'Can you two stop discussing me as though I'm not here? If you want to question me, then question me, but don't expect me to hang around while you decide my state of health.'

'You're happy to be questioned, Mr Collins?'

'Your choice of words amazes me, Inspector. No, I'm not happy to be questioned, but I'm willing to go along with it, at least for the moment.'

The men sat down, Bayliss next to his client and Handford and Ali on the chairs on the opposite side of the table. Ali unwrapped the tapes and inserted them into the recorder, after which they introduced themselves and Handford cautioned Collins that he was not under arrest and free to leave at any time. 'You do not have to say anything,' he continued. 'But it may harm your defence if you do not mention when questioned something which you later rely on in court. Anything you do say may be given in evidence. Do you understand, Mr Collins?'

'I think so, Inspector Handford, I've heard it often enough.' His words were laced with sarcasm, but his voice was void of emotion.

After leaving Jane Collins, Handford had reflected on how he should conduct the interview. She considered her husband suicidal and he didn't want to be the one to give him the final push, yet there was so much he wanted – needed – to know about Collins the person. So many questions had to be asked about his relationship with Jaswant Siddique, with Shayla Richards and with Kerry Johnson, particularly with Kerry Johnson. The problem was where to start: go in hard as Clarke had suggested or gain his trust by beginning with something innocuous about him, his family and his marriage. He decided on the latter.

'Did you always want to be a teacher, Mr Collins?'

Whatever question Collins had been expecting, it hadn't been that. He lifted his head and stared at Handford. 'I wouldn't say it was a life's ambition, but yes, it was something I thought I would be good at.'

'And were you good at it?'

'I think so. I got an excellent report from OFSTED. One of two in the school. I was quite proud of that.' He paused as a smile curled along his lips. 'I think your wife got the other, didn't she?'

'Yes, I think she did. You teach history, I believe?'

'Yes. Not for two years, though,' he added bitterly.

'Where did you qualify?'

'I graduated from Warwick University with a two-one and moved to Leeds University for my teaching qualification. I met my wife while I was there. My first teaching post was in Huddersfield. After I'd been there two years Jane won a promotion and moved to Bradford and I followed her. We married a year later. Then Shayla Richards accused me of sexually assaulting her and I was suspended. She admitted lying, I was pronounced not guilty of anything and I'm still suspended.' He lifted his hands as if to show there was nothing more left, then said, 'There you are, Inspector, my life in a nutshell without you asking a single question. I told you I'd done it before.'

The man was playing with him. Well, if that was

what he wanted, at least for the moment he could have it. 'What about your early life? Where were you born?'

The electricity that had charged through Collins earlier surged again, throwing out sparks of anger. 'What the hell has that to do with anything? Shayla Richards died last week. What has when I was pushed out of my mother's womb got to do with that? You'll be asking me next where I was conceived.' He sank back into the chair.

The solicitor roused. 'I must say,' he said, 'I agree with Mr Collins. I really can't see where this line of questioning is leading.'

'It's leading to me learning about your client, Mr Bayliss. The more I know and the more I can build up a background, the more I can understand where he is coming from.'

'But surely you can get all this from Mr Collins' former file.'

I could if we could find it or if I could get in touch with Slater. But he wasn't about to tell Bayliss that.

'Of course, but I find it's better to ask the questions and hear the answers for myself.' He turned away from Leo Bayliss and towards Graham Collins. 'If you wouldn't mind, sir, perhaps you could indulge me for a little while longer.'

Collins looked towards his solicitor, who lifted his hands in submission.

Handford smiled, his voice conciliatory. 'Now, where were you born?'

Collins' voice flattened again as he recited his answer. 'My name is Graham Samuel Collins. I was born at Catterick in North Yorkshire in April

1973 to Martin and Rebecca Collins. I have no brothers or sisters. My father was in the army and we moved around a lot, so when I was ten I went to boarding school in Stow on the Wold – Beech Tree Grove School. Dad was killed in the Gulf war while I was preparing for my A-levels. After I'd completed them my mother told me she had advanced breast cancer. I'd been offered a place at Warwick to read history, but I put it on hold to care for my mother.' He threw Handford a malevolent look. 'Do you want to know about that? About how much pain she was in? How I had to listen to her cry, administer her morphine and how in the end I had to let her go into a hospice because I couldn't cope with not being able to help her? Perhaps you'd like to know exactly how she died?'

Handford shook his head.

Collins smiled enigmatically, his lips barely parting. Eventually the smile slid away and he continued in the same monotone as before. 'Afterwards, I took up my place at university. I was there three years, came out with a two-one, decided I wanted to teach and went to Leeds where I got my PGCE.' He stopped and slapped his hands on the table. 'There, Inspector, now you have it: my life in that same nutshell. I hope it tells you where I'm coming from.'

Handford wasn't sure it did. The words were there, but it was almost as though Collins had learned them by heart. There was little emotion, hardly any sign of him losing composure, his expression as neutral as his voice. Perhaps Shayla Richards had knocked it out of him, although not

284

entirely if the size of the bruise on his wife's cheek was anything to go by. No, Handford didn't know where he was coming from, but he intended to find out.

Gill Handford was walking towards the staff cloakroom when Brian Atherton appeared from his office. 'Could I have a word, Mrs Handford?'

Gill sighed; she had a pile of year seven essays to mark before tomorrow, which she knew before she began would be awful, and she wanted to get home and do them so that she could spend the rest of the evening trying to patch things up with John. Last night he wouldn't even meet her halfway on the investigation. She accepted it was unlikely he could be relieved of it, and even if he could, he didn't want to be. But it wasn't so much that that upset her, it was the questions and the fact that, because she was his wife, he assumed she would automatically answer them. This time he was wrong. She *would not* discuss staff members with him, however obnoxious they might be. He was putting her in a difficult position by even asking, couldn't he see that?

She watched Brian Atherton's back as he walked towards his office. When he'd first come to the school, he'd been upright, confident in his position. Now he stooped slightly, weighed down by the pressures of running a school like Cliffe Top and the events of the past two years. She almost felt sorry for him.

Almost. Certainly not sorry enough to need a chat with him to end a day that had begun badly with a run-in with Jaswant Siddique and then gone on to grow steadily worse. Kerry Johnson and another of her gang in the classroom hadn't helped; they'd seemed out to cause trouble from the moment they walked in the door. Nor had the atmosphere in school made things any easier. It was still one of shock and disbelief, mingled with a certain amount of sadness, and all she wanted to do was get away from it and go home.

Dispiritedly, she followed Atherton, slipping past him as he held the door open for her. Once inside he moved behind his desk and sat down. She waited, hoping she wouldn't drop the thirty-odd books in her arms. Finally he leaned forward and steepled his fingers, then suddenly realized Gill was still standing, struggling with her burden, and said, 'Oh, I'm sorry, please sit down.'

She took the bright orange visitors' chair and perched the books on her knee.

He leaned back. 'I've been looking through your file, Gill, and it seems to me you haven't been involved in any personal career development lately. Perhaps we ought to think about it for you.'

She waited. If he hoped for a comment she wasn't about to give him one. Personal career development meant a course, a course meant supply cover and supply cover meant spending money, and Brian Atherton hated spending money. As far as she was concerned a course would be great, give her the opportunity to work her brain for a change, but she'd been turned down for more than she cared to think about because of the cost, so why now? If he was offering her one of his own volition, then he had to have another agenda and she wanted to hear what it was.

'So what do you think?'

There was no point turning it down out of hand. 'Yes, why not?'

'Good.' Brian Atherton almost rubbed his hands together. 'I've been looking at courses that would be suitable for you. There's one here: Teaching Shakespeare and Pre-twentieth-Century Literature to Children in the Inner City School. I rang through and they still have one or two places left.'

Gill wasn't sure exactly what expression covered her face, but if it was similar to her thoughts, then it would be one of amusement mixed with amazement. Teaching Shakespeare and pre-twentieth century literature to children in the inner city school! God! She couldn't think of anything worse. No wonder they had places left. She almost laughed aloud. 'I think we do quite a good job of teaching Shakespeare and pre-twentieth-century literature, Brian. I can't see what I could bring back that would help the staff and I'm at a loss as to how this would further my career.'

'Really? I thought you would have been keen to improve your skills, Gill, I'm disappointed in you.'

'I'm sorry, Brian, but if I thought it would be of any use to me, I would jump at the chance. Perhaps someone else in the department would like to take you up on it?'

'No, this was specifically for you.'

'Why?'

'As head of department.'

She sat back and thought for a moment. 'When

is the course scheduled for?'

Atherton's face brightened. 'It starts tomorrow.'

'Tomorrow?'

'It is short notice, I realize that, but all the better in its spontaneity.' He smiled, showing a row of brilliantly white teeth. When he first came the staff had had bets that they were false. *No one has teeth that white unless they're specially made.*

'And how long does it last?'

'Two weeks.'

'Two weeks?'

'A week of Shakespeare and a week of pre-twentieth-century literature,' he said as though that made perfect sense. 'You'll love it. Two weeks away from school in beautiful surroundings. Now shall I ring them and say you'll take the place?'

Two weeks away from school in beautiful surroundings? 'Where is this course, Brian?'

'That's the beauty of it, Gill; it's residential and at the conference centre at Windermere. Think how you could steep yourself in the Greats while looking out on the lake.'

Windermere in November as well as Shakespeare and pre-twentieth-century literature? She didn't think so. She gazed at him. The man was impossible and she didn't know whether to laugh or be angry. She settled for astonishment that he hadn't considered the problems such a sudden arrangement might cause for her. Not only were there her classes to organize for whoever stood in for her, but how did he think she was going to organize the family while she was steeping herself in the Greats? 'You expect me to drop everything and go up to Windermere for a fortnight? It may have escaped your notice, Brian, but I have two daughters at home. What do you suggest I do with them while I'm away in Windermere?'

'Your mother...'

'Yes, she would, but she and Dad are in New Zealand. And even if they weren't, I couldn't expect them to drop everything at a moment's notice.'

Atherton opened his mouth to speak, but anticipating his next suggestion she denied him the opportunity. 'John's parents live in Suffolk and since he's investigating Shayla's murder, there is no way he would be able to step in to look after the girls. They'll be lucky if they see him before bedtime.' She paused, then leaned forward, grabbing the books that threatened to slither off her knee. 'I can see your point though, Brian, it's one way of getting him off the case, although I can't see his senior officers being thrilled with him, can you?' Anger had taken over and she found herself trembling. If he'd allowed her to go now, she doubted she could have stood up, let alone held the books.

But he didn't. Instead he said, 'You're putting me in a very difficult position, Gill.'

She'd known it; this was nothing to do with her career development or the need to examine new methods of teaching Shakespeare and pre-twentieth-century literature. It was to do with Brian Atherton, and over the past ten minutes all he'd been doing was attempting to manipulate her.

She waited and he squirmed in the silence. Eventually he said, 'You know the staff are holding a meeting tomorrow to discuss how they can persuade the governors to allow Mr Collins back in school?'

She didn't know. It hadn't been mentioned to her. Obviously she was not to be invited.

'They're also concerned about the way police are harassing him–'

And there was the reason she had not been invited: part of the agenda concerned her. 'You mean the way they consider my husband is harassing him?'

He ignored the comment, but his eyes shifted onto the surface of his desk and he picked up a paperclip from a small dish. He pulled at it until it became a twisted piece of wire. 'They're also asking for a vote of no confidence in me for cooperating with the police.' So that was it. That was the reason he wanted her in Windermere: to remove her from the school and make things difficult at home so that John would have to hand over the case. He obviously knew nothing about the police service, or about John, or indeed her.

'You had no choice but to cooperate, Brian. One of our pupils has been murdered.'

As she watched, he dropped the one-time paperclip onto the desk and sank back into the chair, which now seemed to engulf him. 'This morning your husband came into school; I invited him in. I had something I thought he ought to see. While he was here he asked to talk to Mr Siddique and I had no choice to allow it, otherwise he would have waited and taken him down to the police station. Mr Siddique sees what I did as disloyal and has spoken to the unions. That's why they want to hold this vote of no confidence in me.'

Gill Handford was struggling to keep both her temper and the tone of incredulity out of her voice. 'And that's why you want me out? To give you a chance of avoiding a vote of no confidence?'

'Just until all this blows over.' He was almost pleading. 'I'm not thinking of myself, Gill. I'm thinking of the school. It will cease to function if the staff do not accept my authority.'

She felt like saying that it had functioned well enough so far, but refrained. She might be angry with him, but that was no reason to rub his face in it. Instead she contented herself with saying, 'I think that's your problem, not mine.'

'And that's your last word. You won't help?'

Gill stood up and clasped the books tightly. 'You know, what really gets to me about all this, Brian, is that none of you care about Shayla Richards. She's dead, murdered, probably quite brutally. All of us should want her killer caught; you should want him caught. Yet all you can think is how it's going to affect you. The rest of them are more concerned with Graham Collins than Shayla. I don't think he killed her, but God knows, even you must realize he has a motive. John is not harassing him, he's checking him out.' She turned to go and then spun back. 'If anyone is guilty of harassment, it's Jaswant Siddique. He's a teaching assistant for goodness' sake; you should be able to eat him for breakfast. Get rid of him, Brian, not me.'

chapter fifteen

Collins slewed his chair so that it was at forty-five degrees to the desk. It rested on its back legs, the rear framework hard against the wall. His body language suggested he was bored with the whole business, although the constant moistening of his lips with his tongue gave the lie to that. 'Let's cut the crap, Inspector,' he said derisively, turning his head towards Handford. 'Stop trying to worm your way into my confidence and instead ask me the questions you really want to ask. Because to be honest I'm not falling for your tricks. I'm not interested in trusting you. I did that before with Slater and it got me nowhere.'

'All right, Mr Collins. If that's what you want, I'll do just that.' Handford paused, working on his timing as any actor would. Collins needed shocking, showing that this was serious and that to cooperate was in his own interest, so rather than teasing the information out of him, Handford would take him by surprise and place him directly at the edge of the abyss so that he had no choice but to look down into it. His eyes rested squarely on the man opposite. 'Why did you meet Kerry Johnson in the cemetery this morning?'

Collins was shaken by the question and Handford watched as his expression ranged through various emotions before settling on venomous. He banged his chair onto all fours. 'What kind of a question is that?'

'A serious question, Mr Collins, and one you'd be well advised to answer.' Handford paused for a moment and then in a quiet voice repeated, 'Why did you meet Kerry Johnson in the cemetery this morning?'

Collins wavered and Handford could almost see the tape of lies and excuses unfurling in his mind. He waited as the teacher's eyes made a circuit of the room, avoided those of the two police officers and came to rest on the recorder. 'I didn't.'

He'd chosen the lie. 'You didn't?'

'No.'

'Mr Collins, you were caught on CCTV this morning.'

Collins turned white, not just pale but a greenish-white, and for a moment Handford thought he was going to be sick. The man turned wildly to his solicitor, then back to the detectives. 'I don't believe you; there is no CCTV in the cemetery.'

'You didn't know?'

Collins shook his head. Obviously he had been too absorbed in his own problems to notice.

'Cameras were installed a few weeks ago when there were problems with pupils from the school. Mr Atherton or one of the deputies checks them over daily. You visit the cemetery every morning; today you met Kerry Johnson and handed over what appeared to be an envelope.'

'That's rubbish. I was running this morning.' At least he hadn't questioned Kerry Johnson's identity.

'Where were you running?' Ali broke in.

Collins turned to him. 'I did a circuit of the roads.'

'Which included the road up to the school?'

'No.' He hesitated. 'No, I was nowhere near the school. I've been told to stay away,' he added bitterly. 'They've got to be careful. I might attack one of the girls on her way in or on her way home.' The sarcasm slid away and he hunched over the desk, his fingertips glossing his eyebrows as though he were soothing a headache. For a moment his eyes closed and the last of his energy seeped into the tears that escaped him. Handford watched as he brushed them away. He would have liked to feel some sympathy for Collins – God knows he knew where he was coming from – but the image of Shayla Richards' body layered itself over sentiment, demanding he reserved his compassion for her. Collins was lying; it was probable he'd been lying from the start – even about the sexual assault.

'Mr Collins, you *were* in the cemetery this morning and there you met Kerry Johnson. Now why?'

Collins opened his eyes and looked squarely at his opponent, but this time there was no animosity, no bravado, just defeat. 'It wouldn't matter what I said, would it? You've decided, just like the others decided.' The insolence was gone, the monotone restored.

'No. It wouldn't matter, not this time, because you were caught on CCTV.' Handford pulled a cassette from an evidence bag. 'Do you want to see the tape?'

Collins shook his head, but Leo Bayliss said, 'I think we should.'

Handford nodded at Ali who pushed it into the player. The static, juddering image of Collins pacing the path appeared on the screen, followed by his meet with Kerry Johnson. It took no more than a few minutes. Ali turned it off and ejected the cassette.

'Is that you, Mr Collins?'

Collins turned to his solicitor, who nodded.

His answer was barely audible. 'Yes.'

'For the tape, sir.'

He cleared his throat. 'Yes.'

'Can you now tell me why you met Kerry Johnson in the cemetery this morning and what it was you gave her?'

Silence stretched the length and width of the room, so that the only sound was that of the recording equipment humming in the background. At first Handford thought Collins was taking up the rights of the caution and refusing to say anything, but eventually he exhaled and said, 'Postcards.'

'Postcards?'

'I was giving Kerry postcards.'

'Of what?'

'Old Bradford.'

Handford was tempted to laugh. As an explanation this was one of the better ones he'd been privy to. 'You were giving Kerry Johnson photographs of old Bradford? And you expect me to believe that?'

'I don't expect you to believe anything. I've learned the hard way, remember?'

They could go on like this for ever and Handford was becoming tired of Collins' whingeing about his treatment by the establishment. He shot a glance at Ali, who took up the questioning.

'Why were you giving Kerry photographs of old Bradford?'

'She's interested in local history.'

'Kerry Johnson is interested in local history?'

This was beginning to take on the nature of a tennis match, each player connecting with the ball and lobbing it back and forth, none of the strikes taking it nearer to a result.

'So why lie? Why, if all you were doing was passing on some photographs, did you not tell the truth about your meeting with her?'

'You know why.'

'No.'

'Until the governors have held their inquiry, I'm not supposed to go near the school, let alone meet with the pupils.'

'So why go there? Why meet with her?'

'Because I haven't done anything wrong. I was found not guilty. I'm a free man, and I can't see why a group of people with nothing more than an inflated sense of their own importance should take away that freedom.'

Handford would like to have suggested that these people could take away more than his freedom if they decided he was a threat to the children in school. Instead, he said, 'Nevertheless, so close to the inquiry, it would seem foolish to go against their wishes. Unless of course the importance of the meeting overrode the importance of their advice.'

Collins made no reply.

'You saw the tape, Mr Collins. I'll admit it was not as clear as we would like it and we will have it enhanced to give us more, but from the kind of movement Kerry made, I would have said she was counting money.'

Collins shrugged.

Handford persisted. 'There were no photographs of old Bradford in that envelope; there was money. Why are you giving her money, Mr Collins? Is she blackmailing you?'

Seconds passed and as the blood drained from Collins' face again, his hands began to tremble. He was an animal caught in a trap. It was not the first time Handford had seen that kind of reaction. It nearly always came when a person was aware the police had got it right and had very little in the way of fight left with which to counter it. 'No, you're wrong.' He tried to sound firm but his voice was too high-pitched. Again he cleared his throat. 'I was not giving her money.' He placed increasingly hysterical emphasis on each word.

As though ignoring the frantic denial, Handford continued. 'What does she know that gives her the ability to blackmail you?'

Leo Bayliss, who had been silent up to now, turned to Collins, placed a hand on his arm and shook his head to warn him not to answer any more questions. He turned to Handford. 'This has to stop, Inspector. You have absolutely no evidence to substantiate any of this, except some grainy CCTV footage. I am advising my client to leave, unless of course you intend to arrest him for meeting and talking to a girl in the cemetery.' The solicitor pushed the top on his pen, stood up and began to pack away his notepad.

Handford pushed back his chair. 'I have no intention of arresting your client at the moment, Mr Bayliss, and certainly he is free to go.' Again he paused. 'It's just that I wonder why, if the meeting was so innocent, Mr Collins hasn't seen fit to mention it to his wife. When I spoke to her this morning she had never heard of Kerry Johnson, neither was she aware that she was a pupil at the school or that her husband was helping her with her interest in local history. What I'm asking myself is why, if the meeting was so innocent, does your wife have no knowledge of the girl you say you are helping?'

Collins sat for a moment, his right hand compressing the knuckles of his left, then, unable to contain his anger any longer, his ability to fight returned and he threw back his chair. In one leap he was over the table. Handford dodged as best he could in such a confined space, raising his arms for protection, but Collins was close to him and rained blows at his head and body, some making contact, some not.

Leo Bayliss leaned over the table in an attempt to grab at Collins, but the man was punching wildly and he couldn't get a hold. In less than a second, Ali had slapped at the alarm strip on the wall, then as Collins flailed his arm once again to hit out at Handford, the sergeant caught it, thrust it behind the man's back and pushed him down towards the table, his face contorted amongst the graffiti. The door flew open and four or five police officers in uniform rushed in. Ali stood back. 'What kept you?' he asked breathlessly, then waved them away. 'It's all right, we have it under control.'

As the door closed behind them, Collins' anger dissipated and he stopped struggling. Ali pulled him to his feet. 'Sit down and stay there,' he said, not unkindly, then turned to Handford. 'Are you all right, sir?'

He wasn't; he was too old for attacks of this kind, but he said, 'Fine.'

Collins raised his head. 'You bastard,' he shouted his voice breaking up. 'How dare you bring my wife into this? Leave her out of it; she's done nothing.'

More calmly than he felt, Handford leaned over him. 'Then tell her, Mr Collins; tell her whatever it is you're hiding, and then when you've told her, come back and tell us. Because until you do, I will not leave either you or her alone.'

Without being invited, Ali followed his boss into his office and banged the door closed. He marched towards him. 'What were you doing just now, John?'

Handford sat down behind his desk, but remained silent.

'You saw him; you saw the state he was in. You shouldn't have been so hard on him. It's no wonder he went for you.'

Handford concentrated his gaze on the sergeant. 'Anything else?'

'Yes. You broke every rule in the book in that interview. You told him what we suspected and

299

then when you had every reason to keep him here, if only to let him calm down, you released him.'

Handford felt the anger in the words and the atmosphere thickened. 'Is this a bollocking?'

Ali stiffened. 'If you like.'

Handford glared at him. 'No, Sergeant, I don't like.' He let the words hang in the air for a moment, making sure Ali knew that he meant them, then said, 'I knew what I was doing.'

'Did you? The first thing he'll do is contact Kerry Johnson, tell her what we know, and they'll get their stories straight. It'll be a waste of time questioning her.'

Handford objected to being under siege like this, having to explain his every action to his sergeant. 'Don't you think they've already got their stories straight? Neither of them is going to risk the other saying something different. I'll bet they've had their stories straight since the first blackmail demand.'.

Ali grabbed a chair. 'Can I?'

Handford nodded.

'What is it with this obsession that she's blackmailing him? You have no proof.'

'For God's sake, Ali, you saw the tape and you saw his reaction. She was counting money and why else should he give her money – or if you insist he wasn't, photographs of old Bradford – and not tell his wife? She's blackmailing him I tell you. I just don't know why. She has something on him, something he doesn't want anyone to know, but whatever it is, it's enough for him to pay her to keep quiet.'

Ali settled himself. 'I don't agree with you, John, but let's say for the sake of argument you're right. Perhaps what Shayla Richards said was true and he did assault her and somehow Kerry knows it.'

'It could be that; it would make sense of her persuading Shayla to change her story. If she hadn't and he'd been found guilty, the money would have dried up.'

'But why wait so long? Why let it get to trial?'

'I don't know.'

'And why would Shayla agree?'

'Because Kerry was the only friend she had.' Handford pondered. 'The trouble is, I'm not convinced that's the reason for the blackmail. I have a feeling that whatever the hold is that Kerry Johnson has over Graham Collins, it's not the assault, it's something else. My intention at the interview was to shock him into telling us.' For the first time he let his eyes slide away from Ali's. He took a deep breath which he let out slowly, then said, 'You're right, Khalid, I did break every rule in the book, but I was trying to make something happen.'

'You certainly did that. The man's at flashpoint and he could have hurt you badly. It was stupid and dangerous to do what you did, John. I just hope for your sake it doesn't backfire on you in a way you don't expect – like a complaint.'

Handford hoped so too. He pushed himself from the chair and wandered over to the window. The storm that had broken over the city had moved on, leaving in its wake a fine drizzle. A wintry sun pummelled at the thinning blanket of clouds to bring some brightness to the day, but the wind that had been forecast was beginning to make its presence felt. Handford watched as a woman tried to control her umbrella and at the same time avoid the pools of water that had gathered where the flagstones were in need of repair. He turned. 'Kerry Johnson was in school today – Atherton told me. Yet when I spoke to her on Sunday morning she said she doesn't do school. So why go today?' In spite of the suffocating warmth of the station's central heating system, he shivered. An image of Gill edged its way into his mind. How had she fared? Had she kept herself to herself, or had she had to run the gauntlet of Siddique's bitterness? He shivered again as the teaching assistant's words came flooding back. *Before I've finished I'll have both you and your wife out of Cliffe Top Comprehensive, and I won't do it quietly.* Handford determined that come what may he would be home early today, just in case.

He regained his seat. 'You'd better pay a visit to Kerry Johnson. She'll be expecting it.' As Ali opened his mouth to argue, Handford lifted his hands. 'I know, I know, but we need something from her for the record, even if it's only that he was giving her pictures of old Bradford. And find out why she was in school.'

'What are you going to do?'

'I don't know yet.' He pointed to his in-tray. 'There's plenty of this.'

Ali stood. 'I'll leave you to it, then.' As he walked to the door, it opened and Warrender side-stepped past him.

'Don't you ever knock?' Ali asked.

He grinned at the sergeant, ignored the question and said, 'I gather you saved our esteemed DI from a fate worse than death this afternoon. I didn't know you had it in you. I shall have to watch it from now on. You can't be too careful with you people.'

Before Ali had a chance to bite back and in the process become the subject yet again of another of Warrender's double meanings, Handford said, 'I can't imagine you came to tell us what we already know, Warrender.'

'No, boss, as much as I'm in awe of Sergeant Ali, this is a lot more interesting. The school Collins went to was destroyed in a fire shortly after he said he left. It wasn't suspicious – an electrical fault, apparently. All records were lost, so there's nothing to say he was there at all. Also the military police got back to me. The only Major Collins to be killed in the Gulf War was thirty-one – too young to be Graham Collins' father, *and* he was a bachelor – so there was no Mrs Collins or a young Graham Collins in any of their records. In fact I haven't managed to trace a Mrs Collins who died of breast cancer in 1992 at all yet, or indeed confirm Graham's birth in 1973; I've got a lovely lady at the Family Records Office working on it for me and I'll let you know as soon as she gets back to me.' He winked at Ali. 'Pity she's in London. She sounds just my type.'

Ali glared at the constable. 'I'll get on, guv,' he said.

Handford indicated his agreement and as the door closed, he said, 'Give your lady a call,

303

Warrender, and ask her to look for Graham Samuel Collins, parents Martin and Rebecca Collins.'

'I'll pass it on to her, guv. In fact it'll be a pleasure.'

'Now we've got his full name, we might get somewhere.' He sat back and put his hands behind his head. 'Am I the only one who can see that there's something very wrong here, Warrender? Sergeant Ali thinks I'm obsessed with what he calls Collins' non-existent past. He has just made his feelings very clear to me. The trouble is, I can't argue with him, because all I have is an instinct.'

Warrender sat on the chair Ali had vacated. 'Anyone would think he'd never worked on instinct before. He's always doing it. The trouble is, his instinct isn't as experienced as ours.'

Handford ought to stop Warrender there, not give him a chance to criticize Ali. But it was too late; he already had, so he let him continue.

'If Sergeant Ali thought about it, he'd realize we've got a man in our midst called Graham Collins, middle name Samuel, whose parents seem to be a figment of his imagination and who, as far as I can see, didn't exist before he went to university in Warwick in 1992. You don't need instinct to know that something's not right here. And if it's not right, it could be important. Don't you let it go, boss, because I'm with you on this.'

Graham Collins stared in front of him as the windscreen wipers flashed across the glass. Backwards and forwards, tick tock. Jane, Kerry. Shayla, murder. The rhythm lodged in his brain

304

like a monster he couldn't rid himself of. Death, prison. He slapped his hands against his ears. Incarceration, blackmail.

He'd rung Kerry, told her what Handford knew. She was furious. Her words reverberated round in his brain. She held him responsible. It was his bloody fault. Why hadn't he known there were cameras in the cemetery? He was a fucking teacher after all.

He'd countered. Why hadn't she? She lived next to the cemetery.

Yeah, lived next to it, but hardly ever went into it. Why should she? She wasn't a bloody stiff.

She'd sworn at him, blamed him, told him that if the police accused her of blackmail she'd tell all she knew, go to Mrs Richards, go to the papers, shout it from the top of City bloody Hall. She might as well; he'd be no use to her when she was banged up in fucking prison.

He'd babbled; if they stuck to the story they'd agreed, the police wouldn't be able to prove anything. The tape wasn't that clear.

They'd take it, have it made clearer and then they'd frigging know.

He'd pleaded with her again to stick to the story, not to tell them. He'd give her more money, anything she wanted. He'd said she couldn't tell, it wouldn't be legal, not after what the judge had said. The papers wouldn't print; they'd be in trouble. *She'd* be in trouble.

What did she care? 'Watch me,' she'd said, then, 'Piss off.' And she'd cut the connection.

He played out the scenario. The police would accuse her of blackmail. They had to. It was on

305

record. It had been alleged, so it had to be followed up. They would ask why and she would tell them. He felt himself beginning to hyperventilate; he inhaled and blew a lungful of air into the car, misting over the windows. He rubbed them clear. Tried to think. Even when they knew, they couldn't do anything, not after what the judge had said. But Jane would find out – Kerry would tell her. And then she'd tell Mrs Richards, who'd bring her posse down to the house again. This time there'd be snarling vigilantes, their faces contorted with hatred, no one believing him, everyone believing her. Bricks and stones through the windows, filth painted on the walls, just like before, only worse this time. Jane would blame him as well; she'd leave him. And even if she didn't, he saw the rest of their lives stretching ahead of them, contaminated, infected, and he recognized his future for what it was – inexorably linked to his past, a past he would never shake off, but most of all a past he couldn't encumber Jane with. It had stomped back into his present with a fury he thought he'd learned to contain. The animal in him was still alive. Now he knew for certain it was time to do something about it. He'd stared into the void for too long.

He saw Mr Heywood looking at him from the window. He'd watch over Jane, see she came to no harm. Graham Collins waved and put the car into gear. He knew exactly what he was going to do, what he had to do. If he was honest he'd always known it would end like this.

Jane Collins drove home after her shift. It hadn't

been a good day. She ought to have called in at the supermarket, but she couldn't stomach the thought of the people and the queues. The other nurses had talked behind her back about the bruise on her face; she knew that's what they were doing because they stopped, embarrassed, as soon as she approached the nurses' station. She'd ignored them as best she could, but it was only because they were so busy that she'd got through the shift without breaking down. She hadn't been able to ignore the fact that the police had taken Graham to the station though. She'd been desperately worried about him since Inspector Handford had left. She had heard nothing and didn't know if he was still being interviewed or even if he would be home that night.

The house seemed deserted. The curtains were open, the windows dark. No car in the drive, the garage doors down. Her heart lurched; they'd arrested him. Or he was out running. Fingers crossed, he was out running and had forgotten to close the curtains. Not surprising with so much on his mind. She'd leave her car on the road, so that he could put his in the garage when he returned. She pressed the electronic fob and as the hazard warning lights flashed she walked towards the front door.

There was a noise. A chugging. The air was suddenly cloying, clogging in her throat. For a moment she didn't understand, then realized. She threw her bags onto the ground and wrenched at the garage door. As it opened a choking mist met her. She coughed, spluttered as she forced herself between the vehicle and the wall. The windows were wound down and through the haze she could make out Graham's shape, his head slumped onto the steering wheel. Pray God he wasn't dead. Frantically she pulled at the door, falling backwards as it flew open and Graham slumped sideways.

Turn off the ignition.

Get him into the open.

She manoeuvred herself into a position where she could kill the engine. Graham's body slipped further. She slid her arms under his armpits and as far round his chest as she could stretch, then dragged him with all her strength out of the car, his feet bouncing onto the concrete of the garage floor as they slid off the edge. Even with the garage door open, the air was heavy with fumes. She felt his pulse. It was there, weak, but there. She needed to get him out of the gas, let him breathe oxygen. She took a deep breath and heaved him for one last time onto the driveway. Finally they were outside in the cold and the rain and she pulled out her mobile.

As she finished the call she felt a tap on her shoulder. Mr Heywood. He handed her a coat. She smiled her thanks and draped it over her husband, then sat beside him on the wet concrete. Mr Heywood sat with her, his arms round her shoulders until they heard the screaming siren of the ambulance.

John Handford was deep in paperwork when the news of Graham Collins' attempted suicide came through. Clarke brought it in to him. 'Graham Collins,' he said. 'He's in the Royal. He tried to kill himself.'

Handford looked at him in horror. 'When? How?'

'An hour or more ago. Shut himself in the garage and turned on the engine. Would have succeeded had his wife not got home. She was supposed to be going to the supermarket but decided against it. Just as well she did. He'd have been dead if she'd been much later.'

'Is he going to be all right?'

'I think so, providing he doesn't go into respiratory failure. I'm not sure about mentally though. He's attempted to kill himself and failed. Keeps asking why they didn't let him die. They've got him sedated – not enough staff for suicide watch – but even so he's on fifteen-minute observations. Not that his wife's moving an inch until she's sure he'll not do it again. He'll see a psychiatrist when he's well enough, but we all know that what he needs is for us to stop treating him as a suspect, and we can't do that. Anyway, Jane Collins has said she will keep us in touch; I've given her your mobile number in case you've gone home when she rings.'

'Did he leave a note?'

'More a letter really – personal to Jane. She won't let us see it, not yet.'

Handford dropped his head and cradled it in his hands. 'This is my fault,' he moaned when he looked up. 'I pushed him too far this afternoon. Everyone warned me he was close to the edge, even his solicitor.'

'No, John, it's not your fault; you did what you had to do.'

'I don't think Ali will see it that way. Does he know?'

'Not yet, no.'

Handford pushed back his chair. 'I'm going to the hospital.'

Clarke put his hand on his boss's arm. 'I don't think that's a good idea, John. You don't want to inflame the situation. Leave them be for the night. You can visit in the morning. Everyone will know more then. Anyway, I thought you wanted to get home for Gill.'

'I did. I do.' Handford picked up his briefcase and began to push in the files from his desk. 'You're right; I'll go tomorrow on my way in. Do me a favour, though: let Khalid know what's happened, but for God's sake keep him away from the hospital as well.'

'Leave it to me.'

Handford shrugged into his coat. 'Oh God, Andy, how stupid.'

'You or Collins?'

Handford grinned ruefully. Andy Clarke never minced his words. 'Both, I suppose.' He moved towards the door. 'You know, Khalid warned me that the interview could backfire but I don't think even he envisaged just how much.'

chapter sixteen

Gill Handford handed her husband his whisky, then poured herself a generous measure of red wine. 'You know they're going to blame you for his suicide attempt, don't you?'

'Probably,' he said, 'but I'm thick skinned.'

She settled herself in the corner of the settee and curled her legs beneath her. 'Were you hard on him?'

'Khalid thinks I was.'

'Too hard?'

He attempted to explain. 'He wasn't helping himself, Gill. I had to try and break him open.'

'Well, you certainly did that.'

'Yes. But not before he got his own back by attacking me.'

Her eyes widened. 'Graham did? He attacked you physically?'

'He jumped over the table and laid into me.' For the first time that evening, Handford smiled. 'Believe you me, he can pack quite a punch.' He emptied his glass and savoured the warmth of the whisky as it drained into his stomach. It was just what he needed to relax him. Attacks on police officers of the kind he had suffered at the hands of Graham Collins were not unknown, but he wasn't a young copper any more and the older he got, the harder they were to take.

Gill unfurled herself from the settee and

poured him another drink. 'I hope you didn't arrest him for it.'

'No, I didn't,' Handford said, mildly offended that her sympathy appeared to be directed towards the teacher instead of him. 'Khalid thought I ought to have done. In fact he wanted me to have him charged and kept in the cells until he'd calmed down.'

If the comment had been meant to show Handford in a better light, it failed miserably as Gill said softly, 'Perhaps if you had he wouldn't be lying in the Royal now.'

Slighted, he set his glass down on the coffee table with more force than he had meant to. Gill had always been his conscience, but she had also always been his support. Now for the first time he felt he was losing that. 'What do you want, Gill? For me to charge him, or not to charge him, to leave him alone or not leave him alone? Because it seems at the moment I can't do right for doing wrong. The man could be a murderer. What do you think I should have done? Pussyfoot around him? Or perhaps you'd rather he goes free anyway, just to please Cliffe Top Comprehensive? Never mind that he might have killed Shayla, never mind that Mrs Richards may never get closure on her daughter's death.' He pulled himself up sharp, immediately regretting the words; he shouldn't have spoken to her like that. A pain struck him between the eyes and he massaged his forehead with the fingers of his right hand.

Gill stretched over and placed a hand on his arm. 'No, of course not,' she said. 'It's just that the staff will blame you and I will catch the

312

fallout, and to be honest it doesn't matter how many times I say you're only doing your job, it will make no difference.'

Handford made no comment. There was no comfort he could give her, except to say he was sorry, and he knew that would appear shallow without an agreement to pass the case to another officer tacked on to it, so they sat in silence until Gill said, 'The boss asked me to go on a course today. In aid of my career development, he said.'

'Are you going?'

'It's a two-week residential at the conference centre in Windermere; it starts tomorrow and it has nothing to do with developing my career. No, I'm not going.'

Handford frowned. 'He's trying to get you out of the school until all this blows over?'

'It would seem so, although my departure would give him more than just breathing space. There's to be a vote of no confidence in him at a staff meeting tomorrow and I imagine he hopes that by getting rid of me, he can show where his loyalties lie and it will go his way.' Her gaze remained steady on Handford's and he knew there was more. 'They're also intending to discuss the best way of helping Graham as well as bringing to an end what they see as harassment of him by the governors and the police.'

'By the police they mean me?' His face tightened with annoyance and the grim smile he attempted was hard round the edges.

'Yes, I think so.'

'What are they hoping, Gill? That the DCI will take me off the case?' He shook his head. 'It

313

won't happen. Russell isn't going to allow the public to decide who investigates a murder. And even if he did give into the pressure, someone else would be assigned.'

'But not someone who is sleeping with the school's head of English and who might indulge in pillow talk. Even now...' Her exasperation seeped between them. 'I'm confirming their worst fears by telling you about the meeting. That's why I haven't been invited to it, in case I pass on information.'

He stared at her. 'Can they do that – leave you out?'

'I don't know. It's been called by the unions and I'm a union member, but if they think my attendance might be prejudicial or embarrassing, then yes, I suppose they can.'

'And the unions are behind this?'

'They've called the meeting, but as far as I understand it, it was Jaswant Siddique and his cronies who asked them to. The truth is the unions might have tried to persuade them against it if you hadn't come into school today.'

'You saw me?'

'No, in fact I was the last to know.' The bitterness of her tone was that of someone who had bitten into a fruit to find it rotten on the inside. 'The boss told me he had something he wanted you to see.'

Handford made no attempt to answer the implied question.

'Well, whatever it was,' she said finally, 'at the end of the meeting you asked to speak to Jaswant. When he arrived at the office, he heard you thank

Atherton for his cooperation and didn't like it. He saw it as disloyalty on the Head's part and went to the unions, who gave into his demands and called the meeting. I imagine he said that if they didn't he would, and since there's enough concern for Graham Collins and dislike of Brian Atherton among the staff, they had to agree.'

Handford downed the last of his whisky. He held onto the glass, rotating it between the palms of his hands while he considered the implications for himself and for Gill. What was going on in that school? More than concern for Graham Collins and dislike of Brian Atherton, he was willing to bet.

'What gives Siddique his power, Gill?' he asked eventually. 'He's a teaching assistant, yet he has the unions at his beck and call and Atherton is terrified of him.'

'He's a militant. He always has been, from the first moment he set foot in the school. He has forceful views and articulates them well; he takes people with him.'

'But why does he make you into the monster? And more to the point, why was he harassing you during the allegation investigation when I wasn't involved? Whatever his reasoning, I can't help thinking that his current behaviour is more to do with you than with me.' He placed his glass on the table and leaned towards her. 'I wonder if he believes you know something about him that you didn't pass on last time and he's afraid that this time you might – perhaps to do with the original assault. Do you?'

'No, absolutely nothing. Why on earth should

315

he think I do?'

'I don't know. Perhaps he believes you either saw or heard something that would tie him in to the allegation.'

'No John, you're seeing something that isn't there. Jaswant is a good friend of Graham's. He's seen what all this has done to him and all he's doing is trying to right what he believes to be an injustice.'

'I don't think he is, Gill. Jane Collins has never heard of him. If he was such a good friend surely her husband would have mentioned him.'

Angrily, his wife stood up. 'You're being ridiculous. You seem to have forgotten they've had a hell of a two years when he hasn't been allowed to communicate with the staff. I should think very few names have cropped up during that time.'

Handford looked up at her, sadness clutching at him, then he grabbed her hands and held them between his, before pulling her gently back onto the settee. 'Maybe you're right,' he said. 'But even if I accept Siddique's reasons for fighting to have Collins reinstated, I'm still left with the question of why he is going to so much trouble to get me off his back and you out of school.'

Gill made no reply. Her expression was strained and he hated himself for it, but he couldn't stop now. 'Think back. Is there anything you have seen which could be prejudicial to him, perhaps a relationship he had with Shayla Richards that you could know about? Was he ever over-familiar with her at any time?'

'No, I can't think of anything,' she said im-

316

patiently. 'And I don't think you should be asking me, either. I've told you once before I won't discuss colleagues with you.'

'And I'm sorry, Gill but you might have to.' His words were measured and regret wrenched at the knots in his stomach. 'The link in Shayla Richards' death is Cliffe Top Comprehensive and the original assault. There's a lot I don't understand yet, but what I do know is that Siddique sees you as a threat. He did before and he does now and the only way I can account for it is that somehow he was or is involved in what happened to her.'

'So now you're saying he murdered Shayla?' Her voice was laced with sarcasm and she pulled her hands abruptly from his.

Handford flinched. 'I don't know. The pathologist insists it would have taken two to smother her. She was killed some time on Thursday. Collins' alibi is weak to say the least and Siddique doesn't work in school on that day. He told me he was at the college and I'm having that checked out, but if he wasn't then it's not beyond the bounds of possibility that the two of them are involved.' He paused as if making up his mind. 'I'm going to tell you something now that I really ought not to.' Was he taking her into his confidence or absolving himself from the guilt he felt? He didn't know. 'The information Brian Atherton had for me was a CCTV tape from the cemetery. It showed Graham Collins meeting Kerry Johnson and giving her an envelope. She checked the contents in the way you would check money. Collins won't admit it, but I think she's blackmailing

317

him. I don't know what she knows and he's not telling me. Today she was in school – for the first time in a long time, I imagine.'

'Except for Friday, yes.'

'Friday? The day the news about Shayla's murder broke?'

Gill sighed. 'There's nothing sinister in the day, John. It's typical of truants to turn up for no apparent reason.'

Handford wasn't so sure. 'While she's been in school has she met up with Jaswant Siddique at all?'

Gill nodded. 'He's not there Fridays, but I saw her talking to him a few times today. Surely you're not suggesting she was involved in Shayla's death?'

'No, I'm not. But she knows something about Graham Collins and if he *is* charged with her murder, then the blackmail money will dry up. Siddique, for his own reasons, doesn't want Collins investigated; Kerry knows this and joins with him to muddy the waters. You and Atherton are the scapegoats.'

'I don't believe you. Kerry is a fifteen-year-old kid who's had a tough life. Yes, she truants and shoplifts and is streetwise, but a blackmailer? I don't think so. And as for Jaswant; he's not a favourite of mine, but to suggest he has had some involvement with Shayla is ludicrous.'

Handford fought his way through her fury. 'Nevertheless, Gill, I intend to find out why he's treating you like this and what he thinks you know.'

'So you'll question him again, no matter how it

affects me?'

'Yes, I'll question him.' He hesitated, hardly daring to put into words what was in his mind. 'And you.'

'Me?'

Unable to speak, he nodded. With two words, he had turned his wife into a possible witness – although of what he wasn't sure.

'But I don't know anything.'

Handford was persistent. 'No, Gill; you *think* you don't. We can use cognitive interviewing techniques. They're designed to help with memory recall. Warrender's trained and if there's anything there he'll bring it out. I hope we won't have to and I promise I'll leave it as long as I can.'

'And if I refuse?' There was a hint of defiance in her voice.

Tiredness engulfed his body. 'Then I'll have to think again,' he said quietly. 'But I hope you'll consider carefully what might be at stake if you turn me down.'

Kerry Johnson clutched the cushion to her body and glared at the two police officers sitting in the armchairs across from her. She was taller and older than Ali expected and had an air of maturity about her that no fifteen-year-old should have. It wasn't just the red lipstick or the heavy mascara, or indeed the cigarette she was smoking, it was the expression in her eyes, eyes packed with knowledge and experience built up over her few short years – most of it bad, he shouldn't wonder. As he studied her, he determined more than ever that his own children would never come into

319

contact with the kind of lifestyle she had suffered. They would be protected in a way she had never been.

Sean huddled next to her in the corner of the settee. Ali had insisted he stay since she was only fifteen, but it was obvious he was going to be of little use either to her or to them. He appeared terrified, sure perhaps they were going to accuse him of killing Shayla. Ali had tried to reassure him that it was Kerry they'd come to see, but he wasn't to be mollified. Ali understood his fear; the man had had to live with it ever since he'd come out of prison on parole. He'd tried to calm him, telling him all he had to do was to sit in while they questioned Kerry and make sure she was all right. And that's exactly what he was doing, sitting hunched up, unnoticed, pulling on one of his roll-ups, a mug of tea on the floor next to him. Even when Warrender had asked him how he was, he'd grunted but not moved.

Ali glanced at his watch. He didn't want to be here either; he had better things he could be doing. He'd told Handford it would be a complete waste of time and sitting here with Kerry's defiance, he knew he'd been right. She was too sure of herself for Graham Collins not to have been in touch with her. Their stories would match, probably word for word and there would be nothing Ali or anyone else could do about it except go through the motions and get it over with as quickly as possible.

'You were in the cemetery this morning?' he asked.

'So?'

'What were you doing there?'

'What's it got to do with you?' She wasn't going to make it easy for them. 'And anyway, how did you know I was in the cemetery?'

'You were caught on CCTV.'

She looked surprised. 'There are cameras in the cemetery? Since when?' Either she hadn't spoken to Collins, which he doubted, or she was playing games with them and Ali, for one, didn't take kindly to being wrong-footed by a fifteen-year-old. 'The footage showed you meeting Mr Collins. He gave you an envelope.'

'So?' It was a word she liked.

'What was in it?'

'Mind your own fucking business.'

Ali ignored her expletives. 'You seemed to be counting something. My boss thinks it was money.'

'Well, your boss needs his eyes testing.'

Warrender said, 'So what was in the envelope?'

She turned to him and grinned. 'What did you say your name was?'

'Detective Constable Warrender.'

She pointed to Ali and said, 'Is he *your* boss?'

Warrender leaned forwards. 'Between you and me, he thinks he is, and I let him go on thinking that; it's good for his ego. So, if you don't mind I'd be grateful if you'd humour him, otherwise he'll get annoyed and when he's annoyed he slows down and if he slows down we'll be here for ever and I've got a hot date tonight.'

He winked at Ali, who shifted in the chair. Whatever the situation, the man never missed an opportunity to embarrass him.

'So do me a favour luv,' Warrender went on, 'and tell him what was in the envelope.'

'It's like pulling teeth questioning me, isn't it?' She seemed proud of her ability to lead them on. Slowly she picked up an ashtray from the table and flicked the ash from her cigarette into it. 'Go on then, I'll tell yer. There were some pictures in it.'

'Of what?'

She sighed as if it was all too much. 'Well, they weren't mucky if that's what you're thinking; they're of Bradford in the olden days.'

Warrender turned to Sean. 'She interested in local history then, your niece?'

Sean shrugged and sank further into the upholstery.

'There's no point asking him,' Kerry interjected. 'He's a moron. Yes, I'm interested in local history. Anything wrong with that?'

'No, nothing.'

Ali had had enough of the banter between Warrender and Kerry Johnson and took over. 'How long has Mr Collins been giving you postcards?' he asked abruptly.

'A while – from before he was kicked out of the school.' She waited for a reaction and when none was forthcoming she said, 'He knew I was interested in local history, and one day I met him when he was out running and we got talking and he told me he would look out for photos and things for me. Do you want to see those he gave me this morning?'

Ali should have expected that. 'You've got them?'

'Of course I've bloody got them. There'd be no point him giving me them if all I was going to do was throw them away.' She turned to Warrender. 'Is he always like this?'

'Only on Mondays and Thursdays. The rest of the week he's worse.'

She walked over to the sideboard and picked an envelope out of the drawer. From it she pulled a series of cards and handed them to the sergeant.

He glanced at her coldly, then carefully and methodically took a quick look at each picture before turning the card over: Lister Park 1914; Bridge Street from the bottom of Sunbridge Road, circa 1900; Darley Street in the late nineteen twenties; back to back housing, 1910; and a picture of a horse-drawn fire engine belonging to Bradford City Fire Brigade, 1905. They were certainly what she had said they were. He handed them to Warrender, who flicked through them and nodded. 'Can I take them with me?' Ali asked.

For the first time her confidence faltered. 'Why?'

'To let my boss see them.'

She didn't seem too certain. 'Well, you take care of them. He went to a lot of trouble to get me those.'

'I will, don't worry. The envelope as well, please.'

Reluctantly, it seemed, she handed it to him. It was brown, rectangular, and similar to the one on the tape – nothing unusual, they could be bought anywhere. Warrender took a plastic wallet from his pocket and dropped the postcards and the envelope into it. For the first time in the interview Kerry's self-assurance fractured and the smirk that had been there throughout slid away. She took a final drag on her cigarette and stubbed it out in the ashtray. Without speaking she picked up an open packet from the mantelpiece and fumbled inside it. It was empty. Angrily she threw it back, but it bounced from the ledge and onto the threadbare rug.

Warrender bent forward to pick it up. He felt in his pocket. 'Here, have these,' he said. Without thanking him, she grabbed at the packet, opened it and pulled out a cigarette. She slipped it between her lips. Picking the box of matches from the table, she attempted to extract one, but her hands were shaking and they showered onto the floor. Warrender crouched down to rescue them and return them to the box. One he struck and held to the tip of the cigarette. The tobacco glowed red and she pulled the smoke and the nicotine into her lungs.

Ali watched the scenario. He doubted he would ever really understand Warrender. The man hated smoking almost as much as he hated the Asian population, yet he always carried a packet in his pocket for just such an occasion and it didn't concern him that he was giving them to an underage girl. Many a nervous suspect or witness had reason to be grateful to him. And there was no doubt that when the postcards and the envelope had been dropped into the plastic packet, Kerry Johnson had become nervous.

Ali capitalized on it. 'You didn't know about the CCTV cameras?'

She shrugged again, calmer now. 'Might have

done. I don't make a habit of going into the cemetery.'

'You don't make a habit of going to school either, do you?'

'No, don't like school. It's a waste of time.'

'So why were you there today?'

'Felt like it.'

'Your gang as well – they felt like it, did they?'

Suddenly her patience snapped and she shouted, 'What you getting at, copper?'

Sean started, snatched out of his stupor. He made to pull himself out of his chair, but stopped when Ali lifted his hand as though he was halting traffic.

'I wondered why you were all there today, when mostly you truant,' Ali said steadily, his eyes still fixed on Sean.

'Sometimes we don't feel like it, sometimes we do.'

'I'm told you felt like it on Friday as well. The day Shayla Richards' body was found.'

Before she could answer, Sean said, 'No she wasn't, she was 'ere.' The colour had faded from his cheeks and he coughed as he pulled hard at his cigarette.

Kerry kicked out at him, catching his foot and he shuffled back into the settee. 'You checking up on me?' she snarled at Ali. 'You've no right. I've not done anything. I just met Collins in the cemetery to get some photos.' She tried to snatch at the plastic packet. 'I've changed my mind,' she said. 'You can't have them.'

But Warrender was quicker and slid it away from her. 'I think not,' he said.

'You got a warrant? You can't take them if you've not got a warrant.'

'Yes we can. You agreed.'

'And now I don't agree.'

Warrender smiled. 'Too late,' he said. 'We'll let you have them back when we've finished with them.'

She was breathing heavily now. 'You see you bloody well do.'

'Can we have a look in your room?'

'No, you fucking can't.'

He turned to Sean. 'What about yours?'

Sean lifted his eyes to Kerry. Fear filled them like a lake.

'His neither.'

Ali stood up. 'I think that's all for now,' he said. 'We'll be in touch if there's anything else.'

As the door shut behind them, Ali turned to Warrender. 'You don't believe her, do you?'

'Do you?'

'Actually, yes, I am inclined to.'

'You've got more faith in her than I have, Sarge. Personally I go with the boss on this. She's cunning, I'll give her that. She must be if she can get one over on you. But give it time. For all her posturing she's still a kid and she's not as clever as she thinks. She'll make a mistake eventually and then you'll see. In the meantime...'

Ali forced a smile. 'I know, you have a hot date. Don't let me stop you, Warrender. I'll take you back to the station to pick up your car and then I'll see you tomorrow – early.'

When the two detectives had gone, Kerry

326

mashed what remained of her cigarette in the ashtray and fled upstairs into her bedroom. She banged the door shut and flung herself on the bed. Why had that stupid cemetery got cameras? Why hadn't Collins known about them? Why had those coppers come and done this to her?

Bloody, fucking, stupid Collins.

Bloody, fucking, stupid coppers.

She was crying now with uncontrollable sobs. She wanted her mother. Why wasn't she here? She screamed, 'Mum, come back. I want you,' and she banged her heels on the bed like an angry child. And then in her head she pleaded with her, 'Come back, Mum, please come back.' And when there was no answer she sobbed again into her pillow.

After a few moments she heard a gentle knock at the door and ignored it, but it came again louder and Sean said, 'Kerry, are you all right?'

'Go away.'

Either he didn't hear her or he ignored her for the door opened and he stepped in. He tiptoed towards her and sat on the edge of the bed. 'Don't, Kerry,' he said. 'I don't like it when you cry.'

She wanted to push him away, but she couldn't and instead she turned and grabbed him, hanging onto him as though her life depended on it. His flesh was soft and flabby from too much beer, but its very slackness reassured and consoled her.

He stroked her hair. 'Ssh now. Come on love, don't cry; the cops 'ave gone. They won't be bothering you again.'

They sat together, her clinging to him, him

patting her hair, and she drew comfort from the odour of his body as she clung to it. Eventually the sobbing diminished and she wiped her nose with the back of her hand. 'I want my mum,' she said at last.

'I know you do, lass,' he said.

'Sometimes I think she's here and then I hear them fighting in my head and then she's screaming and I know she's never going to be here again.'

'Don't. You'll only upset yourself.'

'Everyone I love leaves me.'

'Except me. I know I'm not your mum, and I'm not always much use, but I love you and I'm not going anywhere.'

She laid her head on his chest. 'I miss Shayla as well.' And the tears came again. 'She was a right bitch sometimes, and most people thought she was a waste of space, but I miss her. We were alike, her and me. She'd lost her dad and wanted him back, and I'd lost my mum and wanted her back.' She looked up at Sean. 'There's nothing wrong with that, is there?'

'No, there's nothing wrong with that; it's natural.'

'Shayla shouldn't have died, Sean. Nothing was her fault. She didn't deserve to die.'

'No, she didn't.'

'Why did she have to die?'

Sean made no reply.

'I should have looked after her better.'

'These things 'appen luv, but you can't blame yourself.'

'I know, but–'

'No buts, Kerry. You were 'er friend and you looked out for her. She was lucky to 'ave you because if she 'adn't died, you would have gone on looking out for her. Now me...' he added. 'I was no use to you at all when the coppers came.'

She smiled through her tears and sat back and punched him in the shoulder. 'No, you weren't; in fact you were bloody useless.'

He hugged her. 'That's better, that's more like my Kerry.'

She pulled away from him and sat up, letting her legs hang over the side of the bed. 'Those coppers gave me the shivers today. Do you think they really do know about the money?'

'No, I think they're like all coppers: they decide what they know and then go about stitching you up for it. But they're going to be 'ard pressed with this one. Collins said he'd given you postcards; you showed them postcards. They don't have no choice. They've got to believe you. And *he's* not going to say anything is he, 'cos if he does, 'e's finished. Nah, forget 'em.' As if to add credence to his words, he slipped off the bed and said, 'I'll tell you what. You do your face while I make us a cup of tea, and then just for once we'll spend some of that money Collins gave you. How about the cinema first and a curry on our way back?'

chapter seventeen

Handford followed the directions the receptionist had given him. It was early, not yet breakfast
time, and the hospital's corridors were quiet,
only the occasional nurse or doctor breaking the
silence as they passed him and disappeared
through the doors into the wards. He'd tele-
phoned the sister before he'd set off to be told
Graham Collins' condition was stable and he had
passed a reasonable night. His wife had stayed
with him and was still in the hospital. In truth, he
wasn't looking forward to meeting Jane Collins;
she as much as anyone would blame him for her
husband's suicide attempt. Worse, she would
want answers from him and he was not at all sure
he even had the questions, let alone the answers.

He tried to shake away the fog clouding his
brain so that he could think more clearly, but it
lined it like cotton wool. He'd hardly slept last
night. High winds and rain had lashed at the
windows, adding their fury to the assortment of
memories, guilt trips and images that kept him
awake. He'd revisited over and over again the
argument he'd had with Gill, an argument in
which he'd seen again the concern in her face and
heard the anger and the disappointment in her
voice, but it had made him all the more determined to work the case to its end. Then eventually
the recollections had blurred into images of

Graham Collins slumped in his car as it filled with noxious fumes and the sound from his wife's screams as she tried to free him.

As a result, he'd dozed and cat-napped but mostly he'd tossed and turned, pummelling at his pillow in an attempt to find some comfort. Finally, in the early hours, exhausted, he'd dropped into a deep sleep to awake with a start and a headache to the shrill tones of the alarm. Two paracetamol and a strong mug of coffee had cleared the headache, but left behind the cloud of confusion. Gill had been asleep when he'd left and he'd reset the alarm and laid a note on his pillow. It said 'Sorry'. She'd gone up to bed early last night and was asleep when he finally turned in, so he hadn't had the chance to say it. It wasn't right to end the day with an argument.

Graham Collins was in a side ward. The door was ajar and Handford could see Jane sitting on a chair next to his bed. He tapped and went in. Her husband was asleep.

'How is he?' he asked.

Jane turned. She looked wretched. 'I could have lost him,' she said.

'I know, I'm sorry.'

'Are you? I doubt it. I told you what he was like, yet you had to push him that little bit further.'

Suddenly he was tired of being the one considered in the wrong and tired of apologizing. Anger sparked through his stupor. 'I was not pushing him, Mrs Collins; I was trying to get at the truth.'

'That he killed Shayla Richards?'

'If that is the truth, then yes.' He pulled up a

331

chair and said more quietly, 'It's not as simple as him denying that he killed Shayla. He needs to help himself by being more cooperative. Yesterday I was hoping to persuade him to be just that, but for whatever reason he refused. It was as though he'd anticipated the questions and rehearsed his answers but wasn't prepared to explain or elaborate. I don't know whether he killed her or not, but I do know he's hiding something – not just from me, but from you as well, and somehow what he is hiding or the reason why he is hiding it is preventing us from eliminating him as a suspect. When he's feeling stronger it would be in his best interest for you to persuade him to confide in you, because it's the secrets that are killing him, not me.'

'What secrets?' From behind him Peter Redmayne's tenor tones cut through the silence.

Handford turned. From the reporter's dishevelled appearance and his need for a shave it was obvious he'd been in the hospital for some time. He was carrying two Styrofoam beakers, one of which he handed to Mrs Collins. 'What secrets?' he repeated.

Handford ignored the question and said, 'How long have you been here?'

'All night. Jane rang me when they brought him in.'

Collins stirred. Mrs Collins turned towards her husband and Redmayne grabbed Handford's arm in an attempt to ease him from his chair and manoeuvre him towards the door. 'I don't think it would be a good idea for him to see you just at the moment,' he whispered.

Angrily, Handford snatched his arm away. 'Don't even think about it, Redmayne,' he warned. 'I came to see how Mr Collins was, and now I intend to continue my conversation with Mrs Collins, so unless you're keen to be arrested for obstructing the police I would appreciate it if *you* would allow us some privacy.'

Redmayne was equally as stubborn as Handford. 'That depends on her,' he insisted. 'If she wants me to stay, I will, and I can promise you, John, I'll not allow you to pressurize her as you did Graham.'

Handford's patience was wearing thin. Peter Redmayne had done nothing but get in the way since the discovery of Shayla's body. It was so easy for him to stand there and pass judgement when he hadn't been privy to what had taken place; perhaps if he had to do the job instead of just write about it, he would understand more and criticize less. But Handford wasn't prepared to argue. If the journalist wanted pressure, he would show him pressure and to hell with the late edition. 'I'm not answerable to you, but if you insist in interfering, I'll take her to the station. Here or at the station – which do you think she would rather? It's your choice, Mr Redmayne.' He emphasized the reporter's title, using it as a weapon from his rapidly diminishing arsenal.

Before Redmayne could answer, Jane Collins said, her voice weary, 'It's all right, Peter, I'll talk to the inspector. You go home, get some rest – and thanks for coming. I don't know what I would have done without you.'

'If you're sure?' Redmayne went over to her and

kissed her on the cheek. 'I'm only at the end of a phone if you want me.'

She nodded.

When he had gone, Handford said, 'Do you want to talk in here or shall we find somewhere else?'

'I'm not leaving Graham.'

He glanced over at the still-sleeping man. 'As you wish. We'll do it here.' He moved back to the chair and sat down, but before he could ask his question, she repeated Redmayne's. 'What secrets?'

For a moment he hesitated. Where to start? He could ask about the suicide attempt or he could talk to her about the man she thought of as her husband and eventually get round to his untrace-able past and the fact that he was probably being blackmailed. Whatever he did would be hard on her, but if he waited until both she and her husband got over this present trauma, he could be waiting for some time and he needed answers now, not next week. Given what she'd been through, he felt it was only fair to show some consideration.

'Tell me what happened first and then I'll answer your question.'

'I don't know, exactly. After you'd said you were taking him to the station, I didn't hear anything and I was worried about him, so instead of going to the supermarket at the end of my shift, I came straight home. The house was in darkness and I thought at first he was still with you or perhaps he'd gone running, until I passed the garage and heard the car's engine.'

'What time would this be?'

'I finished work at four, so it would be about half past when I got home. He couldn't have been in the car long, because he still had a pulse and although it was shallow he was breathing.'

Handford said, 'He left me about three o'clock. He would probably spend time with his solicitor after that, so let's assume another half an hour. From there he would drive home – say twenty minutes at that time of day. That makes it about ten to four and you got home at half past?'

'About that.'

'I will have these timings checked of course, but if he'd only been in the garage for a few minutes – and generally it takes about five for a lethal dose of carbon monoxide to build up – then what was he doing between him getting home and you arriving?'

'Probably sitting in the car deciding whether to kill himself or not.'

He caught the bitterness in her voice. 'No, I doubt it,' he said calmly. 'In my experience if he'd been sitting in the car for that length of time, he wouldn't have done it. Generally suicides who decide to jump, jump; they don't sit around wondering whether to or not. If they sit on the rooftop and wait for someone to rescue them, it's a cry for help, not a serious attempt. What I'm saying is that if Graham had had to decide whether to kill himself or not, then the chances are he would still have been sitting there when you got home. What I don't understand is why, if this was a serious attempt, he didn't show any signs of being suicidal when he left me; if anything he was angry, angry enough to attack me.'

Jane Collins put one hand over her eyes. 'No. Please no.'

Handford wished he hadn't mentioned it, but it was done now. He attempted to limit the damage. 'Don't you think, Mrs Collins, that his anger, rather than his suicide attempt, is a sign of him not coping with the interview? When he left us he was an angry man, not a defeated man. I believe something happened afterwards which decided him finally that he really couldn't cope any more.'

She challenged him. 'He hasn't been able to cope for a long time; it was being arrested and pulled into the police station by you that was the last straw.'

'He wasn't under arrest,' he countered. 'I told you that and I made it quite clear to him before we began. And he had his solicitor with him. Whatever it was that pushed him that bit too far, it was not as simple as a visit to the police station. I believe it has much more to do with what he isn't telling us. I just wish I knew what that was.' He changed direction. 'Are you sure Graham has never mentioned Kerry Johnson?'

'I told you yesterday, I've never heard of her. Who is she?'

'She was a friend of Shayla's. It seems she persuaded her to change her evidence about the allegation and admit that she lied.'

'Graham never told me that.' Her frown brought a small vertical crease to the middle of her forehead. 'Did he know?'

'I couldn't say. Perhaps that's something else you should ask him when he's well enough.' He paused, then said, 'I think he spoke to her after he left the station yesterday. Does he have a mobile?'

'Yes, it's with his belongings.' She opened the bedside cupboard, ferreted around for a moment, then pulled out a small phone. She handed it to Handford.

'I can't check this out in the hospital, so I'd like to take it with me if you don't mind.'

She shrugged. It seemed she was past caring.

Handford took a deep breath. He hated what he was about to do; Jane Collins was the victim here, and with his next question he was about to compound the belief that victims are of little importance.

'How much do you really know about your husband?'

The question caught her on the raw. 'As much as I need to know, Inspector; that he's loving and caring and that he's neither an abuser nor a killer. How much do you know about your wife?'

Handford couldn't prevent a smile hovering at the edges of his mouth. She was resilient and spirited, he'd give her that, but he was not about to reply to her question. 'When we begin a murder inquiry, we look into the background of anyone who may be involved in some way. It can't come as any surprise that we've done that with your husband. Our problem is that we cannot find any trace of him or his parents prior to October 1992 when he went to university. Even the school he says he attended was destroyed by fire shortly after he left and all records burnt. As far as we can see, he didn't exist as Graham Collins before he went to university, after which we've had no problem checking him out.'

Handford was glad to be out of the hospital. He hated the places; they had a smell all their own which seemed to cling to him for hours. It was raining heavily now and he stood in the entrance wondering whether to wait until it eased or make a dash for it. He decided on the dash and hitching his coat over his head, he ran through the deepening puddles to the car.

Struggling out of his wet coat, he threw it onto the passenger seat and clambered in, closing the door behind him. He wiped the rain off his face and hair, then opened up the plastic bag and took out Collins' mobile phone. Evidence-gathering dictated he should wait for the scientists' examination of the SIM card, but that would take an age, and for once he wasn't prepared to when there was a common sense way, so he turned it on and scrolled through the services until he came to the Call Register. Only one was listed, made yesterday afternoon following his visit to the station.

It was to Kerry Johnson.

Thank God for modern technology and that it hadn't occurred to Collins to delete that information. He would have it corroborated forensically, but it seemed she had been the last person Collins had made mobile contact with. He checked the length of the call. Ten minutes forty-six seconds. It would be interesting to know what they had found to talk about for all that time. A pity the SIM card couldn't tell him that. While he was about it, he checked text messages and voicemail, but both were empty.

He picked his own mobile from out of his jacket pocket and rang the station. Clarke answered.

Handford dictated Collins' service provider and number. 'I need his records for the last six months, up to and including yesterday. Set it in motion, will you?'

'Yes, guv. How is he?'

'Sleeping when I saw him.'

'And Mrs Collins?'

'As you would expect. Redmayne was with her; he'd been there all night from what I can gather.'

'Had he indeed? He gets everywhere, that man. He needs the hard word.'

'I've already given it to him, but I don't suppose it will make an iota of difference.'

Clarke laughed. 'Probably not. I'll make a start on requesting the records. Are you expecting anything special from them?'

'The last call was to Kerry Johnson. I want to know how many times he's rung her or she's rung him.'

Handford closed his phone and sat for a few moments watching as the rain streamed down the windscreen. It was the fifth of November; the kids would need better weather than this if they were to light their bonfires. There was to be one at his daughters' school tonight and he'd promised he would go, if he could. He always added that premise. Three words of a get-out clause when the job became more important than the family. He wondered if Kerry Johnson would be out watching the fireworks. He couldn't see Sean suggesting it, unless they had an ulterior motive and joined the crowd to snatch handbags under cover of darkness.

His mind wandered from fireworks of the explosive kind to those more metaphorical. Those that would be ignited once the news about Graham Collins filtered through to the school. Both Kerry Johnson and Jaswant Siddique would have the reason they needed to give Gill a hard time. It would have been easier for her not to go into school, but he was sure that if he'd suggested it she wouldn't have agreed. She had pupils taking exams and she was too much of a professional to let them down.

And Jane Collins. What about her? Was she too loyal a wife to wonder about her husband? She'd supported him through the allegation, but was the murder of the fifteen-year-old a step too far? Did she have any concerns at all eating away at her? He thought so. She'd scoffed when he'd told her they could find no trace of a Graham Collins prior to him going to university and said they obviously hadn't looked hard enough, but mingled with the mockery in her eyes was a patch of apprehension. As much as she didn't want to believe him, Handford was fairly sure she wouldn't leave it there. She was an intelligent woman and she would think about it, probably go hunting for his birth certificate, photographs – anything that would prove to her that Graham was who he said he was. And what if she found something? Would she keep it to herself or face him with it? Or would she bring it to Handford? He couldn't risk her doing nothing, which meant he had no choice but to apply for another warrant and invade her privacy once again.

Handford switched on the ignition and put the car into gear. He had to get back to the station for the briefing – perhaps there would be something from that to take them forward. One could but hope. They needed a break, something that would open up the cracks. It was well past the forty-eight-hour limit when information usually began to dry up. Then there were the extraneous issues clouding the investigation. Before he was forced to explain to the DCI why they were not progressing he had to bring some order to the chaos, investigate more diligently family, friends, acquaintances and the weeks Shayla was missing, while at the same time unravel the tangled threads and come at the case obliquely by keeping up the pressure on anyone who was attempting to damage the investigation for their own ends, like Jaswant Siddique and Kerry Johnson.

Particularly Kerry Johnson, for there was little doubt in Handford's mind that she was the last person Collins had spoken to before he closed the garage doors and turned on the car's engine.

When Gill Handford drove into school that morning, her stomach was a mass of quivering coils. She had considered ringing in sick, but only for a few seconds. It was not in her nature to admit defeat, which was exactly what not turning up would be. And anyway, there were her GCSE and A-level students to consider.

It shouldn't be like this; Shayla Richards' murder was nothing to do with her. She'd done nothing wrong. Yet from every perspective it seemed like she had and that she was in some way letting down her colleagues. She ought to have taken the head up on his offer of the course, because the way she was feeling at the moment, even two weeks discussing methods of teaching Shakespeare and pre-twentieth-century literature at a conference centre in Windermere in November appealed.

John had left early and when she had woken she had seen the note he had left her. She smiled at the thought. That was exactly the kind of thing he would do, and he would mean it. Sadly it was the argument he was sorry about, not the fact that he was helping this case elbow its way into their lives. She understood he couldn't hand it over to someone else, but it would have been better had he stayed away from school and refrained from questioning her. His only saving grace at the moment was that he'd left her a message on the telephone pad to say he'd rung the hospital and Graham was responding well to treatment and should be home soon.

As she drove into the car park, she caught a glimpse of Jaswant Siddique standing outside the front door. He was talking to the staff as they arrived and judging by the looks on their faces, he was telling them about Graham Collins. Fleetingly, she wondered who had told him. She turned off the engine and let her eyes span the exterior of the school. She could see the windows of her classroom, which today didn't seem that welcoming.

Annoyed at herself for her nervousness, she

gathered her things together, put up her umbrella and walked towards the entrance. Jaswant Siddique was waiting for her. He barred her way into the building, standing so harassingly close that she could smell his aftershave.

'You've heard?' he said. Before she could answer, his lips curled and he sneered, 'Of course you've heard. You would be one of the first.' Insolence rolled off him.

Gill tried to push past, but he stood in her path. 'Thanks to your husband Graham tried to kill himself last night. If he dies you can consider yourself married to a murderer.'

Had it not been for the intensity of Siddique's tone and the hatred in his eyes, Gill could have been almost amused by his words, so ridiculous were they. Or were they? Did others have the same perception of what had happened or was it just him adding his own brand of poison to the situation?

She attempted to remain impassive. 'I'm sorry to disappoint you, Jaswant, but Graham is not going to die. In fact, according to my husband who saw him this morning, he's doing well and should be home soon. So if you're going to make an accusation of murder against someone, perhaps you ought to get your facts right first. Now if you don't mind...' and she attempted to push past him.

For a moment he seemed fazed, but then said, 'That's rich coming from you. If your copper husband doesn't think Graham killed Shayla Richards, why did he have him arrested?'

'He didn't. He doesn't know who killed Shayla

343

and Graham went to the station of his own free will. And I have nothing to do with any of this, so I'd be obliged if you'd let me go into school. If you don't mind getting wet, I do.'

As he stepped to one side, he said, 'We'll see what the meeting says about you having nothing to do with any of this.'

'Yes, we will.'

He grabbed her shoulder. 'You're not invited.'

Angrily she pulled away from him. 'It's been called by the unions, Mr Siddique; I am a union member, so I don't think you can stop me. Now, if you will excuse me.'

He stood his ground and at first she thought he wasn't about to move, but when several senior students walked up the path he stood to one side to let them pass. One of them held the door open for her and she smiled her thanks.

Inside the ladies' cloakroom, she allowed herself to tremble, although she wasn't sure whether it was through anger or fear. She ought to have said more to him, asked him the questions John put to her yesterday, but the school entrance in the pouring rain at the beginning of the day was neither the time nor the place. She would wait until the meeting and ask them then. In the meantime she had a classroom to prepare.

The head was having a purge on wasting electricity and the corridor on the first floor where the English rooms were located was in semi-darkness. She looked at her watch and clicked her tongue. None of the department staff up here yet. They ought to be, and usually were. Perhaps the proposed meeting was taking their attention in the staff room. She switched on the lights and as she did so, heard a noise behind her. She wasn't sure why, but she was suddenly frightened. She turned. Facing her was Kerry Johnson, and behind her the rest of her gang.

'What do you want, Kerry? You shouldn't be up here, you know.'

She pulled her keys out of her bag and slipped one into the door lock. Kerry was close now and grabbed the key. 'How can you live with a murderer?'

Gill felt like hitting back at her with, 'You tell me,' but refrained and said instead, 'I don't, Kerry. Now give me the key.'

Kerry took a step closer, her eyes flashing. 'Mr Collins killed himself last night because of your husband.'

This had to be Siddique's doing. 'No, he didn't. Mr Collins is not dead. In fact he's much better.' She tried to stay calm. 'We don't know why he did what he did, Kerry, except there are likely to be a lot of reasons, not just one. So whoever you got your information from, you'd better put them right. Now, my keys.'

Kerry threw them to Kylie, who caught them and passed them over to Lindsay and from there to Gemma. Gill refused to play their game. She certainly wasn't going to run around like a bullied schoolgirl. They would get tired if she waited.

Suddenly, Kerry stopped and dangled them in front of her. 'Go home, Handford; you're not wanted here.' She dropped the keys on the floor and as Gill was about to tell her to pick them up, they crowded round her, chanting, 'Go home, Handford.' From nowhere it appeared others – boys and girls – crowded in on her and the chant became, 'Home, home, home.'

Gill tried not to appear frightened, but the truth was she was terrified, trapped between the semi-circle of baying students and the corridor wall, unable to push her way through, unable to retreat. Fear settled in her stomach. She tried to shout at them to go away, but even if they heard her, they took no notice.

Suddenly the bell rang, echoing along the corridor. For a moment some of those in the circle were unsure as to what to do next. One or two stepped back. The doors at the end of the corridor slammed open and Gill heard her deputy shout. 'What do you think you're doing?' He pushed his way through the melee, flinging them to one side as he did so. 'Go to your classrooms. Go on,' he yelled.

Slowly they moved, but Kerry stood her ground. 'You too, Kerry Johnson. Go to your classroom.'

The crowd had moved off, leaving Kerry standing over Gill, with Kylie, Gemma and Lindsay waiting a few paces away. They stood in silence monitoring Kerry's reaction, ready to stand their ground if she stood hers or run if she ran. Casually, she sauntered towards them. 'Come on,' she said and as she neared them she kicked at the keys. They slid across the corridor and came to a halt against the opposite wall.

'Go.'

She turned and gave the two teachers a finger, then said to the others, 'Fuck them, we're going,' as though it was her idea.

They laughed and set off along the corridor. They had taken only a few steps when Kerry turned round. 'We'll get you later, Handford,' she said.

chapter eighteen

John Handford stepped through the door of the incident room and frowned. It disturbed him that the atmosphere had deteriorated so soon from one of expectancy to one of apathy. The team's interest in the case was floundering and indifference was setting in. Except in the media, there was a noticeable lack of concern at the death of Shayla Richards and that was petering through to the investigators. He couldn't blame them; by now they should be sifting through anomalies, not still scrabbling for information.

He took in the scene, annoyed that Warrender was missing and hardly anyone working. Apart from an officer in one corner who was busy cross-checking intelligence in HOLMES, the national major enquiry database, and another entering material into the local Crime Information System computer, very little was happening. Officers stood in groups or lounged on chairs, their feet resting on the desks. Most had a mug of coffee or tea in their hands. All seemed reluctant to answer the telephones when they rang. Three computer screens gyrated coloured shapes, suggesting they had at least been turned on; the rest displayed the West Yorkshire police logo, suggesting they hadn't. Typed up reports and statements not yet filed had accumulated on tables where there wasn't a computer, and where there was, they were perched precariously on top or draped over it like antimacassars.

As a raucous burst of laughter came from one group, Handford decided it was time to step in and bring them back to the task in hand.

He stood for a few minutes and then said, 'Good Morning,' loud enough to be heard. He waited while they straightened themselves or scurried to their places before slipping between them to the front of the room. 'Where's Warrender?'

Clarke answered. 'Taking a statement, guv, from someone he saw earlier this morning. Apparently, the chap's going abroad today but he agreed to come in on his way to the airport. He'll be up as soon as he's finished.'

Handford leaned against a table. 'Do we know who this person is?'

'No, guv.'

'Or how long Warrender's going to be?'

'No, guv.'

'Then we'll not wait for him. Ali, you can bring him up to speed if necessary.'

Ali nodded.

Handford turned his attention to the rest of them. 'I've been watching you for the past few minutes and I'm left with a distinct feeling of lack of interest. It's a bit early in the investigation for that, don't you think?' The temperature in the room chilled as he let the words hang in the air for a moment and the detectives glanced at each other and shifted on their seats. 'Shayla Richards' body was found at midnight on Thursday; it's now Tuesday and we've practically nothing to bring us any nearer to knowing, let alone proving, who killed her. I know there's not been much cooperation, but that shouldn't stop us; we've all experienced it before and we know that what we have to do is get back out there and push for answers. It's the only way we'll get results.'

'Most people who knew her think she brought it on herself, guv, and the staff at the school believe we're just out to get Collins. It's a case of them and us. Neither the teachers nor her so-called friends are going to cooperate, however much we push for answers. They just don't care.'

Handford felt his facial muscles stiffen and the veins in his neck pulsating above his shirt collar as they did when he became angry. 'Then we've got to make them care by caring ourselves,' he said quietly. 'I know she was a nuisance and a troublemaker, always running away, causing us no end of grief, but if uniform hadn't taken the attitude they did, we probably wouldn't be here now investigating her death. We've let her down once and we're not going to do it again.'

Handford paused to allow his anger to dissipate. It didn't, not completely, and when he spoke there was a slight tremor to his voice. 'Have we any idea yet where she was during the weeks she was missing?' He looked towards a couple of detectives in the centre of the room.

They made a play of checking their notebooks. Finally one of them said, 'No, sir, not yet.'

'Perhaps her devils hid her,' someone whispered to his neighbour.

Handford glared at him. That was exactly the attitude adopted by uniform when she'd gone missing and he wasn't going to allow it here in

CID. 'You think the devils seized her, Constable, killed her, took her up to Druid's Altar, where they arranged her body, lit a fire and then dialled 999?'

The detective flinched and lowered his eyes to stare at the rim of the table. 'No, sir.'

The silence deepened, no one else offering to comment.

'She must have been somewhere,' Handford went on, slowly shifting his eyes to those tasked with the job of unearthing her whereabouts. 'Someone must know where she was. Find out.' His voice remained tightly controlled. He was probably being unfair – it was difficult tracing someone who hadn't wanted to be traced – but from the scene when he'd arrived and the earlier uncalled-for comment, he decided, fairness didn't come into it. 'I want you to re-interview family, known friends, neighbours, in fact anyone who came across her and played a part in her life. And this time I want you to come up with something. Ask about Druid's Altar as well. Do they know what it represents? This time, ask all the questions and when you get the answers, probe deeper. Someone out there knows something, and I want you to find that someone.' He turned to Ali. 'Are we any further with the hoax caller?'

'Not yet. I've put Jarvis and Keller on to visiting known jokers, but so far they've come up with nothing. Short of questioning and recording the voice of every Afro-Caribbean male in the district and comparing it with the 999 tape – and I can't see that going down well – there's not a lot we can do. We could put it out to the media. Perhaps someone will recognize the voice.'

'Then do it. See what comes back.'

'Sir.'

He looked over at a DS on the far side of the room. 'Put your team on checking alibis, Steve. Let's see if we can come up with anomalies second time round.'

Clarke put his hand up to attract Handford's attention. 'What about her clothes in Collins' wheelie bin?'

'Mrs Richards has identified them as Shayla's but the preliminary forensic report that came back yesterday gives us nothing scientific to link them to Collins. He insists he didn't put them there and we've nothing to prove he did.'

'I was thinking more about the clothes that weren't there. What happened to the puffa jacket? She's wearing it on all the posters, Mrs Richards told uniform it was her favourite, yet we haven't found it. It was October when she went missing; it's unlikely she'd have been wandering around without it. In fact her mother's statement indicated she had it with her. So where is it?'

Handford frowned. What was the matter with him? He should have noticed that himself. 'It wasn't in the wheelie bin, nor was it found on the moor, so any suggestions?'

'Wherever she was when she was missing or where she was killed.'

'In that case we're back to the weeks she disappeared. It seems to me they're vital to finding out who killed her.' He turned to Ali. 'I want more people on it; I want to know where she was.'

Once in his office, Handford turned on his sergeant. 'Why wasn't the fact that the puffa jacket wasn't with the skirt and the blouse considered earlier?'

They stood face to face and in close proximity to each other as Handford waited for a response.

Ali took a deep breath. 'I don't know, John. Probably because we're too busy rushing about checking on Collins' background and the possibility – the very questionable possibility – that he's being blackmailed by Kerry Johnson, that it never occurred to us.'

Handford slowly lowered himself into his chair, but left Ali standing. His eyes narrowed. 'You're saying it's my fault?'

His voice was cold and at first Ali made no reply. Then his jaw worked as though he was chewing over the words until eventually he said, 'You saw how the team are. They're frustrated at the lack of progress and you blaming them is not helping. There are murmurings that you're holding back because Gill is a teacher at Cliffe Top. They know what's going on and what's happening up at the school and they know she asked you to give up the case and you refused.'

'Do you think I'm holding back?'

'Probably not consciously, but I think subconsciously you might be.'

Handford felt himself begin to fray round the edges. This was becoming personal, yet Ali was articulating no more than what he had been wrestling with since the telephone conversation he'd had with his wife on the first day of the investigation.

'They're sympathetic, John, but that won't last. You're involving yourself with dubious peripherals because they take you away from the essentials. Forget Collins' past, forget the idea of blackmail, and concentrate on what's important.'

However accurate Ali might be about his dilemma over Gill, he was wrong about this. Handford was too experienced to assume correlations without concrete evidence, but that didn't mean that somehow Collins' past, Kerry Johnson's blackmail and Shayla Richards weren't linked. He didn't know how or why, but speculating on unknown connections was part of the investigative process and whether Ali liked it or not he intended to stay with it. 'You don't think his past or the blackmail important?'

When Ali finally answered his voice was calm and well-modulated. 'No, I don't. If you want my opinion, I think you're obsessed by both, and because of it you're losing sight of the larger picture. I think what *is* important is the allegation and the events of the last few days. In fact, I think if you'd brought Collins in when the blouse and the skirt were found in his bin, we'd have a confession by now and he would be in our cells rather than lying in a hospital bed. Instead of concentrating on breaking his alibi you've been clouding the issue by your fixation on an untraceable past and blackmail and we've been wasting time on it.'

Handford slapped his hands on the desk top. He objected to being accused of being misguided and incompetent. 'I think you'd better stop right there, Sergeant, and remember who you're talking to. You know full well why I didn't bring him in.'

For the first time there was a modicum of nervousness in Ali's manner, but not enough to stop him. 'I'm not sure I do, and nor do the rest of the team. But if, as you say, your motive was no more than that we hadn't the evidence at the time that they were Shayla's, then I'm sorry I think you were wrong and you lost us an opportunity to close this case.'

'Close it with a lot of unanswered questions. Come on, Ali, you know as well as I do the CPS wouldn't have let us proceed on what we had, even with a confession. The defence would crucify us in court. It may be that Collins did kill Shayla – heaven knows he had the motive – but we've a long way to go before we can prove it.'

'Then we concentrate on that and we forget about a past that wasn't considered relevant by Mr Slater and shouldn't be by us, and Kerry Johnson blackmailing him. She isn't a blackmailer, she's a kid. What can she possibly know about him that he would pay her money to keep quiet?'

'I don't know; that's what I'm trying to find out. And if I'm wrong then think on this: just what *is* her relationship with Collins? Because I tell you, there's something between them.'

'It's what they both said: she's interested in local history. She's an intelligent girl, so why not? When he comes across a picture she might like, he gives it to her. When we visited her she told us immediately she'd got them from Collins.'

Handford stabbed at Ali's naivety. 'When?'

'When what?' The sergeant sounded surprised.

'When did she get them from Collins?'

Ali sighed. 'Monday morning in the cemetery.'

'You're absolutely sure about that, are you? All I saw was an envelope in which he and she said there were postcards. We have no evidence one way or the other that they were.'

'Or that it was money.'

'All right, or that it was money, but you've only got to look at the CCTV tape to know that what Kerry was flicking through was not as thick as postcards. He could have contacted her and told her what had happened when he'd been with us – in fact, according to his mobile he probably did. That was why she was prepared when you called on her. He could have given her those postcards at any time and you know it. Have you checked where he got them from? A car boot sale? The Tourist Information Centre? Are they still available? You don't know because you haven't checked, have you?' Handford fixed him with a loaded stare. 'Do your own job properly, Ali, before you complain about how I'm doing mine. I am telling you now, until we know what was in that envelope, my "obsession" as you call it is still part of the investigation, and that includes Collins' untraceable past. Is that clear?'

Ali lifted his hands in submission. 'If you say so, but,' his arrogance returned, 'I want it noted that I don't agree with you.'

'It's noted,' Handford acknowledged curtly.

It was a good quarter of an hour after Ali had left that Warrender knocked on Handford's door and walked in to his office, his expression triumphant. Handford groaned inward. He'd had enough of detective superiority for one day.

'What is it, Warrender?'

'Sorry I missed the briefing, boss, but I was taking a statement.'

'Yes, Clarke told me. What was it about?'

'I've been checking Siddique and his movements.'

'Was he at the college on Thursday?'

'Yes, he was.'

Pity, he would have liked to have something to throw at Jaswant Siddique.

'He's been a part-time student there for a while,' Warrender went on. 'He took GCSEs for a few years, a couple at a time, and this year he enrolled for A-level maths. The taught sessions take place Wednesday and Friday, but in the last month he's missed more than he's attended. Thursday mornings he's timetabled to spend in the maths workshop. He was there on the day of Shayla's death but not on the list for the previous three weeks. They don't like to make a fuss with mature students, but when his tutor challenged him on his absences he said he'd been ill and produced a doctor's certificate. I rang the deputy head at the school and she corroborated it. He'd had a virus, apparently. I haven't spoken with the doctor yet, but I'm willing to bet when I get through the doctor–patient confidentiality bit, I'll get the same answer. I'll push it if it becomes necessary.'

'You think it will?'

'I think it's a possibility, boss.' The smile had disappeared and the constable's expression was serious. 'I don't trust either Siddique or Mustafa.

357

Did you know Siddique's flat is in the same building as Mustafa's consulting rooms?'

Handford was interested. 'No, I didn't.'

'Mustafa's rooms are on the ground floor, Siddique's flat on the first floor and a freelance photographer, a Gerry Cavendish, lives on the second floor. According to him, when Siddique's not at college or at work he helps Mustafa with his clients and at any other time when Mustafa wants him.'

'So Siddique may well have come across Shayla out of school?' A crack – at least Handford hoped so.

Warrender pulled up a chair and sat down. 'If he helped out Thursday afternoons, which he probably did, he couldn't have missed her. Cavendish remembers her because of the noise she made. So if Siddique was in the building at all he must have heard her. And if Cavendish is right about him helping Mustafa with his clients, the likelihood is that he was in the room with her or close by. Even though he lives on the top floor he said he could hear her screaming and shouting.'

'Wasn't he worried about what was happening down there?'

'He was. At one point he thought about telling the police or social services.'

'So why didn't he?'

'Partly because since Mustafa is a counsellor, he reckoned the girl was probably very disturbed and it was natural she would make a lot of noise, and partly because there appeared to be someone with her, who he assumed was a relative.'

'He's sure about all this?'

'Oh, yes, and he's made a statement.'

'Why didn't Calvin tell us about Siddique?'

'Probably didn't know. Mustafa's office is next to the consulting room with a door separating the two. All Siddique had to do was remain in one or other of the rooms. Calvin would never see him.'

'Why didn't Shayla mention him?'

'I don't know. Both Calvin and Cavendish said she screamed and shouted a lot and Mustafa's explanation was that it was because the devils were leaving her body. I think it's more likely the two of them were beating them out of her – or worse.'

'The pathologist said there were no signs of injury on her.'

'Sex, then. There were signs of sex. I've worked with the vice squad, guv, and you wouldn't believe the reasons given by some men – and women – for having sex. Ridding a girl of devils is as good a one as any. There are groups who look upon it as a vital part of their religion, Tantrism, for instance.'

'You're saying that Mustafa could make a case for his methods from a religious standpoint?'

'Not Islamic, but certainly from the perspective of his black magic. We know he's into it and Shayla would probably be too terrified to say anything. She'd already made one complaint of sexual assault and look where that got her. Were she to try it again no one would have believed her.'

'Have you passed any of this onto Sergeant Ali?'

'No, not yet, boss; I thought I'd better come to you first.' Warrender grimaced. 'He'll probably tell me I have a one-track mind.'

'Probably, but he needs to be in on it.' Handford picked up the phone and dialled the incident room. 'Ask Khalid to come in, will you?'

As soon as Ali was seated Warrender related what he had gleaned from Gerry Cavendish.

'What do you think?' Handford asked.

Ali thought for a long moment. 'It's possible,' he said hesitantly. 'It would make sense of Shayla's screams and the fact that the pathologist said she had either been abused systematically or was into frequent boisterous sex. But it's not enough and it doesn't tell us where she was in the four weeks before she died.'

'Not on its own, it doesn't,' Warrender said. 'But Cavendish is fairly sure someone has been living in Siddique's flat – at least up to last week when everything went quiet.'

'What did he mean by quiet?'

'When someone's around the floors creak–'

Ali interrupted. 'If that's so, then Cavendish would hear Siddique. He was at home ill.'

Warrender wasn't to be distracted. 'At home probably, but ill? I don't think so. I'm sure Mustafa knows some doctor who is prepared to hand out certificates for a fee.'

'You've no proof of that,' Ali said tersely.

'No, except that while he was at home ill for three weeks – the weeks Shayla was missing – Cavendish heard a woman's voice. And before you tell me she could have been looking after him, he insists that almost from day one there was a lot of shouting, which he assumed was them arguing. More importantly he thinks he recognized the woman's voice as that of the black girl who came to Mustafa for counselling.'

'You're saying it could have been Shayla in his flat? That's something of a leap.'

'Maybe so, and since he never actually saw her it's only conjecture, but he'd heard enough of her over the past weeks to say that it could have been her. He told me as well that one day when he passed by the flat he thought he heard crying. He'd seen Siddique go out so he knocked on the door but the crying stopped and no one answered.'

'When did it appear that whoever had been in the flat had gone?' Handford asked.

'Shortly after that, in the last week, the twenty-fourth or twenty-fifth, because from then on he heard nothing.'

Handford needed to bring all this together, to see whether there was something in it or nothing. 'Okay, for argument's sake let's assume Mustafa and Siddique have been holding Shayla. If they moved her, we have to find out where to. And if they moved her did they kill her to stop her talking? Placing her at Druid's Altar and arranging the body would be just the kind of thing Mustafa might do.'

'What about the hoax calls?' Ali said.

'They don't feature and we can forget them.' Handford stood up and walked over to the window, remained motionless for a moment and then turned to face the detectives. 'If, however, what Cavendish says is accurate, then either she was being held against her will, or for some reason she was hiding and didn't want Evelyn and Calvin to know where she was. If she was there as part of her treatment, surely Mustafa would have put them out of their misery by telling him she was safe. He would have no reason not to.'

'Perhaps she was embarrassed by the events at the trial and couldn't face anyone.'

'Possible, but if that was the case, why did Mustafa insist on helping Calvin to look for her? It would have been better to leave well alone. My gut feeling is that she was being held against her will. The question is why.'

'Mustafa was waiting to take her to Pakistan.'

Ali was adamant. 'No, Warrender, her father wouldn't want her. If it were true she had been sexually assaulted she wouldn't be considered marriageable.'

Warrender snorted.

Ali rounded on him. 'I didn't say I agreed with it; it's just how it is.'

For a moment the constable made no reply and then said, 'All right, if Mustafa wasn't keeping Shayla to send her to Pakistan, he was still intending to have the boys shipped off. She found out and threatened to tell her mother so he was keeping her hidden until they were safely out of the country.'

Handford smiled to himself. That was probably the nearest Ali was going to get to an apology. The two were making progress. 'If just for the moment we accept Warrender's version,' he mused, 'let's take it a step further and ask why she wasn't in the flat during the last week of her life, and if she wasn't, where was she? Had they moved her or had she escaped?'

'Cavendish was becoming suspicious, or she was too noisy, so they moved her. If she'd escaped, she'd have gone straight home, told her mother what Mustafa intended to do,' Ali offered.

Handford would have preferred not to disagree with his sergeant, but there were reasons why Shayla would not have gone home. 'If she'd been a normal girl, Khalid, I'd agree with you, but she wasn't. She'd have been too scared that they wouldn't believe her, think it was a ploy on her part, even think it was the work of the devils. They trusted Mustafa, remember, and didn't know he was a friend of Qumar's. He would have been able to talk his way out of anything Shayla might accuse him of. She would be terrified they would send her back to him.'

Warrender turned to Ali. 'I agree with the boss. I think she escaped and went to someone else or slept rough. Stella said Mustafa appeared a lot more concerned about Shayla than Richards was, which might suggest that somehow she had got away. He would want her back. He might even have got her back and killed her.'

Ali wasn't convinced. 'Or it might suggest she had gone back home, Richards had believed her story and was hiding her himself and therefore knew where she was.'

'And let his sister think she was still missing?' Warrender scoffed. 'I don't think so. He wouldn't do that to her.'

'Then she knew as well.'

'No, Ali, she'd never have been able to keep up

the pretence. She'd have told everyone her daughter was back, including us, *and* she'd have told us about Mustafa; she wouldn't have been able to stop herself.'

Ali turned to Handford. 'Sir?'

The last thing John Handford wanted was to involve himself in a duel of one-upmanship between the two of them. But equally he wasn't prepared to sit on the fence. 'You might be right, Khalid, but from what I've heard and from what we know about the Richardses, I'm inclined to go along with Warrender. I think when Calvin went to Stella's he believed Shayla was missing. I don't think either he or Mustafa knew of her whereabouts and Mustafa's concern was more for himself than for her. It would be worth talking to both Calvin and Evelyn Richards again to make sure, but I don't think that, given what Mr Cavendish has said, we can afford to assume Jaswant Siddique and Shahid Mustafa are not somehow involved in Shayla's disappearance, even her murder. I'm not saying that Cavendish's statement shouldn't be properly checked out, but I think that even at this stage we have enough to work on. Bring both of them in, Siddique first. Warrender, you go up to the school with a couple of uniforms. Give him the opportunity to come voluntarily, but arrest him if you have to. Then once we have Siddique here, Khalid, you and Clarke bring in Mustafa. While you're waiting you can organize search warrants for the flat and the rooms.'

Ali stood up and made to leave, but Warrender remained where he was. 'There's something else you ought to know, guv.'

'Go on.'

'Mustafa must be his professional name, because according to the electoral roll, the man who lives in his house is one Shahid Siddique.'

Handford and Ali stared at each other. 'Are you saying Jaswant Siddique and Shahid Mustafa are related?'

'They're brothers, guv, and if Gerry Cavendish is to be believed they have a very close relationship, spend a lot of time together. What I'm wondering is why neither of them thought to mention it.'

The meeting was a noisy one. The school's drama hall was old, with poor acoustics, and the shouts and applause from the sixty-strong staff bounced and echoed around the walls. The unions had chosen it because it was more private and more suited to their needs than the staff room and although Brian Atherton could have refused them his permission to use it, it would have been foolhardy, given that on the agenda was a vote of no confidence in him. His altruism, however, did him little good for the vote against him was passed unanimously.

Gill Handford's head ached with the noise and the memory of the mass barracking she had suffered before school. She had positioned herself towards the back of the hall, away from the majority of teachers who had crowded into the rows of seats closer to the stage. So far it had gone pretty much as she had expected – hard on both her and John. Graham Collins' attempt at suicide had angered the staff and Jaswant Siddique was doing all he could to lay the blame squarely at her husband's door, citing her as his accomplice. She wasn't certain he was succeeding, for while all had agreed with him about the vote against the head, she sensed a level of embarrassment when her name was mentioned. To vilify Brian Atherton was one thing, but for some, to vilify her was quite another.

Seemingly unaware of the shift of feeling, Siddique was shouting and gesticulating as though at a political meeting. 'Graham Collins has done nothing, yet the governors and the police insist on harassing him and, far from standing by their colleague, both Gill Handford and Brian Atherton cooperate with them. She hands out information and yesterday the head invited her husband into the school and gave him a CCTV tape. I don't know what it showed, but whatever it was, Graham was arrested and taken to the station where police harassment went too far because from there he returned home, drove into his garage, shut the door and switched on the car's ignition.' He was well into his stride now and seemed to be taking a delight in pushing his point home. 'A police officer who can do that to a man shouldn't be a police officer. I don't think we have a choice but to make a complaint against him and demand he is taken off the case.'

As the applause rang in her ears and her headache lifted a notch, Gill's anger against Siddique grew. What he was saying was nothing more than misrepresentation of the facts and conjecture, but by using the attempted suicide as a lever, he was taking the staff with him. She couldn't let the man get away with such blatant falsification.

For a moment it seemed as though she'd left it too late. Siddique stabbed his fist in the air and shouted, 'Come on now, let's take a vote on it. All those in favour?'

Not everyone was, and as hands went up round the hall, the vote was by no means unanimous. One of the union representatives pulled himself from his seat and waved for silence. 'No, I'm sorry, Jaswant, we can't do that without giving everyone a chance to have their say. We have to be seen to be fair. Does anyone have comments to make?'

Gill stood up, her heart beating wildly in her chest.

The rep pointed to her. 'You have the floor, Gill.'

Siddiqué interrupted. 'Before Mrs Handford speaks,' he said, emphasizing her name, 'it is worth reminding everyone that since it is her husband we will be complaining about, she has a vested interest in the result of this vote.'

Anger flooded her cheeks as she walked towards the front and stopped a few feet from the stage. 'And you don't, I suppose?' she said bitterly. 'At least you have the advantage of me, Jaswant; you know of my interest.' He made as though to reply, but before he could do so, she swallowed hard and said, 'I told you this morning, I'm a member of the union and as such have the same right as you to be here and to speak. And since you are determined to conduct a smear campaign against my husband, I think it's only fair you give me the chance to put everyone right on a few facts.

Firstly, I am John's wife not his informant and secondly, Graham was not arrested. He went to the station of his own volition. You say he was harassed; I wasn't there any more than you were, but I tell you the likelihood of that is remote, since his solicitor – brought in by the union – was with him the whole time. My husband may be hard when he's interviewing – that's his job; he has to get to the truth – but he doesn't harass to do it. He works by the book.'

'The police book,' Siddique scoffed.

'Yes, that's right, Jaswant, the police book. It's called the Police and Criminal Evidence Act and it's there to protect all of us, including Graham Collins.'

A buzz of conversation broke out amongst the staff, but Gill couldn't be sure whether they were agreeing with her or backing Siddique. Nor, it appeared, was Siddique for he shouted above the noise, 'Then why did he attempt to kill himself?'

'I don't know. Only he knows that.'

'So you can't say for certain,' Siddique countered, 'that it wasn't your husband's questioning?'

'There's always more to an attempted suicide than one event. And we all know–'

She got no further, for she was interrupted by the double doors of the drama hall banging open. She spun round and as she did so, her heart sank deep into her stomach. Brian Atherton appeared, followed by two uniformed police officers and another in plain clothes. She recognized the latter only slightly, but the copper hair suggested it was DC Warrender, and since he was a member of the investigating team, this had to be John's doing. His timing couldn't have been worse.

Atherton's eyes looked around the room. 'I'm sorry to interrupt your meeting, ladies and gentlemen, but these officers would like a word with Mr Siddique.'

Warrender winked at Gill as he passed her and climbed the steps onto the stage. He flashed his warrant card and introduced himself, then said, 'Mr Siddique, Inspector Handford would be obliged if you would come in to Central Police Station. He has a few questions to ask you regarding Shayla Richards.'

Atherton smiled and the staff glanced round, searching each other for answers.

Siddique's eyes frisked the man in front of him. 'No,' he said calmly, 'I'm not going anywhere with you, certainly not to a police station. You can go back and tell Detective Inspector Handford that if he has any questions he can come to me. Now if you don't mind, we're in the middle of a meeting.' He turned his back on Warrender and then almost as an afterthought he spun round to face Gill. 'You knew about this, didn't you? Which is why you kept the meeting going with your trivial comments.'

Warrender, who hadn't moved, was unruffled. 'I can assure you Mrs Handford knew nothing of our visit. Now, Mr Siddique, if you please?'

As Warrender took a step towards him, Siddique's control exploded into fury. 'Don't you lot ever listen?' He let fly with both hands, slapping at the detective's shoulders, propelling him backwards along the edge of the stage.

The hall descended into a horrified though fascinated silence, no one moving either to help or hinder. In a flash the uniformed officers clambered on the stage while the union reps, roused from their astonishment, scrabbled backwards to avoid the skirmish. One made a half-hearted attempt to pacify Siddique, but the man shrugged him off and continued to push at Warrender. 'I know my rights,' he snapped, the words in time with each thrust of his hands. 'You want me; you'll have to arrest me.'

Warrender turned his head to look behind him. 'I think that can be arranged,' he said and as he moved beyond the table and the chairs, he side-stepped upstage, giving the officers space to jump forward and snatch at Siddique. One pinned his hands behind his back while the other took up a position in front of him. 'Jaswant Siddique, I'm arresting you for assaulting a police officer. You do not have to say anything. But it may harm your defence if you do not mention when questioned something which you later rely on in court. Anything you do say may be given in evidence.' He tugged at Siddique's arm. 'Now please, sir, if you would come with us.'

It was doubtful whether the majority of those in the hall had ever seen a real live arrest and mesmerized, their heads turned as, flanked by the police officers, Siddique was led down the steps. When he passed Gill, he gave her a look meant to threaten. 'You'll not get away with this,' he said, his voice trembling with anger.

Warrender, walking behind, threw her a smile that told her not to worry.

It was at that moment the camera flashed and

everyone turned in its direction.

For a second or two Gill was blinded by the sudden explosion of light, but as her vision cleared she saw the photographer readjusting his camera and Peter Redmayne standing behind him, a small recorder in his hand. The press were in attendance and probably had been for some time. Warrender pushed them aside, but it was too late. Siddique turned his head towards her, a wide grin splitting his face in two and she knew without a doubt that it was he who, against all the rules and without the knowledge of either the unions or the staff, had invited them to the meeting. It had paid off. Not only had he trapped John with his accusations from the stage, but he had forced him, albeit unwittingly, to endorse Siddique's view of the heavy-handedness of the police by sending Warrender and two uniforms to interrupt the meeting and bring him into the station.

Why couldn't John have waited? Done it quietly.

She hoped to God it was worth it and he had a good reason, for she could hardly see the press leaving it alone. They had their story and even if it didn't make the late edition today, it would certainly be front-page news tomorrow.

Wearily, she slumped into an empty seat and closed her eyes, wishing she was anywhere at that moment but at Cliffe Top Comprehensive.

chapter nineteen

As Gill Handford ran the gauntlet of Jaswant Siddique's attempt to malign her and her husband, Jane Collins searched her house to find some scrap of evidence that would prove to the police – and herself – that her husband was who he said he was.

How much do you really know about your husband, Mrs Collins?

Although she'd scoffed at the inspector when he had asked the question, the words had stayed with her. How much *did* she know? All the time they'd been married, Graham had barely talked about either his parents or his childhood. She had asked him about his family when they had first met, but he had changed the subject and she assumed it was something he didn't want to talk about. Now, knowing him so much better, she could understand his reasons. So much of his youth had been spent at boarding school that he'd hardly known his mother and father. And when he was close to becoming acquainted with them again, his father had been killed and his mother eaten up by a cancer that had eventually taken her life. It wasn't surprising he wanted to move on and keep his past exactly where it was – in the past. She had never asked again, nor would she. Nor should the police. Whatever his past, it had nothing to do with Shayla Richards.

She pulled a file from the top shelf of one of the fitted units in the bedroom. In it were their birth certificates, national insurance documents, their GCSE and A-level certificates – his in the name of Graham Samuel Collins – her nursing qualifications and Graham's degree and PGCE certificates. Admittedly, his birth certificate was the shortened version and didn't have his parents' names on, but perhaps he preferred it that way. And if he did it should be enough for the police and for her; they should respect his wishes.

So, why did she feel uneasy? Why did she feel this wasn't enough? Was it simply the inspector's words, or had she had this feeling of unease for some time and pushed it to the back of her mind?

Perhaps photographs of him as a young boy would stem her disquiet. At least they would give him something the police didn't seem to think he had: a past. She delved into the bottom of the wardrobe and pulled out a wooden box. It was filled with photographs she had intended to put into albums when she had time, one of many jobs she had never got round to doing. Sitting cross-legged on the floor, she scoured through them. Wedding and holiday snaps, some of their honeymoon. In one envelope were a few of her as she grew up. School photographs, pictures of her at ballet class, with family and friends and on her eighteenth and her twenty-first birthdays, images that spanned her life from babyhood to the gawky young girl who blossomed through her teens into the nurse Graham fell in love with. But that was it: lots of her, few of her husband except those taken at university with friends, one taken at his degree ceremony and others since they were married. None of him as a child.

Then she came across it, tucked in a small envelope. It was a black and white image of Graham. He must have been about nine or ten when it was taken. He was sitting on a wall, a large grin on his face. Stretching up towards him, its front paws resting on his knee, was a golden Labrador dog. She scrutinized the photograph and her heart skipped a beat as she recalled what had first endeared him to her. That infectious smile. It was there back then and even in this old photograph it worked its magic on her.

As she sat on the bedroom floor surrounded by pictures of their lives together, DI Handford's question came back to her. *How much do you really know about your husband?*

Enough, Inspector, enough.

When she saw the policeman again she would show him this picture, prove to him that he was so wrong about her husband.

Handford strode into the interview room. 'Mr Siddique,' he said, 'thank you for coming.'

Siddique looked up, a mixture of contempt and insolence in his eyes. 'You didn't give me much of a choice.'

'It was a pity it took place so publicly; I'm sorry about that. It wasn't my intention. But since it did and since you assaulted a policeman, it would have been remiss of the officers not to arrest you, particularly as there was no provocation on the part of DC Warrender.' Handford's voice was smooth.

As usual, the teaching assistant was full of himself and saw no danger in his questioner's tone. 'Prove it.'

'I think we can do that; we have several statements corroborating the sequence of events. All insist there was no provocation.'

'No doubt your wife has given one,' Siddique said, his voice overflowing with sarcasm.

'No, Mr Siddique, as much as you would like that to be true, they came from the union representatives and several teachers. Not everyone is happy with the way you conducted yourself, not least when you brought in the press.'

Before Siddique could answer, the door opened and Warrender entered.

The teaching assistant's eyes followed him as he sat down. 'If you think I'm going to allow him to question me, then you're mistaken.' He turned to Handford. 'Nor you, if it comes to that.'

Handford smiled as he settled himself in the chair. 'I'm sorry, there's no one else. As you can imagine we're very busy at the moment. However, if you insist then you'll have to wait until someone is available, I'm afraid.' He made to stand up. 'I'll get one of the custody officers to take you back to your cell.'

The threat worked. 'No,' he said quickly. 'No, don't do that. It's all right. You two can question me, but it's under protest.'

Handford took off his jacket and hung it over the back of his chair, smoothing out the creases with slow deliberation. It was a trick he often used. It was intended to unsettle the interviewee, suggesting as it did that they might be here for some time. 'Would you like a drink or anything?'

Siddique shook his head. 'No, I wouldn't. And stop messing me about, wasting time, pretending you're concerned for my welfare. Just get on with it.' He sat back and folded his arms. He was on the defensive and that was exactly how Handford wanted him.

He nodded at Warrender, who unwrapped the covering film from the two cassettes, entered them into the recorder, switched it on and then proceeded to caution Siddique.

'Do you want a solicitor?' Handford asked, after Siddique had agreed that he understood what had been said.

'No.'

'Are you sure?'

'I've said so. Look, I haven't got time for this. Just ask your questions and let me go.' He uncrossed his arms and crossed them again; he was becoming nervous. He was not used to being the underdog. He liked power and at this moment, in the small interview room, he had none. Handford was in no doubt that at some time during the afternoon he would try to reclaim it.

He began gently enough. 'How long have you worked at Cliffe Top Comprehensive as a teaching assistant?' An easy question.

'Four years.'

'Part time?'

'Yes.' Siddique feigned boredom. 'I've answered these questions before.'

'Not for the tape, sir; we need everything on tape. It's a long time to be in a job part time. Can't pay very well. Haven't you ever wanted something full time?'

'I want to train as a teacher, but I need qualifications for that, so I work part time and go to college part time.' He glared insolently at Handford. 'Satisfied?'

'How old are you, Mr Siddique?'

'Twenty-eight, although I don't know what that has to do with anything.'

'Just interested. How well did you know Shayla Richards?'

'I told you before, I hardly knew her. I work with students with special educational needs; she didn't have any, so I didn't come across her.'

'When I spoke to you at the school you said her father had brought her up as a Muslim but she had renounced Islam by uncovering herself and sleeping around.'

Siddique shook his head. 'I can't remember saying that. In fact I would never have said it. How could I possibly have known how she spent her time when I didn't come across her?'

'How indeed, Mr Siddique? I did remark at the time that you seemed to know more about her than the rest of the staff. Do you remember that?'

'No.'

'You answered me by saying that her lifestyle was common knowledge.'

'It was.'

'You remember that.' A statement rather than a question.

Siddique made no answer. He had fallen into Handford's trap and he knew it.

'So your knowledge of her came second hand?'

'Yes. From talk in the staff room.'

Handford furrowed his brow in perplexity. 'No, I don't buy that,' he said as though he were taking Siddique into his confidence. 'Because what worries me about it is that except for the truanting, the other teachers seemed not to know anything about her. Philip Sutton, her head of year, told me about the break-up of her parents' marriage and the attempted suicide, and I got information on her very questionable lifestyle from her friends. So how did you know if the other teachers were unaware of her background and lifestyle, and you never came into contact with her?'

Again Siddique offered no reply.

'Let's look at this chronologically, then – see if we can jog your memory. You and Shayla would have joined the school at about the same time. Her parents split up in the April before she was eleven. It was then she began to show signs of rebellion, missing lessons, that kind of thing, but at that time she was at the primary school. Once she came up to Cliffe Top, she settled, although there were still signs of disturbance, which became more pronounced the older she got. It was probably her attempt at bringing her parents back together. You know the kind of thing: if she could convince them how unhappy she was, they would be sorry and become a family again. It didn't happen and when they finally divorced and her mother was given custody, her father went back to Pakistan. It was then that Shayla really went off the rails. She truanted almost permanently, joined Kerry Johnson's gang and as a result became involved in petty crime, slept

378

around, even attempted suicide. Finally she was forced back into school by education welfare, after which she accused Mr Collins of indecent assault. Are we in agreement so far?'

Siddique's tongue flicked over his lips. 'If you say so.'

'But do you?'

He shrugged his shoulders. 'Yes.'

'Then I repeat, how did you know all this, when other members of staff who had more contact with her than you did had no idea?'

Siddique began to fragment. 'Is this how you harassed Graham Collins before he tried to kill himself?'

Handford ignored the question. 'How did you know, Mr Siddique?'

There were only two ways out of this; one was to take up his right of silence and the other was to answer. Handford kept his fingers crossed that Siddique would choose the latter. He did, but the answer he gave was unexpected.

'Kerry Johnson told me.'

'Kerry Johnson?' Handford glanced at Warrender. They seemed to bump into Kerry Johnson everywhere.

'Yes. Kerry and I share the same resolve to stop the police harassing Graham Collins. It's called justice. She told me about Shayla ages ago. Shayla Richards was a liar and a slag and deserved everything she got.'

It was afternoon break when Kerry Johnson joined the rest of the gang to lean against the wall behind the drama hall. It was cold and windy, but it was hidden from prying eyes.

Gemma shivered and wrapped her coat tight round her. 'Bloody 'ell, it's cold out here, Kerry. Can't we go inside?'

'No, I'm dying for a fag,' Kylie gasped. 'You'd think they'd let us have a fag break.' She pulled a packet out of her pocket and looked inside.

'Give us one,' Gemma said.

'I can't, this is me last.' For a moment she regarded the filtered end of the cigarette as though it was some well-loved object, but finally she pulled it from the packet, which she screwed up and dropped on the floor. Positioning the cigarette between her lips, she turned into the wall and flicked at her lighter, sheltering the flame with her hands. When the tobacco reddened, she pulled hard to maintain the glow and once she was satisfied, she guillotined the flame with the top of the lighter and blew a cloud of smoke into the air. 'You can have a drag if you like,' she said and handed the cigarette to Gemma, who pulled on it and handed it back.

'Are you two finished?' Kerry snapped.

'We're only having a fag,' Kylie said.

Kerry glared at her. 'Well, just be careful where you're blowing that stuff.'

Kylie dragged at the cigarette again, blew out another mouthful and watched it twirl and dissipate around her. 'It's not my fault, it's the wind. Do we have to meet out here?'

'We do if we don't want someone listening in.'

Lindsay shivered and rubbed at her legs. 'I'm getting fed up of being in school; it's boring. I don't understand half of what they're saying.'

'That's because you're thick,' Gemma said.

Lindsay was just about to lift her fist at the girl when Kerry stopped them. 'Will you two stop it?' They took a step back, glowering at each other.

'The coppers took Siddique in at dinnertime,' Kerry said.

Kylie giggled. 'Yeah, I heard. Pushed one of them off the stage, someone said.'

'Yeah, they had to take the cop off to hospital,' Gemma added.

'Serves him right.'

'I was told they wanted Siddique at the cop shop to talk about Shayla.' Kerry's tone was casual.

'You mean they think he killed her?' Kylie's voice went up a notch.

'I don't know whether they think he killed her or not, but I do know who grassed him up. It was that Handford woman. They had a big row before school, the two of them, and she hates him, so she got her husband to send the coppers in.'

Lindsay frowned. 'She hates us as well. You don't think she told him about this morning, do you?'

Kerry gave her a pitying look. 'Don't be stupid; she's not interested in us. She told him about Siddique to disrupt the meeting.'

'Why should she want to do that?'

Gemma heaved a sigh. 'God, how thick can you be? Everyone knows the meeting was about getting her husband taken off the case. One of the cleaners told me that. She lives down our road,' she added by way of explanation. 'Anyway, she said the teachers don't think he cares who killed Shayla. They think he's trying to fit someone up

381

so he can look good. It won't matter to him whether it's Collins or Siddique.'

Lindsay's brows knit closer together. 'How do they know that's what he's doing?'

'They know because that's what the police do,' Kerry answered. 'Why do you think Gemma's brother's banged up?'

'I thought it was because they caught him robbin' a jeweller's.'

Gemma took a step towards Lindsay. They stood face to face, barely two or three centimetres between them. 'I'm warning you,' she growled.

Kylie pulled on her cigarette. 'I don't know why we're so bothered. We only came into school to have a bit of fun and it's getting boring now. I vote we go home.'

Kerry grabbed at her. 'We're not going home and if you go on saying we are, I'll pull that stupid cigarette out of your stupid mouth.'

She let go of the jacket and Kylie took a step backwards and brushed herself down. 'All right, we're staying, but I still can't see why you're bothered.'

'I'm bothered because if the copper can't get them he'll come for Sean and Sean's scared enough as it is. And,' she emphasized the word, 'if he fits him up for it, I'll have to go and live with some stupid foster parents or in a grotty children's home and that will be the end of *us*.'

'So what we gonna do about it?' Gemma said, still glaring at Lindsay.

'We 'ave another go at Handford. We get at him through her. If we scare her enough, he'll have to back off. We'll do it tonight after school – in the car park.'

'You mean we've got to hang around 'til she decides to go home?' Lindsay was aghast. 'It's fireworks tonight.'

Kerry was losing patience. Her life was unravelling and with it her ambitions and all the stupid cow could think about was fireworks. Kerry's father had laughed at her when she'd announced one day she wanted to be an accountant. She'd been watching a television play in which one of the characters had been an accountant. She had a lovely house and when she came home from work each day she sipped a glass of red wine while she listened to her messages on her answer phone. That was what Kerry wanted. Her father had told her that jobs like that were for kids with middle class parents with money, not for the likes of her, but she had determined that if she couldn't have the job, she'd have the lifestyle. Graham Collins was the beginning of that dream.

Listening to Kylie, Gemma and Lindsay quarrelling and moaning, she wondered why she bothered with them. She might not when this was over. But for the moment she needed to get everything back to where it was – the police leaving Sean alone and Collins paying his whack – and she couldn't do it on her own. Siddique would have been more use to her because he had more clout, but since he'd managed to get himself banged up, they were all that was left. She didn't know why Siddique wanted Collins off the hook; she'd never wondered and had never asked him. It was nothing to do with her. All she knew was that she wanted him around until she had enough money to get out of this godforsaken city and live her own life. Kerry's ambitions didn't include Sean, or Collins, or Siddique and they didn't include the gang. But if she was to carry it off, she had to have them with her, and since they were like kids, the only way was to bribe them.

'I tell you what, we'll have another go at Handford tonight,' she said, 'then we'll take tomorrow off, go into town and see what we can grab.'

John Handford sat back and scrutinized Jaswant Siddique. Here was a man who lived by his own code, the one which said, 'Look after number one.' He cared nothing for Shayla Richards, alive or dead, nor – although he would no doubt deny this – for Graham Collins. He used people, and he was articulate and impassioned enough to convince them of his viewpoint. But perhaps not Kerry Johnson. She was too streetwise to be taken in by him. She was perfectly capable of persuading him into her world to use him just as he used her.

'You're friendly with Kerry Johnson?'

Siddique shrugged. 'We share the same values.'

'And what values would they be?'

'I told you: a need for justice and disgust at police harassment.'

'Is that why you refused to cooperate with my officers when they tried to question you about Shayla? After all, we were talking to everyone who knew her.'

'You twist things.'

'Aren't you concerned that Shayla's dead?'

'I'm more concerned that you're trying to fit up

384

Graham Collins as her murderer.'

Handford smiled. He had been hoping Siddique would say that. 'How well do you know Mr Collins?'

'He's a good friend of mine.'

'And his wife?'

'Of course.'

'Then how is it that she insists that not only does she not know you, but that she's never heard her husband mention you?'

Siddique looked as though someone had suddenly pulled the plug on him. Any sparks that were there when he arrived were extinguished by the question and for a long moment he didn't know what to say. Then he reverted to type. 'See what I mean? You twist things.'

Handford sat back, allowing Warrender to take over.

The detective leaned forward, his forearms resting on the table. 'I'm sorry, but I don't understand. You said you were a good friend of Mr and Mrs Collins, and the inspector said that Mrs Collins told him she had never heard her husband speak of you, let alone met you. How is that twisting things?'

Defeated, Siddique slapped his hands down. 'All right, so I don't know Mrs Collins as well as I know Graham. But that doesn't mean anything.'

'It means,' Warrender explained, 'that by pretending a relationship that doesn't exist, you are able to enhance your profile among your colleagues in order to persuade them to go along with your belief that Mr Collins has been and is still being badly treated by the police and I wonder why you have done that. Are your reasons purely altruistic, Mr Siddique, or do you have another agenda?'

Jaswant Siddique sneered. 'I always did think the police were stupid and this confirms it. I don't have to raise my profile to show how corrupt you all are, how you try to set people up – you do it perfectly well yourselves.' He sat back, his confidence returning.

Handford stared at him in concentrated reflection. Finally, he asked, 'Where do you live?'

The question threw Siddique off guard. 'What?'

'Where do you live?'

'I have a flat in the city.'

'Is it yours or do you rent it?'

'I'm a part-time teaching assistant; of course it's not mine,' he said derisively. 'I rent it.'

'From whom?'

'This is why I don't answer your questions; they're a waste of my time.'

Handford persisted. 'Who do you rent your flat from?'

Siddique sighed. 'From an Asian gentleman called Shahid Mustafa. He owns the block. He's a practising counsellor and has consulting rooms on the ground floor. I live on the first floor and a writer and freelance photographer lives on the top floor. There. That's saved a bit of time.'

'Do you know Mr Mustafa well?'

'No, he's my landlord. I hardly ever see him.'

Siddique was digging nicely.

'You live alone?'

'Yes, I live alone.'

386

'Have many visitors?'

'No, why?'

'None over the past few weeks?'

Siddique shifted in his chair, his arrogance beginning to slip away. 'No. I work and I study. There's no time for entertaining.'

Handford turned to Warrender. 'I think it's only fair we tell Mr Siddique what we know, Constable. It will save him from continuing to lie to us.'

Warrender nodded. 'I agree, sir.'

Siddique shifted his gaze between them, the smirk on his lips swallowed as his mouth tightened. For the first time Handford could smell his fear.

He regarded him narrowly. 'You see, lying makes us wonder what you have to hide.'

Siddique remained silent.

It was now Handford had to take complete control. Siddique had come into the station believing he had the upper hand; now Handford wanted him to know that he was in a position of weakness, because they had more on him than he could ever have imagined. 'We know, Mr Siddique, that far from not being acquainted with Mr Mustafa and hardly ever seeing him, he is your brother and you are very close.'

Siddique made to argue, but Handford stopped him. 'You are right that Mr Mustafa is a counsellor, practising certainly, but whether he is qualified is another matter. Also Mustafa is his professional name, not his family name. He is in fact Shahid Siddique.'

Siddique curled his lip. 'You have been busy,' he sneered.

Again Handford ignored him. 'Now, as for you not having visitors. For the first three weeks in October, someone was staying in your flat. You were not at school, nor at college. You told the maths tutor and the deputy head that you were suffering from a virus. Indeed, you gave them a doctor's certificate to that effect. Last week your flat was empty while you were at school and you returned to college. Your visitor was no longer with you.'

Finally, Siddique's self confidence snapped completely and he began to bluster. 'This is rubbish,' he ranted. 'You can't prove a word of it.'

Handford leaned forward. 'The floorboards of your flat creak, Mr Siddique. Quite loudly, apparently. The walls are paper thin and the gentleman who lives above you knows when you are there, when you are not and when someone else is in the flat while you are at school. Several times he heard you arguing with a female. He also heard shouting and screaming and one day when he was passing your door, he heard what sounded like someone crying.'

Siddique looked like a cowed dog. 'He's lying,' he said, but the words were barely audible.

Handford pushed him further into the abyss. 'He's given us a statement. And in case you are thinking of intimidating him into withdrawing it – because I know you are good at that – he left the country this morning on a photo shoot. He could be away for some time.'

He knew he shouldn't be, but Handford was enjoying himself. He had the upper hand and there was more to come. 'I'm going to make a great leap of faith here, Mr Siddique. I'm going to suggest that it was Shayla Richards who was in your flat during those weeks. I'm also going to suggest that she wasn't there of her own free will.'

Siddique snorted. 'You're going to be hard pressed to prove that, Handford.' Then he sat back and tried to look unconcerned, but his face was taut and the muscles beneath his skin visible.

Handford was sure he was right; the visitor had been Shayla Richards. 'I think not. I'm going to search your rooms.'

At this Siddique roused. 'Oh no you're not, not without my permission and I have no intention of giving it.'

'I don't need your permission, Mr Siddique. I have a warrant signed by a magistrate. I shall bring in a forensic team and they will examine anything and everything. Have you ever heard of Locard's Principle?'

Siddique shook his head; he was way beyond words now.

'It says that every contact leaves a trace of him or her self. If she was there at all, we'll know. For the moment I'm going to arrest you on suspicion of the false imprisonment of Shayla Richards – which, in case you didn't know, also gives me the right to search your flat. Before I do, however, I would urge you to consider further having a solicitor, because I think you're going to need one.'

A murky haze had settled over the city. One of the two security lights in the staff car park was out and the other did no more than bruise the gloom. Had it not been for the half darkness and

389

the fact that she was huddled against the wind, Gill Handford might have noticed the four figures creeping furtively round the vehicles.

She flicked the electronic fob and as the signal receiver sounded and the orange hazard lights flashed, they told her – and them – where her car was located. She opened the back door and threw in the pile of books and papers she was carrying. She wasn't sure whether she would have time to do any marking tonight. Her daughters' school was holding a bonfire party and she had promised to go; in fact she was looking forward to it. John had promised as well, but she doubted he would be able to keep that promise, not now. She hoped he would try. That the job was important to him had never been in doubt, and she'd always tried not to make it a bone of contention between them, but this time it seemed more important than anything else. For him to send DC Warrender and the two uniformed constables in to the school at a time when they would inevitably disrupt the meeting in which both he and his wife were the main subjects of discussion was at best unfortunate. At worst it seemed to her heavyhanded.

She'd never thought of John as an unkind man, but he must have known, given it was Siddique he wanted, that it could have backfired on her. It was no thanks to him that it hadn't. In fact, it was Siddique himself to whom she had to be grateful. Many of the staff were appalled by his reaction and his aggression and while they had not gone as far as apologizing to her, they had not blamed her.

She closed the back door and was just about to climb into the driver's seat when she heard a sound behind her. She spun round. Kerry Johnson stood close to her, her followers a few steps away. 'What do you want, Kerry?'

'You, Handford. We always keep a promise.'

Gill was too tired for this. 'Go away, all of you,' she said wearily. She sat on the seat and pulled her legs in to the well. When she attempted to close the door, she felt resistance and looked up to see Kerry's hand grabbing at the handle. 'Let go, Kerry.'

Kerry held on tight. Gill wrenched hard at the door, snatching it out of her grasp, closed it and pressed down the lock. Starting up the engine, she put the car into gear and moved carefully out of the parking space.

At first Kerry and her mates pushed against the bonnet in an attempt to prevent her from continuing, but the car rode on slowly. No doubt fearing they would be run over, the girls jumped to the side and Kerry waved Gemma and Kylie to the left of the car while she and Lindsay shifted to the right.

Gill kept going, praying they wouldn't do anything silly.

The girls ran beside her.

Slowly she approached the exit to the parking area, but at the driveway to the school she had to stop. It was then that Kerry and her friends whacked at the roof of the car and didn't stop.

The thudding of their fists hammered over her again and again and the sound echoed around her like the beat of a bass drum. Terrified, she put her hands up to her ears to block it out.

Then others joined them and they bounced and rocked the car. Gill pulled her hands from her ears and tried to get back into first gear, but her hand kept slipping off the stick. The car stalled and she turned the key to switch on the ignition, but nothing happened. The crowd grew bigger and noisier and she heard their insults and their abuse.

The Golf rocked more fiercely.

One or two of the boys had shielded their faces with scarves or hoods, not that it would have made any difference; she was too frightened to recognize anyone. She was trapped. The car might tip over at any minute.

A bus drew up on the opposite side of the road and the driver jumped from his cab and ran towards the seething mass of school kids, his mobile to his ear. Simultaneously a group of teachers dashed out of the school and over to the mob. They grabbed at flailing arms and pushed and pulled at the bodies surrounding the vehicle, moving them on as best they could. Some fell over each other; others slipped on the wet ground; others just ran. One stopped to spit on the windscreen before he too turned and disappeared.

Gill wasn't sure where Kerry Johnson and her crew were.

The noise that had resonated through the car was silenced. Only the staff and the bus driver were left. She couldn't move. She was shaking and tears were rolling down her cheeks. Someone signalled that she should release the lock. Her hand trembled but she did as she was asked. She heard the click of the system. A teacher pulled at the door and she felt arms surround her to help her out. The assistant head of English, who had been there for her in the morning, climbed in and said he would drive the car back to the parking area. It was safer than leaving it here. She didn't know whether she thanked him or not.

'I've rung for the police,' the bus driver said. 'They'll be here any time.'

Gill tried to argue; she didn't want the police, but the deputy head disagreed. 'We've got to, Gill.'

The bus driver handed a sheet of paper to the deputy. 'I can't wait, but here's my name and address if they want a statement from me. Bloody hooligans; I don't know how you teach 'em.' And he crossed the road to the bus.

Gill had no idea how long it was before the police arrived and were shown into the deputy's office, but it couldn't have been more than five or ten minutes. One of the teachers had made her a cup of tea, and it rested untouched on her knee.

One of the officers recognized her. 'You're Mrs Handford, the DI's wife?'

She nodded. 'You don't need to be here; it's over and I'm fine.'

'You don't look fine, if you don't mind me saying so. Look, you finish your tea and I'll get some information as to what happened, then me and Barry'll take you home.' He smiled at her.

'You don't need to do that. I've got my own car.'

'And you're in no fit state to drive. Barry'll take it and you can come with me.'

Despite herself, Gill felt relieved. The last thing she wanted to do at the moment was return to the car park. The chances that Kerry and her gang were still there were remote, but she would prefer not to risk it. Even so, to take her home would mean the officers going out of their district and they could get into trouble. She said as much.

'Yeah, the sergeant might not be very pleased, but the DI will be less pleased if we don't make sure you're all right. And I know who I'd rather face when I get back to the station. You finish your tea and I'll be back in a minute.'

chapter twenty

Sergeant Ali and DC Clarke sat in the car and stared up at Mustafa's house. It was in darkness except at the far end of the building, where a light gleamed from the ground-floor window of what Ali assumed was the housekeeper's flat. He stretched over to press the intercom. After a few moments a woman's voice answered.

'Mrs Harris, it's Sergeant Ali. Can you let us in? We'd like to have another word with Mr Mustafa.'

'Mr Mustafa's away, Sergeant.'

Ali glanced at Clarke. 'Can you let us in anyway? I'd like a quick word with you.'

The housekeeper released the lock on the gate and they drove towards the flat, where she stood waiting outside the door. He introduced Clarke, who smiled at her.

'I'm sorry you've had a wasted journey,' Mrs Harris said as she led them into her sitting room. It was small and welcoming, but not in the same league as Mustafa's. There were no logs burning in the grate, just a small gas fire with red electric flames spiralling over the fake coals; nor were there expensive statuettes or porcelain figurines housed in cabinets, but cheap ornaments arranged on open surfaces, probably given to her at Christmas and birthdays by the children in the photographs, and, Ali was willing to bet, all the more treasured for that. The television was playing silently. It was an afternoon quiz show and as Ali watched, the picture danced from one apprehensive contestant to another. Incompatible with the rest of the room, a computer system was tucked away in a corner.

'Mr Mustafa left this morning,' Mrs Harris explained. 'He said he was tired of the weather and wanted some sun.'

'Sensible fellow,' Clarke returned affably. 'Does he often do this? Go away on the spur of the moment.'

'Sometimes, although this wasn't quite the spur of the moment. He had to cancel his clients and he did that yesterday. Mind you, I wish he'd given me more notice. I'd done a big shop over the weekend and now a lot of it will be wasted. I said to him, I said, "You can only freeze so much, you know." But he doesn't really understand the ways of a house and said he knew I'd do my best. I'll have to, won't I, if good food is not to be wasted.'

Ali allowed her to end her protest before asking, 'Where's he gone, do you know?'

'He didn't say. Just that he wanted some sun. It could be Egypt – he likes Egypt – or it might be Pakistan, but I can't be sure. Mr Mustafa said he'd email me and let me know when he was coming back. My grandson persuaded me to get a computer. I'm having lessons, you know,' she added proudly. 'I shouldn't worry, Sergeant. Mostly when he goes away suddenly he's home in a few days. Sometimes it can be a month or more, but not often. He doesn't like to leave his patients too long.'

'Perhaps you can let us know when you hear from him. It really is important we speak with him.' Ali hesitated. 'I don't suppose we could have a look at his house while we're here? I'd like Mr Clarke to see his paintings. He's a bit of a collector himself.'

Mrs Harris was unsure. 'Oh, I don't know, Sergeant. He's always insistent that when he's away the house is closed to everyone but me. He won't even allow workmen in. I don't think he'd like it if I opened it up for you. He trusts me, you see.'

It had been worth a try. The warrant to search covered the consulting rooms and Ali could hardly use it as leverage to check the house as well – certainly not with someone as trusting as Mrs Harris.

'Never mind,' he said. 'Perhaps you'll let me know when Mr Mustafa is back.' He walked towards the door and then stopped, unsure whether to mention the search warrant and the offices. He decided against it. 'Do you have a spare set of keys to Mr Mustafa's consulting rooms?'

If she thought the request strange she didn't say anything. 'No I don't, but his solicitor has – that's Suleman Khan.' She walked over to the small telephone table. 'I'll write his number down for you.' As she handed him the paper, she laughed and said, 'I must be going stupid in my old age, Sergeant; Mr Khan will know where Mr Mustafa is. He always keeps him up to date with where he's going, in case anything comes up.'

Ali took the piece of paper. 'We'll give them a ring. Thank you, Mrs Harris. You've been very helpful.'

The housekeeper beamed as she showed them out, then stood and waved at the car as it manoeuvred its way down the drive. Once into the road, Ali pulled up to look back at the house. 'It's a pity we didn't include it in the warrant,' he said. 'I would have loved to have got in and had a good look around without Mustafa there.'

'You think he may have had Shayla here?'

'No, I doubt it. He wouldn't want to sully his possessions and anyway Mrs Harris would have known. She doesn't exactly look the type to be involved in anything sordid. No, I was wondering if there was anything to tie him in with bounty hunting. I bet he doesn't keep that information in his consulting rooms.'

'You think he's a bounty hunter?'

'It's only a gut feeling. I haven't heard anything, but it wouldn't surprise me if he is. He doesn't get his wealth from counselling, that's for sure.' He indicated and pulled out into the traffic. 'I'm willing to bet some of the girls he counsels are those trying to get out of an arranged marriage. Their parents will have sent them to him, or perhaps Siddique has heard things in school and passed on the information. Mustafa approaches the parents as he did with the Richardses and the girls are shipped off to Pakistan – by force if necessary.'

Clarke sounded unsure. 'That's a hell of a theory, Sarge, if you don't mind me saying so. Have you put it to the boss?'

'No, not yet. Warrender has an inkling. He mentioned it in the car on our way back from talking to Mustafa.'

'But you've no evidence?'

'No. To be honest we haven't tried to get any. But now ... well, we have Siddique and he's bound to know what's going on. I'm not surprised Mustafa has ducked out on him. That young man's a loose cannon if ever there was one and he's hot-headed. If he hadn't been so obstructive and had answered our questions when we first went into the school, we'd not have pursued him and he'd not have been in custody now.'

'Except that he's Mustafa's brother.'

'We can't charge him for being someone's brother.' Ali allowed his thoughts to swirl around his mind and for a while they drove on in silence. Eventually he said, 'When we get back to the station, ring Mustafa's solicitor, tell him what's happening and ask him to send someone to the consulting rooms with a key. Also, see if he does know where his client is. If he doesn't or won't say, contact the airlines. If he's in Pakistan we'll ask Race Relations to try and track him down through their contacts. In the meantime I'll make a start on executing the search warrant.'

Although Handford drove home at speed, faster than either the conditions or the law allowed, he hit every red traffic light and every black spot and became more and more anxious. The news had come through just after they had finished with Siddique and he had dropped everything and rushed out of the station.

Fireworks burst above him, sending out showers of falling stars. At any other time he would have enjoyed them, but tonight the resonance as they exploded and the sudden illumination took him back to the riots sparked by his arrest of Mohammed Aziz. The memory of that night might have dimmed, but he would never forget it. It was the unexpected, even the trivial which brought it back and he knew the noise, the abuse, the petrol bombs bursting on the ground behind and in front of the police in riot gear, and the fires, would always haunt him, just as he knew Gill's experience tonight would never leave her. In her dreams she would feel the motion of the car as it rocked beneath her and remember the students who had hidden their identity with scarves and hoods. He would have given anything for her not to have gone through it. Anger took over from anxiety and he banged his fist on the steering wheel. If he ever caught up with those kids...

He drew up behind his wife's Golf, jumped out of his car and ran towards the house, unsure what he would find. The constable had said that even though Gill hadn't been hurt, she was in a state of shock. She'd warned him that she expected trouble, but he'd assumed it would be from the staff, not the pupils, and it would be insults, not violence.

As he pulled his key from the lock of the front door, one of the officers came to greet him. 'She's more frightened than hurt. The deputy head doesn't doubt Kerry Johnson and three others were at the bottom of it, because there'd been a problem with them in the morning, but by the time we got there, they'd disappeared. Do you want us to pick them up, sir? I doubt we'll be able to prove anything; they'll have their stories well sorted by now, but it might frighten them.'

'If I thought that I'd say yes, but Kerry Johnson is not easily frightened. I'll talk with my wife and then if necessary, I'll see to it. Where is Gill now?'

'In the sitting room, sir. Barry's keeping her company.'

'And my daughters?'

'They've gone off with friends to the fireworks party at their school. They wanted to stay, but I told them we'd look after their mum until you got back.'

'Thank you, Constable, and thank you for bringing Gill's car home.'

'Thought it best not to leave it overnight, sir. If they'd decided they hadn't finished the job, they could have come back and it'd be a burnt-out wreck by morning.'

As Handford approached the lounge door he saw Gill huddled on the settee, a mug clasped in her hand. She held it against her lips, but was not drinking from it. It was as though she was gaining comfort from its warmth against the tenderness of her skin. She was pale to the point of being translucent and it was obvious the experience had affected her badly. Barry sat opposite her.

She looked up when he entered. 'Why, John?' she pleaded.

He sat beside her and tried to put his arms round her, but she stiffened, resisting him. For a moment he felt he was looking at her through the wrong end of a telescope – she was so distant from him. 'I don't know, Gill, but I *will* find out.'

Her eyes penetrated his. 'Why did you send those police officers in to disrupt the meeting?'

401

He stared at her in disbelief. He'd thought she was asking why four school kids and their mates had put her through hell, but she wasn't. She was asking why he had. She was blaming him.

No doubt sensing the heightened tension, Barry stood up and tiptoed out of the room. Handford heard the front door close as the two officers left the house. Again he made to touch his wife's arm, but she pulled it away from him.

'I never intended they should disrupt the meeting, Gill. They could have waited until it was over, *would* have waited had not Brian Atherton insisted.'

'But why come into school at all? I asked you not to. Why did you?'

'Because it's my job and because–'

She continued for him. 'You can't let family interfere with that; in fact you can't let anyone interfere, can you? Not the people out there, not your wife, not your children. It doesn't matter how your job affects them.'

Before he could answer, she hurried on. 'It was round the building in minutes, John. Everyone blames me. They think I grassed him up.'

He cringed at her terminology. It was almost as if he was the enemy. 'Not everyone. We have willing statements from the union reps and from several teachers. Not everyone is happy with the way Siddique has conducted himself.'

'Kerry Johnson and her friends blame me; the other kids blame me. Tonight wasn't the first time I've been taunted and heckled.' Tears began to run down her cheeks. 'This morning they caught me in the corridor. They blamed you for Graham's suicide – they thought he was dead.' She was crying properly now, her voice catching in the sobs. 'They shouted at me to go home and then when the others turned up all I could hear was them chanting "home, home, home".' She stopped and as their eyes met Handford felt the intensity of the emotions swirling round his body.

He took the mug from her and pulled her to him, refusing to allow any resistance. 'They're getting at me through you and I'm so sorry. I never intended anything like this to happen.'

She pushed herself away from him. 'Like you didn't intend to break up the meeting? You know Jaswant invited the press?'

'Warrender told me.'

'It'll be in tomorrow's papers. There'll be pictures of him being led away by three policemen – three! And there'll be comments and quotes about police harassment and the reason behind the meeting and my name and yours bandied about.'

For the first time since he'd arrived home she had colour in her cheeks, but this time, he knew, it was the colour of anger. He felt the same anger.

'So there might be, Gill, but they'd be wrong. I arrested Siddique this afternoon on suspicion of holding Shayla Richards against her will.'

Her voice was hollow when she spoke. 'On suspicion of? Is that all you could manage? You're not even sure?'

He flinched. She seemed to have lost everything: her determination, her sparkle and, worse, her belief in him. He walked over to the drinks and poured out two brandies. 'Not until I have forensic evidence; we're searching the flat.'

'And if you find nothing?'

'I'll have to let him go. But that's not going to happen. Shayla was in his flat for three of the four weeks she was missing – we have a witness.' He handed her one of the glasses.

She took a sip. 'Did he kill her?'

'I don't know. We don't know where she was during the final week of her life.'

Nothing seemed to satisfy her. 'So now you're going to be accused of running round in circles not knowing who killed her and of fitting up Jaswant as well as Graham Collins?' There it was again, the street terminology. She banged the glass on to the small table. 'What do you think it's going to be like for me in school?'

'It will be fine.' The comment was trite and not worthy of him, but he didn't know what else to say to her.

'No, it won't be fine,' she snapped back. 'It will never be fine again. You've taken that away from me. The school will be different. It will look different, smell different and feel different. Each morning when I arrive I look up at my classroom and think how lucky I am. This morning the windows were different; they weren't welcoming me. For the first time ever, I didn't want to be there. You know what I mean. You said the same after the riots and the inquiry.'

He couldn't argue with her, only support her, as she had done with him. But he suspected their relationship might never get back to what it was. She felt he had let her down. He hoped he was wrong. He would do everything he could to take them back to where they had been, except the thing she wanted most: him off the case. He couldn't do that, particularly now. If he didn't uncover what had happened to Shayla Richards, it would be an albatross not only round his neck, but also round Gill's.

He turned the conversation. 'What about Kerry Johnson? Do you want her charged?'

'No, of course not. She's a child.'

Suddenly frustration took over. 'Oh, come on. She's no child, except in years. What she did wasn't a childish prank; she knew exactly what she was doing. Have her charged.'

'You can't do anything if I don't make a complaint?'

'No.'

'Then I won't.'

'She'll look on it as weakness on your part.'

'I don't care. She's gone through a lot and I'm not going to add to it.'

'You've gone through a lot and she won't care if she adds to it. The constable drove your car home because he knows Kerry Johnson. She would have torched it as soon as look at it. All right, she might be a kid, but take my word for it, she's a criminal in the making. And she's cunning with it. She thinks about what she does before she does it.' Handford wanted to tell her what he suspected Kerry of, but couldn't. 'Why do you think she's reacted towards you in this way, Gill?'

'Because she thinks I told you about the row Jaswant and I had this morning. She wants what he wants: Graham back in school.'

'Why? Why does she want him back in school?

405

She's hardly ever there. She's a troublemaker and she's making trouble for her own reasons.'

'Don't be ridiculous. What reasons could she possibly have?'

Handford sighed. 'She has reasons, believe me. It's just that I can't tell you what they are because I can't prove anything. Have her charged, Gill. Let's get her out of the equation.'

'No.'

'Then I'll do it some other way – with or without you.' He stood up and picked up his car keys.

She spun round. 'Where are you going?'

He hated what he was going to do. 'Back to the station,' he said abruptly. 'I'll be back as soon as I can.'

She shouted after him. 'Are you going to bring Kerry in and question her? Because if you are, make sure she realizes this is not what I want.'

'I'm not bringing her in, I'm not questioning her and I'm not arresting her. Not today at any rate. But I am going to make sure she doesn't get away with this.'

On his way to the car he thumbed a number into his mobile. When it was answered he said, 'Warrender, I want you back in the station, now.'

Ali wasn't quite sure why he'd diverted via Warrender's house on his way home. He had no reason to, except that he wanted to see where the man lived, place him in situ so to speak. It wouldn't take long. It couldn't take long because he'd promised Amina he would be home in time to set off the children's fireworks. When he'd left Clarke he'd spent what was left of the afternoon and part of the evening at Mustafa's rooms. The solicitor had arrived with the key and a protest at what the police were doing, but there was little he could do about it except object and stay while the search took place.

To say the rooms were clean was an understatement. Mustafa's appointments book had gone, as had any papers relating to his clients. In fact, considering the man was a counsellor, there was little to prove it, not even books on psychology. Ali had never needed the services of a counsellor himself, but those he'd had to visit as a police officer had always had shelves of books on behavioural analysis, developmental and applied, clinical and cognitive, even forensic psychology. All that seemed to be left in Mustafa's consulting rooms were a few magazines in English and newspapers in Urdu on the coffee table in the waiting room. There was little doubt he'd been quick to make himself scarce. Once Shayla's death had been announced and the police had questioned him, he had set about tidying his affairs and disappearing out of the country. Ali wondered if Siddique had been told of his brother's sudden exit. That news might just be enough to make him talk.

The cul-de-sac in which Warrender and his sister lived was quiet and secluded. Even in the dark, it gave the impression of comfortable tree-lined suburbia. Ali was willing to bet Warrender was the only detective constable who lived here – the others would be bank managers and businessmen, those well enough off to afford the mortgage, the council tax and the fees at the golf club.

According to Clarke the bungalow had been customized for his sister's needs and from what Ali could see that was true; certainly the front door was wide enough to take a wheelchair. Warrender's car was parked against the kerb and another smaller estate was in the drive. That was probably Katie's. He would have loved to take a look at it, see if it was specially adapted for a disabled driver, but to approach it at all would have activated the security light and Warrender would have been out in no time. No, he would have to be satisfied with imagining the man and his sister living there. At least it was one step closer to understanding him.

He was about to leave when the front door opened and Warrender came out. Ali slid down in his seat. He heard the sound of the car's locking system and then one of the doors open and close. The engine spluttered and Warrender drove away, apparently unaware of Ali's car.

What possessed Ali to do what he did next, he would never know and if he could have rewound his life he would have gone home to the fireworks, not left his car and walked up Warrender's drive. But he needed to see for himself. He needed to understand and more than anything else he needed to meet Katie. He made his way to the front door and knocked, then waited the few minutes before it was opened. When it was, he looked down on a young woman in a wheelchair. In the light of the hallway he saw the same features, the same coppery hair as Warrender, but whereas he was stocky, she was thin to the point of anorexia. The exertion of manoeuvring the wheelchair had made her breathless. She greeted Ali with a smile and said, 'Can I help you?'

For a moment he was rendered speechless. Even her voice was similar to her brother's, but friendlier. There was no tone of distrust.

'I'm sorry to bother you,' he faltered, 'but I'm Detective Sergeant Ali. I was wondering if I could have a word with DC Warrender.'

She smiled at him. 'So you're the infamous sergeant. I've heard a lot about you. I'm sorry, you've just missed him; he's been called back to the station. The inspector rang a few moments ago.'

Ali wasn't sure how to react to what she had said – whether to feel slighted at her description of him or to be annoyed that John had called Warrender in without letting him know.

'Look, I'm sorry to have bothered you. I'll catch up with him later. Tomorrow, probably. It wasn't so important that it can't wait.' He was babbling and he knew it.

'Why don't you come in for a moment?' Another smile lit up her face. 'I'd like to know if you're as bad as Chris makes out.'

Her smile and the tone of her voice were infectious and Ali grinned back. 'You know, I might just do that. I'd like to know if I'm as bad as he makes out.' She propelled her wheelchair out of his way and he stepped over the threshold.

Handford arrived at Central before Warrender. While he was waiting, he read through the latest information in his in-tray and then listened to the messages on the answerphone. There were three from Redmayne. Would John please get back to him? No, John wouldn't. If he wanted a quote about this afternoon, then he could await John's convenience. And if it missed tomorrow's deadline, then tough.

He took in a deep breath. What was he doing? He wasn't thinking straight, that was what he wasn't doing. Redmayne would print something, even if it was only that the police had refused to comment and that would be worse than a quote from him; it would look as though they had deliberately gone in to the school to disrupt the meeting and that they were, as suspected, heavy-handed.

He picked up the phone and punched in Redmayne's number. It was answered almost immediately. 'I'm sorry I haven't been able to get back to you until now. I've been busy,' Handford said abruptly.

If Redmayne noticed his tone, he said nothing. 'I wanted a quote from you about the arrest of Jaswant Siddique at the meeting held in the school. It's only fair you give your side of things.'

'It wasn't my intention to disrupt the meeting. Mr Atherton took the officers into the hall where it was being held.'

'So you think it was the head who wanted the meeting disrupted?'

Handford cursed. 'I can't say what was in Mr Atherton's mind at the time,' he said.

'Are you still holding Mr Siddique?'

'Yes. He's been arrested on unrelated matters and is currently helping us with our inquiries.'

'Are you going to tell me what these unrelated

410

matters are?' Handford could hear the smile in Redmayne's tone.

He relaxed. 'No, you know I'm not, Peter. Now if that's all...' He crossed his fingers, hoping that Redmayne had not heard about the later events at the school because he really didn't want to discuss them, or have to think up some euphemism to describe them.

It appeared that he hadn't, for the journalist said, 'No, that's all, thanks. Talk to you soon,' and cut the connection.

A few moments later, Warrender tapped on the door and walked in.

'I'm sorry to bring you back,' Handford said, indicating he should sit down. 'But I want you to do something for me, and I don't want anyone to know about it, least of all Sergeant Ali. You can refuse, because what I want you to do may not be strictly within the terms of the book.'

Warrender frowned. 'Has something happened, boss?'

'You could say that.' Handford explained the events of the afternoon and evening.

'Sounds nasty,' Warrender said. 'Is Mrs Handford all right?'

'She seems to be. Well, physically at any rate. I'm not sure about emotionally. She was very frightened.'

Warrender settled back in his chair. 'I'll help if I can, boss. What do you want?'

'Gill refuses to press charges, but I want that girl; I want her for what she did to my wife and I want to know why she did it.' He leaned across the desk. 'This is between you and me, Warren-

411

der. I'm aware most of the team think I'm being paranoid when I keep insisting Kerry Johnson is blackmailing Graham Collins; Sergeant Ali has made that perfectly clear. Nevertheless, I think that is what she is doing. I need her arrested and I need the house searching. I can't bring her in for the attack on my wife because Gill won't complain and you know what that means: no complaint, no crime. So I want her brought in on something else. I'd rather it was done legitimately, but if you have to push the boundaries to do it, then I want you to do just that.'

Warrender sucked in a mouthful of air and blew it out slowly. 'Blimey, this isn't like you. A by-the-book man normally.'

Handford let his eyes slip away from the constable. 'I know, and I can't say I'm proud of it, but I need this now. Perhaps I wouldn't if she hadn't involved Gill, but she has and she has a reason for that. I believe the reason is that she wants me off the case because she thinks I'm too close to proving that she's blackmailing Collins. In her childish way she assumes that if she can get to Gill, she can get to me. I don't even know why she's blackmailing him, although it must have something to do with his background – something in his past we know nothing about and she does.'

He lifted his gaze back to Warrender and let it settle firmly on him. 'I'm asking you to do something I shouldn't and you can refuse. There'll be no hard feelings.'

'No, boss, I'm with you on this. The book's not always right. We'll get her, don't you worry; I'll think of something. For one thing, it's unlikely she'll be in school tomorrow. She'll want the fuss to die down. She might even be expecting a visit from us, but if we don't give her that privilege, then she'll be out and about. She hasn't been up to her old tricks for a few days, so she'll probably be short of money. Friday and Saturday we were down in the city questioning people, so she wouldn't risk it then, and yesterday and today she's been in school. I reckon they'll all be out seeing what they can pinch. I'd say that was our best bet – catch her in the act, so to speak.'

Handford leaned back in his chair. 'Thank you, Warrender. I'm grateful. As I said, I'm not proud of what I'm asking you to do, and I promise if it goes pear-shaped, I'll take the flak.'

'It won't go wrong, boss. But I will ask you to do something for me. Keep Sergeant Ali off my back. I can't turn round at the moment without him being there.'

Sergeant Ali stood up. 'I really must go. I promised my wife I'd be home to set off the children's fireworks.' He bent over to shake Katie Warrender's hand. It looked so frail he was afraid he might break it, but she had a surprisingly strong grip. 'I'm glad I've met you but I think it would be better that your brother doesn't know.'

'He won't hear it from me. And Sergeant Ali, the feeling's mutual. You're not a bit the person Chris makes you out to be. He'll come round eventually; it's just that he saw the reaction of the man who ran me down as well as that of his family and friends and I didn't. Because I didn't see it, I

413

can let it go. He can't. He's still very angry. And however he comes over to you, I've a lot to be grateful to him for. Without him, I'm not sure I would have survived, let alone had a comparatively decent life. He's given up a lot for me.'

Ali made no reply; he could think of nothing that wouldn't have sounded either trite or insensitive.

'He's trying to find someone who can help me play tennis again,' she went on as though she hadn't noticed. 'I'm not sure I'll be able to because I'm not always well, but Chris thinks I will and he's so positive that he'll probably be right.' She smiled, lighting up her face. 'You never know, you might see me in the Paralympics one day.'

Ali returned her smile. 'I'll look forward to it.'

She made to release the brake on the wheelchair.

'No, don't move. I'll see myself out.'

The security light illuminated the drive and as Ali set off to walk to his car he saw the darkened figure coming towards him. It was Warrender. He groaned. This was the last thing he had wanted to happen.

'What the hell are you doing here?' The words fractured the silence.

Ali attempted to explain. He began with the same lie he had told to Katie. 'I wanted a word with you.'

'A word about what? If it was that important, you could have rung me on my mobile. You didn't have to come here. You don't come to my house. You're not welcome.'

Perhaps the truth would be better. 'Clarke told

414

me what happened to your sister and your parents – the accident. I just wanted to talk to you. Then I saw you go out. Call it pride, call it arrogance, call it stupidity on my part, but I felt I had to make myself known to your sister. Apologise to her, show her we're not all like the driver of that car.'

'We don't need your apologies, Ali, we just need you out of our lives. Leave her alone. Leave me alone.' Warrender prodded at the sergeant's chest, propelling him backwards. As Ali tried to maintain his balance, Warrender suddenly grabbed at his lapels and spun him round.

'Stop it, Chris. Stop it!' Katie must have heard the fracas and wheeled herself to the door. 'Leave him alone.'

Warrender, his gaze still firmly fixed on Ali, shouted at his sister. 'Go back inside, Katie.'

She remained immobile, making no attempt to wheel herself back into the house.

Warrender grabbed Ali's chin and turned his face towards the woman in the wheelchair. 'Look at her. Go on, look at her; look what your people have done to her. They might just as well have killed her. However you try to dress it up, Ali, you're all alike. You do what you want and expect to get away with it. And you do, because we're all too afraid to face up to you. But not me, Ali, not me. How dare you come to my house, talk to my sister!' He let go of the coat and pushed him backwards. 'You keep away from her and away from me.'

At first Warrender walked away, then without warning, he ran back to the sergeant and punched out with his fist, hitting him square on the jaw. Ali spun round and slammed face down on the concrete. It was wet and hard. At first his head bounced and then as he looked up, tried to take in what was happening, a fireball seemed to burst in his brain. The sky lit up and coloured stars rained down as one after another fireworks exploded above him. His head spun, but through the noise he thought he heard Katie's voice. 'Chris, stop it! What are you doing?'

'What I should have done years ago.' Warrender was breathing heavily.

Gingerly, Ali moved his head, then his jaw. As the pain caught he grunted. He lifted his fingers to feel the damage. A large lump was forming at his hairline and he could taste blood. Irrationally, his thoughts centred on how on earth he would explain his condition to Amina.

Warrender came closer to tower over him. Ali covered his head, waiting for the next attack, but when it didn't come, he looked up. Warrender was holding out his hand. Cautiously Ali took it and found himself being pulled upright. He touched his mouth and surveyed the blood on his fingers. Slowly he lifted his eyes to meet Warrender's. 'Has that made you feel better?' he mumbled through swollen lips.

'Much better,' the constable answered and he turned, walked over to his sister and pushed her into the house.

chapter twenty-one

Handford sat at his desk the next morning and stared into space. In front of him was a stack of reports he had made several attempts to deal with, but while his eyes read the words, his thoughts wandered to the events of the previous evening.

He wasn't at all sure he had done the right thing by involving Warrender in his desire to punish Kerry Johnson. It had been no more than a knee-jerk reaction to get back at the girl who had hurt his wife so badly and he ought to have thought it through before dashing to the station. Gill was right: Kerry *was* still a child and one who had had to cope with more in her short fifteen years than most people had in a lifetime. That didn't absolve her from acts that were either criminal or downright dangerous, but neither did it mean he could exact revenge. He could tell himself as many times as he wanted that she was a blackmailer and that as a police officer he had to bring her to book, and that what she had done to Gill was somehow mixed up with what she was doing to Collins, but deep down he knew Gill was his real focus, not the teacher.

He ran his hand through his hair. He could stop it right now if he wanted – bring Warrender in and tell him to forget it. That would be the rational thing to do. But what Kerry had done was not rational and there was no saying that left to herself she wouldn't try something else, something considerably more dangerous. He wished Gill had not insisted on going into school this morning. While Warrender had said it was unlikely the Johnson gang would be there, he would have much preferred her to stay at home.

But she had been adamant. 'Of course I'm going in. If I don't they'll have won. Wouldn't that be your argument if it was happening to you? Wasn't that your argument when you were fighting the community after you arrested Mohammed Aziz?'

'That was different, Gill.'

'No, it wasn't. It was the same – a group of angry people showing their feelings in the only way they knew how.'

He wished he could agree with her, but he couldn't. With Kerry Johnson it was different; he knew it. It was a pity he couldn't yet prove it. Gill blamed him for putting her in this situation and for the moment he would have to live with that. But only for the moment. He sipped at his now cold coffee. He needed evidence, evidence to confirm Kerry Johnson's involvement in all this. And that, he knew, was the reason why he wasn't picking up the phone and calling Warrender.

He would have to live with that, too.

In the meantime he had to concentrate on the inquiry and what they already had. Without authorization from a senior officer, the Police and Criminal Evidence Act allowed Handford to keep Jaswant Siddique in custody for twenty-four hours. The clock was ticking and he would have to re-interview him. A night in the cells and the revelation that his brother had bailed out on him

418

might be enough to loosen his tongue. After that Handford had to decide whether to charge him, bail him while their enquiries continued or let him go. With what they had at the moment it would be imprudent to charge him. The statement given by Mr Cavendish was littered with too many perhaps and maybes; there was nothing to prove Siddique had held Shayla against her will or even that it had been her in the flat.

He phoned down to the custody suite. 'I want to interview Siddique later. Has he given any more thought to having a solicitor?'

'He's still adamant he doesn't need one,' the custody sergeant said. 'Do you want me to try again?'

'Yes. You'd better. At least then he can't say we have denied him his rights.'

As he replaced the receiver there was a knock on the door and he shouted for whoever it was to come in. A seemingly embarrassed Detective Sergeant Ali entered and walked to stand in front of the desk. Handford stared at him.

Ali was ashen. His forehead had swollen along the hairline, the skin distended so that it was the shade of sallow ivory. A deep-coloured bruise followed the contour of his left eye, fading as it reached his cheekbone and a livid cut crossed partially puffy lips to nestle in the cleft of his chin.

'My God, Khalid, what on earth happened? You look as though you've gone three rounds with Prince Naseem.'

Ali attempted a laugh, but caught at his breath as the pain snagged at him. 'I slipped on wet

419

leaves,' he said, lisping as he spoke. 'It looks worse than it feels.'

Handford leaned forward to scrutinize him more closely. This wasn't the first time he'd seen injuries like this and he was sceptical about the sergeant's explanation. 'It looks to me more like you met someone's fist,' he said. 'You haven't been mugged, have you?'

'No, I haven't. I told you; I slipped on wet leaves.'

Embarrassment had given way to defensiveness. There was little doubt in Handford's mind that someone had hit Ali or that he'd been in a fight, but if he didn't want to say, that was up to him. He couldn't force it out of him.

With a final check on Ali's bruised face and a deep sigh, Handford told him to sit down before he fell down, adding, 'Have you seen a doctor? Do you want the police surgeon to take a look at you?'

Ali shook his head. 'No, I'll be fine. Amina patched me up.'

Handford wasn't sure. 'You don't seem fine to me. Promise me if it gets too much you'll go home and rest. In the meantime, you stay in the station today. I don't want you out and about in that state.'

Ali relaxed visibly, 'As I said, John, I'll be fine, but thanks anyway.'

'If you're sure.' Handford handed him the lists of the day's actions. 'You can take charge of the tasks that can be completed in-house and hand the others out to team leaders.'

There was a tap on the door and Clarke's head

appeared. 'John, I've just heard...' His voice faded as he caught sight of Ali. 'Good God, Khalid, you look to have been in the wars. What happened?'

'He slipped on wet leaves,' Handford said before Ali could answer.

'Did he? That was careless.'

Ali blushed as Clarke held his gaze moment-arily, then abruptly the constable turned towards Handford and said, 'I've just heard about Gill. Is she all right?'

'She says she is, although she didn't look it this morning. It was a nasty experience, but she's determined to go into school today.' He would have preferred it wasn't common knowledge around the station.

Ali's eyes switched from the DI to Clarke and back again. 'What's happened?'

Handford told him.

'Is Gill pressing charges?'

'No, I've tried to persuade her, but she's adam-ant. As I said, she's gone into work; she refuses to be frightened by them. Not that I think Kerry Johnson will be there – not even she's that arro-gant.'

'It might be a good idea for someone to keep an eye on them, though, just in case,' Clarke sug-gested.

For a moment Handford wondered if he should mention that Warrender was already doing that, but decided against it. Better they didn't know. 'Uniform has promised to keep a watch on the school, drive by occasionally,' he said. 'I'm not sure even that's necessary, but the duty inspector thinks the students may well be a bit twitchy and

421

could try something else. He's concerned that it might not take much to set them off again.'

Warrender glanced at his watch for the fifth time in as many minutes. Ten o'clock. He'd been sitting in his car watching Kerry Johnson's house since eight and he was bored, stiff and hungry. He pulled a chocolate bar from his pocket and took a bite. One thing was sure: she wasn't intending to go into school today. He only hoped she was intending to get out of bed.

If he knew her as well as he thought he did, he was confident she would want to get back to mugging unsuspecting shoppers. Social security benefits were their bread and butter – hers and Sean's – and proceeds from street robbery their jam. He wondered briefly what the money from Graham Collins was for. Did they spend it as soon as they got it, or did Kerry have something else in mind? Certainly there was nothing to show in the house for however much they were screwing from Collins; they hadn't even got a car, which would have been the obvious choice. Before Sean had killed the kid, he'd been into pinching cars.

As it was, Kerry had had five days without earning, so the chances were she would go into the shopping centre today. Wednesday was a good day for them. Middle of the week, housewives were in town replenishing their larders before the weekend. For the gang morning was better because, though busy, it was not too busy. Enough people to give them a choice of victim, but not enough of a crowd to hinder their escape. He knew Kerry of old, knew how she operated. It would be this

422

morning – it was just a matter of being patient. It wasn't as though he hadn't plenty to think about while he waited. Detective Sergeant Ali for one.

Katie had been furious with him for hitting Ali. She'd made him apologize, bring him into the house and clean him up, after which she'd added to her brother's ignominy by insisting he drive the sergeant home. They'd gone in Ali's car, had hardly spoken a word during the journey, then when he'd dropped him off he'd had to ring for a taxi to take him back to his own home. It had been a Pakistani who had come for him. When he'd finally walked into the house she had told him what she thought of him and his behaviour. It was like being back at school. He hadn't argued with her, just listened, told her he was sorry and put her to bed. This morning he'd hardly spoken to her, just waited for the carer and left for work. Then he'd come straight here, hadn't gone into the station.

He was angry with Ali for forcing the issue, but he was also angry with himself. For the first time since the accident he'd let his rage and resentment get the better of him. Many a time he'd wanted to hit out, let them feel what he felt. Katie coped better than him, but then she'd been unconscious while he watched their mother and father die of their injuries. She hadn't been aware of him while he sat by her bedside for weeks not knowing whether she was going to survive, or when the doctors had told him that if she lived she would be paraplegic. Who else was he to blame for all that? Logically, he knew it wasn't Ali, but grief was illogical. He'd watched the

423

arrogance of the defendant in the dock and felt the disdain of those outside. They had hated him, and he hated them. He'd coped because the only Asians he'd come across had been law-breakers and each time he put one away he purged a little bit of the debt owed to Katie and his parents. Then Ali had come along. Not a crook, but a police officer, a detective and a sergeant. One of them. And from their very first meeting he had been as conceited and supercilious as the driver of the car and his family and friends outside the court.

Ali had no right to ask Clarke about him and Clarke had no right to tell him. And he'd no right to hit the sergeant. Yet when he'd helped him off the ground, in a strange way he'd had the feeling that Ali understood why he had done what he had done. He hoped that now he'd slept on it he still understood. It was one thing Warrender having fun at his expense, making comments, quite another punching him in the mouth. Even so, he couldn't help smiling when he thought about it; the man had gone down like a felled tree.

As he replayed the images, the smile faded and suddenly nervous, Warrender began to sweat. Once Ali had thought about it overnight, he could have him disciplined, charged even. Bending the rules for the DI might be the last job he ever undertook as a police officer. He hoped to God he was wrong, but if he wasn't then he'd make bloody sure it would be a job well done.

He glanced up at Kerry's house. The curtains in the upstairs window flickered and then a few minutes later those in the front room were drawn back. Kerry stood looking out. She was dressed. There was no sign of Sean.

He waited.

Some fifteen minutes later she emerged through the front door, a slice of toast in her hand. As she walked she pulled at the bread and chewed. Warrender slid down in his seat. If she saw him she would recognize him, and being Kerry Johnson she would come over with a mouthful of abuse.

She didn't.

He watched as she sauntered down the hill, making no attempt to hide herself from the school, and then switched on the ignition. He held back until she was out of sight before slowly moving off. As he turned the corner he saw her at the bus stop. She was perched on one of the narrow seats in the shelter. She finished her toast and then lit a cigarette.

He pulled up.

The service here was frequent and within minutes a double-decker rattled down the hill. She stubbed out her cigarette, blew the last vestige of smoke out of the corner of her mouth and climbed onto the step. He saw her pay her fare and move inside. On the journey down into Bradford, he remained two cars behind the bus.

Once in the city, Warrender parked and followed her on foot up Darley Street to the Arndale Shopping Centre. Gemma, Kylie and Lindsay were waiting for her by the steps. They talked for a moment, mashed out their cigarettes underfoot, walked to the automatic doors and disappeared from view.

Warrender slipped in after them and once inside

grabbed the first security guard he saw. Keeping a close eye on the girls, he waved his warrant card in front of the uniformed man and explained that the police were mounting a purge on street robbery this month and he had reason to believe the four girls over there were about to commit one. He suggested that he contact his controller and ask for two or three more guards. They shouldn't make themselves conspicuous, but should monitor the suspects' movements. He used official language and watched the guard preen himself. For once, the police wanted their help.

Once the girls had their prize there were various means of escape – straight out the way they had come; through Boots, which had its own street entrance; the exit at the far end of the centre or up the escalator. He was pretty sure they had their directions of flight well worked out, and he discussed with the security guards what they should do. One guard should take on one girl, but until then they needed to keep all of them in their sights. If and when anything happened, Warrender continued, they should apprehend Gemma, Lindsay and Kylie; Kerry Johnson, he said, was his.

As he maintained his observation, he couldn't help but feel some kind of warped admiration for the four girls. They were good at what they were doing, professional almost; it was no wonder they'd never been caught. They weren't in any hurry, placed themselves strategically near one of the cash machines and took their time selecting their victim. Gemma stood as close to the machine as was sensible and watched as the shoppers asked for and got their money. The others stationed themselves further away.

The first five shoppers Gemma ignored. It seemed that whoever she decided upon had to ask for enough money to make it worth the girls' while and be vulnerable enough not to fight back. Her interest was finally heightened by a youngish woman with a pushchair in which there was a baby and by her side a toddler whom she was desperately trying to hold on to. The little boy was curious, wanted to wander. She told him angrily to stay with her while she got some money or she wouldn't buy him any sweets. He began to wail, then to scream and then to lie down on the floor. Pulling him upright, she struggled to put her card in the slot and finger in her pin number, followed by the amount she wanted. The machine bleeped and the card and the money appeared almost simultaneously. She battled to put them both away in her purse and the purse in her bag while still keeping hold of the struggling boy.

Gemma waved her hand as though she had seen someone she knew. That had to be the signal. Kylie moved quickly, smoothly snatching the woman's bag.

For a moment the young mother stood bewildered, almost paralysed, then she screamed out loud, 'She's got my bag! The cow's pinched my bag.'

Frightened by the sudden noise, the toddler cried even louder.

Kylie threw the bag to Kerry, who set off at a dash for the far entrance. Gemma fled towards the main exit, Lindsay into Boots and Kylie disappeared up the escalator. The security guards sped after them.

Kerry was Warrender's.

She was fast, he had to admit, but he was fit himself and as he pushed his way through the shoppers he began to advance on her. She threw the bag to one side. A young man in dirty jeans and trainers picked it up. Finally Warrender caught up with her at the door, grabbed her first by her anorak collar, then as she tried to pull herself out of it, by her arm. This time he held on tight. He spun her round and marched her back to the main entrance, taking the bag from the youth, who held it out to him as he passed.

Breathing heavily, she screamed at her captor. 'Get off me, you bastard. Get off me.' She appealed to the shoppers who were watching open-mouthed. 'Help me. He's hurting me. Somebody help me.' No one moved and only one woman spoke. 'Serves yer right, yer little slag,' she shouted. 'He ought to give yer a good 'iding. That's what I'd do if I were your mother.'

Kerry yelled at Gemma and Lindsay, who were being dragged along by the guards. 'Don't say owt; they can't do nothing to us.' She turned her head. 'We'll be back here this afternoon, then we'll have *your* bag, you stupid cow,' she shouted at the woman, who gave her a finger.

Warrender pulled at her. 'Shut it,' he said. 'Stand there and shut up.' Maintaining his grip, he spoke to the guards. 'Where's the other one?'

'She's gone. Up the escalator and disappeared.'

Kerry smirked.

'Not to worry,' Warrender said. 'We know who she is; we'll get her. What about the victim?'

'One of the assistants from the jeweller's has taken her inside, given her a cup of tea.'

'Right. Take them up to the manager's office to wait for transport while I have a quick word with the lady, return her property and organize a statement.'

Kerry glared at him. 'You can't keep us. We haven't done anything.' It was a futile comment which drew a smile from Warrender.

'I think you'll find that I can,' he said. 'In fact, Kerry Johnson, not only am I going to keep you, but I'm going to arrest you and your friends for street robbery and then, since I have reason to believe that you may have the proceeds of similar robberies at your house, I'm going to do a search. Will Sean be at home, do you think?'

It was almost eleven when Ali knocked on John Handford's door. He had hoped he would have heard from Warrender by now, although he knew the detective would be unlikely to contact him unless there was something worthwhile to report.

The sergeant still didn't look too good, but behind the physical discomfort, Handford detected an air of excitement, tinged with something else he couldn't quite put his finger on.

'I've just picked up a message for Warrender,' Ali said, 'from the Family Records Office. His lady friend has found the records of Graham Samuel Collins. He was born as he said in Catterick on 21 April 1973 to – and here's where it becomes interesting – a Private William and

Mrs Sarah Collins...'

'Not Martin and Rebecca?'

'No.'

'Nor Major, or even Lieutenant, as he would probably have been then?'

'No. I checked with the military police and they got back to me. Private William Collins served at the Infantry Training Centre at Catterick until he bought himself out of the army after his wife had a severe mental breakdown after the death of their son from meningitis at the age of nine months. They emigrated to Australia some twenty years ago. So I checked again with the Family Records Office. Graham Samuel Collins did indeed die of meningitis at nine months old and the woman confirmed there *was* no other baby of that name born on that date.'

'And that means?'

'That means I owe you an apology. The Graham Collins we know does not have a past as Graham Collins. For whatever reason, he has borrowed or has been given the name of a dead baby. I'm sorry. You were right.'

Handford waved away the apology. 'It's more important to know what this means. Witness protection perhaps?'

'I thought that as well, so I contacted West Yorkshire's witness protection. He's not on their books and they don't know anything about him. The only other place we can be sure he has been is Warwick, so I rang them. Ditto. So if he is in a witness protection scheme, I don't know which, and whichever one it is, it's been well organized because according to admissions at Warwick

University he applied as Graham Samuel Collins and his GCSE and A-level certificates were valid. I've got a couple of DCs trawling through big trials from 1986 through to 1992, when he went to university, to see if he might have been a witness in one of those. It's not going to be easy or quick. It might be better just to ask him.'

'I knew he was keeping something from us.' Handford sat back and there was a long pause before he continued. 'Do you think it's possible Kerry Johnson is aware of any of this? Maybe that he's given evidence against someone Sean knows or met while he was in prison? Sean might have recognized him as the crucial witness and Kerry is using the information to blackmail Collins, threatening to disclose his identity and tell whoever where he is. Does that make sense?'

Ali shook his head. 'It's a hell of a long shot, John. Sean Johnson's not the brightest star in the sky and it's a good few years since he was inside. I doubt he'd recognize his mother any more, let alone someone he might – *possibly* – have seen in a witness box all those years ago. No, that doesn't make any sense at all.'

'Then what does she have on him?' Handford let out a long sigh. 'All this gets murkier by the minute and it doesn't get us any nearer to finding out whether he killed Shayla Richards. I didn't want to, not yet, but I think the time has come to have another word with our Mr Collins – or whoever the hell he is.'

Kerry was plainly nervous – and aggressive. 'I want a solicitor.'

'You can have a solicitor when we get back to the station. *After...*' Warrender emphasized the word. 'I've completed the search.'

'I don't want you in my bedroom, you pig.' She turned to her uncle. 'Sean, tell him. He's only here to go through my knickers, the mucky beggar.'

Sean leaned against the door jamb and dragged on his roll-up but didn't reply.

'Sean!'

Warrender was becoming tired of this. 'Look,' he said. 'We can do this the hard way or the easy way. It's up to you. You're under arrest; I think there are stolen goods in this house, I can search for them now or, like I said earlier, we can sit here while I get someone to get me a warrant. But one way or another, with or without it, I'm going to search your room. So what I suggest is you sit quietly on your bed, while I get on with it.'

She slumped down.

Like those in the rest of the house, the room was small and the furniture cheap, but also like the rest of the house it was clean. Quite the little housewife, mother, lover? Warrender couldn't be sure. The bed that rested against the wall and behind the door wasn't quite a single, but not a double either – more like a three-quarter. Big enough for two if necessary, Warrender thought. Nestled into the corner between the window wall and the party wall was a white wooden wardrobe and next to it a dressing table and stool, both probably bought from some second-hand dealer. Kerry was tidy, he'd give her that. Her cosmetics were carefully arranged either side of the mirror, together with photographs of a woman.

432

'This your mum?' he asked.

Kerry scrambled over and snatched it from him. 'You leave her alone, copper.'

Warrender shrugged. He might want to find something to tie her in with the street robberies, but he didn't want to upset her, particularly where her mum was concerned. He knew how she felt.

He opened the top drawer and carefully pushed the lingerie to one side. Even through his latex gloves, he could feel its softness. While it was not expensive, it was not cheap either – certainly more than the Johnsons could afford. Probably bought with the proceeds of the robberies, but impossible to prove. Pushed up to one side were three packets of cigarettes and a couple of packets of condoms. He'd been right about the lover. Warrender ran his hand along the base of the drawer, inside and out. Nothing attached. Similarly with the second. She obviously wasn't into drugs. He pulled open the third. It was deeper than the others and held several jumpers. To one side was a cardboard box, which he lifted out and opened up. Photographs, letters and a post office bank book. Normally he would have tipped everything out without thought, but he didn't want to disturb the photos, so he took them carefully from the box and spread them on the bed. He glanced through them. Most were of her, or her mother, or her and her mother. There was one of a man whom Warrender recognized as her father. So in spite of herself she hadn't let him go completely. The letters were still sealed and had the prison address on the back. She might not want to read them but she couldn't bear to throw them away either. Poor kid. As he picked up the bank book, she made to snatch it from him, but he pulled his hand away. He opened it. It was made out in her name. £2,347. One hundred pounds every month as regular as clockwork, with a few other bits and pieces at other times. Some of it might have come from some poor old lady's handbag, but not the rest. Much more likely it was what she'd wrung from Graham Collins.

'Where did you get all this money?'

'Mind your own fucking business.'

'Oh, I think it might well be my business, Kerry. Where did you get it?'

'Saved it. You never heard of saving?'

He looked towards her uncle. 'You know anything about it?'

Sean shook his head. He was beginning to take on a greenish hue.

Warrender placed the book in a plastic bag and pushed it into his inside jacket pocket. 'I'll keep it for the moment. Perhaps when we get down to the station you'll both be able to tell me a bit more.'

At this Sean turned and fled downstairs. Warrender heard the front door open and bang shut. Kerry made to follow him, but the detective grabbed at her arm. 'Oh, no you don't. We haven't finished here yet.' They could pick Sean up later.

He replaced the photographs and letters, put the box back in the drawer and then turned his attention to the wardrobe. He opened its door. Trousers, jeans and blouses hung from plastic hangers. Warrender picked them out. Again, while they were not top of the range, neither were they jumble-sale material. He examined them

434

carefully, feeling in all pockets. Again nothing. He was about to return them when he saw another garment tucked away in a dark corner: an anorak, he thought. He stretched in to pull it out. It wasn't an anorak; it was a puffa jacket. He let his eyes do the questioning.

'It's mine. I don't wear it any more; it's old.'

He examined it carefully. It was grey with a red lining and like everything else in her wardrobe, in pristine condition. In one of the pockets was a paper handkerchief, in the other an envelope. The address on it was Mustafa's consulting rooms and the stamp foreign – Pakistan, he thought. There was no letter. He held up the jacket and checked the inside. Clean and well kempt. There were two labels – one at the neck, the other sewn into a side seam. The first was the manufacturer's, the second the washing instructions. He wasn't sure what made him look at the latter more carefully.

Between the printed lettering was a name scrawled in black biro.

Shayla Richards.

He stared at Kerry. Whatever he had expected to find, it wasn't this.

He turned to her, pushed the label under her nose. 'That you, is it?'

Colour fled from her cheeks and she began to tremble. She looked up at him, pleading, then shook her head.

Maintaining eye contact with her, Warrender pulled out his mobile. 'I'm at Kerry Johnson's house, boss. I think we need a SOCO team down here. I've just found Shayla Richards' puffa jacket.'

chapter twenty-two

It was stuffy in the interview room. Humidity clung to the walls and the ceiling like cotton wool and Handford could feel sweat building up between his shoulders. The strip light flickered and hummed. Ali threw two painkillers into his mouth and swallowed them.

'Are you sure you're all right to do this?'

'Yes, I'm sure. Once these kick in I'll be fine. Anyway, there's no one else.'

Although he would prefer not to, he offered, 'I can bring Warrender in, or Clarke.'

Ali was adamant. 'No need to do that.'

True, it would have been awkward. Warrender was finishing off at Kerry Johnson's house and Clarke was following up a promising lead from a woman who had rung in to say she had heard the recording of the tape on her car radio and thought she knew the identity of the hoax caller.

Even so, Handford was concerned. 'All right, Khalid, but let me know if you need a break.'

Ali smiled his thanks as the door opened and Jaswant Siddique appeared, accompanied by one of the custody officers. He looked as tired and as jaded as Handford felt, but in spite of that had lost none of his arrogance. If they had hoped a night in the cells would change the man's attitude, they were sadly mistaken. He had hardly entered the room before he attempted to hijack

436

proceedings. 'You had no right to keep me here overnight,' he snapped.

Handford stood up and offered him one of the chairs at the opposite side of the table. 'I had every right, Mr Siddique. I believe you to have been holding Shayla Richards against her will and until I am satisfied one way or the other, there are more questions to be asked. Now, are you sure you don't want a solicitor? These are serious accusations and I would strongly advise that you consult one.'

'You're the one who'll need a solicitor when I sue you for wrongful arrest for, what do you call it – holding me against my will,' Siddique retorted.

Handford had had enough already. 'Yes, whatever,' he said. Then, 'Perhaps we can get on.' He nodded to Ali, who unwrapped the tapes and slipped them into the recording machine and switched it on. At the beep, Handford recited the preliminaries, reminding Siddique that although he had been advised of his rights to a solicitor, he had declined. He was asked to verify for the tape that this was so, which he did in a voice tinged with boredom.

Handford's first question was to the point. 'What was your relationship with Shayla Richards?'

Siddique leaned back in his chair and hooked his arm over the top corner so that he was half skewed away from his interrogator. The body language was familiar to Handford: seeming indifference.

'I'm tired of answering this question,' he said. 'I didn't have a relationship with Shayla Richards.' He emphasized each word.

Unconcerned, Handford continued. 'You say you work at Cliffe Top Comprehensive all day Monday and Tuesday and Wednesday morning?'

'Yes.'

'What do you do the rest of the week?'

'I've already told you this. Thursday and Friday I'm at the college.'

'Morning or afternoon?'

'Morning.'

'So what do you do in the afternoon?'

'Homework.'

'What does that mean?'

'It means that I come home from college and I work on the various exercises I have been set.'

'You don't help your brother with his patients?'

After a moment of hesitation, Siddique let out a long sigh. 'I don't know where you've got that from. And they're clients, not patients.'

Handford ignored the addendum. 'It wouldn't be surprising for you to help out, though, would it? You live in the same building as the consulting rooms, Mr Mustafa doesn't have a receptionist, and...' he paused, 'from what I hear, some of the patients – clients – are quite distressed. Perhaps he needs your help to calm them down. After all, Mr Siddique, you work with students with special needs. I'm sure you're used to settling distraught pupils.'

Siddique offered no reply.

'As far as I understand it, Shayla Richards was often distressed. Did you help him with her?'

Still he remained silent.

'It's my understanding that you did.'

Siddique scoffed. 'And who told you that?'

438

'Witnesses.'

Siddique pulled his arm from the back of the chair and leaned across the table. 'Cavendish.' His tone was mocking.

Handford sat back, restoring the space between them. 'I'm not obliged to tell you at the moment who they are. If you bring in a solicitor or if I charge you, the information will go to him. In the meantime it's enough that you know we have one witness to the fact that you do help your brother when you are not at school or at college, and more who are prepared to state that Shayla was very distressed during her sessions. In fact she screamed and shouted most of the time. For goodness' sake, even your brother admits that.' He leaned forward. 'I repeat, do you help your brother each Thursday and Friday?'

Siddique's confidence slipped. 'And that's a crime, is it?'

'Not unless you're helping in a crime. Were you?'

'Now you're saying my brother is a criminal?'

Handford ignored the comment. 'Did you help your brother with Shayla Richards?'

Silence. Not even a 'no comment'.

Handford waited. Then, tired of playing the man's games, he banged his fist on the table. 'Did you help your brother with Shayla Richards?'

The action startled the man into an answer. 'Yes, all right. I did, although why it's such a big deal, I don't know.' He scowled, then said, 'I object to the way you are questioning me.'

'Your objection is noted on tape,' Handford said, and before Siddique could make further

439

comments, or ask for a break, which they would be obliged to give him, he nodded to Ali to take over. The last thing he wanted was for Siddique to regroup his thoughts and his answers.

Ali took his time. 'If it's not such a big deal, why didn't you tell us that when you were first asked?'

Siddique shrugged.

'Perhaps he pays you? Cash in hand, don't let the Inland Revenue know.'

'He doesn't pay me.'

'So you helped him simply because he was your brother?'

'If you like.' It was a begrudging agreement, which for now Handford was prepared to accept. If necessary, he would come back to it later.

Ali continued. 'Why did Shayla Richards shout and scream?'

'She got a bit upset from time to time, but she didn't shout and scream.'

'Her uncle sat in the waiting room while she was being treated. He said she did.'

Again Siddique shrugged. 'Family members are emotionally involved. Their feelings are heightened; they often hear what isn't there. It's not unusual.'

A good answer, but not good enough. 'According to Calvin, your brother told him that the distress she was in was because the devils were leaving her body. Apparently they were deep-rooted and their extraction caused her some pain.'

'As I said, relations often misunderstand. I shouldn't take too much notice of what Calvin says. Ask my brother if you don't believe me.'

This was what Handford had been waiting for.

440

His next words, he hoped, would open Siddique up.

'I would, Mr Siddique, but your brother has disappeared.'

The two detectives watched his reaction. It was obvious he was struggling to keep his emotions in check. He couldn't, however, keep the incredulity from his voice. 'What do you mean, disappeared? When?'

'According to his housekeeper he's gone off to Egypt or Pakistan; she's not quite sure which. Nor, it appears, is his solicitor. He locked up his house, cleared his consulting rooms and left yesterday morning, apparently. Didn't he tell you?'

Outside, the storm broke. A sheet of lightning flashed across the skies, eliminating for a moment the gloom blanketing the city and a few seconds later, a roar of thunder erupted overhead and rolled across the heavens.

On cue, Siddique's temper exploded. 'The bastard!' he yelled, replicating Handford's action as he banged his fists on the table. And then, as though all his energy had been taken from him, he repeated more quietly, 'The bastard.'

Now it was time for a break.

Kerry Johnson had never been in a police station before. Never in the reception area, never in an interview room and never in a cell. Some would say it was more by good luck than good management, but she knew that it was because she was careful; she had everything worked out and that made her better than the cops and better than the security guards – until today. She didn't know

441

what had gone wrong. It was almost as though they had known they were going to be there and had been waiting. It was that detective, that Warrender. He was a sly bastard; she'd thought so the first time he'd been to her house. Then he'd wanted to search her room, and now he'd got his way.

After he'd found the post office book and the puffa jacket, he'd made her watch while the men and women in white coveralls had ransacked her bedroom and then the house. They had bagged all kinds of things up, including the cushions from the settee in the sitting room. Then she'd been brought here. But she'd fought them. When they tried to put her in a cell – a secure room they'd called it – she'd kicked and screamed and the social worker they'd brought in had insisted that she was so distressed she had to be seen by a doctor. He had given her a couple of pills to calm her down.

The room she was in was small. Too small. It gave her the creeps. She'd hated places that were small ever since her mother's funeral. They'd buried her in a grave that was narrow and deep. She was dead, Kerry knew that. They'd done a post-mortem – cut her up to find out how she'd died. Even at twelve, she understood what that meant and that without her heart and her lungs and her brain inside her, her mother had to be dead, but that hadn't stopped the nightmares in which her mother was in the coffin suffocating, unable to breathe, desperately trying to fight her way out to rejoin Kerry. This room made her feel like her mother felt in the dreams.

When Warrender had brought her in, he'd charged her with the street robbery and then said they were keeping her. Then the solicitor had come and almost immediately disappeared with the cop – to talk, he'd said. The social worker had gone for a cup of tea. When they came back she was told she was being arrested on suspicion of obtaining money with menaces. They'd not make that stick. She'd never needed to menace Collins, just let him know the score. The solicitor also said they would want to question her about the jacket found in her wardrobe.

They could question her all they liked – she was saying nothing. She'd show 'em.

She lay down on the bed and closed her eyes. If they thought she was asleep, they'd think the pills had put her out and they'd leave her alone for a bit. She didn't want to answer any of their questions, but deep down she knew she couldn't sleep for ever; they would come for her eventually.

She had never been so frightened.

She wished Sean was here with her instead of that wanker of a social worker – her appropriate adult, they'd called her. Sean shouldn't have gone, not when she needed him. Detective Warrender had said not to worry, they would find him eventually. But she was worried. She didn't know what he would do. He was terrified of going back to prison. He would kill himself first, he had once said. She didn't want that. She didn't want another death. There had been too many.

During the break, Handford asked Jaswant Siddique again if he wanted a solicitor. This time he accepted and asked for Suleman Khan. Mr Khan turned up within half an hour and spent some considerable time with his client. Eventually, he agreed they were ready and that Handford could continue the interview.

As soon as he appeared in the room, it was obvious Siddique had shed his arrogance and his posturing. He refused to make eye contact and when he was asked if he was ready, his voice cracked and he had to clear his throat in order to answer the question. When he sat down, he rested his arms on the table and fiddled with a piece of detritus he found next to his fingers.

'My client wishes to make a statement, Inspector, regarding the unlawful imprisonment of Shayla Richards,' Suleman Khan said, his accent flawless.

Handford took in the solicitor for a moment. He was not a man he knew, certainly not the kind of criminal lawyer Handford came across too often. Probably more involved with cases like tax evasion or fraud or even litigation – those that would bring in the money. There were solicitors who were in their element in a police station interview room, but not Khan. He seemed as out of place and as uncomfortable as a Ming vase in a junk shop. The very sparseness of the room, its characterless decor, plain furniture and recording machine were meant to cow suspects, not entertain men like Suleman Khan. Handford almost expected him to flick the chair free of dust with a handkerchief before he sat down.

Every inch of him breathed success: his impeccably groomed hair, his expensive and perfectly

444

tailored dark suit and his slim, expressive fingers. But what really fascinated Handford was his tie and he found his eyes drawn to the sheen of the small red and black pattern woven into the silk. Ties were Handford's downfall. Gill loved shoes; he loved ties. Ties could make a man's appearance, and there was no doubt the one Suleman Khan was wearing did exactly that.

As he watched Khan unlock his briefcase and bring out his notebook and gold fountain pen, he wondered why he had taken on such a case and how Jaswant Siddique, on a teaching assistant's salary, could possibly afford him. No doubt he'd send the bill to his brother – if he could find him.

Handford nodded to Ali, who switched on the recording machine, asked each person to identify himself and reminded Siddique he was still under caution.

'You wish to make a statement, Mr Siddique?' Handford said.

The man nodded, still avoiding eye contact. Handford was certain he was about to shop his brother, but whether they were going to get a murderer out of it, he wasn't sure. He sat back, giving Jaswant Siddique the platform – probably the only platform he'd ever been unhappy with.

'It was my brother's idea,' he began. Handford had been right; he *was* about to shop his brother. 'Shahid was in the process of organizing the removal of Qumar's boys, Dion and Aaron, to Pakistan and Shayla found out, told him she knew what he was doing and threatened to tell Calvin and her mother.'

Handford interrupted. 'How did she find out?'

445

Siddique lifted his eyes. 'It was during one of her sessions. There was a letter on the desk from Qumar. Shahid had gone out of the room for a moment to talk to some parents. She must have recognized the writing and read it.'

'Where were you?'

His eyes dropped again. 'I went for a smoke. I told her to stay where she was and made sure the door to the waiting room and the door I used were locked. There wouldn't have been a problem if she hadn't gone snooping and he hadn't been so stupid as to leave the letter on the desk,' he added angrily. 'Anyway, she knew too much and had to be kept out of the way until the boys had gone. My flat was handy. Shahid didn't give me a choice. Once he'd got the boys away, we'd let her go home, he said. I looked after her, but she was gone for a week before she turned up dead and I had nothing to do with that. That's someone else.'

Siddique sat back.

'That's all my client has to say, Inspector,' Suleman Khan said. 'We agree Shayla was held against her will, and you can charge him with that if you wish. We will of course apply for bail and since there was obviously coercion on the part of his brother, we will plead not guilty. Other than that I have advised him to use his right to silence, so any more questions will be irrelevant.'

'I think not, Mr Khan. Shayla Richards is dead and you cannot expect me to take what Mr Siddique has said without inquiring further. It's up to him whether he answers or not, but I can assure you I'm not leaving it at that.'

'Then if that's what you intend I may need a little more time with my client.'

'You can have all the time you want, sir, but he's not going anywhere until I have asked my questions and maybe not then. It might be worth you reminding him that a right to silence is a right an innocent man almost never uses and that if he insists on doing so then, if and when it comes to court, he must expect the jury to wonder why he didn't take the opportunity to prove his innocence when he had the chance.'

Khan whispered to Siddique, who hesitated for a brief moment, then lifted his hands in resignation. For the first time ever, probably, he had lost the will to argue.

Handford lifted his eyes interrogatively at Suleman Khan, who nodded.

It was difficult to know where to start, but if Siddique was blaming Shahid, then Shahid was the obvious place. The two of them might not be joined at the hip exactly, but neither were they mutually exclusive. 'Is your brother a bounty hunter, Mr Siddique?'

'No, he isn't.' Siddique sounded aggrieved. 'He helps parents whose daughters run away because they refuse to accept their choice of a partner or who marry surreptitiously and out of the faith, and more particularly fathers who have been denied their children when there is a split in the marriage.'

Handford tried to keep his temper. 'You mean he stalks the young girls until he finds them, then forces them against their will to return to their parents, or in the case of the children, kidnaps them and takes them abroad?'

'Something like that.'

'For payment?'

Siddique shrugged. 'My brother never does anything for nothing. He'd squeeze the last drop of blood out of someone if he had to.'

'And you help him?'

'Don't answer that,' Khan broke in quickly.

Siddique offered no reply.

Ali said, 'For the tape Mr Siddique has declined to answer.'

'Your brother wasn't interested in Shayla?'

'Of course not. Neither was Qumar. I've told you, she was a slag, gave herself to any man who wanted her.'

Handford felt sick. 'Yet he counselled her as a client. Why did he do that?'

'Calvin had asked him to help her. He thought she was possessed by devils; Shahid had no option but to go along with it.'

'And was she possessed by devils?'

Sarcasm laced his words. 'She was possessed by something. Whether it was devils or not is doubtful.'

'How did he counsel her?'

'The usual way; they talked about her and her life, her fears, her aspirations, and then eventually discussed the devils and what had allowed them to take hold. Then he attempted to remove them from her body.'

'How?'

Suddenly Siddique was on the defensive. 'He used the tried and tested methods.'

'Which are?' Handford wasn't sure he wanted

to know.

'Chanting, imploring them to leave her, in language they understand.'

Handford thanked God Warrender wasn't co-interviewer.

Ali interrupted. 'I assume that didn't work?'

'No.'

'So what was the next step?'

Siddique licked his lips. 'A gentle massage.'

Handford frowned. 'What kind of massage?'

'Usually at the point at which the devils entered. If the person had been fed evil thoughts by another person, then it would be around the ears, moving on to the skull. If they had entered through the eyes, it would be the eyes. It depended on how they had got in.'

'And Shayla?'

Without lifting his eyes from the notes he was making, Suleman Khan said, 'I am advising my client not to answer that question.'

Relief showed on Siddique's face. 'I shall take my solicitor's advice,' he said. 'I have no comment.'

A pity, but there was time.

Ali said, 'You don't like your brother, do you, Mr Siddique?'

For the first time during the interview Siddique looked straight at his questioner. 'No, not much. He's always been the favourite with my parents. They're proud of his success, whereas they feel I have let them down. He married well; I have not yet accepted any of the wives they have found for me. He is a counsellor and people come to him for help; I am a teaching assistant. They pretend to relatives that I am a qualified teacher, you know, so that they're not too ashamed of me. It doesn't matter that I like my work. They're proud that Shahid has made it in this country, with his big house and his wealth. I'm not allowed to live there, of course. Instead I have a flat in a building he owns, which he lets me have at a reduced rent and I'm expected to be grateful. No, I can't say I like him.'

'So why are you protecting him?'

The force of the question took him by surprise and Siddique began to unravel. Unable to speak, he shook his head.

Suleman Khan replaced the top on his pen and placed it carefully next to his notepad. 'I really do think my client needs a rest, Inspector. Perhaps some tea.'

Handford nodded his agreement and Ali turned off the recording machine.

As Ali left the room to organize the refreshments, Handford turned to Siddique. 'You do realize that should you be found guilty of holding Shayla against her will, even as an accessory, and even if the judge is lenient and doesn't send you down, you'll never be able to return to the classroom or work with children.'

'Yes, I do know what happens.' Insolence oozed from him. He had become the old Jaswant Siddique. 'Don't forget I've seen how you've all harassed Graham Collins.'

The comment didn't deserve a response, but if that was what it took to keep the conversation going, then he could have one. 'He can claim harassment because he wasn't guilty, although I doubt he'll get anywhere. You, on the other hand, have admitted to being involved in Shayla's disappearance.' Handford leaned over the table. 'For goodness' sake man, use some common sense. You claim you were forced into it by your brother. If that's so, and I can see that it might be, you owe him nothing. He's even left you to shoulder the blame. So tell us what happened.' He paused. 'Or are we talking family honour here?'

Siddique shook his head, but made no reply.

'Are you offering my client a deal, Inspector?'

'I'm not offering him a deal, Mr Khan; I'm simply trying to find a spark of humanity in him.'

Before the solicitor could answer, Ali returned with the drinks and handed them round. 'Are you ready to continue, Mr Siddique?'

He nodded and Ali switched the recording machine back on. Then, rather than sitting down, he leaned against the wall, his arms folded. He looked like someone at rest, but the action was deliberate.

Handford took a sip of his drink, then sat back. His earlier comments had been off the official record but in front of Suleman Khan, and he hoped Siddique had taken them in. He doubted the man in front of him was evil, but as sure as hell his brother was. Jaswant Siddique disliked his brother, was maybe jealous of him; he'd shaken his head at family honour, so why had he gone along with what Mustafa was doing to Shayla Richards? He could just as easily have taken her home or even gone to the police. But he didn't. Why? A sudden thought jolted him.

Another gut reaction. Ali wouldn't approve. But it would make sense of everything that had happened so far.

His next question was meant to shock, give some indication of what they knew. 'Shayla Richards had been the victim of what the pathologist said was systematic sexual abuse, some of it old, some of it more recent, all of it rough. Do you know anything about this?'

Khan looked at his client and shook his head, advising him not to reply.

Siddique said nothing. He was holding on – just.

'She was with you for three weeks before the final week of her life. One of you had sex with her. Was it you or your brother?'

That was too much and he answered so quickly that Khan had no time to stop him.

'My brother.'

'You really don't have to answer these questions,' the solicitor interjected.

Siddique turned to him. 'Yes I do, or I shoulder the lot like he said.'

'That was no more than a threat.'

'It was the truth. My brother's gone and is unlikely to be back. I know him.' He pointed at Handford. 'He's said they have evidence that she had had sex with someone. She was with us; it couldn't be anyone else but me or my brother, unless we were using her as a prostitute, which we weren't. I'm sure Gerry Cavendish wouldn't have missed that if it was happening,' he added bitterly.

'And you? Did you have sex with her?'

'Once or twice, but not like Shahid. He didn't give her the choice.'

Handford struggled to keep a hold on his

temper. 'You are saying you had sex with a girl who was both a minor and a pupil at your school, and your brother raped her?'

Again he was on the defensive. 'It was part of her treatment.'

'Sex with Mustafa was part of her treatment?'

'It's not unusual. He said the devils were deep seated. It was one way of forcing them out.' As Siddique scrutinized the faces of the two detectives, he declared, 'It's well documented – soul transference through sex, ridding the body of evil through sex. He took the devils into his own body because he was strong and could cope with them. Chanting was enough for him to dispose of them from himself. Sex isn't only there for bodily gratification.'

Warrender had been right. He had talked about groups that looked upon it as a vital part of their religion. What was it called? Tantrism? Was that it, or was it part of the black magic Mustafa's card suggested he performed? How many more children did he use this on? No wonder he'd made a run for it.

'And Shayla accepted this?'

'No, she struggled and shouted and screamed. She didn't want it at all.'

Handford would like to have picked up Siddique and beaten him to a pulp. He kept his voice as calm as he was able. 'She was fifteen and he was raping her. Of course she didn't want it.' A multitude of emotions crowded in on him. He wanted to leave it there, get his head round it. He swallowed hard and asked, 'What did you do while she was trying to fight him off?'

At this Siddique dropped his eyes. 'I held her down,' he said, almost inaudibly.

'Louder please, for the tape.'

Siddique's voice intensified. 'I held her down,' he shouted. 'Is that what you wanted to hear?'

No, it wasn't what he wanted to hear. Handford closed his eyes for a moment and then stood up and walked over to Ali. 'I can't take any more of this,' he whispered. 'You have a go.'

Ali returned to his chair; Handford remained where he was.

'Some time ago you suggested that Shayla had renounced Islam by uncovering herself and sleeping around. What did you think you were doing by helping your brother in this way? There is nothing in our faith that allows for what you were doing.'

'I didn't have a choice.'

'Of course you did. We all have choices.'

'He knew something about me, something I'd done. If he told anyone I would probably have been arrested, lost my job and been despised by my colleagues. The school is the first place I have ever, ever been respected. It would also have brought more shame on my family than they could have expected – even from me.'

'You've already done that, so what was it Shahid had on you that made you do such awful things to Shayla Richards?'

Siddique deflated like a pricked balloon. He shook his head.

Handford knew. It was obvious. He pushed himself from the wall, walked over to the table and leaned over it, his face close to Siddique's. 'It was you, wasn't it? You assaulted Shayla two years ago.' It was a statement of fact, not a question. 'It wasn't Graham Collins at all. That's why you've been so insistent that he was innocent and so uncooperative with us and that's why you've been harassing my wife.' He shouted the last two words.

Siddique pushed his chair back and tried to stand up. 'She saw me. I was in the room as Shayla ran out.'

'No, she didn't. Gill has no memory of it at all. You've been making her life a misery for no reason. She could have been killed last night when Kerry Johnson and her friends tried to turn her car over. Was that your idea as well?' And before Siddique could answer, Handford turned and walked out of the interview room, taking care not to bang the door.

Sean Johnson stood opposite Evelyn Richards' house. Although it was still early afternoon, the streets were dark enough to trigger the lamps, which threw an amber glow over the pavement. There was a light on in the front room, but the rest of the house was in darkness. From time to time a figure crossed the window. A black woman. Mrs Richards. He recognized her from the papers. Suddenly the door opened. A woman copper walked out and closed it behind her. She waved at Shayla's mum. Probably one of those cops families got when someone was killed. Did Catherine's mum have one to stay with her? He hoped so. Catherine had been so pretty; he hadn't meant to kill her, just play with her. He watched

Mrs Richards for a while. She had a cup of something in her hand and took a drink.

Sean would have given anything for a cup of tea. He was cold. He shivered. He should have brought his coat. He had rushed out of the house without picking it up. He was also frightened – frightened at what was going to happen to Kerry and frightened for himself. He couldn't face life without her. She had kept him together for so long now. He pulled his cigarette tin out of his pocket, opened it and took out a roll-up. He lit it and pulled hard at it to drag the smoke into the back of his throat.

The copper had found the post office book. Why couldn't she have told him there was so much in it? Over two thousand pounds. She'd never said there was so much. No way would the copper believe she'd saved it. He would put two and two together and work out that some of it was from Collins and the rest was nicked. Why had the silly bitch gone into town to thieve? Why couldn't she have left it for a few days? They'd have managed.

And the jacket. Why couldn't she have got rid of it when she knew Shayla was dead? If he hadn't been so drunk...

Well, he wasn't drunk now and without Kerry it was up to him.

It was Collins' fault, no one else's, and Sean knew exactly what he was going to do about it. First he'd tell Mrs Richards. She of all people had a right to know what he had done. According to Kerry she and her friends had protested at his house once before, insisting he'd killed Shayla, but the cops had turned them away. This time more people would join her. They would band together and march round to his house, hound him out of Bradford. And serve him right.

A sheet of lightning crossed the skies, lighting up everything around it in a translucent glow. A few seconds later a roar of thunder erupted overhead and the rain began, big drops that came faster and faster, bouncing off the pavements and running down the gulley. It wet him through. His hair plastered to his forehead and water dripped from the end of his nose. He wiped it with his hand, then set off across the road. For a moment he stopped, collecting his thoughts, working out what he was going to say. When he was sure, he knocked on Mrs Richards' door.

'Mrs Richards,' he said, when she answered. 'My name is Sean Johnson. Kerry was Shayla's friend. Can I come in? There's something I need to tell you about Graham Collins.'

John Handford was in his office when the call came through to say that Jane Collins was at the front desk and would like to see him. He wasn't sure he could move yet. His nerves were still thrashing about in his stomach and he felt sick. He had come so close to attacking Jaswant Siddique. What he and his brother had done to Shayla Richards was obscene, and Handford had had a belly full of obscene during his time in the service. As he'd left the room, he'd seen the combination of disgust and horror in Suleman Khan's face. He hoped the man would refuse to represent either of them, but he doubted it. Everyone

457

deserved representation. Did they? Handford wasn't sure.

As he walked through the door next to the front desk he saw Jane Collins standing looking out of the windows. He'd been half expecting her at some time. She would have gone back home to search for documents and old photographs that would give her husband what the police thought he didn't have – a past. Handford wondered whether he should tell her what they had learned from the Family Records Office, but decided against it. They needed to know first what it was they didn't know. He'd give it another twenty-four hours. After that if there was still nothing then he'd do what Ali had suggested and ask the man outright.

He approached her and smiled. 'How can I help, Mrs Collins?'

She returned his smile. 'You know the last time I was here was when Graham was charged with the assault on Shayla Richards. I vowed there and then that I'd never come through those doors again. You should never say never, should you, Inspector?'

'Perhaps it's not a good idea. Time has a habit of making fools of us and our promises.' He took her arm. 'Come over here and sit down, or we can use an office if you'd rather.'

'No, this is fine.' She sat down and faced him. 'I have something for you,' she said and thrust a large brown envelope towards him. 'Proof that my husband does have a past. In there are his birth certificate and his GCSE and A-level cer-tificates.'

He took the envelope and turned out the papers inside. The birth certificate was one of the small ones, proof of nothing except that a boy, Graham Samuel Collins, had been born on the twenty-first of April 1973. Not to whom he had been born. The educational qualifications were as the admissions officer at the University of Warwick had said: in his name and valid.

He placed them back in the envelope. 'Thank you for bringing them. Would you mind if I kept them for a little while?'

She shook her head. 'Not if they prove to you that my husband is who he says he is.' She opened her purse, pulled out a small envelope and handed it to him. 'If they're not enough, perhaps this will be.'

He opened it and took out a photograph of a young boy sitting on a wall, a large grin on his face. A golden Labrador dog stretched up towards him to rest its front paws on his knee. 'My husband as a little boy,' she said.

As he scrutinized it, a frown creased his forehead and then in spite of the central heating he shivered. The image was familiar. He didn't know why or where from, but he knew beyond a shadow of doubt that he'd seen it somewhere before. Not recently, but a long time ago. A happy scene with sinister connotations – he'd thought that then and he thought it now. But why? He flicked through the recesses of his mind. A picture of a boy and a dog ... where *had* he seen it?

He'd been quiet for too long and was suddenly aware of Mrs Collins. 'You think this isn't him, don't you?' She was angry.

His expression changed and his eyes rested on hers. 'No, Mrs Collins. Of course not. I can see it's him. It's just that...'

'What?'

He smiled. 'Nothing. A bit of déjà vu, I think. It reminds me of the kind of photographs my parents took of me and I had a dog similar to this one.' It was worth the lie to allay her fears, if only for a while. He waited and then said, 'Is this the only one you have of Graham as a boy?'

'Yes.' Her expression became wary; she seemed to know where he was going and pre-empted his next question. 'I'd rather you didn't keep it.'

He shifted on the plastic chair, uncomfortable, embarrassed almost. 'I'm sorry Mrs Collins, but I think I'm going to have to – for a while at least.'

chapter twenty-three

Handford sat at his desk, his feet resting on the half-opened bottom drawer, his body angled backwards. He stared at the photograph Jane Collins had given him and tried to recall where he'd seen it before, why it was familiar to him. A boy, a winning smile and a dog? He closed his eyes and attempted to visualize it, not as a snap from an album but in another form. Perhaps in a newspaper or on television?

As the memories returned he opened his eyes and looked at it again. Images formed in his mind. First of the boy, smiling, stroking his pet dog and then of a little girl in a party dress, and later one of a woman, grief-stricken, dressed in a black suit, ill-fitting on her anorexic frame, clinging onto a man who was crying unashamedly.

Then, suddenly as if caught in the light of a photographer's flash bulb, his brain cleared and simultaneously his stomach lurched. He slid his feet off the drawer and sat up straight. What he was looking at was a photograph of Todd Bright-man, whose case had been so controversial in the early eighties and then again at the end of the decade. He turned to his computer and typed in the name. The answer came back: access denied.

Recognition sparked, neuron to neuron, and confirmation fought with denial. For the first time since the death of Shayla Richards all that

461

had happened in house made sense – Super-intendent Slater investigating the alleged assault and then when he should have been putting Handford in the picture, dashing off to monitor a case elsewhere; the file going missing.

They hadn't wanted him to know.

For a long moment he stared at the words: *access denied*. He didn't want this. Not on his patch and not in this investigation. But like it or not, it *was* on his patch *and* part of the investigation – an integral part. And although they must have known what it could mean, they'd dumped it on him without warning. Their excuse would be that the information would cloud his judgement and his impartiality. They were right there, because if it hadn't before, it sure as hell did now. The waters Ali had described as muddy had with this one picture become even more polluted.

Handford's immediate reaction was to march into Russell's office and demand to know why he hadn't been told, why he'd had to work in the dark. But there was little point; he'd have to do what he'd told Ali to do with his problem with Warrender – deal with it. If there was any time he felt the weight of rank, it was now, when events had overtaken him. Half an hour ago he'd had a suspect without a past. Now that same suspect not only had a past, but a dirty and complicated one.

This, he knew, was something he ought to keep to himself, just as Slater had, but a fifteen-year-old girl was dead and he had two suspects with similar backgrounds: Sean Johnson and Graham Collins, both of whom had been involved with

462

her and with each other. He had been expected to work without the full facts; he would not expect the senior members of his team to do the same.

He pushed himself away from his desk and strode into the incident room. It was empty except for Ali and Clarke.

'I think we might have our hoax caller, boss,' Clarke said, looking up from his computer screen.

John Handford waved the comment aside. 'Later,' he said and thrust the photo in front of Clarke.

Clarke took it from him. He stared first at it and then at his DI, holding his eyes for a long moment. 'Where did you get this?'

'Collins' wife brought it in a little while ago. She wanted to prove to me that her husband has a past.'

Clarke handed it back. 'If that's Collins, he has a past all right and one he obviously hasn't thought to mention. Are you going to tell her?'

Handford avoided the question. That was something he didn't want to think about. 'I'm right, then? The boy on that photograph is Todd Brightman?'

'Yes, it's Todd Brightman.'

Handford flopped down on to the nearest chair. 'Are you absolutely sure, Andy? I don't want us to be wrong on this.'

Clarke drew in a deep breath and exhaled slowly. 'I wish we were. We've got Todd Brightman living on our patch.'

Ali closed the filing cabinet drawer and walked over to the two men. 'Who's Todd Brightman?'

463

he asked.

Andy Clarke threw a silent question to Handford. The DI nodded.

'Todd Brightman was a ten-year-old lad who killed a four-year-old girl,' Clarke told Ali. 'Jennifer Kirton, I think she was called. It's a good few years ago and he would have been about ten at the time. The story is that he picked her up in the shopping centre near his home, took her to some wasteland, where she screamed and called for her mummy. He was frightened she was drawing attention to them, so he hit her with an iron bar, several times. When she was quiet, he hurled stones at her. He said it was to make her get up, but when she didn't he left her and went home. She died of multiple injuries.'

Ali was aghast. 'A ten-year-old. Surely it wasn't his intention to kill her?'

Clarke shrugged. 'Who knows? Kids can be cruel and it's probably not that far a step from bullying to killing. Some take it, most don't. At the trial the psychiatrist said that as young as he was, he had the makings of a psychopath – didn't know right from wrong and didn't care. Brightman was in court but wasn't called to give evidence. He sat and cried most of the time, by all accounts. The murder and the trial got lots of media coverage and a lot of editorial comment when it was over. The main thrust of the argument was that he should never have been tried in an adult court with all the wigs and ceremony. In fact, as far as I remember, it went to appeal for that very reason – as a young kid in Crown Court there was no way the trial could be fair on him.

He lost the appeal.'

'He never went into adult prison, though.' Handford broke in. 'He was in a young offenders' institution until he was eighteen and then given parole. It seems he charmed everybody. One social worker said you had to know him to believe in him. He'd been a model prisoner, thrown himself into his education and in spite of what the psychiatrist had said, was filled with remorse at what he had done to young Jennifer. Everyone who worked with him said he deserved the chance to live a normal life, the board agreed and before Brightman came out he was granted a High Court injunction to preserve his anonymity for life. Judging from what *we've* managed to come up with, they must have been working on it for months, if not years before he was released. Graham Collins has a protected identity and there's not a damn thing we can do about it.'

'I don't suppose they ever asked William and Sarah Collins if they could give their dead son's name to a convicted killer,' Clarke said bitterly.

'No, I don't suppose they did.'

For a while there was silence, each man concentrating on his own thoughts until Ali said, 'If Collins really is Brightman, how is it he was allowed to become a teacher?'

'They didn't have the same checks when he qualified, or at least any they did would have been cursory. I doubt he would be flagged up with a protected identity. In fact when I typed Todd Brightman into the computer, I was denied access. And except for the sexual assault case which collapsed because Shayla admitted to lying, there is nothing on Graham Collins at all. One thing is certain, though. If it becomes common knowledge and *if* he has killed Shayla Richards, then there'll be all hell to pay.'

Ali screwed up his eyes in concentrated reflection. 'I'm not sure I understand. If he has anonymity, how can it become common knowledge?'

Handford regarded him narrowly. 'You've forgotten Kerry Johnson.'

Ali stared at him. 'Kerry Johnson?'

Handford stood up. 'Yes, Khalid,' he said firmly. 'Whether you believe it or not, she is blackmailing Collins and now we have the reason for it.'

Ali shook his head. 'I don't agree. How could she have knowledge that is not in the public domain? We didn't.'

Handford sighed. As good a detective as Ali was, he didn't always use his head. 'Sean Johnson spent three years in a young offenders' institution after he killed the little girl and the chances are he was in the same one as Brightman. Coincidences happen.' He lifted his eyes as if to make the point. Then, coming to his decision, he added, 'We need to talk about this some more, but there's something I have to do first. Ali, I want you to check out where Sean Johnson and Todd Brightman were institutionalized and the years they were there. If I'm wrong, I'll apologize, but I don't think I am.' He glanced at his watch. 'We'll meet in my office in three quarters of an hour and I want Warrender in on it, too. Bring him up to date, Andy.' Clarke nodded. 'When we've decided how to proceed,' Handford continued, 'you and I

466

will visit Collins, Andy. Khalid, you join up with Warrender and interview Kerry Johnson. If I'm not back in time you can stand in for me at the briefing – but not one word of this to anyone else, you understand. This information is on a need-to-know basis.'

Handford returned to his office and picked up the phone. For a moment his fingers hovered over the buttons. He shouldn't do what he was about to do, but he needed the information and there was only one person who could get it for him at speed.

Redmayne answered almost immediately.

'Peter, it's John. A favour, please. I want it yesterday and I don't want anyone else to know.'

Redmayne chuckled. 'Of course you do and of course you don't. What is it?'

'Everything you can find on Todd Brightman.'

Redmayne conjured with the name for a while, repeating it out loud. 'That's the kid who killed that little girl, isn't it? Why would you want information on him?'

Handford sighed. Couldn't the man, just for once, do as he asked without so many questions? He was always asking questions. 'I can't tell you, Peter. And I mean I can't as in not allowed – legally. Just get it for me, will you?'

'He's not here is he? In Bradford?' The man was too quick for his own good. 'God, John, what are you telling me?'

'I'm not telling you anything, because I can't tell you anything. I'm asking you to do this for me because you can get the information quicker

467

than I can get it myself. And there'll be hell to pay if anyone finds out, so please, for once, do as I ask and do it discreetly.'

'Half an hour do you?'

It was exactly half an hour later when Peter Redmayne was shown into Handford's office. He carried two large envelopes. 'I've got what you want,' he said and handed over one of them. In it were photocopies of reports and editorial comment on the murder of Jennifer Kirton and the trial of Todd Brightman, as well as pictures of the two of them. One of Brightman was identical to that Jane Collins had given Handford and the rest were either head or shoulders prints taken from the original or school photographs. Handford scrutinized each one. There was little doubt that what he was looking at was a youthful Graham Collins.

Redmayne handed over the second envelope. 'I'm sorry, John, but I took what you wanted a step further.'

Handford opened it and pulled out a picture. It resembled Graham Collins. He lifted his eyes in a question.

'I know you,' Redmayne said. 'You wouldn't have asked for information on Todd Brightman without a good reason. So I had the pictures age-enhanced.'

As Handford made to protest, Redmayne said, 'Don't worry, I did them myself – no one else knows.' He placed two side by side on the desk. 'That is Todd Brightman aged ten, and this is as Todd Brightman might look aged twenty-nine.'

He focused on Handford, his eyes unflinching. 'Is that what you wanted, John? Confirmation that Todd Brightman is Graham Collins.'

Handford made no reply.

Redmayne leaned towards him. 'You know what you've done, don't you?'

Handford knew exactly what he'd done; he'd given information that he shouldn't have to a journalist who was inquisitive enough to take it a step further. He could argue he'd done it obliquely, but he'd known Redmayne a long time and was well aware that you never gave him anything you didn't want him to have, however obliquely you did it. If it ever came out, he would be in big trouble.

Again he made no reply, but Redmayne answered his own question, 'You've handed me the best scoop I've had in years and I can't use it. Not only is child-killer Todd Brightman living in Bradford but he's a teacher in one of our schools and I can't say or write anything. I can't even leak it.'

Ali, Clarke and Warrender met in Handford's office. Ali and Clarke sat on chairs in front of the desk, Handford behind it. Warrender leaned against the wall, his arm resting on top of the filing cabinet.

'Well?' Handford asked Ali.

'It took some finding,' he said, 'but you're right, sir. Johnson and Brightman were at Barton Grange Young Offenders' Institution at the same time. Brightman had been there about twelve months when Johnson was sent down. They spent

469

approximately three years together. There's little doubt that Johnson would know of Collins, may well have recognized him, if not through the school, then certainly through the pictures in the newspaper or on television – there were plenty of them, particularly after Shayla admitted to lying. There's no way Sean will have kept information like that to himself, so Kerry is bound to know.'

'Where is Johnson now?' Handford asked Warrender.

'Don't know, sir, not yet. Uniforms are keeping an eye out for him, but so far there's nothing.'

'Any idea where he could have gone?'

'Not really. He's not in any of the pubs he normally frequents and for all he's been out twelve years, he's a bit short on friends.'

'Do you think he had anything to do with Shayla Richards' death?'

'I've no idea, boss. But if he had and he thinks we're on to him and Kerry, there's no saying what he'll do.'

'Meaning?'

'He's desperate not to go back into prison. Last time he was there as a child-killer and the other prisoners gave him a hard time. If what I know about him is accurate, if we charge Kerry with blackmail and she's locked up, he'll be useless; he's nothing without her. It ought to be the other way round, but the fact is she's the mother, the thinker, the planner and he's the child and the follower. If I'm honest, I'm worried as to what he might do.'

'You think he might commit suicide?' Ali said.

'That or if he's stronger than I think, he'd get

the spotlight off his niece and turn it onto Collins. He does not want to go back into prison. For him it would be a living hell.'

Ali smiled. 'I expect it would be, Warrender, for anyone.'

Handford watched as Warrender flushed and picked at the corner of the papers in the wire tray on top of the cabinet, but said nothing. For whatever reason, the man was ill at ease. Handford frowned. He didn't know why and he wasn't about to ask but perhaps for once, Ali had the upper hand. 'If you really think Johnson's likely to kill himself or try to implicate Collins, then we need to find him quickly.'

Warrender lifted his eyes. 'I've done what I can, including suggesting uniforms keep a lookout near the railway line, the river, even Evelyn Richards' home, and bring him in if they see him.'

'Then there's not much more we can do for him at the moment,' Handford said. 'We'll leave him to uniform. We need to consider how the new information affects the investigation. Whatever we do, we mustn't assume that what we now know about Graham Collins makes him Shayla's killer.' He waited until he was sure they had understood. There was no reason why they shouldn't have – they were all experienced, used to being impartial – but not one of them, him included, had been in a situation like this before.

He suggested they look at the problem logically. 'Collins is a known killer and Johnson is a known killer, but except for the assault, neither of them has been in any kind of trouble since they came out. The MO for Jennifer Kirton's death was

471

nothing like that of Shayla Richards. Johnson, on the other hand, suffocated his victim. Both of them were acquainted with Shayla, Collins through school and Johnson through his niece. Of the two of them, Collins has the obvious motive and his alibi is weak. As far as we know, Johnson has no motive and currently the better alibi, but the main part of it is backed up by Kerry, who we are well aware would lie through her back teeth if she had to.'

'The pathologist said post-mortem evidence suggested two people were involved in her death,' broke in Clarke. 'So if we assume that, the big question is who would help either of them? I can't see Jane Collins giving her husband a hand, can you? Or if it comes to that, Kerry Johnson. She'd be more likely to have pulled Sean off.'

'Jaswant Siddique might just have gone along with it with Collins. Both had a reason for wanting rid of her,' Ali offered.

'Or even Mustafa and Siddique,' added Warrender. 'She'd been with them for three weeks before she escaped. Given we found the puffa jacket in her wardrobe, the chances are she was with Kerry Johnson for that final week. Could Kerry have told Siddique where Shayla was? If not for the same reason, there's no doubt they're both of the same mind when it comes to Collins, so it's quite likely she would have let him know that Shayla was with her. Siddique and Mustafa pick her up and not wanting to risk her escaping them again, they kill her and dump her on the moors. Then Mustafa disappears off to Egypt or Pakistan – it doesn't really matter where – leaving

472

his brother to take the flak.'

'And the arrangement of her body up at Druid's Altar. You think that was Mustafa as well?' Handford said.

'No, guv, you can forget that. I'm pretty sure the arrangement of the body has nothing to do with Shayla's murder or murderer,' Clarke said. 'That's what I was trying to tell you when you brought in the photograph. The woman I saw earlier is a care worker in the community. She said the voice belonged to one of her patients, George Philips, a twenty-eight-year-old West Indian. He's a schizophrenic and unless he's carefully monitored, he forgets to take his medication. When that happens he hears voices, hallucinates, does weird things. According to her, he's harmless, but he does have a fetish for fire engines.'

'And you've spoken to him?'

'Yes, she took me to see him. I'm almost sure the voice is his. He's coming in later to give me a taped statement and we'll have it analysed, but I'll give you a pound to a penny it's him. I've already got an explanation of sorts, but he's not the brightest button in the box and I doubt it would be much good in court. He admitted to making the calls – the voices told him to do it, and to hide while the engines drove up. They were very specific about Druid's Altar apparently. I said he must have dashed up the hill at quite a speed to get there before the appliances and he told me he could show me how quickly he can run. He was quite proud of it. Anyway, last week he found Shayla. She was lying on the ground semi-naked and he said she'd been left for him by the voices. He was told to lay her on the altar and to light a fire to keep her warm until the gods came for her. Luckily for him the appliance was returning from another shout and took longer than normal to get up there. Even so the fireman arrived before the gods, followed by the policemen and he became frightened and ran off. I'm fairly sure he was telling the truth – he didn't kill Shayla.'

'I don't think so either. What about you two?' Handford said, looking first at Ali then at Warrender. 'Presumably you're of the same opinion? We can discount George?' They murmured their agreement. 'In that case we need to concentrate on Collins, Siddique and Johnson. Let's see what Clarke and I can get from Collins; Khalid, you and Warrender have a go at Kerry. I can't. Given her encounter with Gill last night it would look too much like revenge. Make the blackmail a priority, but ask her about the jacket. And for God's sake let's find Sean Johnson before he does anything stupid.'

Graham Collins sat in the half gloom. Even though it was mid afternoon, the mist outside had hardly lifted and the room was dark. He should switch on the light, but he couldn't be bothered. Doing anything had become an effort.

Jane had gone to work. She was on the early shift and would be back soon. She hadn't wanted to go, but he'd promised her he wouldn't try it again. His life, her life and their baby's life were all too precious to him, he'd said. And he wouldn't because he'd promised, but his emotions and his reasons had been all too false. He cared about nothing. Sitting in the car with the carbon monoxide building up, his eyes closing and his breathing shallow, he'd been at peace. For the first time in years he'd felt at ease with himself. She should have let him go; it would have been over, his past dead and buried, no one, not even her, ever the wiser.

He'd never wanted Jane to know. He hadn't wanted his past to come between them. Now it was inevitable. The very fact that the detective couldn't find it would mean that he would go on trying and eventually he'd get the information he needed. Maybe from Sean Johnson. He'd told Kerry; why shouldn't he tell Handford? If there was half a chance he was suspected of killing Shayla, he'd want to move the limelight off himself and on to the only other person he would consider capable of killing. He'd been like that inside, dropping everyone in it to get himself out of a mess.

Kerry would be hard pressed to say anything – he'd been a nice little earner for her. He stirred, anger shifting inside him – the first emotion he'd felt since he came out of hospital. She'd had him trapped in a cage for too long now, unable to move. He wished it wouldn't come out, but if it did, then she would be the one in a cage because he wouldn't think twice about shopping the little bitch as a blackmailer.

Sean Johnson was pleased with himself. If there had been any doubt in Evelyn Richards' mind as to who sexually abused and killed her daughter, it was wiped out after his visit. Graham Collins was a murderer and a pervert – and Sean had given her all the proof she needed.

The march to Collins' house began with her and the two boys. It gathered momentum as neighbours and friends joined her, until by the time they reached Silverhill Grove it had the makings of an angry, yelling mob. The loudest voices were from the hangers-on, those who had been standing on street corners, drinking cans of lager or beer and smoking spliffs – some as young as twelve or thirteen. This was something to take away their boredom, to give them a buzz that the cannabis and the booze was no longer doing.

Sean hadn't explained and they hadn't thought to ask how he knew about Collins. They had believed him, because that was what they wanted to believe and now their focus was Graham Collins, alias Todd Brightman.

As the crowd swelled he dropped behind. He would be there at the kill, but at the back, easily able to slip away.

Jane Collins opened the door to John Handford and Andy Clarke.

'Can't you leave us alone?' she whispered. 'He's not well enough.'

'I'm sorry, Mrs Collins,' Handford said. 'Leaving him alone isn't an option. I do have some good news for him, though.'

'Then you'd better come in.'

She led them into the lounge. The room was in the same pristine condition as it had been when Handford had last been there, except that now the walls, the carpet, each piece of furniture exuded an atmosphere of dread and the sense of desolation was palpable. Graham Collins sat hunched in an armchair. The television was on, but the sound had been turned down and he seemed unaware of the two chefs scurrying around the studio-built kitchen. Collins was a man who didn't care any more, a man so deep in the clutches of despondency that Handford wondered if anything he said would make an impression.

He walked over to him and crouched down, touching his arm, and although Collins didn't respond, Handford said, 'We know for sure you didn't assault Shayla Richards, Graham.'

Collins made no reply and it was Jane who answered for her husband. 'How do you know?'

'Because we have the man who did in custody.'

'And are you going to tell us who it is?'

Handford stood up. 'I shouldn't, but yes, I think you deserve to know. It was Jaswant Siddique.'

For the first time since they had arrived, Collins reacted, lifting his head to look up at them. His wife asked, 'The teaching assistant who professed to be our best friend?'

Handford nodded.

'So why did Shayla blame Graham? Why did she lie?' Bitterness stalked her words.

'I don't know, but I suspect she was persuaded into it.'

'By Jaswant Siddique?'

'Possibly.'

'And what will happen to him? Will he be charged?'

Handford shook his head. 'No, I'm sorry. We

can try, but it's doubtful the CPS will pursue it. Shayla is dead; she's not there to be cross-examined and that means by definition there are no witnesses.' He didn't mention Gill. 'His confession isn't enough, I'm afraid. We've charged him on other counts which I really can't disclose and we'll try and get it out in court if we can.'

Jane Collins took a pace towards him. 'Did he kill Shayla?'

'I don't know, Mrs Collins.'

'Then my husband is still a suspect?' She was considerably smaller than Handford, hardly came up to his shoulders, but at this moment her presence towered over him. He didn't want that; he needed to be in control. There were things that had to be said.

'Yes, I'm afraid so. Look, I do need to talk to him. Here rather than at the station, but in private if you don't mind.'

'I do mind, but I don't suppose it will make any difference.' She walked towards the door. 'I'll make us some tea – isn't that what I'm expected to do at this juncture?'

Clarke made sure the door was closed behind her and then turned off the television. He joined Handford on the settee. Collins stared at the darkened screen. Somehow Handford had to bring him back into the room and as much as he hated to do it, there was only one way and that was to shock him.

'Why didn't you tell us that your real name is Todd Brightman?'

What remained of any colour in Collins' cheeks drained away and he closed his eyes.

'It would have saved an awful lot of trouble if you had done.'

Collins roused. 'For whom, Inspector? For you perhaps, not for me. It would have got me charged with Shayla Richards' murder.' As depressed as he obviously was, the strength needed to fight back was there. That was good.

'As I told your wife, we know now it wasn't you who assaulted her, but I don't know who killed her, and until I do I can't take you off my list. What I can promise you is that until I am a hundred per cent sure, I have no intention of charging you with anything.'

Collins attempted a smile, but it was taut and crowded with suspicion. He trusted no one. 'How did you find out about my alter ego? Did Slater tell you?'

Handford decided against telling him about the photograph his wife had brought in. It would serve only to antagonize both of them. 'No, in fact I haven't either seen or spoken to Superintendent Slater. You were telling us so little that we had to check your background for ourselves. Dig deep enough and it's amazing what you find.' At the look of horror on Collins' face, he continued hurriedly, 'I promise you there are only four of us at the station who know; the rest of the detectives will not be told. However, I would like to ask you again what you were giving Kerry Johnson in the cemetery. And please don't tell me it was photographs of old Bradford, because we both know it wasn't.'

This time Collins didn't offer a denial. 'No, it wasn't photographs – she said they were our get-out should anyone ask. It was money, a hundred pounds every month. I knew her uncle; we were both at Barton Grange together. Sounds like a public school, doesn't it?' he added acerbically. 'Anyway, he recognized me either from the pictures in the paper or at an event at school. I'm one of the unlucky ones, apparently. I haven't changed that much, just grown older. People often think I look familiar, but never go further than thinking. Johnson was the exception and once he'd worked it out, it was inevitable he would tell Kerry, and being her, she couldn't wait to taunt me with it.' He sank into himself. 'Believe you me, blackmail was the easy way out.'

'You could have told us; we could have stopped it.'

'You might have stopped the blackmail, but you wouldn't have prevented her from passing on what she knew. Money is the only way to keep her quiet. As soon as that dries up either she or Sean will make sure everyone knows. Neither of them will care that there's a court injunction to preserve my anonymity.'

'Does your wife know that you're Todd Brightman?' The question was blunt, but Handford didn't have time for niceties.

Collins looked at him in horror. 'No, of course not.'

'Don't you think she ought to? The police will say nothing; we are bound by the injunction, but you've said yourself that neither Kerry nor her uncle will give a jot about that. Kerry was arrested for street robbery this morning and when we searched her house, we found her post office book. There are over two thousand pounds in it. You've given her a lot, Mr Collins, *and* without your wife's knowledge. Kerry will be questioned about it. She'll no doubt deny that it came from you but Sean won't know that. We don't know where he is at the moment, but my guess is that to get Kerry out of trouble he'll stir it up for you. All he's got to do is tell Mrs Richards what he knows and if she reacts in the same way as before, she'll be down here with her information, her friends and her stones. Before that happens, tell your wife, Mr Collins; don't let her find out that way.'

Terror built up in Collins and he trembled visibly. 'I can't,' he said. 'She'll leave me. I'll take anything that Mrs Richards throws at me, but I won't risk that.'

Handford pressed further. 'If I'm right, it won't just be a stone through your window, you'll be vilified in the worst possible way. Believe me, if you thought it was bad last time you had a mob outside your house, then this time you'll really know the meaning of the word. They'll terrify you, your wife and your neighbours. She at least has a right to know why from you and not from them.'

'Know what?' Jane Collins came through the door carrying a tray.

Handford held Collins' gaze. 'Tell her, Graham. If you don't, I will.' It was a threat he shouldn't have made and he hoped he wouldn't have to carry it out.

Panic filled Collins' eyes. 'You can't. There's an injunction. You'll be in trouble.'

481

With his fingers psychologically crossed, Handford said, 'I'll risk it.'

At that Clarke grasped Handford's arm and pulled him away. 'Leave him, John. You can't do this.'

He snatched away from Clarke and glared at him. Friend or not, how dare he undermine him?

Still clutching the tray, Jane Collins turned first to her husband and then to the two detectives. 'Is someone going to tell me?'

Handford twisted away from Clarke and back to Collins. 'Tell her,' he urged. 'It's going to come out sooner or later. We've already charged Kerry with street robbery. As far as the courts are concerned, it's her first offence. She'll get community service or a supervision order. She's not going away. Even if we charge her with blackmail she'll get bail, and injunction or no injunction I can't stop either her or her uncle from spreading rumours, nor can we keep an eye on Evelyn Richards twenty-four hours a day. Tell your wife yourself, Graham, before someone else does.'

Jane Collins looked round wildly. 'Graham? What injunction? This is frightening me. Please. Tell me.'

Clarke took the tray from her, placed it on the small coffee table and led her to the settee, where she sat facing her husband.

Handford felt the silence as Collins struggled to come to a decision and then to find the words.

He looked up at his wife, his eyes filled with tears, his world fallen in around him. 'I... My...' Then he shook his head. 'I can't.'

'Tell her,' the detective said softly.

Handford's tone must have given him some strength for he said, 'I couldn't believe my luck when I met you and once or twice I tried to tell you, but the words weren't there. Now I don't want to tell you because I'm afraid you'll leave me.' He paused and took a deep breath to gather in more strength. 'As much as I loved you – and I did, I do – I married you with a lie. I'm not who you think I am. I'm not Graham Collins. For years I've lived with a borrowed name. I only became Graham Collins when I went to university.'

Jane's head turned to Handford. 'Lots of people change their names. Why is this so bad? I don't understand,' she said. 'And anyway the birth certificate, the GCSE and A-level certificates – I've seen them; you've seen them, Inspector Handford. They're in Graham's name.'

Collins said, 'I was Todd Brightman when I took those exams. They were awarded in the name of Graham Collins because ... because I had to change my name.' Before she could ask why, he said, his voice barely audible, 'I was in a young offenders' prison, Jane.'

'In a prison for young offenders? Why? When?'

Handford watched as Collins struggled to answer the questions. 'I was there eight years, until I was eighteen.' He had answered the when, but the why had been too difficult.

'Eight years.' Her voice rose in panic. 'What had you done that kept you in prison eight years?'

When Collins didn't answer, she repeated the question more slowly. 'What had you done that kept you in prison for so long?'

He shook his head.

483

'What?' she screamed.

He began to sob uncontrollably. 'I'd killed a little girl.'

For a moment she sat quite still, then suddenly jumped up and ran out of the room, holding her hand to her mouth. They heard the downstairs toilet door slam and her vomiting into the bowl. Clarke followed her. It was minutes before she returned wiping her mouth with a tissue. She held onto the back of the furniture as she guided herself to the settee. As she sat down, Clarke handed her a glass of water. She looked up at him. 'Why did you have to tell me?' she asked. 'We were all right as we were.'

He perched next to her. 'Because it's possible that there are those who have been informed about Graham and are on their way here to protest,' he said gently. 'Inspector Handford thought it better that you heard the reason why from your husband and not from an angry crowd.'

She turned to her husband. 'Is it true? You're a murderer?' she asked quietly.

He pleaded with her. 'I was ten; I didn't know what I was doing.'

'How did you do it? How did you kill her?'

'I hit her.'

'You hit her and she died? Just like that? Don't take me for a fool, Graham. I'm a nurse.'

'I'm not sure the details are important, Mrs Collins–' Handford broke in.

'Of course they're important,' she flung at him, her eyes remaining on her husband. 'I'm his wife and I'm having his baby. I need to know what kind of a monster he is.'

Collins flinched. Suddenly, her head flew round to face Handford. 'Why wasn't I told before?' she shouted. 'Why did no one think to tell me?'

He shook his head. 'He has an injunction from the High Court. It gives him anonymity for life. His real identity is protected. He did well in prison and they felt he needed the opportunity to lead a normal life,' he added lamely.

'And what about me? Am I not allowed a normal life? They – whoever they are – are happy to let me marry a murderer without having the decency to give me the choice.' She was still shouting.

Collins pulled himself from the chair and came towards her. He attempted to take her hands in his, but she pulled away. 'No. Don't touch me.'

He crouched down beside her and grabbed at her legs. 'I love you, Jane. Please.' This time she let him hold on to her.

'Where did the name Graham Samuel Collins come from? Is it made up? Did you pore over names in a baby book until you found one you liked, just as we were doing last night?'

Handford took over. 'It doesn't work like that. They had to use a name that gave Graham a birth certificate. He won't have been told whose name it was. And I can't tell you either.'

'But that person is dead?'

'Yes.'

'A child?'

'Yes.'

She stood up and pulled herself away from her husband. 'I'm sorry, I can't take this in. I need – we need to be alone.' Her eyes fell on Handford.

485

He couldn't return her gaze and he stared in front of him. 'You've destroyed what was left of our lives,' she said. 'I can't possibly see that there is anything else you can want from us. Please go.'

Both detectives stood up. 'I'm sorry, Mrs Collins,' Handford said. 'I would have given anything to prevent you going through this. I know how awful it must be for the both of you.'

'I doubt it, Inspector.' Her voice was laced with contempt and the comment was well deserved. Nevertheless, there was a good chance of violence soon and he had to protect them from it. 'DC Clarke will get an area car here just in case there is any trouble and arrange for back-up if it gets nasty. We will go, Mrs Collins, once they arrive. In the meantime we'll wait in the hallway.'

Handford sat on the chair by the telephone and Clarke on the third stair.

'I didn't mean it to be like this,' Handford said.

'Just how did you mean it to be, John? How did you expect her to react?'

'I was trying to save her hearing it from a mob of vigilantes. You think I should have let them tell her?'

'You don't know there is a mob yet.'

'Don't I? If we don't catch up with Sean Johnson, I'm pretty damn sure there's going to be, if not tonight, then tomorrow or the day after.'

Clarke shook his head. 'I hope you're right. Because if you're not you're going to have to live with what you've just put her through.'

It was only a few minutes later when the shouting hit the street, at first an incomprehensible mantra in the distance and then as it came closer and louder and louder, the words became clearer.

Pervert.

Murderer.

He ought to have suggested the Collinses leave; now it was too late. There was no way to get them out of the front door, and the back led only to the garden.

Handford peered through the corner of the curtain pulled across the door. He couldn't make out faces, just a huge, angry crowd. Someone pushed open the gate and marched down the drive, followed by a stream of others, men and women. They banged on the front door.

'Come on out, coward. Come on out!'

Clarke dashed into the lounge to be with the Collinses. Handford stayed in the hall.

Where the hell was the area car?

At first the wail of the siren was insignificant in the clamour, but as it screeched louder announcing its arrival some of the crowd turned; the rest remained as they were. This was their problem, their fight.

In seconds the lights of the police car flashed into view and simultaneously the first stone smashed through the lounge window. The second crashed into the hall.

chapter twenty-four

Warrender and Ali waited for the custody officer to bring Kerry to the interview room. It was not a comfortable wait. The central heating system masqueraded as a sauna and in its heat the tension between the two men mixed uneasily with the smell of stale sweat.

Ali scrutinized the constable as he leaned against the wall, his hands behind his back, his gaze fixed on a stain on the floor. He was worried, that much was obvious – and so he ought to be; as much an invasion of privacy as it was, going to the house last night didn't warrant the vicious attack. The accident had ruined so many lives and Warrender had a right to be angry, but he hadn't the right to take it out on any Asian who happened along. Ali wanted to say something, make his feelings clear, but this was the first time today he'd been alone with Warrender and had they been anywhere else but in an interview room awaiting a fifteen-year-old girl with whom they would have to be as one, he would have done so. In the event Warrender took any decision out of his hands.

He shifted his position. 'Thanks,' he said, without looking up.

'Thanks for what?' Ali knew what he meant, but wasn't about to make it easy for him.

'For not telling anyone what happened last night.'

'You mean that you attacked me and I could have you charged with actual bodily harm?'

'Yes.'

'I should have done.'

'I know. I owe you one.'

'Oh, I think you owe me more than one, Warrender.' He paused for a moment. 'And you can start by thinking on this. You didn't hit me last night because I came to your house; you hit me because I was an Asian who came to your house. I don't know how prejudiced you were before the accident – I didn't know you then – but I suspect the feelings were there, covertly if not overtly. The accident was not my fault; it was the fault of the man driving the other car, and the reaction of his family to the sentence and to you, was not that of my family. Your problem is yours, not mine.'

Warrender made no reply.

Ali contemplated his fingers. 'Let's get one thing clear, Warrender. I'm not letting you off the hook for your sake. If I had my way, I'd hang you out to dry. I'm doing it for Katie. The last thing she needs is her brother in prison. But make no mistake, do anything like that again and Katie will not be part of the equation. In your own vernacular, I'll have your balls. Do I make myself clear?'

Warrender nodded.

'Of course,' Ali added with a slight smile, 'the other reason I'm not taking it any further is that I promised Amina I wouldn't. She was furious with me for going to your house in the first place. I tell you, she told me off in no uncertain terms.'

Warrender looked up. 'Same here. I got a hell of a dressing-down from Katie when I got back.'

'In that case we both probably got what we deserved.'

Ali wondered if either of them believed that, and if, now that he was off the hook, Warrender would return to type. More than likely; he had a reputation to keep in the station. Perhaps as a parting shot, he should give him something to think about.

'One thing for sure, Warrender. Despite the difference in our colour, our culture and our faith, we do have something in common – we're both under the thumb of the women we live with.'

Warrender walked over to the table and pulled out a chair. 'Maybe so,' he said as he sat down. 'The difference for me is that when Katie had chewed me up and spat me out, I had to put her to bed.'

There was nothing Ali could say to that, no answer that would make things any better. He was saved from trying by a knock on the door and the custody officer entering with Kerry Johnson, her solicitor and the social worker called in as her appropriate adult.

The situation at twenty-seven Silverhill Grove was growing more serious by the minute. Initially the crowd had been made up of friends of Evelyn Richards, parents from the school and the few hangers-on they had picked up on the way, but now it was swelling with those more interested in the fight than the cause. As Handford watched, a cluster of youths charged down the road, shouting and jeering. Where they had come from he couldn't be sure, but they had little to do with either Evelyn Richards or Graham Collins. Swathed in scarves to avoid recognition, they climbed over the bonnets of the cars parked along the roadside and the police vehicles forming a barrier on the fringes of the crowd. It was only a matter of time before they would begin to turn them over. Their argument was with the police and with the help of mobile phones they had taken the opportunity to continue it. He wondered if Mrs Richards had any idea what she and Sean Johnson had started with their desire for revenge, or what Superintendent Slater had done by not telling him about Graham Collins. Had he done so this might have been prevented.

The area car and one other had managed to get through before the mass arrived, but the rest could only park on the rim of the crowd, pulling away and arresting those on the fringes. The ambulance was stoned as it tried to force its way through and drew back until it was safe. The helicopter had been called and was on its way and an armed response vehicle had been brought in on stand-by.

What they really needed was rain. That was often more than enough to disperse a crowd, but although the atmosphere was heavy and dank there was no sign of the weather breaking and Handford was afraid of what might happen if the situation couldn't be contained. He'd seen and heard it all before – the missiles, the petrol bombs and the incessant, ear-splitting clamouring. People were injured in these situations and in an area that was far too small for the growing mob, those already there were being forced to jostle for position. Already some were having difficulty keeping their feet and eventually, if it wasn't brought to an end, the weakest would be trampled under foot.

Jane and Graham Collins were relatively safe in an upstairs room with the curtains drawn, but Handford was worried about the neighbours, particularly the old man across the road. For the moment there was nothing he could do for any of them other than keep in telephone contact and warn them to keep away from the windows.

Missiles cascaded through the Collinses' already shattered panes. The chanting was continuous.

'Murderer.'

'Pervert.'

'Coward.'

'Come outside. Show yourself.'

Collins wanted to face them. He hadn't done anything, he said. He would talk to them, tell them.

Angrily Handford turned on him. 'The chances are they know you're Todd Brightman, otherwise they wouldn't be here. They're vigilantes, Graham, and vigilantes don't listen to discussion. All they want to do is mete out their own justice. You stand out there in front of them and there's no way I can prevent them getting to you and pulling you apart.'

As Handford pinched the curtain aside, he glimpsed an officer pushing his way towards a youth, poised to throw a missile at the house. Even from this distance he could make out the shape of a petrol bomb. Women near the boy screamed and the crowd tried to part. The officer made a grab for the attacker's arm, but his attempt did little more than skew the aim and prevent the petrol-filled bottle from connecting with the house. Instead it exploded and burst into flame in the garden, igniting the wet grass around it. At the sight of the flames, survival was the only thing that mattered and the crowd struggled to get away, fighting and pulling at each other, their shadowed bodies gyrating in frantic waves.

Handford knew he could not allow things to deteriorate further. Someone would be badly injured or worse still, killed. It was the last thing he wanted to do, but as he turned back into the room, he made up his mind. 'I'm going out,' he said. 'They want someone, they can have me.'

Clarke shook his head. 'No, John. With them in this mood, it would be suicidal.'

'With them in this mood,' he countered, 'we'll have a full-scale riot on our hands if we don't do something.' He looked at Jane and Graham Collins. 'I'm going downstairs with DC Clarke. You are to stay up here and away from the window.'

When they reached the hallway, he said, 'As soon as I get outside, Andy, you close the door. Stay here, but make sure you're safe.' He looked into his friend's eyes. 'Do you understand?'

Clarke nodded. 'I can't pretend I like it, but yes, I understand.'

Handford took a deep breath. 'Right, open the door.'

At first the crowd assumed it was Collins, for they surged forward, some flailing baseball bats, all shouting abuse.

'That's him! Get the bastard. Murderer!'

As the door closed behind him, Handford stood his ground, pulled out his warrant card and held it up. At first they were too incensed to notice, until someone shouted, 'It's not Collins; it's the copper.'

The noise wound down like an engine coming to a halt and to Handford the silence was almost worse, for it was as taut as a violin string. He spoke, hoping his voice sounded less nervous than his stomach felt. 'I'm Detective Inspector John Handford and I'm asking you all to go home,' he said. A futile comment, as he knew it would be.

'Bring him out, and then we'll go.'

The clamouring began again.

'I'm not bringing anyone out, and if you continue to disturb the peace like this you are likely to get hurt and will almost certainly be arrested,' he shouted.

'He's a pervert! He attacked my Shayla and now he's killed her,' Evelyn Richards screamed at him and then looked round at the crowd, demanding agreement.

'He didn't attack Shayla, Mrs Richards, and we don't yet know who killed her. If it was Mr Collins then he will face the courts, not a mob taking the law into its own hands.'

'How do you know he didn't attack her?' a tall Afro-Caribbean man standing next to her shouted. 'Because he told you he didn't?'

The crowd jeered.

'I know because we have the man in custody

who did.'

'You're lying, copper,' the self elected spokesman came back.

'I'm not lying. He has admitted it and he's in custody.'

'You tell me who it is,' Evelyn Richards demanded.

'I'm sorry, Mrs Richards. I'm not allowed to do that.'

The jeering continued and the crowd pressed forward. As they did so, Handford held tight on to all his reserves to prevent himself from banging on the door for Clarke to let him in.

They changed tack. 'That man in there – we know he's Todd Brightman. Are you going to deny that?'

The crowd surged again, and the chant began. 'Child killer, child killer.'

'I can't comment on that,' Handford shouted above the din. 'If and I repeat *if* he is Todd Brightman then there is a court injunction to prevent his identity and his whereabouts being divulged. I am bound by that.'

Mrs Richards shook her fist at him. 'It's him and you know it's him! You'd say if it wasn't.' Her voice was gaining in intensity. 'How can you protect him when he's murdered my Shayla?'

There were cries of 'that's right' and the chanting began again. 'Child Killer. Todd Brightman child killer.'

By now they were beyond reason and Handford saw no point in arguing with them. 'I'm not bringing Mr Collins out,' he hollered, 'so you might just as well go home. There are already officers here and more can be brought. The helicopter is on its way and there are armed police on stand-by. Don't make this any worse than it already is. If you go now and go quietly, you will not be arrested. Go home to your families before anyone gets hurt.'

As they ignored him and surged forward, the sound of the helicopter roared overhead. They stopped to look up and as the light from its search-lamp illuminated the crowd, most attempted to flee, scuffling with the few who were still pushing towards the house.

At first the spokesman tried to urge them on, but they were panicking and there was little he could do but let them go. He yelled, 'We'll leave, Handford, or whatever you call yourself. But I'm warning you, if you don't get that child killer out of our city we'll be back and this time not your police or your helicopter or your gunmen will stop us.'

He waved at the others, indicating they should disband. A few shouted abuse and another stone was flung in the direction of the house, but as the helicopter continued to hover over them, all turned and walked away.

The front door opened and Clarke came to join Handford on the step. 'Don't ever do that to me again, John. I don't want to have to break the news to Gill that you've been dismembered by a crowd of rioters.'

Handford collapsed inside. 'Do me a favour, Andy, don't tell her. This case has given her more than enough grief already.'

Clarke laid a hand on his boss's arm. 'Don't

worry, old buddy,' he said. 'I'll not say a thing.'

The lights of a police car bounced along the road. It pulled up outside the house and an officer jumped out. 'I know you said not to arrest anyone, sir,' he said as he greeted Handford, 'but Sean Johnson was at the edge of the crowd and we'd been told to keep a look out for him. He's in the back of the car, a bit worse for wear. Shall we let him go or take him to the station?'

'Take him in, Constable. Sit him in the custody suite and I'll be down in a bit.'

'Oh, and sir, there's Peter Redmayne at the top of the road. We wouldn't let him through, but he says he would like a comment on what's happened.'

The interview with Kerry Johnson was not going well. She continued to deny blackmailing Graham Collins and that the envelope he had given her in the cemetery contained money. The solicitor, Michael Graham, an elderly man with a benevolent demeanour, insisted they discontinue the line of questioning; it had gone on far too long. Janet Strang, the social worker and appropriate adult, intervened to say in her opinion Kerry was becoming anxious and the interview ought to be halted to give her the opportunity to calm herself.

Kerry grinned at them.

Ali smiled back at her. 'We'll stop for a drink. Perhaps a Coca Cola, or would you prefer something hot?'

Kerry said a Coke would be all right and could she have a biscuit – chocolate?

The solicitor and the social worker refused refreshment and the former asked both the detectives to leave so that he could have a word with his client.

Ali and Warrender walked to the drinks machine. As the can clattered into the drawer, Warrender said, 'I swear if she carries on like this, I'll wrap this Coca Cola round her neck.'

'If we're going to shake her at all,' Ali mused, 'we'll have to be much stronger. She's tough and she's playing with us.'

'Her solicitor won't let us and the social worker will hang us out to dry if we try.'

'Does that worry you, Warrender?'

Warrender grinned. 'Not in the least, Sergeant.'

'Then let's do it. You first.'

Once they were resettled and the recording machine was switched on, Warrender asked, 'Coke all right?'

Kerry nodded.

'And the biscuit?'

'It'll do.'

He paused an instant before continuing. 'You're very careful, aren't you Kerry?'

She grinned. 'Well, you've never caught me before.'

'I'm not talking about the muggings – although I have to admit you had it all worked out. No, what I mean is that you're methodical, know what you're doing, keep track of things.'

She eyed him quizzically. 'What you getting at?'

'The money in your post office book. Every month a hundred pounds. Occasionally a bit less, sometimes a bit more, but as regular as clockwork for nearly two years. Two thousand three hundred and forty-seven pounds: that's an awful lot. What's it for?'

'Mind your own business.'

'It's become my business, Kerry. Is it for you and Sean?'

When she didn't reply, he asked again, 'What are you intending to do with it?'

Suddenly she was on the defensive, exactly as Warrender wanted her. Defensive interviewees made mistakes. 'It's nothing to do with Sean, and you're not to say anything to him,' she said.

'Why?'

'Because I don't bloody want him to know, that's why.'

'So what *are* you intending to do with it?'

She took a long drink from the can before answering. 'I'm saving it so I can get out of here. As soon as I've got enough, I'm going as far away as possible. To London, most likely,' she ended triumphantly.

'London? That's an expensive city.'

'I haven't finished saving yet. There's more where that came from.' Michael Graham placed a hand on her arm and shook his head.

'Where did it come from, Kerry?' Warrender attempted, but Graham's intervention was enough for her.

She sat back and clasped her hands behind her head. 'My solicitor says I don't have to answer that question, so I'm not going to.'

He tried again. 'I'm surprised you don't want to answer it. You seem proud of the amount you've saved. Aren't you proud of how you came by it?'

Again the solicitor intervened. 'I've advised her

not to answer the question, Detective Constable Warrender. That should be enough.'

'Then perhaps you'd better advise her, sir, that if it has come from criminal activities – and I can't see any other way she would have obtained that amount – then she will lose the lot.'

Kerry's head spun forty-five degrees and she glared at Michael Graham. 'What's he talking about? Can they take my money from me?'

Graham nodded. 'If it's the result of a crime the courts can order it to be confiscated.'

Her mouth opened. 'That's thieving,' she declared.

'No Kerry, it's the law. If the police can prove you have obtained it as a result of a crime, it can be confiscated.'

'And this lot have to prove it?'

The solicitor nodded.

'Then I'm saying nothing,' she announced, shaking her head vehemently, and she sat back and folded her arms across her chest.

Ali said, 'In that case we'll talk about the puffa jacket we found in your wardrobe. You said it was yours, but Shayla Richards' name was in it.'

'She pinched it. She was always pinching things and writing her name in them, then saying they were hers.'

'Her mother has identified it as her daughter's. Why should she do that?'

'Because she's as stupid as Shayla was, the silly old cow.'

'Shayla was in your gang. She couldn't have been that stupid.'

'She was; she was useless.'

'So why did you have her in?'

'I felt sorry for her, all right?'

'Why did you feel sorry for her?'

'Because I did. She was twisted and she saw devils.'

'And you felt sorry for her because of that? Didn't it frighten you?'

'Sometimes.'

'When?'

'When she said they were looking at her from the mirror. She was always going on about it.'

'Did you ever try to stop her?'

'Sometimes.'

'How? Shout at her? Tell her not to be so stupid? Cover her face so that she couldn't speak or see?'

Janet Strang jumped from her chair. 'That's enough. You're bullying her.'

Ignoring the social worker, with a conscious effort at self-control, Ali asked, 'Did you kill her, Kerry?'

He was aware of Warrender staring at him as Kerry screamed, a loud, ear-splitting scream. 'I didn't kill her,' she shrieked. 'I didn't.'

'Enough,' the solicitor demanded. 'This stops now. You have absolutely no evidence to suggest that.'

Ali was not prepared to be contrite. 'We have the jacket, which in spite of what your client says, belonged to Shayla Richards. She stayed in Kerry's house at some point. We know where she was up to the twenty-fourth or twenty-fifth of last month; we don't know where she was for the last week of her life. We also know that the last time

501

Mrs Richards saw her daughter she was wearing her puffa jacket – she never went anywhere without it, so she would hardly leave it behind unless she was forced out or carried out of where she was living. Kerry must know something, Mr Graham, and I think it would be a good idea if you talked with her again to persuade her to tell us what it is.'

It was early evening when Handford and Clarke left the Collins house. Jane Collins had refused to move out; if she and her husband were to come to terms with everything they had to be alone. They could go to her mother's, but what would they tell her? The truth? Sarcasm had bitten deep when Jane Collins pointed out that her husband had a protected identity and the truth was no longer a priority. Handford said he could have them moved to a safe house, but both had refused. If they were going to get through this, then they had to be in familiar surroundings. If they wanted to make a drink, they had to know where the crockery was; if they wanted a corner where they could be alone, it had to be a corner they knew. They had to stay here, the only place they would be able to release their feelings without an audience.

Reluctantly, Handford acquiesced, but insisted there would be uniformed officers on duty round the clock in case anyone came back. 'They will be told to be discreet,' he said. He also arranged for their window to be boarded up until next morning when a glazier would come round. Then, before he and Clarke left, they visited the neighbours. Handford spoke to Walter Heywood. The old man was more concerned about the Collinses than he was about himself. He asked the inspector to tell them that if they wanted anything or if he could help, they only had to ask. Handford promised to relay the message.

Clarke drove back to the station. He said Handford didn't look as though he should be in charge of a toy car, never mind one of CID's and Handford was grateful. As he sat in the passenger seat, he was glad it was dark enough for Clarke not to see him trembling. He held his hands, one in the other, in an attempt to pull himself together. Clarke had suggested they go for a quick one to steady their nerves, but Handford refused. Not only had he to question Sean Johnson but there was a likelihood that if he drank anything alcoholic he would be sick.

Once in the station, he went straight to his office. Sitting behind his desk, with only a lamp for illumination, he took a series of deep breaths and reached down inside himself for control. When he found it and his stomach juices had ceased to churn, he began to check the internal mail. Most of it consisted of circulars from headquarters or from the divisional commander, but amongst it was an envelope marked Forensic Science Service. He opened it and read the report. They had a result on the DNA found on Shayla's underclothes and on the two pubic hairs. There was no match on the database for the latter, but the semen belonged to Sean Johnson. So he had seen her on the day she died. It was all beginning to fall into place. Handford slipped the report back in the envelope and made his way down to the custody suite.

Kerry's uncle slouched uncomfortably on one of the benches, looking the worse for wear. He was mumbling drunkenly to himself and occasionally calling out. His words were incoherent and Handford cursed that he would probably not be fit to be interviewed straight away. He asked the custody sergeant if Johnson had been seen by a doctor.

'He's with another prisoner at the moment, but he shouldn't be long.'

'I do need to interview him,' Handford cajoled.

'Not until he's been seen, sir.' Custody sergeants were in charge in this part of the station and there was nothing more that Handford could do.

'Let me know when he's ready, will you?'

'By the look of him it'll probably be tomorrow.'

That would have to do.

He was about to leave when the double doors opened and Ali emerged from the corridor that held the interview rooms.

Handford walked over to him. 'Did you get anywhere with her?' he asked.

'Not really. She's not saying much; she's certainly not admitting to the blackmail and insists the puffa jacket is hers. She talked a lot about Shayla and the devils she saw. I'm convinced that either Shayla was with them during the last week of her life or that Kerry knows where she was, but without something else to go on, we'll never get her to admit it. When I tried to get it out of her she became so hysterical the solicitor and the social worker insisted we stop. I'm afraid I suggested she might have killed Shayla, so there might be a complaint of bullying against me – just warning you.'

Handford handed his sergeant the forensic report. 'This might help,' he said.

Ali skimmed through it and looked up at Handford, excitement in his eyes. 'Are you going to question Johnson?'

'I am when he sobers up. And given that Collins admitted he was being blackmailed by Kerry Johnson and is prepared to make a statement, I want to be in on the interview with her. I know I said that because of the attack on Gill I shouldn't, but things have moved on since then. Is her solicitor still here?'

'He's staying until she calms down. I'm not sure he wants her interviewed again for a while.'

'Perhaps when I've disclosed Collins' admission that she was blackmailing him and this report on Sean, he might change his mind. If nothing else it will give Kerry something to think about. If you don't mind a late night, Khalid, I'd like to get it over with as soon as possible. We won't be able to hold Kerry much longer.'

Ali handed back the report. 'I'll ring Amina,' he said.

Kerry was calmer though still sobbing when she was brought back through custody towards her room, helped by the social worker. The moment Janet Strang saw Handford she marched them over to him. 'The interview with this young girl was a disgrace, Inspector. Both your officers bullied and harried her and I intend to put in a complaint in the strongest terms.'

'That's your privilege, Ms Strang. But you would do well to remember that the accusations against Kerry are serious. For her sake we have to get to the truth.'

'But not by bullying tactics.'

He sighed. 'I'll listen to the tape,' he said, 'and have a word with the officers. Perhaps in the meantime it would be better to take Kerry back to her room so that she can calm down. There is a doctor in the station if you think she needs one–'

He was suddenly interrupted by Kerry pulling herself away from the social worker. 'What's he doing here?' she demanded, pointing to her uncle lolling on the bench. She pounced on Handford. 'You, pig! What's he doing here?'

Handford grabbed her arms and manoeuvred her back to Janet Strang.

Sean slowly became aware of the fracas and smirked at his niece. 'I've done it, Kerry,' he said drunkenly. 'I've dropped Collins in it; I've told everyone who he is.'

Again she snatched herself away from the woman holding onto her, but this time instead of Handford she launched herself at her uncle. 'You fucking stupid fool!' she yelled. 'What you do that for?'

Her fists smashed against his chest, knocking him sideways. Sean flailed his arms in an attempt to ward her off. 'No, Kerry, it was brilliant. They all went down to his house. They've broken his windows and everything. They called him a murderer; they think he's done it.'

Unable to make her blows count, she kicked at

his legs. 'Stop it,' she screamed. 'Shut up.'

Two of the custody officers grabbed at her. As they forced her towards the cells, she kicked out at them. Another joined them. Under the horrified gaze of the social worker and the solicitor, the three officers pinned her down and pushed her unceremoniously into her cell. As they returned, out of breath, she could be heard kicking at the door.

'You fucking bastard. Fuck you, Sean Johnson,' she screamed. 'I'll get you for this.'

Handford looked at the astounded solicitor. 'I don't envy you your client, Mr Graham,' he commented. 'When she's calmer I want to interview her again, but in the meantime I have a couple of disclosures to prepare, so I should pop up to the canteen if I were you.'

The man smiled. 'You're right, Inspector. I think I will have a cup of tea before I speak with her again.'

chapter twenty-five

It was an hour later when Kerry's solicitor sent word that she was ready to be interviewed once again. Sean, on the other hand, was not considered fit and was sleeping.

Before joining them in the interview room, Handford and Ali sat in his office discussing how to proceed. By now her solicitor should have told her what the police already knew: that Collins had admitted to being blackmailed by her and that the DNA of the semen on Shayla's underclothing had been matched with that of her uncle. She could still deny having any involvement with Collins and insist that he was lying, but she would be hard pressed to argue the forensics results. Something had happened in that house and Handford was quite sure she knew what it was.

'I'd like to take it easy with her,' he said. 'If we're too harsh she'll fight us. She might seem hard, but I suspect that underneath, she's vulnerable. For all her bluster she's a young girl who is probably very frightened. It's now she's going to make the mistake if there is one to make.'

'Warrender said something of the sort after we'd visited her.'

'Warrender is no fool; he understands how suspects think.' Handford paused. 'I hope you've sorted everything out because I want no more talk of you transferring. You're too good to lose and so is Warrender.'

'I have,' Ali said. 'We'll never be friends, and I don't suppose he will ever be able to stop winding me up, but I think we understand each other.'

'Good.' Handford pushed back his chair. 'Come on. Let's see what Kerry has to say for herself.'

Ali hesitated. 'Do you really want to do this, John? It's not going to be easy questioning her, given what she did to Gill. Warrender and I can do it if you'd rather.'

For a while the comment hung between them. Handford walked over to the window. Darkness was beginning to spread like a slow bruise across the city and the roads glistened orange under the street lamps. The tail lights of cars spooled out trails of colour as they headed out to the ring road, or sent steady waves of light as they cruised south towards Manchester Road.

'No, I'm fine with it,' he said. 'If this were about what she did to Gill, then I'd step down, but it isn't.' He picked up the file from his desk. 'Come on, let's make a start; I don't want to be accused of questioning her when she's tired. Her social worker has one complaint up her sleeve already and I'd rather not feed her another.'

Kerry was waiting for them, her solicitor next to her, the social worker sitting behind. There was no doubt she was frightened. Her eyes were red and puffy from crying and the smirk was gone. For the first time her air of self-assurance had fractured. This was not the girl who had barracked Gill and who had attempted to turn over her car. This was an insecure, terrified child and he felt for her.

'Are you all right?' he asked when the preliminaries were over.

She nodded.

'If you become too tired and you want to stop, or if you want advice from Mr Graham, you only have to say so and we'll turn the machine off and give you a rest. Do you understand?'

Again she nodded.

'Now Kerry, has Mr Graham told you what we have learned? Can you answer out loud this time, for the tape?'

She licked her lips. 'Yes.'

'So you are aware that Mr Collins has admitted he was giving you a hundred pounds a month to stop you telling what you knew?'

'Yes.'

'Do you agree with his statement?'

She turned to look at her solicitor, who nodded. 'Yes,' she said.

'Can you tell me what it is that you know?'

Fear crept into her eyes. 'What are you going to do to me?'

'Don't let's worry about that for the moment. Just answer the question.'

'I know he's called Todd Brightman.'

'Yes?' Handford encouraged.

'He killed a little girl.'

'How do you know this?'

'Sean told me.'

'And how did Sean know?'

'He was inside with him. Then when he came to work at our school, Sean recognized him. He said he hadn't changed that much. He said he

510

would have known him anywhere.'

'Was it Sean's idea to get money from him?'

Suddenly she became angry. 'No, Sean never suggested anything. It was Collins.'

Puzzled, Handford and Ali stared at each other. 'Mr Collins suggested you should blackmail him?'

'No, he didn't mention blackmail. When I told him what I knew he said I was wrong, but when I said Sean had recognized him he got upset and asked me not to tell anyone – well, he pleaded with me really. Then he said I couldn't say anything, because the court wouldn't let me. When I told him I didn't care about the court and that all I had to do was to tell his wife or Mrs Richards, he said he would give me whatever I wanted if I would keep quiet. So I asked him for a hundred quid a month.'

'And he paid you?'

'He was too scared not to. Everyone thought he had messed around with Shayla; if they'd known he'd been in prison for killing a kid, he'd have been beaten up, no sweat.'

'Did you know he hadn't assaulted Shayla?'

'She said it wasn't him.'

'Did she say who it was?'

'Yes, but I'm not dobbing him in.'

Handford smiled as though he understood. 'So what did you do?'

'I told her she had to tell everyone she'd been lying. I told her if she didn't I would. If Collins had gone down, I'd have lost my money and I needed it to go to London with.' She was beginning to build up some confidence now. 'But I wasn't blackmailing him. It was his idea and if it hadn't been for me, Shayla would have lied and he'd have ended up back in prison.'

Handford sat back and studied her. Sometimes it was hard for people to hold onto reality when it was so overwhelming and to compensate she was beginning to see herself as the one in the right. The ministering angel. She'd persuaded Shayla to do the right thing, saved both Collins and the real attacker from jail and kept the money coming in. He had to admit it wasn't a bad day's work. He was filled with admiration. It was as Gill had said: with the right background she could have gone far. As it was, she was looking at a criminal record and possibly a few years in a young offenders' institution.

'Let's talk about Shayla for a bit. Sergeant Ali here tells me you liked her.'

'She was all right.'

'You would help her if she needed it?'

'Sometimes.'

'How would you describe her, Kerry?'

Kerry looked confused. 'I don't know what you mean.'

'What was her personality like? Was she a happy person or sad? Describe her to me.'

'Most of the time she was sad.'

'Why do you think that was?'

'Because her father had left her. She loved him and wanted to go and live with him, but her mother wouldn't let her.'

'And you understood that?'

She nodded.

'It seems to me you were a very good friend to Shayla.'

Tears began to cloud her eyes. 'Not really.'

'What makes you say that?'

'Because she's dead.'

'And you think that's your fault?'

She nodded.

'Why?'

At this she began to sob uncontrollably. They were close and with anyone less vulnerable he would have pushed it hard, but he was not prepared to force the truth out of her while she was so distressed. He turned to Michael Graham. 'I think we'll take a break here. Perhaps, Ms Strang, you can get her some water.'

The social worker half smiled her agreement and gave Kerry a reassuring squeeze on the arm as she left the room.

'While we're waiting, Kerry,' Handford said, 'would you like me to find out how your uncle is?'

'Please.' The word caught in her throat.

For the tape, Ali postponed the interview and the two of them moved swiftly into the corridor.

'Why did we stop?' Ali asked when they were away from the interview room. 'We were getting somewhere.'

'And we'll continue to get somewhere, but not when she is so upset. So far Ms Strang has kept quiet. If I get too bullish, she'll interfere and I don't want that. Go and check on Sean. See how long it's going to be before he's well enough to be questioned.'

Handford was leaning against the wall in the corridor when the social worker passed him, carrying a beaker of water in her hand. 'I'm glad to see you've taken on board my complaint,' she said. 'It's a pity Sergeant Ali hasn't your patience. Bullying never gets anyone anywhere.'

Handford wanted to suggest there were several ways to bully and that possibly what he was doing was one of them, just more covert, but he held his comment and smiled at her. 'All we want is the truth, Ms Strang.' He indicated the beaker. 'It would be very helpful if you can let Kerry have her drink.'

Janet Strang's lips narrowed into a straight line, but she refrained from comment and disappeared into the interview room.

A few minutes later Michael Graham's head appeared round the door. 'We're ready now,' he said.

When they were settled, Ali said, 'Sean's awake. He has a bit of a hangover, but he'll live.'

Kerry smiled at him. 'He usually does,' she said.

Ali switched on the recorder. 'Does Sean often get drunk?' he asked.

'Not often. Just when he's upset or worried.'

'He was drunk on the day Shayla died. Was he worried then?'

'He must have been. I don't ask; I just put him to bed.'

Handford took over. 'Let's talk about the puffa jacket. It is Shayla's, isn't it? Her mother has identified it and it's being examined forensically at the moment. Do you know what that means?'

'Yes.'

'Do you think it's likely that by examining it, we will prove it's hers?' He smiled at her encouragingly. It was half sincere, half an act. He looked over at the social worker. This is my kind of bullying, Ms Strang.

Kerry clenched her eyes momentarily and then said, 'It was hers.'

Handford held the next question for a moment. 'Why was it in your wardrobe?'

Again Kerry began to cry. 'Because I wanted to have something of hers,' she said through the sobs.

The social worker began to move, but Handford lifted a warning hand to stop her. 'She left it in your house?'

'Yes.' The word was no more than a whisper.

'You remember I asked if you understood what was meant by something being forensically examined. Do you know what semen is?'

In spite of herself Kerry gave him a derisory look. 'Of course.'

'Shayla's underclothes have also been examined and on her pants the scientists found some residue of semen. Do you know what DNA is?'

Fear covered Kerry's face. There was little doubt she knew what was coming next. 'Yes,' she whispered.

'The semen was examined for DNA. It matched with Sean's.'

Kerry crumbled. 'It can't be. They've got it wrong.'

'No, Kerry. They haven't got it wrong. There were also two pubic hairs caught up in her pants. They were tested for DNA and that didn't belong to Sean.'

He watched her for a moment. 'Now I think

515

you know what happened to Shayla. I think she was in your house during the last week of her life. Probably, you were taking care of her, helping her, but somehow she was suffocated and she died. I want you to help Shayla by telling me what you know.'

As he watched her, Kerry's expression said it all. She was beaten. She began to sob hysterically, but this time Handford did not call for a break. Neither did Michael Graham or Janet Strang.

'We didn't mean it,' she cried. 'We never meant her to die. All we wanted was to stop her screaming, but she just went on and on.'

'Tell me what happened. You say it in whatever way you want and if we need to, either I or Sergeant Ali here will ask you a question just to make things clear.'

She turned to her solicitor. 'It's all right, Kerry,' he said. 'You tell it in your own way.'

'We didn't know where she was when she was missing, honestly we didn't. When Mrs Richards came to ask, we had no idea. But then one day she turned up. She was dirty and crying and ever so upset. I asked her where she'd been and she said the man who was helping her kept her and wouldn't let her go. She said he was trying to take Aaron and Dion to Pakistan to live with her father, but he didn't want her. She said she'd tell her mother, so he kept her in a flat so that she couldn't.'

'Did she say whose flat it was?' Ali broke in.

Again she turned to her solicitor. He nodded. 'It was Siddique's.'

'The teaching assistant at Cliffe Top?'

'Yes.'

'Go on.'

Kerry was calmer now. 'They kept having sex with her. She screamed a lot because she kept on seeing the devils and they said sex was the only way to get rid of them.' Suddenly a thought occurred to her. 'I bet those hairs were theirs,' she said.

'Probably,' Handford agreed. 'What happened next?'

'One day when Mr Mustafa, I think he was called, was in the flat, she kneed him in the balls and ran away and came to our house.'

'Why didn't she go home?'

'She was frightened that they would find her there and that anyway her mother and Calvin wouldn't believe her if she told them. She ran away a lot and always had some stupid excuse. No one believed much of what she said.'

'Except you?'

'I tried. Anyway, while she was with us, she got worse. She saw the devils all the time. I said I couldn't see them, but she said they were there, everywhere, in front of her, behind her, looking at her from the mirror. I didn't know what to do. I thought if I could get her to sleep a bit more, she would get better. So I went out to the chemist to get some paracetamol. I had to pinch them because they wouldn't sell me them. The old trout on the counter said I was too young and to tell my mother to come and get her own.'

For a moment she became lost in her own thoughts.

Handford understood, but had to bring her

517

back. 'Kerry?'

'When I got home I could hear her yelling all the way along the road. She was on the settee with Sean on top of her. Kicking and screaming, she was. I pulled him off her and told him to keep his dick where it belonged. He said she was up for it, but she wasn't, I knew she wasn't.' She began to sob again and she ran her hand under her nose. Ali gave her a tissue.

'I shouldn't have left him with her,' she said when she was a little calmer. 'It was the birthday of that kid he killed – like an anniversary – and he always goes stupid on that day.'

'What happened after you'd pulled him off?'

'She carried on screaming. I tried to get the pills down her, but she wouldn't have them. Then...'

Handford closed his eyes; he knew exactly what she was going to say and although it would wrap up the case, he wasn't sure he wanted to hear it. 'What did you do?'

'I put a cushion over her face. She carried on kicking and Sean held her while we had got her quiet. That's all we meant to do, to get her quiet.'

'But she was dead?'

'She wasn't breathing and she was a funny colour.'

'What did you do then?'

'Sean said we had to get rid of her. He borrowed a car from a man up the road – well, he didn't exactly borrow it. He said he'd take her where she wouldn't be found. But she was, wasn't she?'

'What was she wearing?'

'Just her pants and her bra. Oh and a scarf

518

around her neck. It was one her father had bought her when he lived with them. She wore it a lot.'

'What did you do with her other clothes?'

'I took them and hid them.'

'Where?'

'In Graham Collins' wheelie bin. I waited till late so no one would see me. I was going to drop them in his garden, give him a fright, but the bin was outside the gate, so I stuffed them in there. They'd be on the tip before anyone noticed.'

'But you kept the puffa jacket?'

'I wanted something of hers.'

Handford thought the lilac scarf might have been a better bet, but he said, 'And Sean?'

'He got drunk, like he always did.'

Handford stretched out his hand and touched her arm. 'Thank you, Kerry. You've been very brave.'

She looked up at him, her eyes filled with dread. 'What's going to happen to me?'

'We'll send all that you've said, together with the other evidence we've collected, to the Crown Prosecution Service. They're the people who decide what we should charge you with. I'll suggest manslaughter because I believe you didn't mean to kill her. But however good your intentions were, Shayla is dead and you tried to hide the fact. I think you have to prepare yourself for being sent away for a while. As for Sean, he's already on parole. I'm afraid he'll go down for a long time.'

Handford and Ali led Kerry back through the custody suite as an officer was bringing Sean to an interview room. When Kerry saw him, she pulled away from the officers. Ali made to stop her, but Handford shook his head.

She ran up to her uncle and clung to him. 'I'm sorry, Sean. I told them. They know what we did.'

Sean stroked her hair. 'It's all right, baby,' he said. 'It's not your fault.'

'They'll send you back to prison.'

'I expect they will, but I'll manage. Don't you worry about me. I'll be all right.' He pushed her away from him and brushed her tears away. 'I want you to promise me one thing: that while you're inside you'll do what Collins did and get down to some exams. They might even change your name when you come out and you'll be able to get a good job like him.'

She clung to him again. 'I don't want you to leave me,' she sobbed.

'And I don't want to. We'll probably see each other in court and we can keep in touch. I'm not much of a letter writer, but I will try.'

Handford walked over and gently manoeuvred her away from her uncle. 'Come on, Kerry, you need to rest. I'll get the doctor to give you something.'

Reluctantly she allowed herself to be led away.

Janet Strang stood next to Handford. 'It's so sad, isn't it?' she said as she watched Kerry out of sight.

'Yes it is,' he answered her. 'Very sad.'

It was gone midnight when Handford walked in the house. The interview with Sean Johnson had been short and to the point. He had admitted everything, corroborating exactly Kerry's version.

520

After he left the interview room to be taken back to his cell, he turned to Handford. 'Be kind to her, won't you?'

'I will,' Handford assured him.

Gill hadn't waited up for him; she'd stopped doing that a long time ago. He was in two minds whether or not to wake her, but decided he would. It was important she knew what had happened and tomorrow morning they would both be in a rush. For a while he stayed in the kitchen making them some tea and wondering what he would say exactly, and how much he would tell her. He decided on everything.

She stirred as he feathered her arm, opened her eyes and looked sleepily up at him. 'What time is it?' she asked.

'About twenty past twelve. I've brought you a cup of tea.' He sat on the bed. 'It's over, Gill. We know who killed Shayla Richards. We also know she wasn't assaulted by Graham Collins.'

Gill eased herself up the bed and took the beaker from him. 'Who was it, John?'

He laid an arm on hers. 'It was Kerry Johnson together with her uncle.'

'Oh, no. Why? Are you sure? She's only a child.'

'Children kill. We can't pretend they don't. In Kerry's defence, there was no intent.' He explained what happened. 'If only they'd called for some help, instead of getting rid of the body and then leaving her clothes in Graham Collins' wheelie bin. I'm going to suggest a charge of manslaughter to the CPS, but I can't guarantee that's what it will be.' He took a sip of his tea. 'You know, the only person who really cared about Shayla was Kerry. Everyone involved with her, even her mother, blames someone else – the school, the police, her father. And the direction they wandered across her life was stealthy and selfish. It was what others wanted and not what Shayla wanted. So many people turned her into what she had become and only Kerry really understood her. She might have gone about looking after her in the wrong way, but at least she tried.'

'You sound sorry that it was her.'

'I am. In spite of everything she's not a bad kid. I let her talk to her uncle after the interview and he said that when she's inside, she must take the opportunities there are. He told her to get down to some exams, to get herself some qualifications.'

Gill laid her head against the pillow. 'Who assaulted Shayla if it wasn't Graham?'

'Jaswant Siddique. He thought you had seen him because apparently you came along the corridor as Shayla ran out of the room.'

'I don't remember. Will you have to question me?'

'Not now he's admitted it. And anyway, we may not even be able to charge him with it. Shayla was the only witness and she's dead. She did tell Kerry, but that may not be enough. No, he's going to get away with that one. He's been charged with holding Shayla against her will and we have much more evidence to go with that. He'll not be back in school.'

'But Graham will. The governors can't keep him out now.'

Handford had been dreading this. He shouldn't tell her and if he did he had to insist that it was not to go any further. 'I'm afraid they can.'

'But he hasn't done anything.'

'I'm going to tell you something now and it must go no further.'

Gill listened aghast as he told her about the injunction and the reason for it. He said that there were people in the city who knew and had attempted to storm Collins' house. He did not tell her about his part in it. No doubt Peter Redmayne would do that in tomorrow's paper. 'I don't know what's going to happen exactly, but I suspect he and his wife, if she stays with him, will move on under another identity. It can't be much fun living with a borrowed name.'

Handford put down his beaker and held his wife in his arms. 'I'm so sorry for what has happened. It's made life very difficult for you.'

'Yes, it has,' she agreed, 'but I'm sure I can think of a way you can make it up to me.' She twisted to look up at him. 'How about a holiday?'

He smiled. 'That would be good: a weekend away without the girls, me making it up to you.'

'Oh, I wasn't thinking about a weekend, John. I think you owe me more than that. No, I was thinking more about a cruise in the Mediterranean or a holiday in Venice via the Orient Express.'

His eyes widened. 'That's one hell of a making up, Gill.'

She laughed. 'I was only teasing, but it was good to give you a bit of your own back. No, a weekend's fine – providing it's not Windermere in November.'

27 Silverhill Grove
BRADFORD
BD9 7NR

15 November 2002

Mr B Atherton
Headteacher
Cliffe Top Comprehensive School,
Cliffe Top Lane,
BRADFORD
BD3 6TJ

Dear Mr Atherton

It is with regret that I tender my resignation as teacher of history at Cliffe Top Comprehensive School to take effect from the end of the Spring term. In the meantime I shall remain on leave for health grounds.

I loved my work at the school, but as you will appreciate the events of the last two years have rendered my position untenable. Although I was neither guilty of a sexual assault against Shayla Richards nor of her murder I feel that parents will never be sure of me, assuming as they will that I would not have been suspected or charged in the first place had there not been a reason.

The rumours about me that continue to circulate the district make it impossible not only for me to continue in my chosen profession, but also to remain in Bradford. My wife and I intend to leave as soon as it is practicable and I shall not return to teaching.

I consider my resignation to be a case of constructive dismissal and am in discussion with my solicitor as to what course of action I should take against the school, the governors and the local education authority.

Yours sincerely

Graham Collins

Graham Collins
Cc Lawrence Welford, Chair of Governors
    Mr John Reynolds, Director of Education

The publishers hope that this book has given you enjoyable reading. Large Print Books are especially designed to be as easy to see and hold as possible. If you wish a complete list of our books please ask at your local library or write directly to:

Magna Large Print Books
Magna House, Long Preston,
Skipton, North Yorkshire.
BD23 4ND

This Large Print Book for the partially sighted, who cannot read normal print, is published under the auspices of

THE ULVERSCROFT FOUNDATION